SWORD BROTHERS

JERRY AUTIERI

1

Blaring horns announced the breaking of the siege. Ulfrik stumbled out of his command tent into a slash of morning light and searched for the source. Warriors were spilling out of tents all around him, and from the slipshod hall where Jarl Hrolf the Strider resided a stream of armored spearmen flowed out in advance of their jarl. The horns sounded again, like the call of a dying beast rolling up from south of the camp, and Ulfrik's hands went cold. He ducked back into his tent and pulled his chain shirt from the rack.

His arms ached as he slipped the heavy chain over his head. He had no help in donning his mail, eschewing the servants that other great jarls employed. Yet he needed help this morning. The mail shirt was tangled with his hair when someone burst in through the tent flap.

"Gods, Father, the men can't see you like this. They'll be worried you'll trip in battle." Gunnar's voice was low, salted equally with impatience and humor.

"I'll be tripping over piles of enemy corpses, if that's your worry. Now help me get this on and tell me the Franks have their relief force at last."

Gunnar worked Ulfrik's gray hair out of the chain links, then helped settle the mail on his shoulders. The cold weight of it was consoling, like the embrace of a strong, protective friend. He clapped his son's shoulder in thanks. Gunnar was a full jarl in his own right. Fearsome to behold on and off the battlefield, hard lines and a ragged black beard framing a dark, angry face. The first wisps of gray worked through his wavy black hair. His sword arm ended in a stump, having lost his hand to the Franks years ago. He made up for the handicap with a custom shield strapped to his stump and a long-hafted ax in his good hand.

"The Franks are attacking from the south, and the Bishop of Chartres has raised some holy relic over the walls." Gunnar handed him his shield then his sword, and Ulfrik slipped on his helmet to complete his transition into a warlord. He strode from the tent, shield on his arm and sword in hand, and Gunnar followed.

"More Christian nonsense," he said. "But it gives them hope, which is the worst thing in a siege. How much time—"

He did not need to finish the question. The outskirts of the camp were already roiling in combat. The din of clashing iron and screaming men was muffled with distance, but the morning light flashed on their weapons and lit the violence with a stripe of yellow. The relief force marched under bright banners of blue with white or yellow stripes or strange beasts to set apart their various lords. The gleam of their conical helmets was like the glittering scales of a snake crawling through the flat grassland. Across the fields, high on the hill, the gates of Chartres opened.

"Caught in the jaws of a wolf," Ulfrik said. "This siege was a fool's mission from the start. Be ready to get bloody fighting out of this mess."

"No other way to fight," Gunnar said. "I'll get my men to the ships. You'll follow?"

"Not until Hrolf agrees," Ulfrik rubbed his face and looked toward the center of camp where Hrolf's banner of red and yellow dragons caught the morning breeze. Beside the hall, the giant form of Hrolf the Strider loomed over a crowd of armored men. In the distance, more enemy flowed out of Chartres. "But he'll have no choice. Make haste. The Franks are not stupid enough to leave access to the river unopposed."

He parted from Gunnar and he marched for Hrolf, whose men clumped to his sides like flotsam to the shore. He plowed through them on his way to Hrolf, but gathered up his other son, Hakon, and his second, Finn Langson. The two men nodded without a word and fell into stride with him. Hakon now fought under Ulfrik's banner, and while he was the very image of Ulfrik in his youth, he was far less impulsive. Finn still had the freckle-splattered face of a boy, but years of battle had hardened it and dulled the brightness of youth with a tarnish of violence. Both of them shoved away men who crowded Hrolf, until Ulfrik stood at the center of the crowd.

"We have to flee," Ulfrik said. "The men have no heart for this fight and the Franks are going to crush us."

"We haven't sat here all summer just to run when the fight starts." The words came not from Hrolf, but from the man standing beside him, Mord Guntherson. He had once been Ulfrik's foster son at the request of his old friend Gunther One-Eye. He had been the main proponent of this siege of Chartres, so his opposition was expected. However, for years he had opposed anything Ulfrik said or did.

"Look over my shoulder," Ulfrik said to Mord. "Your younger eyes see better than mine. There's not just a relief force. There's all of Frankia's fighting strength bearing down on us. The Franks wouldn't have sallied from behind their walls if this wasn't their big push."

Mord grunted in frustration, shaking his head like a wet hound. Hrolf turned back toward the city and stared at the open gates. All around, the distant roar of the approaching Franks drew closer. Hrolf sighed.

"There is a hill down the Eure River," he said. "If we can retreat to the high ground, we can make a stand."

"Sound the retreat now," Ulfrik said. "Or the only high ground will be the piles of our corpses."

"We can beat them," Mord said, glaring at Ulfrik. Hrolf dismissed him with a wave of his hand.

"Pull back to the ships," he said. "Have everyone gather at the hill."

Ulfrik sprang to action the moment Hrolf turned from the battle. No one wanted to retreat, but the first wave of Franks was already crossing the ditches dug about their siege camp. Their neat ranks were broken up, but Ulfrik knew what would precede their charge.

"Keep shields overhead while the men are falling back," he said to both Hakon and Finn. "They're going to spray us with arrows the moment they come into range. Hakon, you must gather our men to the ships. Finn and I will meet with Einar. The Franks are already working up the riverbanks to cut us off. We'll keep a corridor open."

The next moments were filled with shouted orders, kicking men into action, and organizing a defense. He assembled a force of fifty of his best hirdmen and joined it with an equal number of hirdmen from Einar's band. Together they marched to the riverbanks where at least triple their number of Franks advanced behind their teardrop-shaped shields. The crunch of their armor and the thud of their boots on the muddy banks reverberated through Ulfrik's own mail. He felt their approach like a fist rapping the center of his chest. He set his ranks deep, but wide enough to plug the gap from the riverbank to the slope. He stood at the middle, Finn at his right, and set his banner of black elk antlers against a green field into the soft earth. Down the front rank Einar set his banner of a boar's head with bloody tusks. Even now with his blond hair and beard streaked with gray, he was still a strong, giant man who forsook a shield in favor of a two-handed ax. He smiled at Ulfrik as the Franks approached.

Finn's shield touched Ulfrik's and it was the signal for all of his men to lock shields. The wooden clacks echoed down the line and spear points lowered over shoulders to meet the Frank's approach. There would be no parley, no attempt at peace. These Franks would be their best warriors, given the crucial task of cutting off retreat. Ulfrik was Hrolf's greatest warrior and Ulfrik's hirdmen the finest troops. The battle would be a clash of giants, and Ulfrik was honored to spill the blood of these noble enemy.

Archers detached from the rear of the approaching Franks. Ulfrik raised his shield and shouted, "Arrows!"

The shafts fell among them, thudding into wood or thumping into the earth. Cries of injured men gurgled up from the rear ranks. As the last arrows fell, he lowered his shield. He knew it was nothing more than cover for the charge of the main force.

The Franks were dashing now, screaming to their god for victory. Ulfrik watched patiently, and not one man flinched in his line. Over the years he had distinguished himself among other jarls for instilling battle discipline in his men. Where others would meet the charge, he waited until they were close then shouted again. "Spears!"

From the second and third ranks spears sailed overhead to crash into the charging line of Franks. The long shafts sailed home into flesh, causing the charge to stutter. Franks collapsed, screaming with a spear through their guts or piercing their thighs. Where the spears missed, they formed an obstacle in the ground or stuck to a shield and weighted it down into uselessness. All Northman spears were made with long, flexible blades designed to bend out of shape so they could not be picked up and used against them. A few inexperienced Franks tried, further ruining the cohesion of their line.

Ulfrik smiled as the first enemy crossed the final distance, leaping dead friends and dodging the last flight of spears.

He had waited all summer for a stand-up battle. He braced his shield and widened his stance. He had his sax in hand, a short sword built for the close fighting of the shield wall where a longer blade was useless. The Franks had yet to learn that lesson and fought with their long swords.

The Franks roared, and Ulfrik's men cursed them with their own battle cries. The enemy charged across the gap, red-faced and wide-eyed, swords and spears flashing in the light.

They rammed into Ulfrik's shield wall.

Then all was a red haze.

The battle lust was strong in him, even at his age. A whole summer of simmering energy exploded when those first shields crashed into his own. He felt himself shove backward then stop. The spears behind both sides clamped down across the gap, like the teeth of a great dragon closing on its prey, and men on both sides screamed as they died. The instant he had regained himself, Ulfrik slammed back into the enemy and stabbed under his round shield, aiming for exposed legs.

Nothing was louder than a clash of shield walls; not even the collapse of a glacier rivaled the volume. Men roared in pain and hatred, iron rang and hummed, wooden shields thudded together in an awful song of death. The tangy scent of blood filled Ulfrik's nose, overwhelmed only by the stench of someone's bowels being spilled onto the grass. His hands grew hot and slick with blood, and he sewed his blade into enemy flesh.

The whirlwind battle filled Ulfrik with joy, even as companions fell back bleeding and shrieking. Battle defined him, and in the shield wall he found all the meaning he needed in life. A sharp pain lanced through his shoulder where a spear pierced his mail. He tore it free with a growl, plunged his sword into the throng of enemy, and delighted in the soft resistance he encountered.

Despite his love of combat, he realized the edges of his line buckled. Over the turmoil he saw the Frankish archers scurrying up the hill unopposed. They would set themselves at his unanchored flank and shoot into his rear ranks. Unable to turn to see the progress of Hrolf's retreat, he had to hold the line until he could be sure Hrolf had launched his ships.

A blade clanked against his helmet, shifting his faceplate so his vision was obscured. He returned to the shove and strike of holding the line.

"Step back," he called out. "Give some ground."

He had to repeat the order twice before he heard it echoed in the rear ranks. Reversing a block of men required care, for it could easily devolve into a rout. He was glad Einar held the far line, or else it may have collapsed already. The man behind pulled back and Ulfrik stepped with him, leaving a tidemark of bodies for the Franks to hurdle. This was an advantage as well, forcing the enemy to clear the obstacle.

A dozen or more hand axes flew across the gap to harry the Franks as they rushed forward. Ulfrik saw one well-placed throw sink into a Frank's neck and send him flailing back into his shocked companions. Yet victory was short-lived.

"Archers on the flank!" The warning spread like burning oil across a deck. Ulfrik heard the hum of bowstrings and the hiss of arrows in flight, then the screams of the wounded.

Whether Hrolf had extracted his force, Ulfrik's line verged on collapse. The Franks closed again, praising their god and saints. Finn had moved his standard back, but now it wavered as he struggled to plant it again.

"Forget it," he shouted to Finn. "Fall back to the ships. I've got the archers."

Finn nodded and backed away from the oncoming Franks. His rear ranks were already melting away, but Ulfrik grabbed his front line and anyone at hand. "Follow me. Kill the archers!"

He did not stop to watch who followed, but broke free of his line to run for the archers. They were preparing another volley as Ulfrik and his men charged. The Frankish archers were lightly armored, numbering twenty at most, and unprepared for a fight. Ulfrik expected to chase them off long enough to cover his men's escape.

Instead, they lined up squarely and leveled their bows at his charge.

2

Arrows swept around Ulfrik, one close enough to feel the rush of air as it sped past his face. Behind him men grunted and he heard them crash into the grass. An arrowhead exploded through the wood of his shield and another glanced off his helmet, which was still twisted over his head. Despite the workman-like disposition of the archers, Ulfrik continued his charge. To falter now would send any man following him into a retreat. The archers had to be driven back or his men would be destroyed during their withdrawal. He had no other choice but to pound across the grass into the morning sun where the archers arrayed for their next shots. He did not even know how many warriors had charged with him.

Judging from the archers' patience, he guessed he might have thrown his life away on this gambit. They had their next shots on their strings, and Ulfrik was close enough to read the determination in their faces. One archer had an arrow lined up to his head. He ducked behind his shield and the arrow clanged against the metal boss at the center. His hand went numb from the blow.

That was the archers' last volley and already they were drawing swords. Ulfrik careened into the closest archer, bowling him to the ground and continuing through the ranks. The man behind struggled with his sword caught in the sheath. Instead, he swiped at Ulfrik with his bow staff. It thumped onto Ulfrik's shield then a quick jab beneath it and the archer screamed in agony.

He whirled now, finding he had been joined by only half the number of archers. Behind his on-rushing men, bodies stuck with feathered shafts squirmed in the grass. Beyond them the Franks had pursued Finn and Einar's men down to the waiting ships at the shore. Dead bodies and ruined weapons streamed out behind the Franks like the wake of ship.

An archer fired at point-blank, sending a shaft into the throat of one of Ulfrik's men. He did not falter, but continued through, lopping off the archer's arm at the elbow, then collapsing in death. Each of his men was worth three of the Franks. Filled with pride, Ulfrik bellowed his challenge.

"It is Ulfrik Ormsson come to bring you death! Prepare to meet your god!"

Despite their superior numbers, the archers did not fare well against Ulfrik's heavily armed and armored followers. The swirling combat lasted only long enough for the remainder of the Northmen to charge home. The raving Northmen carved a swathe through the enemy ranks, Ulfrik a bloody-handed devil roaring at their center. His arrow-studded shield collided with the head of one archer while he drove his blade into the leg of another. He would have delighted in nothing more than running down the rest of the fleeing archers, but he witnessed the arrival of the main relief force.

A tide of bright banners and iron flowed across the siege camp and their defiant shouts were like the breaking of waves on a beach.

"To the riverbank," he shouted at his men. A wild-eyed warrior was bent over, tearing the through the belongings of an archer who still lived. Ulfrik grabbed him by the collar of his mail shirt and shoved him back. "Run or die. Look at what's coming."

He left the man to decide if booty or life were more important, and began sprinting for the shore. The Franks had moved past him, now away to his right and crowding the rear guard of Einar and Finn.

He saw their standards waving and thrashing over the chaos, and he prayed they would escape. Ships filled with men were launched into the green waters of the Eure River. The hill where Chartres stood crawled with exultant Franks, and their cheering could be heard over the clash of battle.

Ulfrik arrived at the riverbank. His left leg throbbed in such agony that he had to check for wounds, but it was the old injuries that had never left him. He waved on his men, who dashed toward him as if reaching him would make them safe from attack. Nothing could be further for the truth, for Ulfrik stood on the shore and watched helplessly as Einar and Finn fought to board their ships, which were already pushing into the river.

As men arrived, they shared his realization, but like him simply scowled and turned to face the Frankish army. If they were trapped, then they would all die as heroes and take as many with them as they could. Ulfrik did not need to tell these men; they were the bravest and strongest of his hird and would rather die in glory than to drown trying to reach a ship.

Between him and the approaching Franks, one of his men carried a wounded companion, arms looped across their shoulders as the injured man tried to hobble to their tiny line. Ulfrik cursed their pace, then ran out to help.

"Thank you, Lord," said the injured man. "I didn't want to die under their feet."

"If it's your day to die, then it will be with us at the riverbank," Ulfrik said, rushing the injured man to his line of nine men. "I don't think anyone is stopping to fetch us to a ship."

They stood together and watched the Franks approach. When it seemed they would reach them, they turned their formation and rushed to join their brethren attacking Einar and Finn.

"Over here, you fools," Ulfrik called out to them. "I'm your prize! A jarl! I'm worth more than anyone there."

He shouted in Frankish, but his words could not overpower the din of battle or their lusty cries for blood. He would have made a fat prize for someone, being Hrolf's second. Yet the Franks were more interested in breaking the back of Hrolf's power.

"We're not that tempting," said the injured man, who supported himself with a spear. "I don't think they'll bother."

Ulfrik picked up a broken spear and hurled it in frustration. The only bright spot was that his banner and Einar's were on their ships, and the bulk of Hrolf's ships had slipped away. At least Hakon would be aboard one of those ships.

Now, a line of ships drew close to the shore, and he recognized Gunnar's sleek hull. The sides were bristling with bowmen, and he led six ships' worth. These bowmen launched a volley into the attacking Franks, a blur of black arrows humming across the water to land among the enemy. They screamed in fury, their own archers dispersed and their relief not yet fully engaged. Gunnar's ships sent another volley and the Franks recoiled. It was enough to allow Einar and Finn to launch out of reach.

"That's my son," Ulfrik said, then ran to the shore and began waving. The ships sailed past, strafing the Franks and driving them from the shore with howls of frustration. Ulfrik waded out into the water until it was up to his waist. His men followed, two of them carrying the injured on their shoulders. Gunnar steered his ship close to the shallows, but not close enough to run aground on mud. The crew cast out ropes so that the men could haul themselves to the sides.

Ulfrik was the last one, and now that the shooting had ceased the Franks charged to the shores and sent their own arrows after them. A shaft plunged into the water as he dragged himself to the hull. The fetid taste of it filled his mouth and his hair hung over his eyes. He realized his helmet had fallen off in the water. As he clambered up the sides, Gunnar reached down to haul him over the rails.

"That's the last of these fat walruses," he shouted to his crew. "Get on an oar and row."

The sky streamed past Ulfrik as he wiped water out of his eyes and blew it out of his beard. Gunnar's dark shape hovered over him.

"That was too near for my taste. I'm glad they have no ships or we'd be in a bad way."

"Don't be so sure we've escaped yet," Ulfrik said, content to lie on the deck. "It's not like we've broken into open sea. They only need follow the shore to wherever we land."

"Why not keep sailing all the way home? They'll never catch us."

Ulfrik stared up at Gunnar and blinked. "Because we're not done fighting."

3

Ulfrik sat around the campfire with Hrolf and his jarls and hirdmen. He did not need to hear the scouts' reports to know they were now encircled and trapped. His only curiosity was to learn if the Franks had expended any energy to search for their ships. The lack of any major fires from the south told Ulfrik they had not taken this key step. Yet to glance around the fire he saw every face drawn in tight anguish, as if their beloved ships had been sent to the river bottom. The fire crackled loud against the silence of the early evening. With hundreds of fighting men both on and around this hill, the stillness of the night unsettled Ulfrik.

Hrolf especially seemed drawn after a day of hasty retreat. He squinted into the dancing flames, rotating a drinking horn in his heavily jeweled hand. Beside him Mord stole glances, like a child expecting his father's displeasure. The other jarls rubbed their aching muscles or sipped at their drink. No one would dare a word, and Hrolf would not speak until the scouts had confirmed what everyone guessed.

Finn appeared behind Ulfrik, plucking his shoulder for attention. Even in his mail, Finn could be more of a ghost than a person when he wanted. Ulfrik twisted around to look into his friend's freckled face.

"The scouts are coming, but I already had a look for myself."

Ulfrik glanced warily back at Hrolf, who did not shift his expression. Mord, however, squinted at him across the flames and frowned. Ulfrik got to his feet with a low groan, using Einar who sat beside him for support. Finn guided him away from the others to where the common men huddled and mumbled about their plight.

"What have you seen?" Ulfrik whispered. Finn checked over his shoulder.

"The ships are untouched, at least for tonight. I went down myself and warned the guards. They'll be ready to launch if the Franks attack them."

"These Franks are smart enough not to turn their backs on us to burn our ships. A cornered wolf fights to the death, after all. How bad is it around the hill?"

Finn's bright face darkened. "They must have used the bridge south of Chartres to cross. I guess almost all of their army is here."

Ulfrik rubbed his neck. He had argued with Hrolf to destroy that bridge, but it was stone and guarded with a tower. He carried bad memories from Paris of such bridges. Mord, who was no more than a boy then, weighed in against Ulfrik, too. Now they paid the price for their fear.

"They will have left part of their force to relieve Chartres." Ulfrik stared north at the moonless night where the faint glow of the city stained the sky. "No doubt they will celebrate all night. There's no hope for taking the city now."

"What should we do?" Finn asked. "Gunnar and Hakon want to sneak away tonight, before the Franks attack tomorrow."

"Don't we all? But it's one thing for a single man to move through a forest in complete darkness, and quite another to shift armies in the same conditions. We are stuck here until dawn, when the Franks will attack."

He and Finn stared at each other in the flickering ambient light of multiple campfires. Hrolf had ordered more fires set than needed to make their force appear even larger to the enemy. At last Ulfrik put his arm on Finn's shoulder and squeezed it. "Good work this morning getting the men aboard the ships. Have you counted our losses yet?" Finn shook his head. "Well, time for that when all is done. If we don't escape this trap it will have been wasted effort. But gather my sons. I have a plan, and I will need their help to make it work."

"Really? What is it?" Finn's face lit up again, a return to boyish enthusiasm that the years had ground away.

"I need to convince Hrolf and the others first," he said as he turned back to the campfire. "Or explaining it will have been wasted effort."

Returning to the campfire he drew suspicious looks from a few men, particularly Mord, who in recent years had revealed himself to be a sour and petulant man. Ulfrik blamed his young Frankish wife, being a Christian shrew who thought she was some kind of princess. He had turned out so unlike his aged father, Gunther One-Eye, who would have exulted at the challenges of this battle.

The tableau had not changed and Hrolf continued to stare into the flame. Einar raised his brows and sighed. Ulfrik had seldom seen such defeat in the faces of his peers, but they had also seldom backed into a trap from which escape appeared impossible. The campfires twinkled behind Hrolf as men shuffled back and forth. When the scouts finally arrived with their reports, their white faces told the story before their mouths could. Most hovered at the edge of the circle, but one leaned to Hrolf's ear, appearing like a floating head lit by yellow firelight. When his whispers were done, he withdrew to the darkness and Hrolf closed his eyes.

"As we feared, they have come with enough strength to surround the hill. By morning, whatever can be spared from Chartres will reinforce them." Hrolf drained the contents of his horn, then dropped it at his feet. "We will have to fight to reach or ships, and pray we escape."

Ten men circled Hrolf, each face adorned with the memories of battles: white scars, broken teeth, or missing ears. These were the best of his hirdmen, and the leaders of his warriors. They slumped in defeat at Hrolf's pronouncement, and Ulfrik could scarcely believe they were veterans.

"We will not beg the gods," Ulfrik said, quietly but with as much conviction as he could put into his voice. "But we will delight them with our cunning and bravery."

"Cunning?" Mord said through a sneer. "Shall we all dress as Franks and walk off the hill unopposed? Cunning is a poor substitute for fighting strength."

"And will you be sweeping the Franks away with one slash of your magnificent sword?"

Hrolf stamped his foot on the ground. "Enough! We've no time for this. If Ulfrik has a plan, then I shall hear it."

Mord leaned back with a scowl, but Ulfrik ignored him. He leaned forward, the campfire hot on his face. "We have set these fires to appear even mightier than we are. At the foot of this hill hundreds of Franks are sitting in stone silence afraid we will crash down on them at any moment. I say let's make their worst fears come true."

"You call attacking in the dark cunning?" Mord said, arms folded over his chest. A few chuckled, but the others listened intently. Hrolf peered at him as if trying to guess his plan. Ulfrik licked his lips and continued.

"We cannot let dawn break and reveal our true numbers. Worse still, we can't let them reinforce, which they surely will once Chartres is safe. Tonight we leave with the night for cover. But to succeed, the Franks must believe they are under attack. I will lead picked men into the Frankish camps when their campfires are low and they drift to sleep. Then all at once we will sound our horns and raise the alarm. They will believe we have attacked and are among them. We will set fires and sound warnings, everything to strengthen appearance of attack. In the confusion, the rest of you will charge not for the Franks but for the riverbank and follow it back to the ships, then slip away. Come dawn the enemy will pursue, but they will be on foot. I suggest a barricade thrown together along the riverbank will hinder their advance long enough to allow a peaceful withdrawal home."

He sat back, staring at Hrolf who rubbed his chin in consideration. Mord and any other detractors waited for Hrolf's reaction. Even Einar, usually his staunchest ally in Hrolf's circle, only offered him a quiet pat on the back. Ulfrik had just suggested defeat to the greatest jarl ever to challenge the Franks. He did not care. Hrolf had lost plenty of battles before this one, and to remain on the hill come dawn was not only another path to defeat, but one fraught with death. He preferred escape and trying again some other day.

"That could work," Hrolf said, still staring into the fire as if mulling the plan. The wisps of gray in his beard and the shadow-filled lines around his cheeks lent him a fearsome and kingly demeanor. His jeweled hand sparkled as he continued to rub his chin. "If this plan succeeded, you and your men risk being caught or separated from us. I would not risk a man as valuable as you."

The compliment made Ulfrik's chest warm, and he strained not to watch Mord frown in response. He merely inclined his head. "I have experience in this. I once had to hide among the Franks in order to free your son who was allowed to fall into their hands."

He smiled at Mord, who had been responsible for the grievous error that resulted in the Franks taking Hrolf's son, Vilhjalmer, as a hostage. While that had been more than six years ago, it was still a bleeding wound for Mord. Given his former friend's attitude, Ulfrik could not resist the jab. Mord's face reddened and he decided to study the starless night sky.

"That is true," Hrolf said. "And you've shown a remarkable knack for escaping their grasp. I trust you will do everything to keep up with us, but if you are delayed, I will leave men to cover your escape and a ship to speed you home. I like your plan."

Ulfrik clapped his hands together. "It will work, and we will all be telling this tale to our children's children one day. I will select the men for the task. My sons will be with me, as will Finn. I need only a handful of other crafty men to make this a success. I will need help organizing the rest of the force to retreat in time with our ruse."

"Leave that to me. You worry about getting the Franks to believe we've attacked." For the first time in days Hrolf smiled. He stood and all the others followed. Einar assisted Ulfrik to his feet, the bones in his knees cracking. As each man left the campfire, Einar held onto to Ulfrik's arm.

"You can't run as fast as you used to. Will you be able to escape in time? Do you need me with you?"

"I learned this morning that if a Frankish army is chasing me, I run just fine. No, you have your own men to worry for. Gunnar will lead my men home, while Hakon will attend me. Just ensure Gunnar does not do anything foolish, and keep him focused on escape. You know his temper. He's his mother's son, only a thousand times more fiery."

Einar laughed and clapped Ulfrik's back before they parted. Now Ulfrik turned to Finn, who paced at the outskirts of Hrolf's campfire.

"I can tell you the plan now. You'll love it. It will probably get us both killed."

4

Between the top of the hill and the Frankish camp, total darkness ruled. Ulfrik set each foot down with all the care of laying a sleeping baby to bed. Whatever light thrown by both Frank and Northman camps was scattered by the thin woods covering the area. Each snapping twig or tumbling rock sounded like a crash to him. Yet no sentry challenged him nor did any enemy stir at his approach. From the dead silence he surmised the others of his picked men shared his success.

He crouched behind a tree, watching the low fires for shadows passing before them. He imagined Finn doing the same only with more grace and skill. His knees throbbed and his leg ached, and he leaned on the tree more for support than cover. His mail coat was no longer a welcoming old friend but a heavy ogre riding his shoulders. He and all the others had selected dark cloaks and rubbed their mail with mud to prevent a gleam from giving them away. Finn had daubed his own face with grime, but Ulfrik thought that was too much. They would be blaring horns, after all, with no chance of remaining hidden after that moment.

Satisfied no one moved in this section of camp, he crept toward the next tree. His heart throbbed with the excitement of the stealthy work. He had seldom employed the skills he learned infiltrating the Franks years ago, spending the last six years in a shield wall. Tonight he returned to the heady mix of danger and deceit, and he relished the thrill.

He stepped to the next tree, then a small clearing marked the center of this segment of the camp. Only a few tents marked where the lords slept, and they were billowing masses of gray in the low light. Most of the ground was covered by slumbering men with their cloaks pulled over them. Their snores droned in the night and the odd man shifted in his sleep. He searched for a path through the bodies, but found none. Indeed the Franks had come in the hundreds, and were carefree enough to sleep with enemies nearby.

Sentries would be close, and he waited until the low orange light of small campfires revealed them to him. One sentry wrapped in a cloak and leaning against a tree resolved into view. He was barely visible, but revealed himself when he wiped at his nose. Ulfrik continued to wait until no other shadows revealed more guards, then he made a careful dash to the next tree all while staring at the sentry.

He arrived safely, but decided he had to draw the guard away from the edge of his sleeping companions. He tossed a rock to where he had just been, and it thumped against the trunk. The sentry stood straighter and stared at the tree. Ulfrik threw a second stone when the sentry's interest appeared to fade, then the Frank grasped his spear in two hands and approached the tree. He stopped and stared, shook his head then continued. The sentry examined the tree and began to prod the earth with his spear. Ulfrik had no idea what that would do to detect him, but he was already sweeping up behind the guard.

In the final step he cracked a branch and the sentry whirled, though his spear was not too long for the job. Ulfrik grabbed it with one hand and pulled forward. The guard instinctively tried to hold onto the shaft and thus he fell forward into Ulfrik's waiting dagger. He punched it into the sentry's ribs, then released the spear and clamped his hand over the Frank's mouth. He led him to the ground so the crash would not awaken anyone, then cut the sentry's throat for good measure.

Again he paused, but no one investigated the brief struggle. Across the camp he saw another form slowly pacing, but the distance was great enough to be of no concern. Stooped as if walking behind a fence, he glided toward the edge of the sparse trees where the sleeping men lay. He pulled out his horn and imagined Finn, Hakon, and a dozen other men waiting for him to sound it. Once he blew the horn, he had moments to unleash chaos and make his escape.

There would be no turning back and he would be surrounded by alarmed foes.

The horn pressed against his lips and he drew his sword.

He blew with all his might and the sound burst over the sleeping men. Unseen sentries standing only a few spear-lengths distant jumped in shock. The sleeping men shot up in confusion. In answer to his horn, all the others sounded. Then from the top of the hill, Hrolf sounded his own horn and his men screamed for blood.

Ulfrik leapt into the sleeping men and began screaming in Frankish. "The Northmen are among us. Run! Run! They are here!"

Men scrambled for their gear while others jumped up and fled toward the rear. Ulfrik grabbed men who appeared confused and left them no time to recover from their dreams. "Hurry! We're overrun!"

The ruse reinforced itself, as sleep-befuddled men repeated the lie for him as they fled. All around the camp he heard the same shouts and heard the horns blowing. Hrolf's warriors raised a din to rival any army. Ulfrik flitted through the camp, kicking men to action, rushing any man who appeared to pause in thought, all while declaring their defeat.

Horses charged away without riders. Ulfrik paused in surprise, for no horse would be of use on a wooded hill and thus were useless to the Franks. But their panic aided the air of defeat so he welcomed the beasts. Personally he hated horses.

The pause was his undoing, for as long has he kept moving no one had a moment to consider his identity. Yet the moments it took to watch horses charge past gave the Franks a breather. Now men pointed at him, and one challenged, "Who the bloody Christ are you?"

Ulfrik smiled and flitted away, and the men bounded after him. He had one final task to fulfill. The commanders' tents needed to be set afire. From the yellow blaze to his left, he knew Hakon had probably set his fires. Shadows danced around it in confusion, and Ulfrik had to laugh. He would not have the chance to enjoy that spectacle up close, as his pursuers were close behind.

The confusion was complete and by now the lie of the attack needed no one to repeat it. The Franks scattered either to find safety or to find an enemy. Ulfrik raced amid clusters of determined men forming ranks and heading for the hill. They ignored him for a coward, but after he passed he heard his pursuers calling. "He's the enemy. Get him!"

Ulfrik ran into a man, and whether or not he intended to fight, Ulfrik stabbed him through the thigh while the Frank was on the ground. He blew his horn again, hoping to signal to Hakon and the others his position. He did not hear answering horns, but then he was crashing through bunches of confused and angered Franks and their surly leaders.

There appeared no end to the number of Franks in the rear who were roused by the commotion at the fore. He was not breaking out as he had expected and hoped Hrolf had not encountered the same resistance. Hrolf's escape path had been at the thinnest point of enemy concentration, yet the reliability of estimates made in darkness was not strong.

As Ulfrik was discovering.

After a day of running and fighting, he was amazed he could weave and dodge like a man half his age. The Franks at the rear were either chasing horses, calming their fellows, or forming up for a defense. A knot of warriors readying their teardrop-shaped shields caused him to veer to the right and sprint past like a stag fleeing a hunter.

But this bought him squarely into a line of spearmen ranked up and marching with purpose. They were too wide to skirt and too closely ranked to break. He whirled about to backtrack and found his pursuers were close behind and had gathered more support.

He was in the jaws of a closing trap. He had only a sword and mud-smeared mail for protection. Even in murky light of the campfires he could see the gleam of anticipation in the eyes of his pursuers. Holding out his sword, he touched the silver amulet of Thor's hammer at his neck.

"A bolt of lightning would be good right now," he said, then screamed his battle cry.

5

Mord Guntherson's toes throbbed with pain. He guessed he had kicked every stone and root as he fumbled through the darkness in retreat. Now that they arrived at their ships, he wanted nothing more than to launch his and be away from this horrid mess. Dozens of ships were a jumbled mass along the shore, just as they had left them. Men carrying torches walked among the hulls, directing men to their ships or helping to launch others into the river. Mord ordered his own men to locate their vessel and fetch him once they were ready to leave. He sat on a fallen log and began rubbing his calves.

He had pitched headlong down the hill, along with all of Hrolf's forces, and broke through the thin Frankish resistance. It had not even been a resistance. The Franks were so ready to believe in a surprise attack that they had scrambled at the slightest provocation. Mord and his fellows had only to march through them as the Franks fled the so-called attack. None had pursued them up the banks, probably expecting a trap, and so the enemy had let Hrolf and his hundreds upon hundreds of men melt away into the night.

Another victory snatched from total defeat, all thanks to the perfect and wonderful Ulfrik Ormsson. The man must shit gold and piss silver. Of the years he had spent under Ulfrik's command, Mord had seen a man who made more mistakes than successes and whose choices were questionable. He had an uncanny knack for worming out of trouble and appearing better for it. Men flocked to his banner despite so many of them ending up dead shortly after. Mord had to admit he did at least provide glorious ends for his men.

The mood of his fellow warriors had lightened, and now people hustled about with purpose. Only hours ago they were sodden with defeat, himself included in that number. This adventure in Chartres had gained them nothing, and he had backed it harder than any other jarl. He had only just earned Hrolf's respect after years of being relegated to his backwater for the incident with his bullish, arrogant brat. What had begun as another attempt at Paris to test the new King of West Frankia's resolve had devolved into this siege of a secondary target of Chartres. They would be counting the dead for months, and Hrolf's skeptical eye would be turned toward him once more.

"Has no one seen Ulfrik?" Hrolf himself was calling out for his second in command. Mord scowled at the giant king and his unseemly concern for Ulfrik. If he was such a hero then no doubt he would fight back the entire Frankish army with a stick and then walk all the miles back to Rouen with a sack of booty over his shoulder. Why should the greatest and most powerful jarl ever to rule this land stoop to seeking out one man?

"We've not seen him, Jarl Hrolf," answered another warrior, whose arm was in a sling made from his cloak. "There was too much confusion."

Hrolf waved the man aside then began to shout orders as others filed past him. "You three, begin the formation of the barricade. Fill the space from the riverbank all the way into the tree line with anything you can find. Make it waist high. Use my authority to gather whoever you need. Hurry, there are only a few hours before dawn and the Franks will come."

Mord continued to rub his leg as Hrolf surveyed the progress of the retreat, standing with hands on his hips as if presiding over a victory march. Mord set his leg down and was about to hide himself elsewhere when Hrolf caught him.

"What are you doing sitting down?" Hrolf was to him in two quick steps, a looming giant. Mord leapt to his feat.

"I had something in my boot, Jarl Hrolf."

"You should be leading the men to safety, not tending your foot like some old woman." Hrolf's eyes were hidden in the low light, but his frown was plain to read. "Oversee the construction of the barricade. Put whatever you can find into it. It just has to slow down the Franks."

"Jarl Hrolf, we're wasting time with the barricade. The enemy did not pursue us, so we should get onto our ships and leave. The barrier is wasted effort."

Hrolf had returned to studying the flow of men out of the darkness, nodding with satisfaction. "I thought we'd been backed into a trap we'd not escape. Ulfrik's plan saved us. I only hope he will join us before long."

Mord felt his face growing hot. Of course the unspoken words were that the trap has been Mord's fault and that the failure at Chartres was his idea. Of course Ulfrik would get all the credit for anything good, as he always did. Mord cleared his throat.

"I think we have the gods to thank for our escape tonight."

Hrolf looked down his nose at Mord and squinted. "Yes, Ulfrik and the gods. The two seem to go together, don't they? Would that all my men be so favored, then Paris might have been mine by now."

The jab stung and Mord turned aside, face on fire and heart pounding against his ribs. "I will see to my men, Jarl Hrolf."

"I've not dismissed you," Hrolf said, a hint of irritation in his voice. "See to this barricade's construction and close it up once the last man has come through. When Ulfrik arrives direct him to me immediately, and if he does not, then we will post a guard for him. Do not fail me in this simple task. Build a barrier of shit, but build it high and wide enough to halt the Franks long enough for us to be back at Rouen."

When Hrolf stalked off, the guards following in his wake gave

Mord sly smiles. He shook his head and cursed Ulfrik's ridiculous barrier. Yet it was now his task to make the idea real, and to do it to Hrolf's satisfaction. Swearing as he went, he gathered up all the uninjured men he could find and set them to work.

The effort was more than he had expected, and hours later he had organized dozens of crews to fell trees, gather debris, and assemble a chest-high wall from the banks of the Eure up the slope and into the woods. The men were animated and positive, glad to have escaped with their lives. Whenever he heard Ulfrik's name mentioned, he was sure to interrupt and redirect the men. By the time a vague light stained the eastern horizon, most of the ships had departed, including Ulfrik's whelp Gunnar the Black and Ulfrik's lackey, Einar Snorrason. They had wanted to wait for Ulfrik, but Hrolf insisted they return to safety.

Now Mord presented his wall to Hrolf, who had returned with his full crew at his back. Hrolf nodded and patted Mord's shoulders. "That's a tangled mess if ever there was one. It won't fall over easily. Is that a deer carcass woven into it?"

"Someone threw it into the mix," Mord said. "Anything to keep the Franks from crossing. I've anchored it to the deep woods, where the density of the trees does the same job as the wall. They won't be skirting this."

"And Ulfrik has not come. I fear the worst, but he is the most resourceful man I've ever met. Whatever his fate, he and his band will arrive here, and I will not leave him behind. We owe him our lives."

Mord stared at Hrolf, unwilling to add any more praise. His father, Gunther One-Eye, had told him his contempt and hatred for Ulfrik was too open. He counseled to praise him and show support no matter what he felt. The advice was too hard for Mord.

"You've done all you can," Hrolf said. "Get to your ship and leave. I will select men to stay."

"Allow me to leave some of my own," Mord said. "I was harsh in judging Ulfrik's plan and it's the least I can do now to make up for it."

Hrolf patted his shoulder again. "Good for you. If the Franks arrive before he does, then get to the ship and flee. Ulfrik will either be dead, captured, or following another escape route."

As Hrolf set about his final preparations choosing a guard for Ulfirk, Mord located his own second in command. He had been his father's man, only leaving Gunther because he had grown too old to fight and too blind from the cataract on his single eye. The strong man was devoted to Gunther and had passed the loyalty onto him. He found him now, Magnus the Stone, leaning against the barricade with arms folded and watching him. Magnus had a fiercely weathered face, deeply lined, and a hooked nose with a red scar on its bridge. His dark hair was shot through with gray.

"I have a job for you," Mord said. "Hrolf is assembling a guard for Ulfrik's return."

Magnus did not show any recognition, yet he had served his father once in arranging for Ulfrik's demise. Without having to say more, Magnus simply nodded in acknowledgment of the mission. "I'll be glad to watch for his return. I'll have my bow ready."

"I'm sure a retreat can be very confusing. Be careful to shoot the right men," Mord said.

His hands were cold and his heart racing. Throughout the siege he had few opportunities to remove Ulfrik from the board, as his father liked to describe it. Now it seemed his chance was at hand. With Ulfrik off the board, Mord's competition for Hrolf's favor would be gone and Ulfrik's lands would be in question, particularly if his sons had also died in the battles. He had been waiting patiently for that land, for it was the southern gateway into Hrolf's territory and to defend it was the highest honor. That it held a large concentration of farms was also attractive. They had expected Ulfrik to die as he threw himself into battle after battle in an effort to rebuild his wealth and reputation. No one survived such constant warfare, yet at the end of every summer Ulfrik had a new victory and more glory. Hrolf awarded him with more lands, and when he reached the limit, he awarded Ulfrik with gold and status. Now his own father, Hrolf's most trusted man, took a seat on the rowing bench while Ulfrik replaced him at the steering board. His father had saved Ulfrik from nothing, promoted him, and that was his thanks. It sickened him to think on it.

Years ago his father had recognized the threat Ulfrik posed to their future, and he had worked through others to arrange for his death. It had failed when that young fool, Throst Shield-Biter, had chosen drama over practicality in Ulfrik's murder, and the lucky bastard survived. During the years Ulfrik was away, Gunther had positioned Mord as Hrolf's closest man, and was grooming the young Vilhjalmer to fall under Mord's sway. However, the brat did not get along with Mord, and the disaster that followed was something he did not want to remember.

Gunther insisted that this adventure would be the right moment to have Ulfrik meet his end once more, and this time no fancy traps but a tried-and-true stab through the heart. Mord feared he would have to return to his father with yet another defeat, but this retreat had worked out in his favor. Both Ulfrik and Hakon might either be dead already or, more likely, lagging behind them. Magnus was efficient and unswerving in his purpose, and two arrows would find their marks before anyone understood what was happening.

"It would be good to leave me some help," Magnus said. "Just in case things become difficult."

"Of course, a good idea. Just watch for Ulfrik and report back to me immediately."

Mord left Magnus to attend the details. His hands actually trembled with excitement that this gambit might succeed. If Ulfrik was not dead already, he would be if he showed up here, and Mord would be free of his biggest obstacle to standing at Hrolf's side where he rightfully belonged.

6

Ulfrik flew at his pursuers, five in all, led by a potbellied man with a fringe of frizzy beard and hair surrounding his red face. He screamed for their deaths, sword held recklessly overhead as if he planned to split a tree. In his time, Ulfrik had learned that men who feared death often found it, and those who did not concern themselves with it lived. Besides, no man died before the Fates had chosen his time. Today was not his time. He knew it.

All five enemies skidded to a halt and scrambled to line up. Ulfrik laughed at their reaction, so typical of drilled men who had not learned real combat. He was already cleaving through the links of their potbellied leader's mail as they formed up. The blade cut deep into his neck and the man bellowed as he crumpled to his knees with blood flowing down his chest. Ulfrik slashed right, clipping a shield, punched left and cut his knuckles on the edge of the man's nose guard, then sprang through the opening he had created.

He did not turn to see if he was pursued. He plunged back into the milling confusion and men made room for him to pass. In the predawn darkness they did not recognize him as the enemy. Running in a wide loop through the campfires and confused enemy, he came to the edge of the camp then slipped into the woods. He sought the biggest tree he could find in the slate colored murk, then collapsed against it. His breath was ragged, his heart thumped so hard his eyes pulsed, and his legs burned with the effort. Sweat rolled into his mouth off his nose and he laughed. Behind him he heard crashes and clangs, Frankish curses, and the cries of horses.

The plan had worked. He did not need to see Hrolf escape to know that in such turmoil he would have had no trouble. Now all that remained was for him to round up Hakon, Finn, and the others. That might prove a great deal harder to do, and it was the least considered part of his plans. For the moment, he recovered from the strain. His left leg began to stiffen and he rubbed it furiously.

As the night wore on, the Franks settled down. He did not know exactly what they were up to, but doubtlessly by now they had discovered Hrolf's abandoned camp and would be preparing for pursuit. Dawn was a few hours away yet, but scouts would be sent ahead to start tracking by torchlight. If Hrolf built the barrier, then the Franks would never catch up. Ulfrik finally decided he had to seek out the others. He had hoped they would find him, but he had possibly drifted off to sleep at one point. He did not know. Neither friend nor enemy had spotted him against the wide tree.

Standing again pained his back and legs, and his knees cracked like breaking sticks. His first steps were like those of an ancient man, reminding him of how his old friend Snorri hobbled from one bench to the next. He groaned but forced his legs to move, carelessly kicking through the underbrush. He circled left, which he guessed was toward the riverbank, but in the starless night he had no sense of direction. His only plan had been to meet up with the others behind the Frankish lines and seek the riverbank at dawn. He had hoped Finn would have had more to offer the plan, being the truest woodsman of all his hirdmen. Yet he had been too excited at the prospect of creating the diversion, or else he had no idea how to rejoin the group.

Yet the gods truly loved him this day, and as he staggered past a clump of bushes amid the trees, Finn's familiar voice whispered to him, "You move like a blind bear. We're over here."

He stopped and stared at the dark shapes, needing a moment for Finn's head to come into focus over the tops of the bushes. "Are there others?"

"Hakon, Ragnar, Bruni, and Olen are with me. Alvis and Ketil are watching the Franks for us. Only Gils is missing."

"All those good men," Ulfrik said as he pushed through the bushes to join Finn, "but you couldn't find me. I'm better at hiding than I thought."

"No, you just didn't listen when I told you we'd assemble south of the camp. This is north of the camp, exactly the wrong way."

Finn's smile flashed in the low light, and Ulfrik felt his face grow warm.

"This is north? How do you even know? Never mind. We have to find Gils, then we make our escape."

Finn was already shaking his head. "We'll never find Gils, not now. The Franks are all awake and they've got their wits about them. If we don't go now, we'll be caught for sure."

Ulfrik pushed past Finn toward the dark shapes huddled in a circle and seated on the ground. He stood above them, unwilling to crouch and let them hear his joints snap and pop. Hakon stood and embraced him. "We were beginning to wonder if you'd join us."

"As soon as we locate Gils, we're leaving." Ulfrik could not see anyone's face in the blue darkness, but he read their reluctance in their bowed heads. His voice hissed with irritation. "Don't stain your bravery with cowardice now. None of you left without me, and I have sworn to not leave without all of you. If Gils is dead, then I need to know before I leave. Otherwise, he must escape this camp."

The men nodded, but their hearts were not in it. Ulfrik understood they had already risked much, and finding Gils in such a wide camp was challenging. He was their jarl, gold-giver, and war-leader. They would do as he commanded, but he would not command men to risk their lives for something they did not believe in. Hakon, standing beside him, clapped his shoulder.

"I am with you, Father. If it were me in the hands of the Franks, I'd want to know my brothers remembered me."

"You won't find him without me," Finn said from behind. "So I'll go. In fact, let me spare the others the choice. I say the three of us are enough. All the others should make for the riverbank and try to catch up to Hrolf's ship. Too many men will just get us all caught."

"I'll listen to Finn whenever it comes to sneaking about the woods," Ulfrik said. "You men hold the ship for our return. We will not be far behind."

Decisions made, they all parted with encouraging words. Ragnar begged forgiveness for his cowardly reaction and Ulfrik waved it off. All of his men had been heroes that day. "We all get scared," he said to the young man. "There's no shame in that as long as it does not rule you."

Finn then led him and Hakon through the woods to where Gils was last seen. They had all taken sections of the camp, and Gils's had been directly opposite of their location. Traversing the distance took much longer than it would to walk normally. Finn stopped them dozens of times for things Ulfrik could not see, and Hakon appeared just as confused. Yet Finn knew his work, and he guided them to the opposite end without rousing any guards.

"This is where he should be, but the Franks were like madmen. Gils could've ended up anywhere." Finn checked the sky and shook his head. "We've got little time before the cock crows. I know why we are doing this, but daylight will see us captured or dead. We're of no use to anyone like that."

"Then let's make use of what time we have." Ulfrik moved off to search for likely hiding places. He whispered Gils's name as he went.

Hakon and Finn also separated, and after a short search Hakon give a harsh whisper. "Here he is."

Doubling back to Hakon, he arrived at the same time as Finn. Gils was seated in the bole of a tree looking content and quiet. His flesh was blue in the vague predawn light. One hand gripped his sword, the blade snapped in half, and the other hand rested on his stomach. The blood that flowed out from beneath it appeared like pitch.

"A warrior's death," Ulfrik said. "A man cannot ask for more. Better than dying in a bed."

Hakon grunted his concurrence. Finn knelt beside him and touched his neck. "He's cold. Must've died hours ago."

"Where's the enemy that slew him?" Ulfrik asked the question, but realized the answer was closing in on them. As if in confirmation, a branch snapped behind them. Finn stood and his face was pale. Hakon's hand fell to his sword. "They're all around us. Act as if you don't realize they are near."

The three of them stood over Gils's corpse and Ulfrik felt eyes on him from every direction, but more from Finn and Hakon. When he judged the Franks were closer, he spun around and drew an ax from his belt. He confronted a semicircle of Franks and two had bows with arrows nocked.

"Finn, lead us out of here!" he shouted.

The two bowstrings thrummed as the arrows let loose.

7

Hakon shouted in surprise as an arrow thudded into his gut. Finn jinked aside as the other arrow screamed through the air where he had stood. The Franks were dressed in muted greens and browns and wore only furs over their bodies. Ulfrik picked the closest bowman and let his ax fly. The ax head flickered as it whirled straight into the face of the bowman with a wet chop. Before the Frank collapsed, Finn was already running past Ulfrik.

He grabbed Hakon, who still stood, and together they began to run. "Are you wounded?" he shouted.

"The mail stopped it. Can you believe the luck?"

Ulfrik shook his head, conserving his breath. He had run too often and too hard this day and his legs were already leaden. Were it not for imminent death behind him, he would have rather turned to fight. Yet the alarm horn sounded from behind and he heard the Franks curse him. He pumped his legs through the pain.

They both trailed Finn, which felt like chasing a rabbit as he dashed from bush to tree to open ground. Ulfrik cursed him more than once when he tripped or stumbled over some unseen obstacle. He should not have been able to outrun younger, unarmored men, and after a while he slowed to check over his shoulder. Nothing stirred behind him.

"Hold on. I think we've lost them." He leaned on his knees, gasping and sweat dripping from his face. Hakon leaned beside him.

"Impossible, Father. They're just careful not to be led into another trap. Once they realize it's only us, they'll catch up and bring others. We have to keep running."

"Remind me to never again devise a plan that requires so much running. My legs ... the old wounds. I can't keep running."

Hakon pulled on Ulfrik's chain shirt. "You must."

Now Finn had doubled back and stood panting before Ulfrik. "If you can't run, we make our stand here."

Ulfrik shook his head, too weary to protest. The two hovered over him as he continued to lean on his knees and catch his breath. They shifted impatiently but held their words. At last Ulfrik straightened and wiped the sweat from his brow. "Don't be so quick to throw your life away. There's no glory in dying here. You two travel ahead and get the ship prepared. When I catch up, I'll have an army at my back. For now, I can't run anymore."

"Get rid of your mail," Finn said. "There's no need for it. You'll travel easier."

He grumbled and looked down at his mail. Links were broken and blood mixed with the mud he had smeared on it. "It doesn't seem like much, but this is a fine coat. Besides, Hakon's mail just saved his life. I can't risk taking it off."

"But you would risk being overtaken instead," Hakon said. "Finn's right. Leave it off and let's continue. I will carry it for you."

"It will become twisted beyond repair if you carry it. No, I'll have another coat made, or better still Hrolf will award me one for what I've done. Help me out of it."

He worked out of the shirt, Hakon helping to raise it over his head while Finn held his sword. The relief on his shoulders was immediate and he flexed his arms, enjoying the new freedom. The mail crunched as Hakon dropped it into the underbrush, and Ulfrik gave it one last glance. He sighed then said, "Let's keep moving."

Without the weight on his shoulders and back, Ulfrik moved freely for a short time, then the old wounds in his leg flared into hot pain. He gritted his teeth as he loped after Finn and Hakon. His son constantly checked over his shoulder, and when he saw Ulfrik slowing down, he called them all to a halt. Ulfrik again leaned over, gritting his teeth in frustration. "Fleeing disagrees with me. That damn fall from the tower, so long ago, but my leg feels like it was yesterday. If I keep pushing, I'll go lame. You two hurry ahead and I'll follow."

Hakon straightened Ulfrik and pulled his arm across his shoulder. "I'm not leaving you, Father. Finn, run as fast as you can to the ships. We will be behind."

Finn was about to protest, but Hakon snapped at him. "You won't help us if you stay. The men need to know we are still alive and to wait for us. Go now."

"Just keep the riverbank to your left and you will be all right." Finn stopped and cocked his head. Ulfrik leaned back and heard the sounds of approaching danger. The Franks were not disguising their approach from the noise of shouts and cracking branches.

"Do as Hakon ordered," Ulfrik said, his voice weary. "We will be right behind."

The dawn colored the woods in gray-green hues, and Finn vanished into the trees like a ghost. Ulfrik shook his head, admiring his young friend's uncanny ability to hide. Hakon tapped his shoulder and the two began to trudge forward. Neither spoke, and Ulfrik was both grateful and shamed for the aid of his son. His weakness was a danger to them both, but he did not relish becoming a captive of the Franks. He had sworn to die rather than ever be taken a prisoner again.

Keeping the Eure River at their left, Ulfrik glimpsed sparkles from the water and smelled the wet mud. All the while he staggered along with Hakon to support him, he heard the Franks drawing closer. At one point someone cried out even nearer to them than he had expected.

"They must've found your mail coat," Hakon said, then adjusted his grip around Ulfrik's shoulders. "How do you feel? Can you run again?"

Ulfrik only offered a grunt and powered forward. He conserved his strength for the final push that he expected. His left leg burned with pain, and the front of his thigh had gone numb. His hips creaked and every joint flared with hot fire. If he had to fight now, he could not defend himself against a lame grandmother never mind the limber, angry Franks pursuing him.

They pushed directly to the banks and down the river and he saw the silhouette of a waist-high barrier of debris blocking the way. Behind it, a ship's mast leaned to the side where it had been hauled ashore.

In the same instant, he heard the Franks screaming from behind.

"You've got to run, Father," Hakon said, unhooking his arm from around his back. "They're right behind us."

He did not look back. Their brassy curses were loud in his ears. He just nodded and began to run. Hakon kept pace with him.

The riverbank was muddy and uneven, so they stayed closer to the grass. Ulfrik watched where his feet landed, for one rut or rock would sprawl him out and his pursuers would finish him off. Their swearing was clear now, and one challenged them. "Stop and we will show mercy."

Ulfrik coughed a laugh at the lie and forced his legs to pump. His left leg, the one that had been mangled years ago, was leaden and hot. Yet he managed to kick it forward and continue. An arrow sped past him. He felt the air of its passing on his face and saw the grass ahead of him part as it lodged in the dirt. He wished he had not abandoned his mail coat.

As they neared the barrier, men appeared over the top, and Ulfrik experienced a relief he could not believe. His shouts were weak and breathless, but he started to laugh all the same. They were going to escape.

Their shapes were still indistinct and in the trees' shadows, but Ulfrik thought they were readying arrows. Of course, they could not shoot or they would risk striking him or Hakon, but once they had made the lines, a volley would force back their pursuers.

They were close now, and Ulfrik saw a cluster of figures on the right lift their bows over the barrier and aim.

Their arrows were leveled at him.

"Wait, it's me!" he shouted.

The shafts flew, and Ulfrik dove at Hakon who did not seem to notice. He missed his son, landing face-first in the mud, but scrambled up as fast as he had fallen.

"Hakon, get down!"

His son stumbled with a cry. Ulfrik could hear his heart beating. He dashed for Hakon and flipped him over. His face was covered in blood and an arrow stuck through his right cheek and protruded from the left side of his face. His eyes were wide in horror, but he still lived.

Ulfrik looked behind him. Nearly a dozen Franks charged at him and were a spear-throw away. All his pain vanished and he hefted Hakon off the ground. "You're fine, boy. Get up and run."

He felt a burning tug at the inside of his calf, looked down to see a thick gash through his torn pants, then glared at the men on the barrier. It seemed they had shot again, but now others were wrestling with them. At least a dozen of his own men had leapt the barrier and were now charging for him.

"It's Ulfrik," he called out. The men rushed to him, and Ragnar, who had been so guilty for leaving him, helped to carry Hakon. "What were you thinking, shooting at us?"

Ragnar shook his head. "It was the others, not ours. They must've mistook you for Franks."

More men streamed past and from behind he heard their battle cries and the crash of blades. His only concern was for Hakon, who staggered along in a daze with blood drizzling from his mouth. He choked and coughed on it, but Ulfrik and Ragnar hauled him to the barrier where Finn waited to help them over.

"I don't know why they shot at you. I told them you were behind me." Finn's freckled face was white with shock, and he stared at Hakon's wound with open revulsion.

"They'll pay for that mistake," Ulfrik said. "But after we get on the water. Let's get Hakon aboard then launch the ship."

Hakon's protests were incomprehensible with the arrow skewering his face. The men who had shot at them lingered behind the barrier. There were three and now they were not interested in shooting nor helping their companions drive back the Franks. Ulfrik glared at them, but returned to Hakon. Finn leapt aboard and took Hakon's arms while Ragnar and Ulfrik pushed him over.

In the distance, the Franks were in retreat and Ulfrik's men were shouting victory. He hoped they had sense to return rather than chase down any stragglers. To his relief all of his men were uninjured and Hrolf's men had only taken superficial wounds. The three men sulking by the barrier were Mord's, and having learned that, Ulfrik burned with rage. Once all were at the ship, he ordered it launched.

"That was a scouting party to follow us. The main force is just behind them and we have to flee now." He stopped Mord's men, who had not offered an apology. He recognized one as a veteran, a hard man with a red scar across his nose who had served Gunther One-Eye. His name was Magnus the Stone. Before Magnus boarded the ship Hrolf had left them, Ulfrik grabbed him by the shoulder. He looked as if Ulfrik's touch sullied his armor.

"You should have known better than to shoot at us. If I were a suspicious man, I'd say you wanted to kill us." Ulfrik held Magnus's cold eyes, and he knew he had guessed right. The veteran glanced at Ulfrik's hand.

"We thought you were Franks. Sorry, my eyes are not what they used to be."

"Good for me or that arrow would be in my neck," Ulfrik grabbed Magnus's beard and pulled him closer. "You'll pay the blood money you owe to Hakon. And if I decide you intended to kill either of us, then you'll pay with your head."

Ulfrik released the veteran's beard, whose lined face broke into a smile.

"Of course, Jarl Ulfrik. It's only right." He stepped back and looked at Ulfrik's leg. "How's the old wound? I bet it hurts every day. It's a hard thing to grow so old yet still fight against men half your age."

The veteran mounted the ship without another word, and Ulfrik decided that his disagreements with Mord had taken a deadly turn.

8

Ulfrik smiled as he emerged from the trees and saw his hall seated atop the gentle hill, dozens of buildings spread out beneath it with peaceful curls of hearth-smoke rising from their rooftops. His legs and feet were still sore from running, but he was glad to make the short walk from the Seine River where his ships docked to his hall. Hakon's expression was lost beneath the rust-stained bandages swaddling his face, but his eyes were bright with joy.

"It has been a long summer away from home, hasn't it?" Ulfrik put his hand on his son's shoulder. "I'll be glad to stretch beside the hearth with a horn of fresh mead. No more of that stale piss we had to drink for so long."

Hakon nodded, still unable to speak. It had only taken four days to arrive home from Chartres, and Hakon still moaned with the pain of his wounds. He had lost two teeth, shattered by the arrow, and his tongue had been cut deep. Finn had stitched the tongue together as best as he could while on a rocking deck, but the wound was in an awkward position, and Hakon could not bear the agony. For now, he could only drink and not eat. The puncture wounds on his cheeks would leave deep scars but not affect him otherwise. Ulfrik seethed with anger at Magnus the Stone's ignorance. His heart burned for vengeance, but as a jarl of high standing he had to behave with more grace and accept Magnus's payment. In truth, it was Hakon's duty to demand and collect compensation, but Ulfrik knew that arrow had been for him.

"Do you think they've prepared a feast for our arrival?" Finn asked. He walked at Ulfrik's left, and the rest of his crew fanned out behind them, walking with a light step and full of laughter.

"Gunnar's ships were at dock, so I'm sure by now he's told my wife a lie about how we were only a day behind him. I've no doubt a feast has been ready since he returned, and that he has had one for himself already."

"Well, that's unfair," Finn said.

"You could have left with him."

"What we did was more glorious. I made the right choice."

All laughed, even Hakon through his injuries. At last they came to the stockade walls and found Gunnar, his crew, and the rest of Ulfrik's hirdmen waiting. When the gates swung open, the cries of welcome echoed to the skies and Ulfrik forgot all his pains and worries as they parted for his entrance.

"You'd never guess we're returning in defeat," Finn said.

"After the summer we had and the narrow miss being trapped, I'm proclaiming this a victory worth celebrating."

The men welcomed him with cheers and pats on his back. Families and lovers rushed to each other. At the edges of the crowd Ulfrik saw the forlorn expressions of those whose fathers or husbands would never return. He would later meet them all, pay blood prices, and tell them how bravely their man died, even if he had not witnessed it himself. For today, however, he was content to see his own woman, Runa, standing beside Gunnar with her hands folded at her lap.

Time had stained the tight curls of her hair with gray, but had not diminished the fullness of it. She had at last succumbed to pressure and wore a head covering like every other married woman. Her waist had thickened and lines had worn between her brows, but she was as beautiful to him as ever. He was conscious of the limp bought on from all his running, and struggled to walk straight to her. When he enveloped her in his arms, more cheers went up.

He felt drunk on her sweet scent and her warm, soft body against his tired skin was a salve to all his pains. They kissed deeply, and when they drew apart he looked into her dark eyes. "Sorry I was delayed. It pleases me to find you well and happy for my return."

Her smile deepened, and she put a warm, smooth hand to his cheek. "Welcome home, Ulfrik."

She turned to Hakon, and Ulfrik knew she did not recognize him at first glance. Gunnar also seemed to not recognize him until Hakon presented himself. Runa gave a short gasp and ran to him. "What happened to you?"

"It's not as bad as it looks," Ulfrik said, pulling his wife back from Hakon. "We had some difficulties escaping the Franks. Hakon caught an arrow through the mouth. He's lost a few teeth and his tongue was cut, but give the boy time and he'll be spitting and cursing again."

Runa's face was pale with shock and her dark eyes were like two dots in circles of white. Her hands hovered around Hakon's face, unsure of what to do, but he gently grabbed her wrists and lowered them. He tried to speak, yet only muffled words escaped the bandages. Runa's eyes teared up.

"His tongue was cut? Will he speak again?"

"Of course, Finn stitched it back together." He turned to point at Finn, but discovered he was lost in the arms of his own woman.

"Stitched it back together?" Ulfrik did not think she could grow any paler, but she did. Gunnar shook his head and led Ulfrik away by the arm.

"Father, you've spent too many days talking to warriors and have forgotten how to speak to your wife."

"Well, wasn't she Runa the Bloody once? You know what your mother's history—"

"You're missing the point, Father. Hakon is her little boy. Come with me. You've got grandchildren waiting for you."

They pushed through the clumps of people embracing in

welcome. Some were families reunited, others were younger boys crowding their older peers, others were just tradesmen come to enjoy the happiness of returning warriors. All around them was jovial chatter and laughter, Ulfrik's favorite part of returning from a long raid. His hall dominated a wide swath of crucial farmland and river trade along the Seine. Everyone here had a stake in his successfully demonstrating strength.

Gunnar's wife was a woman he had captured in England during his dark years as a raider. A full-bodied woman who stood no taller than Gunnar's chest, she went by the name of Morgan. She had learned to love Gunnar and gave him many children, though most had not lived. Not until Gunnar settled his own lands next to Ulfrik's did his family begin to prosper and his children survive. He had two girls and a son, and all three were a delight to Ulfrik. The boy was only two years old, but looked like him with bright blue eyes and golden hair that had Gunnar's strong curls.

Standing with his grandchildren was Aren, or Broken-Tooth as others had come to call him. It was a cruel name, for his true father had smashed his front teeth in a fit of rage. Yet he did not disagree with it, and made up bold lies of how he had come by the disfigurement. His wide, inscrutable face regarded Ulfrik with an outward coolness that Ulfrik knew masked a fierce love. Though not his son by blood, Aren was his wife's son, carrying both her passions and her loyalty. To that he bought his own keen intelligence that made him a master of both men and strategy. At twenty-one years of age, Aren had not filled out and remained far less imposing than his half-brothers, nor did he possess Finn's wiry strength.

He stood with arms locked behind his back as Ulfrik approached. Aren's eyes swept Ulfrik's body head to toe, examining all the cuts and scars he had earned on this campaign. Most did not show on the outside, but Aren was adept enough that he would eventually see those internal wounds as well. "Welcome home, Father. You look well."

"That I am," he said, then gave Aren a bear hug that he returned with a weak pat. "No worries while I was gone?"

"I saw to everything as you would," Aren said. Ulfrik had left him in charge, for, though lacking physical strength, his sharp mind and insight into the hearts of men made him a formidable leader. He would anticipate trouble long before even the troublemakers themselves considered it, then stamp it dead at the root.

"I have news," Ulfrik said. "I want your opinions on the matter when we have time to talk alone."

Aren's eyes flicked over Ulfrik's shoulder, and he turned to see Runa fussing over Hakon's injury. "I watched you trying to explain Hakon's wound to Mother. You seemed ill at-ease. Would that be part of our discussion?"

Ulfrik nodded and Aren flashed a small smile. "As perceptive as ever. Tell me, did Vilhjalmer bring you a woman while I was gone? Hrolf seemed to think the two of you would be up to mischief."

Now Aren's face flushed bright red. Despite his ability to read a person, he had little skill with women. He had told Ulfrik it was because he saw through all the women who wanted him for his riches and status. Ulfrik saw no problem with those intentions, but it bothered his son.

"Vilhjalmer is not allowed to do anything without a dozen guards. You know that, Father."

"The lad is fifteen now, that's a man in anyone's eyes. He's become your best friend, and I'm sure he can do as he pleases."

"Your grandchildren," Aren said with a raised brow. "They're patiently waiting."

"Of course!" He turned to Morgan, who smiled then released her three children to run for Ulfrik. He gathered them together as they clamored for his attention. The eldest girl, Hilde, gave him a soft, gentle kiss upon his cheek and Ulfrik laughed with joy. He swept Gunnar's youngest, his son Leif, into his arms and put him on his shoulders. The middle child Thorgerd, a red-haired girl with green eyes, took his hand, and together they all made for the hall.

The reunion celebration lasted all day and filled his hall to bursting. Though he had wished to recapture Ravndal, he had been given Konal's lands shortly after his return. Not satisfied with that parcel of land, he threw himself into conquest and expanded Hrolf's borders south of the Seine. The work of the last six years had been to pacify this area and provide Hrolf a choke hold on the western Seine River. His reward was this massive swatch of land, and he left Konal's old lands to Einar. He built a great mead hall, twice the size of what he had at Ravndal, second only to Hrolf's great hall outside of Rouen. His success and fame attracted people from all over Hrolf's expansive territory, and even from beyond. Whatever he had lost when Konal had betrayed him to his enemies, he regained and then added to it. He never had to tap the fortune in jewels that Runa had recovered from Konal.

The day turned to night and to day once more. Scores of hirdmen and their women were sprawled in the great hall, sleeping off the drink of the prior night's feast. Even Ulfrik had been too exhausted to find his bed and he awoke under the table with Runa tucked into his arms and gently snoring. The scent of mead and smoke was heavy in the hall, and he carefully extracted himself from his sleeping wife. She had celebrated as hard as any man, and paid for it by passing out early in the night. He kissed her forehead, then stood.

A few others had recovered and now sat staring blankly ahead as the fog of the night wore off. He sat at the high table, and a servant roused from the corner of the hall to attend him. The young girl bought a bowl of water and set it before him. He dipped his hands into the cool water and rubbed it on his face. When he lowered his hands, the hall doors opened and three men rushed inside.

He sat back on his bench as the men knelt before him. Above their heads, Ulfrik's green standard of black elk antlers hung from the rafters. "Jarl Ulfrik, a messenger from Jarl Hrolf the Strider has arrived."

"Do not keep him," Ulfrik said. The men hurried back with one of Hrolf's warriors, who likewise knelt to Ulfrik.

"My lord, Jarl Hrolf the Strider has summoned you to attend him at once. Bring a guard of fifty men."

"Fifty men?" Ulfrik straightened on his bench. "Then he is in no danger?"

The messenger shook his head. "We are not sure. I only know what I have been ordered. Yet, the rumor is the King of the Western Franks, Charles the Simple, wants to offer us peace. I think we have beaten them, Jarl Ulfrik."

Ulfrik blinked, his mind racing. "A peace? From the king himself?"

"It is what I've heard, Jarl Ulfrik. You must not delay. We are to travel north again and meet King Charles at the border. I do not know the place, but perhaps you do. The Franks call it Saint Clair sur Epte, if I have spoken right."

"So you have," Ulfrik said, rubbing the back of his neck. "It is not far from lands I once ruled."

The idea of a peace after being defeated was strange, but Ulfrik had seen the Franks give away their victories before. Another king once had them all encircled and yet surrendered and paid ransom. Perhaps this was the same thing. He had only to attend Hrolf to find out.

"I will leave at once," he said. "While I prepare, make yourself welcomed in my hall."

9

The land rolled away to grassland on every side, a bright blue sky shining down as if in blessing of the day. Ulfrik stood to the rear with his men, where Hrolf and his guard of one hundred hirdmen in freshly scoured mail awaited the arrival of the King of the Western Franks, Charles the Simple. They saw the long train of armored Franks approaching. Behind it a stone church dominated the small village of Saint Clair sur Epte. This place had been chosen for the impossibility of launching an ambush. Ulfrik guessed that despite the offer of peace, the Franks still did not trust Hrolf.

He stood with Gunnar and Einar flanking him. Both men had come as part of Ulfrik's guard and had not been invited. If this was to become the momentous day Hrolf promised, he had wanted both of them at hand to witness it. Einar had especially done much to advance Hrolf's power even as he had grown his own. No one spoke, not daring to break the tense silence that gripped Hrolf's men. All wanted to appear mighty and aloof, particularly after having been chased out of Chartres.

A flock of geese flew overhead, heading toward the Franks, and more than one man nodded at the favorable sign. Hrolf himself even looked skyward and he pointed to the flock, speaking to one of his guards. He stood at least a head taller than the tallest man among them, dressed in his finest clothes and jewels and covered in a bright red robe. The jewels upon his fingers sparkled as he pointed. He had planted his banner of yellow dragons on a red flag and it stirred in the light breeze.

The column drew closer and Ulfrik strained to see it. They were still indistinct with the morning sun behind them, another ploy the Franks had for discouraging attack. Ulfrik squinted but was only able to determine where the king rode by the tight cluster of armored horsemen surrounding him. He could still not see King Charles's features. Like everyone else, this would be his first glimpse of the king that had thwarted them since the death of Odo several years ago. He was called the Simple, for he preferred direct, uncomplicated dealings. Ulfrik liked this king, who had been less strident than Odo and far less cunning.

As Hrolf and his men waited in silence, hands resting on their swords or clasped at their backs, Ulfrik avoided glancing toward Mord. Of course he and Gunther One-Eye had been invited. Old Gunther had been a friend from long ago, and was Hrolf's right hand since his childhood. Now Gunther had a white cataract over his single eye, and his once muscular body had wasted with age. He could no longer fight, but he served Hrolf in other ways. His son, Mord, however, had proved to be far less capable than his father. Ulfrik harbored doubts about his man, Magnus the Stone. During this journey to Saint Clair sur Epte, Mord had been cordial, which Ulfrik had assumed was out of respect for both his father and Hrolf. He almost appeared like the young man who had served him for years, and less the sour complainer he had become since taking a Frankish wife. He did steal a glance, finding him staring ahead like the others, looking for all the world a contented and sincere man. For a moment Ulfrik wondered if Magnus had truly made an honest error.

The arrival of King Charles the Simple was preceded by an advanced guard that dismounted and walked to the center of the field. Hrolf sent his own contingent to meet them. Ulfrik wondered at their discussion, for the Franks had many frivolous details about their kings and their god that had to be observed. For their part, Hrolf had ordered peace straps on every man's swords so that no weapon might be drawn in haste, nor was anyone allowed spears, hand axes, or bows. That should have been enough for the Franks, but the parley groups wrangled for what felt half the day.

"I'm growing older as I wait here," Ulfrik whispered to Einar. "I bet they want to dig a hole for Hrolf to stand in so he doesn't appear taller than their king."

Einar chuckled, but Ulfrik was half serious. Soon Hrolf's men returned, and after a brief discussion he ordered everyone to accompany him. "My jarls should attend me, and let the others stay close at hand. Do not be impressed with their displays of strength. Remember we are Northmen and they are but Franks, their greatest power is in talking us to death."

All laughed at Hrolf's jab, and Ulfrik joined Mord, Einar, and a few others at Hrolf's side. Mord led Gunther One-Eye, and Ulfrik allowed him to stand at Hrolf's right hand. "This position is yours, old friend."

Gunther smiled but said nothing, and Mord even inclined his head. Hrolf was too intent on meeting the Frankish king to notice anything else. The Franks moved with practice, as if they had rehearsed this moment a dozen times. A young boy led the king's white horse forward while his armored guards surrounded him. They all wore blue surcoats with yellow designs like arrowheads. A man got on his hands and knees and the king used him as a stepping stool, no doubt a worthless slave to be treated no better than a footrest.

King Charles was not dressed as the others. He wore a simple shirt of cream colored linen, and a brooch of gold pinned a red cape at his neck. His dark eyes were hooded and calculating, sunken into deep sockets. His hair and beard were neat and close-trimmed in the Frankish style. He wore a thin crown of gold embedded with jewels. Ulfrik noted several of them matched those in his own secret horde. Perhaps Konal had not exaggerated their value as a king's ransom.

"His Majesty, King Charles the Third," announced one of his guards. At least one priest also attended him, a bald-headed man with shrewd eyes and a heavy gold cross swinging over his belly. No doubt he would be whispering to the king throughout this meeting.

King Charles was assisted to the ground much like a lady, and Ulfrik heard men snicker behind him. He forced his own face to remain expressionless. Hrolf appeared unsure of the protocol, so he announced himself. "Jarl Hrolf the Strider, master of the Seine."

The bold shout drew disgusted looks from the king's attendants, but Charles himself parted his thin lips in a smile. Ulfrik might have guessed it to be genuine were he not convinced all Frankish royalty were born of snakes and lizards. The king approached with his interpreter, priest, and two bodyguards. Hrolf needed no one to speak for him, but had a young lad who spoke Frankish fluently. Otherwise, he took no bodyguard, confident in strength and safety.

"A fine day for this meeting," Hrolf said. "You've come a long way from Paris."

"I have, and not for small talk, Jarl Hrolf. I trust my emissaries have explained to you the terms of my offer, and your presence here confirms our acceptance."

"I'm here because your messengers interested me. As for agreeing to anything, that depends upon what I hear from you today."

King Charles's wooden smile died and he blinked in quick succession. "You will not have me negotiate with you now. My offer was clear and your arrival here is confirmation."

"You're not my king yet."

Hrolf's statement sent a ripple through his ranks. Ulfrik struggled to keep from staring at Hrolf. Was this a surrender? This was to be victory over the Franks, as Hrolf had promised when he had summoned him.

"Then I shall state the terms again, and you shall either accept or decline as is your right. Do not negotiate, for I will not abide it, nor will I idle here one moment longer to hear it. Do I make myself clear, Jarl Hrolf?"

Ulfrik bristled at the insolence of this man. Hrolf had asked for nothing more than a fair statement of terms, and this pompous Frank derided him like a subordinate. For Hrolf's part, he held his tongue and waited for King Charles.

The king cleared his throat and raised his chin to look down his nose at the assembled Northmen. "As your folk have so long occupied the coast of Neustria and earned deep respect from the people of Rouen, it is clear that you shall not leave. A new generation of your kinsmen have been born to this land, and call no other place home. It is in our mutual interests that we end hostilities of many decades and establish peace. As King of Western Frankia, it is in my purview to offer you a treaty. Provided that Jarl Hrolf the Strider agrees to become my vassal and that he be baptized in the light of Christ Our Lord, then I shall cede all lands and the subjects therein from the Epte River to the coast. This includes the territories of Caux, Talon, Roumois, Evrecin, and Vexin. He shall be named Count of Rouen and rule in my name with my authority."

Ulfrik's head spun. The offer was tempting. Each year they fought harder but conquered less territory. Peace would be welcomed by many. Becoming a count would set Hrolf above all the petty jarls south of his territory, and in fact bring them into conflict. He did not know how he felt about this choice. Hrolf might be trading peace with the Franks to make enemies of his own kin. Yet the choice was not his to make, and from Hrolf's grin, Ulfrik knew how his jarl had decided.

"That is a fair exchange. Let it be witnessed here, by my old gods and the new god, that I swear to be your loyal bondsman and protect your rule in exchange for the land and title promised me."

The oath hit Ulfrik like a punch. Such plain-spoken words, yet they forged the start of a new rule in Frankia. No more were any of them invaders, but now Franks themselves—at least in name. The thought made him numb.

The false smile returned to King Charles's thin lips. He stood straighter and his eyes glinted in triumph. The priest who had lingered behind his monarch now came forward and addressed Hrolf.

"Oaths are not enough to secure this treaty. You must perform an act of homage and fealty to consecrate it."

"An oath is all I need make. A man who breaks his oath is no man at all. What is this act?"

"You must kiss the foot of your king."

"No. As I swore the day I took up my sword, I will never kneel before another man, nor kiss anyone's foot."

"It must be done," the priest insisted. King Charles placed his foot forward in the grass.

"Let a man who represents me do this," Hrolf said. "It is enough respect that the best and longest serving of my men kiss your foot."

Gunther One-Eye stirred beside Ulfrik, and Mord whispered to his father, "You can still see enough to manage it without me."

Then Hrolf called out his choice, "Ulfrik, perform this act in my name."

The choice surprised Ulfrik, and he felt his face warm as Gunther quietly stepped back. To hesitate would bring shame to Hrolf, so Ulfrik stepped up to King Charles and knelt before him.

The king wore soft shoes of leather that appeared as if he had never worn them before this occasion. Ulfrik stared at the foot, and the priest urged him to perform the rite. "Kiss the king's foot as a sign of homage. What are you waiting for?"

Ulfrik reached down and carefully lifted the king's foot from the grass. As he hunched forwards, lips pursed, he felt his stomach clenching in revulsion and anger. Is this what these Franks demand of their warriors, he thought. To see how willing their best men are to debase themselves to prove their loyalty? As he held the king's foot, he decided how he would demonstrate his loyalty.

He lifted the foot, brushed his lips against it, then continued to raise it.

King Charles the Simple lost his balance as Ulfrik raised the foot past his head and sent the king sprawling into the grass. Hrolf and all his hirdmen burst into raucous laughter. Ulfrik stood over the king, his crown askew on his head and eyes wide in disbelief. The Franks gasped and men surged forward to aid their king. Ulfrik returned to his own, offering the fallen monarch a shallow bow.

Tears of laughter stained Hrolf's cheeks and he grabbed Ulfrik into a bear hug. "You acted for all of us. I could not have done better."

Men patted his back and congratulated him. He felt the warm glow of satisfaction, and it deepened as King Charles raged at the men helping him to his feet. He glared at Hrolf as he straightened the crown on his head.

"There is the act of fealty and homage, my king," Hrolf said with a bow. "The treaty is now made good."

With that, Hrolf became Count of Rouen and the land of Normandy was born.

10

"The humiliation still burns!"

Mord flung his drinking horn into the hearth, the ale hissing into steam as it spilled on the fire. His hall had emptied of men, leaving only a Frankish slave cowering in the darkness of the corners. The old man fetched Mord's horn out of the flames before it was ruined, but Mord's eyes saw only Hrolf and Ulfrik laughing together after he had toppled the king to the grass. Though it had been more than a week gone, he still thought of nothing else.

The hall doors were closed against the balmy night breeze, but moonlight slipped in through the smoke hole in the roof. Mord's mouth tasted of a too-salty meal that he had cursed his wife for ruining. The night was truly a waste but for the ale.

"Bring me another horn," he yelled at the old slave, who was already refilling it from a clay pitcher.

"Stop acting like a drunk. You're better than that." His father, Gunther One-Eye, sat along a bench against the wall. His white hair glowed in the low light and his milky eye fixed on Mord. "I'm tired of the constant complaining. You're worse than your wife."

Mord snatched the horn out of the slave's hand, contemplated ignoring his father's demands, but then handed it back. "Here, don't waste it."

"You've chased everyone away," Gunther said, his voice a low grumble. "And your woman won't be giving you another chance at children tonight. Not after the way you shamed her before everyone."

He had not paused to think about his wife, Fara. As usual, his father had mentioned his lack of an heir. His only child, a girl, had died two years after her birth, and Fara had produced no more children.

"She will recover. Besides, I will have to find another woman to give me sons. Fara obviously is spent of her child-bearing."

Gunther shrugged. They sat in silence, and Mord listened to the night breeze blowing against the hall. Smoke clung to the ceiling like a white cloud, and not for the first time Mord wished his hall were larger. He stared at his hands, unsure of what else to say. If he could not complain of the shame he endured at the Saint Clair sur Epte, he had nothing more on his mind.

"Did that spot of silence help clear your thoughts?" Gunther asked.

"Not really."

His father's head lowered and he pinched the bridge of his nose. "I too felt the shame. More than you. I was Hrolf's oldest serving man, but I suppose I was not his best. A lifetime of faithful service, all forgotten."

"And you know why."

"Because I am old and halfway blind and can't do more for him than try to teach his arrogant son how to be a man. I can't deliver grand victories or flip a king on his ass. My usefulness has passed, and I'm set aside to die."

"All because of Ulfrik!"

"Ulfrik is an upstart. I found him when he was nothing, a slave. I saw the potential in him, pushed him before Hrolf, and made him great. He went from being a farmer on some bird-shit island at the top of the world to Hrolf's trusted man. He moved me aside without a look back. I knew years ago that he had gotten too big to let him remain on the board. Now look at him. He has replaced me not only in his position today, but even in Hrolf's memories. It's as if I had never lived."

"I wish Magnus had shot at him first, rather than his son. It would be good to have him dead."

Gunther shook his head. "Ulfrik is the luckiest man I know. I could have told you an arrow would not find a mark on him. Besides, the time is not right for his sudden death, and to have died that way would have brought Hrolf's suspicions to your hall door. Magnus would have died to keep your secret, but Hrolf would learn the truth. He's good at that."

Mord bowed his head. "I saw an opportunity, much like you did once."

Gunther leaned back and laughed. "That was nothing of the sort. I planned for months to put together a scheme that would take Ulfrik off the board. Magnus worked like a bull assembling all the pieces, bringing Throst and Konal together and carefully planning every step of that plan. I had to work on Hrolf myself, so he put the plan in motion without even realizing it. No one ever knew I had sent Ulfrik into his enemy's hands. That's a great deal more thorough than having him shot in front of dozens of loyal hirdmen. What were you even thinking?"

Mord's fists clenched and his pulse quickened, but he turned his head aside. The slave had shrunk into the darkness again, his narrow head lit only with wavering hearth firelight. Mord squinted at the slave and he slid from the bench and fled to the far corner of the hall.

"We had five years to do what we needed," Gunther said. "I had cleared the road then you shit all over it. You let that brat of Hrolf's get captured by the Franks. You were to be grooming him, planting seeds of a future friendship, and you almost got him killed."

"I was letting him have the adventures he desired. It was bad luck that the Franks attacked." Mord knew how lame this excuse was. It was as weak now as it had been the dozens of other times he had fallen back on it.

"Oh yes, so you've told me. Luck can be good or bad, but a man can help which way his luck turns. Bad luck was Ulfrik's return. Even worse luck is he recovered as well as he has. Now look at the land he possesses. He's practically a count himself. Hrolf does not see him as a threat to his rule. He still thinks Ulfrik is his luck."

Gunther stood, then carefully picked his way to Mord's table, keeping his gnarled hand on a table to guide himself. He set his cataract eye on Mord. "That land, those farms and those trade posts, those should be yours. I saw this coming years ago, that Ulfrik would grab the glory and spoils to himself. He would set you aside as he did me. I have served Hrolf all my life, and he has made my old age comfortable. But he has not done well by you. That land is precious, the very heart of Hrolf's fortune. Whoever controls that land controls Hrolf."

"Then Ulfrik is even more formidable than before."

"Ulfrik is a monster on the battlefield and a leader of men. But he is simple, much like the Frankish king. He is an honest man, and will keep faith with Hrolf until he dies. He would never challenge Hrolf, and Hrolf knows this. Before he realizes what power he has, or worse yet decides to parcel out the land to his sons, he must be removed. It's no longer just him, but his three children. Gods be cursed, but they are craftier than he is, especially the youngest one. Gunnar would not hesitate to abuse whatever power he grasps. Ulfrik has a den of wolves in those three sons, and all of them must be cleared out. Killing the dominant wolf alone will not destroy that pack."

Mord's fists clenched tighter. "The the sooner we act, the better."

His father shook his head. "Have you learned nothing from me? Now is not the time to act, but to watch. Everything has changed. Enemies are now allies and old allies have to decide where they stand. You have been too vocal in your opposition of Ulfrik these years. You must become his friend again, or at least lead Hrolf to believe you have set aside your differences."

"Would that I could bury an ax in his skull while his back is turned."

"And if that was the answer, I'd have done it years ago." Gunther felt along the table edge to find a seat beside Mord. "A whole world of revenge would fall upon you. Just think of Einar Snorrason and the way he lops off heads with his ax like a man knocking apples from a tree. Besides, Hrolf would never stand for murder. Ulfrik and his sons must be the cause of their own undoing."

"And how would that come to be?"

"I don't know yet. But here is what you must consider. Hrolf has vowed to become a Christian, and that will mean the return of churches. Have you not paid attention to how the Christian priests build their churches? They settle wherever they wish, and take whatever they want. Your dear wife is a great Christian, is she not? So is Hrolf's beloved wife, and she comes from a royal line. How hard will it be to steer the church toward Ulfrik's lands when those lands are already so valuable? Trouble will follow, and we only need to goad both sides to increasing conflict. Hrolf will have to side with the Church in any dispute, and there is the seed of Ulfrik's undoing."

"As if Ulfrik is fool enough to fight the church." Mord scowled at the vision of Ulfrik in his head, him presiding over his beautiful hall and bountiful lands.

"Yet one more thing you have not considered. Ulfrik is a warrior. He has built a life of fighting and knows nothing else. He is a master of battle, but is he a master of peace? Give him a year or two of collecting taxes and settling petty arguments and he will be ripe for violence again. Peace will wear on him like rust on a knife, and he will break at the first push. We just watch for the right moment, then provide the push."

"It's all too vague, Father. What if he deals better than we expect?"

"Then we adjust our plans." Gunther smiled, his blind eye staring into the distance. "I will see him gone before I leave this world, and see you in his stead. Where you should have been all along."

11

It was after Sumarmál festivities that Gunnar learned Father Lambert was making trouble on his lands. He was standing outside of his hall, hands on hips, watching his son Leif run with the other boys as they played in the grass. The dozen of them were between two to four years old, and now piled upon each other with shouts of glee. Conversely, Gunnar frowned, listening to his hirdman describe the conflict with the priest.

"So the priest has marked out the foundations of the church he intends to build, and it is in Hrothgar's pasture. The old man is trying to negotiate like you've asked, but the priest says it is the best spot for his church." The hirdman was named Bekan, and was one of the few original men to have sailed with Gunnar. Bekan had a craggy face and heavy brow. A jagged scar ran through his right brow, a horrid white line where a spear had nearly removed his eye. He stared after Leif while standing beside Gunnar, who ground his teeth and flared his nostrils.

"He's deliberately provoking me. It's not enough that he had to insist we celebrate his Easter over our Sumarmál? Wasn't that one victory enough for him?"

"Land is worth more than a festival day," Bekan said.

"And the Christians have a festival day for a thousand of their saints. But it's never enough. They want more, and now they want my land."

"Hrothgar is old and quick to anger. I think he might pull out his war gear and bring the fight to Father Lambert."

"I might allow him the chance," Gunnar said.

The children were again chasing each other in a circle, laughing without a care. A year and half had passed since the treaty of Saint Clair sur Epte has been made. Gunnar surveyed the prosperity he enjoyed since that time. His hall dominated a wide field, and around it were open homes and farms without walls. No longer did they fear Frankish attacks. Half the children running with his son were Franks, and they all spoke the same language. Farmers worked a field in the distance, and faint echoes of the blacksmith's hammering reached them. The parcel of land Ulfrik had cut from his territory and bestowed to him was every bit as rich as he had promised it would be. He and his people enjoyed success undreamed by any of them.

Gunnar hated it. Certainly his wife, Morgan, loved the stability and the station of being a jarl's wife. All loved the taxes he collected and the wealth he now possessed. Peace brought trade and good harvests. Yet his belly grew softer by the day and his ships patrolled the Seine to encounter nothing more than boats of adventurous Danes who poked up from the south once a year to test the resistance of their new enemies. He had never expected his days of warfare would end so soon. Even raiding had no purpose other than to risk his life. His father told him to be glad for it, but he saw it in Ulfrik's eyes too. They were both restless and bored. Peace was fine for a season. Not for a year.

Certainly not for a lifetime.

Bekan cleared his throat and Gunnar shook his head. "So I assume you bring me the joyous news because you fear Hrothgar will become violent and that I should put a stop to it?"

"That was the intention. I left a few men with him, but the priest and his flock have gathered in strength. It's complicated. Those are our people too."

"Franks were the enemy not long ago." Bekan glowered at Gunnar from beneath his brow, causing him to chuckle. "But I know times have changed. Hrothgar was on the land first, so he should be compensated for its use."

"Then you had best tell Father Lambert that. Should you ride to him now?"

"I hate horses," Gunnar said. He shared his dislike for animals with his father, for no one in his family had any affinity with beasts but for Aren, who had raised a puppy once.

"But you are more commanding on horseback," Bekan said. "You should look down on this priest as if you might step on him if he displeases you."

"So you say. It is not a bad idea, though. Bring us two horses and we shall see what bold Father Lambert will do."

He returned to the hall while Bekan fetched mounts from the stable. Morgan and his two daughters were spinning wool while other women labored over the looms. Letting them know he would be gone until later, he kissed the heads of his two girls then fetched his sword from his room. Having lost his sword hand years ago to a mad Frankish warlord, he fought with an ax rather than a sword, which had far more utility for his fighting style. The sword was more recognizable as a symbol of authority to laymen, so he chose one for today. Back outside, Bekan had selected two horses with sleek seal brown coats. The beasts snorted at Gunnar as he approached.

"She smells the mead on you," Bekan joked. "You remember how to ride?"

"Help me onto this monster and let's get be gone."

The journey across his lands was effortless from horseback, though Gunnar had only one hand for the reins of his horse. They followed trails that had been worn around old stumps, deep-set rocks, or other unnavigable patches. He waved at the farmers in their fields but did not stop to chat. He was never as good as his father with building relations with his people. He preferred they worked their farms, paid their taxes, and visited him only with good news.

His territory was not wide, but was deep. Hrothgar's farm was at the northern tip closer to the Seine River, and he heard the shouting long before he saw the farm. They crested a rise then paused to review the situation. Gunnar easily spotted the squat, long buildings of Hrothgar's farm and the fences built around it. He scanned east of it to where the shouting echoed and saw the crowds gathered.

"That's right in the middle of his pasture," Gunnar said.

"Something Father Lambert does not understand."

"Let's help him understand."

Gunnar kicked his horse's flanks and guided the beast by its mane. He had difficulty in making it take a direct route. "Did you find the most contrary horse you could find?"

"Ander said she was the most docile one of the bunch."

"He is a liar."

Their horses picked their own path down the slope and, true to Bekan's prediction, their arrival on horseback gained everyone's attention.

Father Lambert stood in his black robes, his hair cut blunt and short, making his fat round head look like melon. His flesh looked like white clay to Gunnar's eyes, and he appeared doughy, as if he had never lifted anything heavier than a quill pen. Hrothgar was his exact opposite, a gnarled mass of lumpy muscle weathered from years under the sun both behind a plow and a shieldwall. He had three yellow teeth, yellow eyes, and a snarl that made a rabid wolf seem tame. Father Lambert had about fifteen followers lined up behind him, mostly men but some women and children, all in simple clothing, arranging rocks in a wide rectangle to mark the location of the proposed church. Watching them listlessly were a handful of Gunnar's hirdmen, who gave him pleading looks.

"It's about time someone in authority showed up," Father Lambert said. Gunnar had only met him once, but his voice was pitched too high for a man and dripped with a whinny sarcasm that made

Gunnar's hand itch to strike him. He stared up at Gunnar on his horse, undaunted by the animal.

"What's going on here?" He looked to Hrothgar, whose red face relaxed upon seeing him.

"Jarl Gunnar, this fool wants to stick his church in the center of my pasture."

"So I see," Gunnar stroked his beard as if in careful thought. "How much did he pay you for it? Such a prime field must have cost the good priest a fortune."

"The old farmer will be compensated for the land. But I have a decree from Bishop Burchard to begin immediate construction of a church to serve our flock in these lands." Father Lambert's cheeks jiggled as he spoke, and Gunnar wanted to kick him in the face. It was an impulse he resisted, but he detested Christian priests, and this one was more odious than most.

"Impressive. The compensation doesn't sound very specific. You seemed to have staked out a wide patch of land, a very specific gain, and offered Hrothgar nothing better than a dream of some future reward. Before I agree to this church of yours, I'd like to know what exactly you are paying for the land and when."

Father Lambert's eyes drew to slits and he cocked his head at Gunnar as if debating whether to throw a punch. His followers put down their rocks and gathered closer. Hrothgar folded his arms in victory. "That's right, priest. How much gold are you offering for my land?"

"Did you not hear who has authorized this?" Father Lambert's voice was a low threat. "Bishop Burchard's decree is all I require to begin construction of my church. You have the Church's promise to compensate Hrothgar for his land. That is enough."

"It's not enough for me," Gunnar said. Bekan glanced at him, probably wondering when he would erupt into violence. Gunnar did not look at him, but stared down at the priest from the horse. "I will summon my hirdmen to put a stop to this. You are on my land and abide by my laws."

"You impetuous boy," Father Lambert said. "This land is held by

Hrolf the Strider, and he his beholden to King Charles. He has demanded the Church rebuild its presence where your kind banished it. Bishop Burchard has his orders from the king, and an even mightier power in Jesus Christ!"

Gunnar had done all he could to dam the tide of anger, and invoking the name of the Christian god to steal his property broke it wide open.

"I'll have your fucking arrogant head on a spear!" He tore his sword from its sheath as he yelled. Father Lambert's eyes went from slitted defiance to wide-open terror, and he sprang back. "This is my land, and if you want to steal it, then bring an army instead of old men and women."

The hirdmen drew their swords and a woman screamed. Father Lambert scampered away, then fell on his back.

In the same moment, Fate revealed its designs.

Gunnar's supposedly docile horse shrieked at the sudden violence and reared. Out of reflex, Gunnar dropped his sword and seized the reins with his one hand. Someone howled and everyone began shouting. The spooked horse bolted and Gunnar could do nothing but hold onto its neck while it charged away. Had it been any other man in another situation, Gunnar would have balled up in laughter, but now his rage turned to fear as the animal dashed back up the slope. Realizing this beast was not going to calm down, he had no choice but to leap from it. He closed his eyes and threw himself clear into a patch of clover. Despite the soft appearance, he landed on rocks that drove the wind from his lungs. He lay staring at the stark blue sky above for long moments before he regained his senses.

The stupid animal had thudded away over the crest, and Gunnar stood up and dusted off his pants. Back down the slope, his hirdmen were chasing away many of Father Lambert's followers, while a small knot of them crowded around something. Bekar's horse had also run off. Stomach tight with fear, Gunnar took the first painful steps downhill then broke into a jog when the pain abated.

He pushed through the crowd and found Father Lambert on his back in the grass. Gunnar's dropped sword had speared the priest's left leg. His face was pasty white, and he shivered with pain. The dark cloth around the sword glistened from the spreading pool of blood. Bekan was cutting away the robe to get a better look at the wound. Gunnar closed his eyes and turned aside.

From behind he heard a woman from Father Lambert's followers accuse him. "You ran him through. You killed Father Lambert!"

12

Ulfrik rushed back across the field toward his hall. A tight pain built in his left leg as he swished through ankle-high grass, but he ignored it. Aren was ahead, pausing to turn and wait for him. The black shape of the long hall still felt so far away, and he feared he would never reach it in time.

"I wish we had horses," Ulfrik called out to his son. "You should've brought one."

Aren's face was red, whether from embarrassment at the mistake or anger at their speed, Ulfrik could not guess. A crowd of people had gathered at the front doors of his hall, and his heart dropped at the sight of it. He redoubled his pace.

They threaded the paths between homes and buildings, mounting the heavily worn track to his hall. He was careful not to step into a rut lest he break his leg. The murmur of the crowd was tense, and Ulfrik glimpsed Hakon emerging from the hall. As he and Aren closed the final distance, the crowd began to disperse. A woman with baggy, sad eyes looked at him mournfully as he passed. Two more men behind her nodded solemnly. He caught up to Aren at the hall doors.

"How is he?" Ulfrik asked.

Hakon shook his head and looked aside. "He lives."

"Thank the gods for that much." Ulfrik glanced past Hakon to Runa who stood in the shadows. Her face was puffy and she did not wear her head cover. He pushed past Hakon and grabbed her by both arms.

Her eyes were wet from crying, and Ulfrik had no words to comfort her. He gently squeezed her arms, and she placed her cold hands over his.

"He has been asking for you," Hakon said. "I don't think it is long now."

Ulfrik swallowed hard and nodded. It was a day he knew would come, but he was not ready for it. He tenderly folded Runa's hands back to her sides, then straightened himself. "I will go to him now, and not leave again until this is done."

Being a jarl of such a large and important territory had proved a demanding task. His decision was required for everything, particularly where the Seine River trade was involved. He had spent the morning sending off an important trader and had to scurry back when Aren arrived with dire news. Fortunately he did not need to accompany the trader to the river, which was half a day's walk.

He crossed his empty hall, limping with the pain of his old wound, but not losing a stride. The tables had been cleared to the sides and he only had to skirt the large hearth at the center. Mounting the rise to the high tables, he passed through the wide door to his room and immediately the scent of death filled his nose. He stopped, not out of reflex, for he had long grown accustomed to the smell of the dead, but from fear of what he might find.

Yellow points of lamplight encircled Snorri as he lay on Ulfrik's bed. He was stripped to his waist, and his thin, frail body glistened with sweat. His gray body hair was like a fine cloud clinging to his skin, and his chest rose and fell with his shallow breath. His age-spotted hands were folded over a sword that Runa had placed over his chest. A wet towel was folded over his brow, and his head rested on a block of pure ash wood to draw off evil spirits. Yet in one glance

Ulfrik understood there was no evil here, only old age and the time Fate had selected for death.

"Is that you, lad?" His voice was weak and strained. Ulfrik swallowed, then entered his own bedchamber.

"It is. Save your strength. I will sit with you until you are well again."

Snorri's laughter was like the crackling of dry leaves. His eyes were sunken into their sockets and his face was more skull-like than the prior day. It seemed overnight he had deteriorated. Ulfrik put his hand on Snorri's forehead and felt the heat emanating from it.

"You should not have traveled here," Ulfrik said, trying not to let blame slip into his voice, though he heard it bite into his words.

"And why not? I am glad to spend my final days with you, lad."

"Don't say it."

"I'm old, lad. Older than I have a right to be. No man dies before his time, but when his time arrives, no man may avoid it."

Ulfrik patted Snorri's shoulder and the two sat in silence. Einar had taken Snorri to visit, as he had not been to Ulfrik's hall in the year and half since Hrolf made peace with the Franks. Snorri had planned to stay a month, then Einar would return to fetch him home. The night after Einar left, he complained of a sour stomach. Within days he was too sick to stand. Ulfrik gave him his bed, and had healers to tend him day and night, but he only worsened. Men were dispatched to call Einar back, but so far he had not arrived. He would not be present for his father's death, for Snorri seemed to have few breaths remaining.

Runa and her two sons quietly joined him by the bedside. Snorri's eyes were closed but he continued to breathe. At last his lids fluttered open and he reached out a hand for Ulfrik. He grabbed it in his own, feeling Snorri's intense heat.

"How old am I?" Snorri asked.

"I'm not sure. Maybe you are seventy, or perhaps older?" Ulfrik tried to think back to his earliest memories, but Snorri had always been a man.

"Does Harald Finehair still rule in Norway?"

Ulfrik laughed. "Of course he does. Why do you ask now?"

"I promised your father I'd never stand for one jarl ruling over all others. Remember how we fought Harald?"

"How could I forget? It was a terrible battle. So many friends were lost that day." Ulfrik had also killed his brother and avenged his father's murder in the same battle, but even after so many years he still could not discuss it. Some wounds never healed.

"So now one jarl rules over all others, but we call him a different name." Snorri's watery eyes fixed on him. "How does that figure, lad?"

Swallowing hard, he could only stare at Snorri's knowing eyes. His face grew hot with shame. The answer was now he had gained too much land and wealth to reject the offer, whereas under Harald he had nothing more than a half dozen farms. Snorri's trembling hand squeezed his.

"It's all right, lad. Your father would not have done any different. Hrolf has been generous and you deserve all you have gained. But be wary of what you trade for it." He paused to catch his breath, and Ulfrik folded Snorri's hand to his chest.

"Rest now," he said. "We can speak again later."

"There's no later. I must use every breath wisely. Listen to me, lad. I don't like the mixing of our people with the Franks. Already we're losing ourselves. Don't grow soft. Remember our people and our ways." Snorri spoke in a rush, his voice rough and tired.

"I can do nothing else, old friend." Ulfrik omitted how many of his people had already begun to intermarry with the Franks and how some spoke Frankish in their own homes.

"Good, and keep the Church out of your lands. I have seen my own son forced to give away property and gold to them. They use Hrolf's authority like a war hammer. Don't let them take what you have built. All they want is your land, your people, and your gold."

"You know I've no love of the Christian priests."

"Hrolf is on their side now. I've seen it. How much blood have our people spilled to make a home here, only to give it to some soft-bellied priest? Promise me you won't let it happen to you. And help my son keep what he has."

"You have my word." Snorri nodded and closed his eyes again. Ulfrik glanced at Runa and his sons, who returned a grave stare. Snorri rested in silence, and when Ulfrik prepared to allow his friend rest, Snorri again opened his eyes.

His spotted, blue-veined hand grabbed the sword lying over his body. "I am seventy years old?"

A smile came to Ulfrik's face. "So I have counted. You're the oldest person I've ever known."

Snorri stared at something only his eyes could discern and smiled. "It was all good. I only wish it hadn't been so short."

Ulfrik's throat seized up and tears stung his eyes. Snorri no longer saw him, and his breathing grew more shallow. Runa began to sob quietly at his back. He firmly pressed both of Snorri's hands on the hilt of the sword laid across his body.

"It was too short, old friend. You were as a father to me." The lump in his throat made his voice break and he could speak no more. He did not want to mar Snorri's final moments with unmanly tears.

"And you were as a son. My last wish for you, lad, is don't die like me. I was a warrior." He paused to wheeze and cough. His eyes still looked at another world. "I should not die in bed. Neither should you. Die on the battlefield with a sword in hand and a foeman's blood on your face. That is how a great warrior dies. Not coughing his final breaths on a bed."

"A sword is in your grip now," Ulfrik said, patting Snorri's burning hands. "You will join the heroes in Odin's feasting hall. I shall see you there."

"No, I am too old for Odin to take me. I will go to Freya's hall, and see my wife. Dear Gerdie, she has waited so long. Odin will want you at his table. We shall not meet again."

Snorri lapsed into silence and his breathing grew more strained. Ulfrik watched his face twitch and twist as he dreamed. Time stretched on as Ulfrik and his family kept a tense vigil.

Then his lips moved in his final whisper. "Tell Einar his mother and I are so proud of him."

His breathing stopped and Ulfrik put his ear to Snorri's chest.

When he heard nothing, tears filled his eyes and he sat up with his fists clenched.

"Good-bye, Snorri. You were the last of the old breed, a great warrior, and greater friend. Your name shall not be forgotten."

The tears streamed freely, and he was glad no one but his family witnessed his shame. Runa's hands embraced him from behind and he folded his arm over hers. She had loved Snorri as much as he did, perhaps even more. His passing made a hole in Ulfrik's heart from which the tears flowed. In time he would fix the hole, but with Snorri's shrunken, pale body lying on his bed, he could not imagine when that would be.

A knock on the door shook him. Immediately his stomach burned and his teeth clenched. "Whatever it is, go away."

Rather than hearing the intruder leave, the door opened. Ulfrik was ready to explode with anger, but Finn poked his head inside. His freckled face turned red as he quickly surveyed the scene.

"I am so sorry, but there is a bishop in the hall and he is like a mad dog."

The words made no sense to Ulfrik. He hadn't invited any of the Church, and a bishop was too important a visitor to not have been announced earlier. "What is a bishop doing in my hall?"

"It's about Gunnar. The bishop says he attacked a priest and cut off his leg. He can't find Gunnar and says you're hiding him. I think the bishop wants his head."

13

Bishop Burchard was taller than Ulfrik expected. He was also younger, with his close-cropped black hair only streaked with gray. Ulfrik did not believe a bishop could be anyone other than the most ancient priests the Christians could find. Yet standing at the center of his hall, hands upon his hips, was a bishop no older than himself. The similarity ended there, for Bishop Burchard had a frail frame and a long, tired face that was clean-shaved and soft. The bishop had spent little time outdoors and certainly never worked at anything harder than counting his gold. His eyes were ringed with dark circles as if he had not slept in days, and his drooping nose and sagging chin made it seem as if his face would slide off his head.

Ulfrik had dried his eyes, though his nose was still filled and his joints still weak with the crushing sadness of Snorri's death. Yet it all burned away at the sight of Bishop Burchard with his coterie of priests and wormy laymen lined behind him as if hiding from storm winds. A dozen of his own men lined the walls and all carried spears and shields, an intimidating display to anyone who didn't believe their god made them invulnerable, as the more ardent Christians maintained.

Finn gestured to the bishop, "Here is my Jarl Ulfrik Ormsson. On your knee, priest."

The bishop put his hand to the large wooden cross that hung over his simple brown traveling robes. His nose curled as if manure had been shoved beneath it. "I kneel before God Almighty and my king, not a heathen murderer."

"So much for peaceful relations," Ulfrik said. Hrolf had admonished all of his men to embrace Christianity, and for those who did not, to be tolerant and kind to those who did. He had ensured the Christians and their priests only sought peaceful relations, which Ulfrik considered one of the greatest lies Hrolf had ever told.

"Yes, how quickly peace is forgotten along with your new duties and obligations," the bishop said. He sniffed and looked past Ulfrik at Aren and Hakon who had followed him into the hall. "So where is he, this Gunnar the Black? No doubt he hides behind you in that room. I demand he be turned over to me."

Ulfrik folded his arms. "Make one more demand of me and you'll only be asking for help finding your broken teeth. Your authority ends at the borders of my lands. Now why are you searching for my son?"

Bishop Burchard narrowed his eyes at Ulfrik and the sycophants huddling behind him pumped up their indignation, but the bishop wisely checked whatever challenge he was considering. Instead, he folded one hand beneath his elbow while his finger tapped the side of his face. "Well, you truly have not heard?"

Ulfrik shook his head. His hands were still balled into fists and ached to slam into the bishop's arrogant face, but he restrained himself. "Tell me before my patience reaches its end."

"Gunnar the Black assaulted one of my priests while performing God's work. Without any provocation, he drew his sword, proclaimed that Father Lambert and all his faithful were vermin to be eradicated, then—again without any reason beyond a sick love of violence—he charged his horse at Father Lambert and hacked his leg off at the hip. He fled the crime, and has not been seen since. His family has left with him as well. Of course, we will find him here."

Ulfrik's teeth ground and his vision hazed, yet he still managed to force his voice down to a low growl. "Your mind has gone soft, priest. Do you even listen to your own story? Whatever happened to Father Lamb-butt was not the work of my son. For one, he would not ride a horse nor would he charge anyone with the intent to fight from horseback. That's not our way. But more telling is your claim he charged the priest and cut off his leg. If you told me Gunnar hacked off his head, I might believe it. But a leg from the back of a horse? That's not possible. And have you ever cut through a man's leg? It's like claiming to chop down a tree with one blow of the ax. If the tree is small enough, maybe, but otherwise it doesn't happen. A man's thigh bone's just too thick to be hacked off in one blow of a sword. So you'll forgive me if I say your story is built on lies."

The bishop's eyes widened. "It is no lie that Father Lambert has lost his leg. This I have seen with my own eyes."

"And the rest of your story was witnessed by others, I assume. So you have but one fact and all else is hearsay. I also have to wonder, what was your priest doing in Gunnar's land? Or do you claim he was just taking a merry stroll when my son charged out of nowhere to cut off his leg?"

"Father Lambert was making arrangements for the construction of a new church." The bishop held up his palm to forestall Ulfrik. "You know Hrolf has ordered the building of churches throughout his lands."

"So now we come to the heart of the matter. Your priest was stealing land from Gunnar and no doubt smashing him over the head with Hrolf's authority. I do not even need to ask where the new church would be established. Your greedy rat would have nabbed the best patch of land he could find and demand it be turned over in God's name. No doubt you made a nice survey of my property as you journeyed here, and I can soon expect grubby priests to pay me the same insult as yours did to my son."

"A priest lost his leg to your son," Father Burchard screamed. He straightened himself and strode right up to Ulfrik. "You are hiding that heathen dog and I will see him brought to justice. Your wild insults and coarse treatment will not be forgotten. The faithful among your people will learn of your transgression and they shall rise up against you."

"You are threatening me in my own hall?" Ulfrik's hands twitched. His eyes hazed red and Bishop Burchard's sneering face filled his vision. "You want to start a rebellion in my land?"

"I am a bishop! Appointed to my holy mission by the king himself! You will learn proper respect, you heathen barbarian scum. Your kind are no better than filth to be washed off the soles of my boots!"

Ulfrik grabbed the bishop's neck with one hand and crushed the breath out of him. The bishop's words became a squeak of surprise and his smug look turned to horror.

His mind buzzed and he had no other thought than to tear the bishop to pieces. He raised his fist and punched the bishop's nose flat. Bone cracked and blood and snot shot down the front of the bishop's robe. He screamed in agony, but that only made Ulfrik enjoy it more. He slammed his fist home again, driving the bone of the nose deeper into the bishop's head.

Then the dam broke.

Ulfrik flung Bishop Burchard to the ground and straddled him. If anyone moved to prevent it, he was unaware. With both fists he smashed the bishop's face over and over, a wet and meaty thump following each strike. His knuckles burned with raw pain from shattering bone, and blood splashed Ulfrik's clothing. He was laughing and beating the lump that had once been a face. At last Runa screamed from behind and he realized he had to stop.

Beneath him was a flattened mass of red with one eye ball popped out and another smeared into jelly. Smiling teeth showed through torn flesh, but the bishop was not laughing. He was dead.

Breathing hard, Ulfrik's knuckles throbbed with pain and his hands were slick with blood. He stood and faced down the bishop's horrified followers. One of the priests had fainted and now hung limp against his companions. Ulfrik's hirdmen had lowered their spears and cut off exit from the hall.

"Fucking bastard," Ulfrik said, nudging Bishop Burchard's corpse with his foot. "Never threaten a man's life in his own home."

Truth was, Ulfrik felt far worse now that the satisfaction of savaging the bishop had drained away. He was left with a bloody mess to clean up, in his hall, and a far worse mess with Hrolf. Now he would have to pay a blood price and probably build a church over his own hall and dedicate it to this pig priest bleeding all over his floor.

"We have to kill these witnesses." The voice of his youngest son, Aren, was quiet at his back, yet in the stunned silence one of the bishop's followers cried out at the suggestion.

He shook his head. "No, there's been enough dying in my hall for one day. Let this not become a place of murder and death. The fool earned this reward for his insult. No one would deny it within my right to punish a man who threatened my life and people in my own hall."

"The Church will see it differently," Aren said, now louder. "Vilhjalmer tells me their priests are untouchable and that even he, Hrolf's own son, cannot escape their grasp. Revenge will be swift and terrible."

Ulfrik did not glance back at his family but pointed to the closest of his hirdmen. "March these scum to the borders and send them back to their holes. If one even raises a voice, you've my leave to take his head."

The bishop's followers huddled together in fear, not comprehending Norse but for one who paled in terror. Ulfrik raised a bloodied fist to them and spoke in Frankish. "You tell your masters the truth of what happened here today. I killed your leader for threatening my life. If I see any of you on my land again, I'll hang you by your feet and use you for target practice, then leave your bodies for the crows. Now be gone and take this corpse from my hall."

None moved and Ulfrik shouted, "Now!" The bishop's followers gathered up the corpse, wincing in revulsion. None made eye contact with Ulfrik. The hirdmen then prodded them out of the hall with their spears, but before the last left, he called back.

"This place is accursed of God. You will feel His wrath." Then a hirdmen butted him with the end of his spear and knocked him outside. The cavernous mead hall was empty once more, but with the iron scent of blood hanging in the air.

He turned to his family, Runa with both hands clasped to her chest in shock, Aren and Hakon both standing ready for their father's next command.

"Have a servant clean the blood. I want this place back to normal once Einar arrives. I will prepare for Snorri's funeral. His was the life lost that truly mattered today. Let us not forget."

14

Mord glanced at his father, Gunther One-Eye, who sat by the hearth fire with his good eye closed as if listening to distant, unheard music. He wished his father would allow a hint of his thoughts. Hrolf sat on his high throne, built for his giant size and carved with dragons and strange beasts called lions. His thoughts were as easy to read as runes carved in stone. He held his head in both hands and leaned on his knees. His jeweled fingers sparkled in the firelight. No one dared speak, not even the three representatives the archbishop had sent from Rouen. Hrolf was known for his good humor and social graces, but was also famous for a deadly anger. Mord had once witnessed him snap a man's neck with his bare hands in a fit of rage. The poor victim had likely died without knowing what he had done to give offense. Hrolf was in a similar mood now.

They had gathered at Hrolf's mead hall outside of Rouen. Though now a Frankish count and a Christian, he still preferred to live as he always had and handle affairs from his hall. The enormous throne was his sole concession to his new role, and Mord thought it out of place. Behind the throne his wife, Poppa, hovered and gave apologetic glances to the three holy men. While Mord had long ago become a Christian at the insistence of his wife, he did not understand the Christian ranking system. He figured the larger the cross the more important the priest, and these three men wore silver crucifixes the size of a big man's hand over their clean black robes. These priests were clearly important.

Hrolf groaned and rubbed his face, sitting back at last and staring at the three priests. He thrummed his fingers on the arm of the chair as he considered. Hirdmen clung to the shadows, Mord barely aware of them but for the errant gleam of mail in the hearth light. His heart continued to pound. This was the night he had long awaited, a night his father had predicted over a year ago. All it had taken was one firebrand bishop and Ulfrik had done the rest.

"I must think upon all you have told me," Hrolf said to the priests. His voice echoed in the silent hall. "There are two matters at hand, and each must be judged according to the crime."

The three priests looked at each other, but their leader smiled as if he were indulging a trite story from a favorite nephew. He was the oldest, with a fringe of white hair surrounding a brown-spotted head. "It would be best to handle the matter in one decision, Count Rollo."

Rollo was Hrolf's new name, taken the day he was baptized a Christian. Mord thought it a fitting name, though his father hated it.

"What is best and what is just are not always the same," Hrolf sat straighter in his chair and his eye twitched. Mord knew Hrolf's anger risked spilling over, but the Church was a terrible enemy and had to be handled with deft care. "I will hear the accounts of my men, and not judge them otherwise. If Father Lambert is well enough, he should provide his own account. Only then can I make a fair judgment."

"Count Rollo, our witnesses can attest to the murder of Bishop Burchard and the maiming of Father Lambert. Ulfrik Ormsson and Gunnar the Black's hostility toward Christianity is well known. Their crimes against God must be judged in the harshest possible light. It is the position of Archbishop Franco that these criminals be publicly executed as both an example of God's justice and your authority."

"My authority is unquestioned! Let your God make his own justice."

The priests hissed at Hrolf's blasphemy, but he sank back into his throne and ignored everyone. The room again fell into silence and finally the lead priest inclined his head to Hrolf.

"We will leave you to your thoughts, if it pleases you, Count Rollo."

"It does please me," he said, then shook his head and adopted a more pleasant demeanor. "I will have you escorted to the church where my Confessor will arrange your lodging. Tonight I shall give you a welcome feast. Forgive my manners, for it is grave news you bring and I have been a poor host for hearing it."

The lead priest again bowed, then turned away. As he did, his eyes met Mord's and they shared a knowing look. All three filed out and the hall remained in tense silence. Mord's heart beat faster, for now it was up to him to carry home the final blow. He glanced yet again at his father who remained contemplative and silent, still listening to his inaudible song.

"You must do as they ask." The words were subdued but firm. Poppa, Hrolf's wife, was the only one bold enough to break into his thoughts. Many men beat their wives. Mord did without hesitation. But Poppa had long ago tamed Hrolf, and if he raised a hand to her it was never witnessed by any.

"They cannot command me in my own hall." The words lacked the fire of only a moment ago. Mord again found his eyes straying to his father and again received no sign.

"Burchard was my cousin. You must deliver justice, for family if not for the Church."

"I know it, woman, and I shall."

"But it must be equal to the crime of murder."

Hrolf hung his head again, and Poppa, still melded with the shadow, lowered hers as well. She gave Mord a knowing look and then shifted to Gunther One-Eye. A small smile pierced the gloom clinging to her. "Mord is here not just to witness. Of course, he is here because you need a man capable of restoring the Church's belief in you. Mord has been a good friend of the Church. He has built churches and gives freely of his wealth to those in need. His wife's family is connected to Paris. He could heal the wound your wild jarl has made."

"Enough of your meddling," he said in a voice more tired than commanding. "I know what needs to be done. But I will not hear it from you. Thank you for soothing the priests, but your presence is not needed. Go back to your idle cares, and let me do the work of ruling over this mess."

Poppa said nothing more, but her shadowy form turned and three women followed her out of the hall to the solitude of her chambers beyond. Hrolf did not face her but instead stared at Mord, hand covering his mouth.

"You're arrival here was convenient," Hrolf said. "You've nothing to do with this?"

"You heard the priests, Jarl Hrolf. Ulfrik and Gunnar have committed their own crimes without any aid from me." Mord's heart flopped. He was truthful to an extent, but once his father had learned of Burchard's relation to Poppa and his temperament, both Mord and Gunther had guided the bishop towards his inevitable clash. Ulfrik had just surpassed their expectations in his response.

"So you are to be my peacemaker with the church?"

"If you wish it so." Mord stood from his bench at the side of the hall and went to his knee before Hrolf. "I live only to serve you as well as my father did before me."

Hrolf rubbed his face and moaned. Falling back in his chair he stared at Mord as he remained on his knee. "All right, get up. You've thrown your lot in with the Church. A wise choice in these new times."

Standing as instructed, he again stole a look at his father and his impatience burned. Why was the old man not helping? This was the moment all their patience and plotting had earned them. Had he finally gone soft?

"You've been silent, old man." Hrolf stood from his throne and approached the hearth where Gunther sat in rapturous quiet. "If you have counsel, I'd hear it now. Otherwise, find another hearth to warm your old bones."

Gunther laughed, but Mord wondered if Hrolf's words were not as playful as they sounded. He watched his father scratch his beard and appear to dig deep into his thoughts. Of course he would support Mord for the role and counsel Ulfrik's and Gunnar's deaths.

"You cannot bow to these priests. Ulfrik has served loyally and we have not heard his statement nor that of other witnesses. What will your men think if you reward your greatest supporter with death?"

Mord's mouth fell open and he was grateful Hrolf's back was turned and his father blind. He schooled his expression, but his hands clenched in rage. The old man had gone soft after all.

"Of course you're right," Hrolf said, his voice brightening. "I will not allow priests to dictate to me. If Archbishop Franco has a command, then let him come out of his golden halls and command me to my face. I'll hear it from him and no other."

Gunther grunted agreement, and Mord cleared his throat. Hrolf turned with a raised brow and suddenly he regretted calling attention to himself.

"They do not work like that, my lord. The archbishops are even greater than the counts, and their commands are laws that—"

"You speak out of turn, like a boy that has not grown up. Yet you want to be entrusted with some of the richest lands in my territory?"

Mord's face burned and he fell silent, stepping back. The scar of his father's destroyed eye twitched, a sign of his anger, but otherwise he said nothing.

Hrolf turned away and clasped his hands at his back. He paced beside the hearth in thought. "I will hear Ulfrik's words. I still must issue some punishment. But death?"

"Death is too great a demand," Gunther said. Now, with Hrolf's back to both of them, he faced Mord and offered a brief smile. "You must fight the Church on this, even if we need break our truce and take to the battlefield once more. If a thousand men must die to show the Church we are not dogs to be brought to heel, then so be it.

Perhaps the Norns never intended anything else but war for our people."

Hrolf stopped pacing and remained still. Gunther closed his milky white eye again and returned to his dreamy silence. Mord's chest filled with warmth at his father's skill. He could see the debate raging in Hrolf's heart as the giant Count of Rouen stood still. When he renewed his pacing, his step was heavier.

"Perhaps I do not have a choice." Hrolf's voice was small and tentative. "There is more to consider than my own pride. A day may come to war with the Franks again, but it is not today."

Neither Mord nor Gunther spoke, but let Hrolf pace in silence. By the time he had rounded the hearth and now stood again before Gunther, his face was drawn and tired, as if he had scaled a mountain.

"I will hear Ulfrik's story." He spoke to no one, his eyes unfocused on the far wall. "Then give my judgment."

He exited the hall as if carrying an anvil on his back. The front doors opened to reveal the yellow light of day, and then slammed shut. Mord stared at his father who remained seated with eye closed. But a wide smile formed on his face.

Mord smiled as well. He realized what his father knew. Hrolf would give his judgment and it would be death.

15

Ulfrik looked to the dark gray sky and felt a pinpoint of cold rain strike his cheek. He turned his gaze back toward Snorri's temporary grave, a wide oval of brown earth in green grass. Two slaves, young Irishmen who barely spoke any Norse, patted the earth flat with their shovels. They were stripped to the waist and heads shaved clean, making them appear like twins.

"Enough," Ulfrik said to them, and though the slaves understood little Norse, they were smart enough lay their shoves aside and back away. Ulfrik knelt by the grave and touched the damp, freshly turned earth. "You will be buried with great honor, old friend. I will have new clothes and a fine sword made for you. You will be the envy of Freya's hall."

His sons surrounded the temporary grave, Gunnar having just arrived with his family the prior night. Runa wrapped herself in a dark cloak and held a fist to her lips as she tried to control her tears. After Ulfrik stood, he kissed her cheek and spoke softly. "We are done for now, so go back to the hall and play with our grandchildren. It will take your mind from this sadness."

Runa nodded, leaned into Ulfrik's hug, then she joined her women who had waited for her further back from the grave. Yet before she did, she cast a stern glance to Gunnar. She had blamed him for all that had happened with the bishop, and though she had not openly accused Gunnar, in her private moments with Ulfrik she had cursed her son's temper. Gunnar had no expression, as grim as his brothers, and watched his mother go.

"We have much to discuss," Ulfrik said. "I am tired of the hall. Let's walk while we decide what happens next."

His sons all nodded and began to fall into line. Ulfrik waved to Finn, who had also stayed back from family matters, toward the hall. He fell in with Runa as they crossed the grass toward the long hall in the distance.

Ulfrik led them away from the center of the village toward the distant line of trees. Gunnar had shared his news, and Ulfrik had caught him up on the death of Bishop Burchard. The exchange had been all time allowed, but Ulfrik had many questions for his son. Another drop of rain hit his nose, and Ulfrik stopped them before they went too far from the hall.

"The bishop said he witnessed Father Lambert's missing leg," he said to Gunnar. "Are you certain they didn't have to remove it after he left you?"

Gunnar growled in frustration. "I told you, we took him to my hall and cared for his wound. If his crazy followers hadn't insisted on carrying him off, he would have been standing again within the week. The wound was nothing, though you couldn't tell for the crying of that priest. I kept it clean, and when he left, he had a fresh dressing. If he lost his leg, it's because his fool followers injured him again."

"It was probably a lie," Hakon said. He had recovered from his arrow wound, though both cheeks bore deep scars where the shaft had pierced him, and his voice sounded thicker from the wound to his tongue. "The bishop wanted any excuse to act like an ass."

"I'll agree to that," Ulfrik said. Now he stepped closer to Gunnar and looked him in the eye. "Why did you run? I can think of no reason for you to have fled with your family, not if all was as you say."

Gunnar's gaze faltered and he looked toward the dark line of trees. Another cold drop struck Ulfrik's cheek as he waited for Gunnar to answer.

"Father Lambert promised the bishop would bring an army of the faithful with him and they would deliver justice," he said at last. "I did not want to expose my family to danger, so I took them down the Seine, just to keep them safe while I figured what to do next."

"A nice story, but the truth this time." Ulfrik folded his arms and watched Gunnar struggle to find his words. Both Hakon and Aren shifted uncomfortably at Ulfrik's bluntness.

"I had a dream that night," Gunnar said, refusing to look at anyone. "I do not put credence into such things normally, but this was the truest dream I ever had. Have you never experienced such a thing?"

He remembered dreams of the ghosts of his brother-in-law Toki and his old companion Yngvar Bright-Tooth during his imprisonment in Iceland. "I've had a few over the years."

"Well, then you understand how the fear grips you like death. The next morning I knew I had to go or something terrible would happen. I told no one where I went, for at that time I did not know where I was headed."

"What did you dream?"

Gunnar gave him a sideways glance. "I dare not repeat it and give the evil a life outside of my own heart. It's best it stays inside me."

"Holding evil only gives it more power. Spill it into the light of day and it becomes weak."

Swallowing hard, Gunnar scanned all of their faces, then described his dream.

"A black adder had slipped into my hall and bit all my men and servants on their legs. They cried in pain and soon died. With each death the snake grew larger until it was fat around as a man. Then it swallowed my children, then Morgan, but it spared me. I was like a stone, unable to speak or reach for my sword. The serpent coiled about the posts of my hall and tore it down about me. Still, I remained unharmed, but when the walls fell I discovered the whole land was aflame. I know not how I came to your hall, Father, but as one does in dreams I found myself suddenly transported. You stood over mother's sleeping body in your mail and helmet, sword drawn to ward off a warrior made of shadow. His spear pierced the mail over your gut and drove clear through. But rather than cry out in pain, you only laughed. Then I was awake, covered in sweat and my heart pounding. I knew I had seen a terrible omen."

Ulfrik's chest tightened at the horrible depiction. Aren frowned with horror, and only Hakon had any words for his brother.

"Surely the gods have sent you a warning. They speak to us in dreams." He searched all of them for agreement, nodding his head. "Remember I had once seen Odin on the night we became lost in battle with the Franks? So, I believe what you say, brother. You did the right thing."

"You saw Odin?" Aren asked, his eyes widening.

Gunnar chuckled. "I had forgotten about that. But thank you, for the support. I didn't dare tell Morgan. I don't have to warn you all to keep this a secret."

"We'll never speak of such ill omens again," Ulfrik said, clapping Gunnar's shoulder. "But I think you were just worried for Father Lambert's threat. At least now I know why you fled."

"Now what will you do about the bishop's death?" Gunnar asked.

Ulfrik shrugged. "I will have to present myself to Hrolf. No sense waiting to be summoned like a wayward child."

"He's a Christian now," Gunnar said. "He's in bed with the Church. Won't he demand your head?"

"He would not. Christian or no, he is one of us. That bishop came into my hall, shit on my honor, and threatened to ruin me because I couldn't tell him where you were. Perhaps death was a stiff punishment, but he was a weakling unable to take the beating he had earned." Ulfrik paused and scratched his chin. He recognized excuses and his claim sounded hollow even to himself. Snorri's dying words had kindled a fire in him, and the bishop had paid for it. "Among our own kind, I'd pay a blood price if I paid anything at all. For the death of a Christian leader, I'll probably be forced to let them build churches and pay a heavy amount of gold. They'll cry about justice, but gold will silence them. I fear the Christians will have their place in my land after all."

"I suppose they baited the trap and we bit," Gunnar said.

"No doubt they wanted us to resist, though I don't think they expected their bishop to die." Ulfrik started back toward the hall and his sons fell in beside him. "But for all I have done for Hrolf these long years, he will treat fairly with me, and with Gunnar. I'm not so headstrong that I can't admit killing their bishop was too much. I'll pay what they ask and give them no trouble. Hrolf will appreciate it, and so we will soon have all of this behind us."

Gunnar nodded and they walked three more paces before Ulfrik realized neither Hakon nor Aren followed. He turned and found Aren with his arms folded and face scowling.

"Stepped in horse shit?" Ulfrik asked.

"I don't like the plan, Father. You are underestimating your enemy and not thinking through the outcome."

Aren was known for plain speech, but hardly had he dared to be so bold. Ulfrik blinked and laughed uncertainly. "Hrolf is not my enemy."

"The Church is," Aren said, and Hakon nodded silently beside him. "They are an incredible power in this land, and you are fighting on their ground now. You are locked in battle, but not the kind you understand."

"Oh well, you will enlighten me then?" Ulfrik felt his face grow warm but clamped down on his words out of respect for his son.

"If you and Gunnar go alone, then it is the same as offering your neck to an enemy. Gunnar was right to run in fear."

"What are you saying?" Gunnar said, bristling at Aren. Ulfrik restrained him with an outstretched arm.

"I say what I mean. The Church is a terrible enemy, as black-hearted for revenge as the worst of our people. They will not be content with a token punishment any more than we would be content for the same from the killer of our own father."

Ulfrik paused at that and Gunnar stepped back. Aren's wide, square face grew red as he pressed his point, but Hakon put an arm on his brother's shoulder to urge him. Aren cleared his throat and continued.

"You should not go to Hrolf at all, but force him to come to you."

"Impossible," Ulfrik said, folding his arms. "I will not have to be collected like a lost sheep."

"But to go alone is to lie down before the Church and surrender. You must take every jarl who opposes the Church. There are many who have no love of Jarl Hrolf's new religion. Without support, the Church will have you alone and then they will do whatever they wish to you. If they have to come here, we can prepare and rally our own support."

"This sounds too much like a battle plan," Gunnar said, and Ulfrik nodded in agreement.

"It is," Aren said. "This will be a fight to decide the rest of our lives."

"Now you are making this into a mountain." Ulfrik wiped his hands as if scrubbing away dirt. "Gunnar and I go to Hrolf, we settle this matter as men, and I pay whatever price he asks. I will even become a Christian if he demands it. I can pray to their god and ours then see who listens."

Hakon now stepped forward. "Aren is the smartest person any of us have ever met. He is a close friend of Vilhjalmer, who has shown him things none of us have seen. If he is afraid, then it's right to heed his warning."

Ulfrik rubbed his face. "There's merit to Aren's thinking. But however much he believes he understands Hrolf's court, he does not know how warriors deal with justice. I must go to Hrolf. So what do you suggest, then?"

Now Aren rubbed his face, unknowingly mimicking his father's reaction to frustration. Yet he kept his face covered while he considered his answer, and they all waited. Ulfrik felt more rain pelting his head and the scent of it filled the air.

"No one knows Gunnar has returned," Aren said. "So keep it that way. For both of you to go is like putting all your game pieces on the board at once. Your opponent will know your strength and plan to counter it. Gunnar has done the lesser crime, and so he remains in reserve while you test Hrolf's resolve. Whatever is judged for you will be less harsh for him. Then, if things go badly, he can organize a response."

Aren glanced at Hakon, who nodded along with the plan.

"You really believe the Church could force Hrolf to take drastic action?" Gunnar asked.

"I do. Hrolf's future is with the Church, not with us." Aren raised his hand when Ulfrik inhaled to protest. "I'm not dishonoring your legacy, Father. But it is the truth. The Church rules everywhere, and if Hrolf desires to sit upon the throne of Frankia one day, then he must be a good Christian."

The silence was complete and Ulfrik could not deny the logic. "Wise counsel from one so young. I will consider it."

16

The grandeur of Hrolf's hold had always impressed Ulfrik. Inside felt larger than it appeared outside, with a high roof supported by posts that climbed away into the dark. His new banner of a yellow lion on a red flag hung from the rafters, its rich colors grayed in the low light of the hall. The long hearth in the center crackled with pulsing orange embers and threw a gentle warmth over him as two hirdmen led him to the back of the hall where Hrolf sat upon his high chair.

The moment he saw the great man piled into his seat, he realized the judgment of his king would be heavy. Hrolf's dark shape leaned back against the chair and his face was drawn and serious, with shadows that clung like ink to the recesses of his eyes. His posture suggested he wanted to recoil, but the chair had trapped him. Ulfrik stopped short at the sight, and the two hirdmen flanking him took three steps before they also paused.

Four priests hovered around Hrolf's chair. One he recognized as Hrolf's personal confessor. The other three were dressed in clean robes as black as night and wore heavy silver crosses that winked hearth light, as if sharing some secret message with him. Their faces were plump and soft, men who had never labored beneath the sun or missed their supper, but their brows were creased from a long acquaintance with frowning. None of the dour men had any smiles today, and Ulfrik chilled at seeing them crowding Hrolf. Like a flock of crows on a corpse. The thought came unbidden to his mind, but the comparison was apt.

One of the hirdmen motioned Ulfrik forward, and they resumed the approach. What had been an admirably spacious hall now seemed like an unreasonably long walk. Hirdmen lined the walls in mail and armed with spears. Yet another sign that caused Ulfrik's guts to burn. His own men had been disarmed and asked to remain outside the hall. While laying aside weapons on Hrolf's property was not unexpected, being refused to accompany their jarl was a strange request.

When he presented himself to Hrolf, he noticed that at the edge of the hall and garbed in shadow stood both Hrolf's wife, Poppa, and Gunther One-Eye. At least the presence of his old friend relieved some of his tension. However, Gunther had grown old, blind, and distant over the years. Perhaps Mord had turned him as well. He had not time to consider, as he went to his knee before Hrolf.

"Jarl Hrolf, I have come to you seeking mercy for my rash actions." He kept his head bowed and acted as contrite as he was able. Though he had come to seek forgiveness, he had been careful to wear his dozen gold armbands Hrolf had awarded for his service as a subtle reminder of his value to Hrolf. He glanced up. "I have caused injury to your reputation and mine."

Hrolf shifted on his throne, the dark wood creaking under his weight. He sighed and motioned Ulfrik to stand. "You have come in good faith, rather than be forced to appear before me. I am grateful for your consideration. You were wise to do so."

Inclining his head, Ulfrik shifted his gaze toward the priests. "I wish only to put this behind us so that we may continue to enjoy our well-earned peace."

"As do I," he said, and these were the only words he had spoken that sounded like the Hrolf of old. Thus far, Hrolf's tone was as drawn and reluctant as his posture. "You are facing your accusers this night. Have you brought no witnesses of your own?"

"Your men prevented them from entering the hall."

Hrolf sat up straighter and scowled at his priest, who shrugged as if he knew nothing of it. Hrolf snapped at one of the hirdmen beside Ulfrik. "Bring only those who have borne witness, and be quick."

The priests organized themselves according to what Ulfrik assumed was their rank, the most important being closest to Hrolf. He was an older man with a fringe of white hair to crown a narrow head. He wore a condescending sneer that made Ulfrik dream of slapping it away. The priest behind him murmured words that this leader dismissed with a barely discernible flick of his hand and twitch of his eye. When he did speak, he sounded as if he were exhausted from explaining the same story to a child.

"You are Ulfrik Ormsson? You are the man who killed holy Bishop Burchard?"

"Holy Burchard? I remember a haughty fool who didn't behave like a proper man."

"Ulfrik!" Hrolf's sudden barking of his name made him jump. "Do not mock these good men. There are no challenge insults here. We're not at parley, but at court." Hrolf's comparison to the pre-battle insults thrown about during the parley was precisely correct. Ulfrik was treating this like the cursing out of an enemy before battle and not like a proceeding of justice. He felt his face heat up.

"Sorry, Jarl Hrolf. I allowed my anger to best me once more."

"A terrible habit of yours. What served you well in battle serves you less admirably in peace." Hrolf sat straighter in his chair and set both of his ring-laden hands on its arms. "These priests, represented by Father Odger, are here to present their account of your crimes."

"But they did not witness anything. How can they accuse me?"

"They are holy men," Hrolf said. "And will swear an oath before God to tell the entire truth as it was given to them by their witnesses."

"That's not the law," Ulfrik said, hands balling into fists. "They must produce witnesses to prove the accusation, and I will have men to speak for me. You must judge according to what the witnesses have told you."

Hrolf slammed his hand on the armrest. "Do not tell me what I must do. A bishop is dead, and you have killed him. Will your witnesses claim otherwise?"

Ulfrik had so focused on Hrolf and the priests he did not see his men arrive behind him. Ulfrik waved them forward. "Let them tell you. Here is Styr Grimmason. Come, tell them of the bishop's visit."

Styr was not a tall man, but wide shouldered and muscular. A lump of scar tissue wound across his right forearm, and it showed pink in the light as he balanced with it when he knelt before Hrolf. Motioned to his feet, Styr addressed only Hrolf as Ulfrik had previously instructed him.

"Jarl Hrolf, the bishop came on Thor's day of a week ago. The hall was closed but the bishop demanded he be allowed inside. Finn Langson told us the bishop should be let in. Once he met with Jarl Ulfrik, he went mad with rage. He threatened to start a revolt, and promised he would get all the Christians in the land to overthrow Jarl Ulfrik. So when Jarl Ulfrik warned him to silence, he just got more insulting. Jarl Ulfrik hit him, and he fell with his nose broken."

Styr had stopped short of describing Ulfrik's maniacal pounding of the bishop, again as Ulfrik had instructed, and he shrugged as if he had said all he wanted.

"Was the bishop dead at that time?" Hrolf asked.

"Maybe he was, Jarl Hrolf. A broken nose bleeds a lot, but the bishop wasn't defending himself and just lying there. So maybe he died in one punch."

"So it could have been an accident?" Hrolf's voice lifted with hope and Ulfrik swelled with it. Hrolf seemed to be searching for an exploit in the case.

"I would say so, Jarl Hrolf. He forced himself inside the hall and then threatened to use his power to overthrow my lord. That'd make any man mad enough to jab someone in the nose. Jarl Ulfrik did not set about killing the bishop. It just ended that way."

Hrolf relaxed in his chair and Ulfrik felt the tension drain from his chest. The three priests and Hrolf's confessor in turn stood taller and their lips were drawn thinner. They appeared to be restraining themselves from speaking out of turn, as the rear-most priest held the back of his hand over his mouth.

"Do you have others who would swear to Styr's account?" Hrolf asked.

"Any of my men will tell you the same account." Ulfrik again turned to the six other of his men allowed inside. All of them had an opportunity to speak and confirm the same story. Once all had finished, Hrolf dismissed them and they were led away. Ulfrik shared a hopeful smile with Styr, and believed his men had rescued the situation. At the worst, he had committed a terrible accident but could not be accused of murder.

"Now for our statement, Count Rollo?" Father Odger asked, his lofty smile reborn. Hrolf waved the priest forward and Father Odger stepped before Ulfrik.

"I do swear before almighty God, His son Jesus Christ, and the Holy Spirit, that I will faithfully convey all that was told to me by our witnesses." The priest placed one hand upon his silver cross as he did so. When no one questioned this, he listed off seven names of witnesses that meant nothing to Ulfrik. He did not know why these men and women could not be present, but it did not matter since Hrolf allowed Father Odger to speak for them.

"I will save us the details, for they vary little from what your witnesses have stated. I will note several facts that vary from the statements of your witnesses. First, I will remind Jarl Hrolf that while Bishop Burchard might have been zealous in his demands to access Jarl Ulfrik's hall, he was in fact invited inside. He did not invade the hall, as Jarl Ulfrik would like you to believe. Also, Bishop Burchard was seeking Gunnar the Black, who had maimed a priest in yet another conflict over the building of a church. We believe Jarl Ulfrik to harbor him, for who else but a father would share in the crime to protect him?"

"Why was the bishop searching for Gunnar and not Hrolf's

warriors?" Ulfrik asked, cutting off the priest. "The bishop wanted me to strike him. That's why he acted like an ass."

The priests shouted protests and crowded Hrolf's chair. Father Odger scowled at Ulfrik, who smiled back at him. Strangely, Ulfrik noticed Hrolf's wife, Poppa, step forward as if to join the opposition. Ulfrik lingered on her, but she retreated to the shadow where Gunther One-Eye held her arm.

"Enough!" Hrolf roared, and the priests recoiled. "Ulfrik asks a good question. I had not considered this myself, but now I wish to know the same thing."

Father Odger stared levelly at Hrolf, like a father deciding the punishment for his unruly son. Ulfrik burned at the thought of these priests having any control over his great jarl, but remained quiet.

"If your son were injured, would you not go yourself to confront the man who had dealt him the wound?" Father Odger spread his hands and Hrolf's face softened at the question, then he nodded. "Of course you would, and so did Bishop Burchard. He was a passionate man, and loved all his followers like his own children. Now, if there have been enough distractions, allow me to make my final point."

He paused then returned a predatory smile to Ulfrik, who suddenly felt as if the priest had grown three feet taller. Panic fluttered in his chest, much like the pangs of doubt and fear before shield walls collided. Yet just like the moments before battle, Ulfrik braced himself and faced his accusers.

"After you struck Bishop Burchard out of impulse, you fell upon him and continued to beat him in the face. You did not stop, but continued to punch him until you tore the flesh of your knuckles on the exposed bones of the good bishop's face. Only until your wife called you to your sense did you cease. That is not an accidental jab in the nose, as your witnesses so carelessly described, but the actions of an enraged murderer. The punishment inflicted on Bishop Burchard far outstrips his improprieties. At best you should have ejected the bishop from your hall if his words displeased you. Instead, you brutally murdered him."

Now Ulfrik understood Aren's warning all too clearly. The hall hung in silence with the four priests glaring down at him and Hrolf brooding upon his throne. He was alone at sea and surrounded by sharks. The best he could do was grab an oar and beat back the sharks.

"Jarl Hrolf, I have served faithfully for many years. I struggled to return to your side when I was lost in Iceland. I protected you in battle and earned glory for your name. I cannot deny I made a grievous mistake in killing the bishop. I did not intend it. He enraged me and not moments after the death of my oldest and dearest friend, a man I might as well call my father. Please consider this in your judgment."

Hrolf ran both of his jeweled hands through the gray hair at his temples and avoided meeting anyone's eyes. Father Odger pointed at Ulfrik while Hrolf remained lost in his thoughts.

"Archbishop Franco has made his will clear. Ulfrik Ormsson is responsible for the murder of Bishop Burchard, a terrible loss for the Church and the good people of Normandy. As God teaches us, 'Whoever strikes a man so that he dies shall be put to death.' Ulfrik Ormsson cannot escape this sentence. By order of the Archbishop Franco of Rouen, I demand the execution of Ulfrik Ormsson."

Though Ulfrik had expected such nonsense, now in the shadowy silent hall with none but priests surrounding him, the threat seemed entirely plausible. He faced Hrolf, and Hrolf returned his stare. He slumped in his chair, eyes vacant and wet.

"Jarl Hrolf?" Ulfrik asked in a small voice. "You can't agree with this?"

17

Ulfrik stared at Hrolf, waiting for his decision. The hall held its breath, everyone waiting for a sign from the great jarl. Hrolf shifted on his seat, eyes scanning the distance like he would before a great battle. Ulfrik could not count the times he had seen that expression upon Hrolf's face, but now it was a shade more desperate. Years ago when the Franks had surrounded them outside of Paris and destruction seemed imminent, Hrolf still did not appear as unnerved as he was at this moment. A bead of sweat rolled down the side of his face and he swatted at it as if it were a fly.

At last he stirred, and his face was set in grim determination. He stood to his full height, making every man in the hall look up at him.

"Ulfrik Ormsson, the crime you have done has grieved me worse than you can imagine. Do you understand what you have done?"

Bowing his head, Ulfrik spoke softly. "I have stained your honor as well as my own."

Hrolf roared in frustration and the four priests surrounding him leapt in surprise. Ulfrik's own heart leapt at the outburst. "Gods, man, you killed my wife's cousin! And a bishop no less. Do you even understand what choice that leaves me?"

Ulfrik's stomach sank and he stepped back. "He was a relation of your wife's? How could I have known? He said nothing."

"It makes no difference." Hrolf emphasized each word through his grit teeth. "The Church and my wife's family have considerable authority in this new world. And you shit all over them."

He bowed his head lower, so his chin rested on his chest. "I am sorry for what I have done. I swear to you, Jarl Hrolf, I will make amends. The Church will be welcomed on my land. I will pay whatever blood price you demand. But you cannot kill me." He stopped short of warning Hrolf that executing him would spark a revolt of his other jarls who did not embrace the Christians. Saying so would be too much like the threats of Bishop Burchard.

"Count Rollo, it is the will of Archbishop Franco that justice be carried out." Father Odger stepped closer as if to urge him, but the huge man put up his hand.

"Remember yourself, priest. I've heard what your archbishop demands, so do not remind me once more. I tire of being told how I should decide." Father Odger bristled but stepped back, his white face turning red. Hrolf's confessor, the only priest not appointed by the archbishop, guided Father Odger away with a soft whisper.

Hrolf returned to his seat, plopping into it as if exhausted. He drew a deep breath and blew it out, staring at Ulfrik. His voice was tired and soft. "You have been the greatest of my warriors and fiercest of my jarls. You carried my fight when others would not. You saved my life, twice that I know of and probably others I've never realized. So to find ourselves at this point is like a spear through the gut."

Ulfrik began to speak, but Hrolf again raised his hand for silence and closed his eyes.

"To satisfy myself, I must render a decision that pleases no one else."

Ulfrik swallowed hard. The priests leaned forward. Even Poppa and Gunther stepped from the shadows.

"For the murder of Bishop Burchard, I banish you from my lands and from my protection."

"No!" Ulfrik shouted.

"I reclaim your lands and will grant the Church property as compensation for the death of their servant."

"This is an outrage," Father Odger protested. "He is to be executed."

"Your sons are banished along with you. The injuries to Father Lambert will be paid from the confiscation of Gunnar the Black's lands."

"You can't do this!" Ulfrik lurched for Hrolf but the two guards at his side grabbed his arms.

"Your men will be allowed to follow you into banishment, or they may remain on my lands providing they swear loyalty to me in person."

"He must die," Father Odger screamed, his face bright scarlet. "The archbishop will be furious at this disobedience."

"Until the transition of lands is complete and to ensure peace, you will be held as a hostage to the good behavior of your sons and hirdmen. Any acts of violence will mean your death." Hrolf paused, eyes never wavering from Ulfrik's. "That is my judgment and my justice."

"He was to die!" Father Odger repeated, and rather than fly into a rage, Hrolf simply looked him over as if noticing the priest for the first time.

"Reputation to our people is greater than life itself. Rest assured, Father, I did just kill him."

Ulfrik struggled with his guards but he was already weakening. Hrolf turned from him without another look and gathered his wife to his side. He then disappeared into the rooms at the far end of the hall. The remaining hirdmen closed around Ulfrik, spears lowered. Some were men he knew by name, and their eyes avoided his. One of them touched his spear point to Ulfrik's belly.

"Please, Jarl Ulfrik, let's make this easy."

He stared at the tip trembling over his gut, then glared up at the quartet of priests. They returned the glares, and Hrolf's confessor stretched out his arms before them like herding children. They followed him around the edge of the hall toward the front doors.

Ulfrik watched them leave until they disappeared from his sight, then he put his hand over the spear at his stomach.

"Put that down before one of us gets hurt. I'll go with you." The guards hesitated, but the lead spearman sighed and lowered his weapon, and the others followed. Ulfrik allowed them to encircle him as they prepared to exit the hall.

"This isn't done yet," he said, to no one. "Hrolf has made a mistake."

18

Gunnar met the thirty hirdmen flying Hrolf's standard at the outskirts of the village. They all rode horses, the rumble of hooves audible across the distance. They followed the same path his father would have traveled to the Seine, where one of his ships would ferry him across the river to Rouen. He had taken thirty crew including his witnesses and about as many of Hrolf's hirdmen now arrived in return. Glints of mail showed in their black shadows and their faces were dark beneath iron helmets.

A stale gray blanket of clouds weakened the light and the scent of rain hung in the air, yet none had fallen in the days since the bishop's death. Gunnar felt as if the sky itself was holding its breath in anticipation of Hrolf's judgment. A swirl of black crows shot up, protesting the passing of Hrolf's warriors. He frowned at the ill omen.

"Remember they are friends," Hakon said from behind. Having received word from the docks of the arrival of Hrolf's crew, Gunnar had gathered his brothers and two dozen hirdmen to intercept the new arrivals. Only one farm sat in the distance where a dog barked and the farmer's wife drew water from a well. Expecting the worst, he did not want panic to spread when Hrolf's men appeared without his father.

"Yes, they are friends. Until they are not," Runa answered Hakon's reminder. She spoke with the bitter resolve of a warrior woman's hard life. She had been many things in life. Slave. Wife. Ruler. Shield Maiden. Widow. But of all her roles, Gunnar most cherished her as a mother, and so had wanted to shield her from bad news. He had forbidden her from accompanying them. However, his mother was never to be swayed where matters of his father were concerned. She dressed in a simple cloak, strapped on a short sword, and joined her sons to face the news herself. People saw how she carried herself and called her mad, but Gunnar loved her for her simple determination to do what she felt was right.

The column drew their mounts to a halt in the grassy field over a spear-toss away. Gunnar smiled at the caution, and wondered if they expected to be resisted. Depending on what they told him, a battle might be in the offering. The leader dismounted, then the others climbed down out of their saddles. The banner man joined the bulky form of the leader then five of them approached.

"Let's hear their news," Gunnar said, not bothering to look behind. "Hakon, Aren, and Mother, with me. Let no one else approach yet."

Halfway across the grass Gunnar stopped, forcing Hrolf's men to cross to him. As their leader approached, a fire flared in his stomach. He recognized the leader's hooked nose with a red scar on its bridge and the weathered, lined face sizing him up was assured and cool.

"Magnus the Stone," Gunnar said. "What a misfortune to see you again."

Magnus rubbed his legs and groaned, apparently unused to riding. His voice was as rough as his namesake. "I see your brother has recovered. Sorry about the scars."

Gunnar held his arm across Hakon's chest. "We're all glad you are not a good shot. Now, why have you taken the pains to cross the Seine with two dozen riders and head straight to my father's hall?"

Magnus ignored the question, cold eyes flicking past him to study Gunnar's hirdmen lined up beyond. His gaze landed on Runa, and he pursed his lips. "Glad the whole family is here. I've got news for all of you, the wife especially."

Runa stepped forward and Gunnar fought his instinct to drag her back in line. If it had been any other, he would not have tolerated another stepping before him.

"You fly Hrolf's banner, but you are Mord Guntherson's man. Who do you speak for?"

"Jarl Hrolf, or as the Franks call him, Count Rollo." He played with Hrolf's baptismal name and his companions chuckled at the mangled pronunciation. "He selected me especially for this task. Didn't want men too attached to your husband to deliver this news."

They all stiffened at the hint, and Magnus smiled to reveal yellow teeth. Runa alone dared to challenge him.

"Deliver your message then take yourself from my lands. You are not welcomed here, no matter who you represent."

"Ah, the famous bitch-wife of Ulfrik Ormsson and her equally famous tongue. You are still a good-looking woman for your age. Maybe you'll want to bed down with another man before this day is done. You've still got the face to trap a man."

Gunnar's hand flew to his sword, Magnus and his men matching him. His vision hazed red with rage, but Aren threw his arms around him from behind, preventing him from drawing his sword.

"Don't! It's what he wants. You're falling into the same trap. You strike him and we are all dead." Aren squeezed, but it was his words and not his strength that prevented Gunnar from struggling. Magnus kept his hand on the hilt of his sword.

"We are evenly matched. I'd split this bastard's head in two before he can beg forgiveness."

"And there could be a thousand men waiting across the Seine to follow up on your rash action." Aren released him and stepped between them. His wide face was red. "Let him deliver his news. Look at Mother. She has not even moved."

Runa stood with arms folded across her chest, unruffled but stern, glaring at Magnus. Gunnar felt the shame for his stupidity, but felt better when he noticed Hakon dropping his hand from his own blade. "Out with your news, Magnus."

"For the murder of Bishop Burchard, cousin to the Lady Poppa, Ulfrik Ormsson is named an outlaw and banished from Normandy. Furthermore, all his direct relations," Magnus paused and stared at all three brothers as if they did not realize he meant them, "are also outlawed and banished. Lands will revert to Jarl Hrolf the Strider. Your men will have to decide to either follow you into banishment or swear a new oath to Hrolf. During this time, Ulfrik is held hostage to your peaceful behavior. Any violence to Hrolf or his representatives will mean Ulfrik's death." Magnus paused again and smiled playfully at Gunnar. "Too bad you didn't get your cuts in. Would make it a lot easier to string up your Da and have done with this."

Gunnar felt his entire body brace as if he were about to jump into battle. The same breathlessness that comes before facing death seized him now. Yet he did not reach for his blade nor lash out. He had expected a judgment like this and had been prepared. Next he looked to his mother, who had turned away and lowered her head. She said nothing more but retreated from the meeting.

"Jarl Hrolf did not set a time for you to clear out," Magnus said. "But I wouldn't take too long. Best to get these things over before they get out of control."

"Go back to your master," Gunnar said. "And tell him we'll not do anything until my father is released."

His brothers whirled to face him, but he ignored them and focused on Magnus's widening smile.

"You're in no position to make demands, but I'll deliver your message anyway. I'm sure he'll enjoy it."

Magnus and his companions returned to their horses, where they all remounted then rode away.

"I'll take the men and follow on foot," Hakon said. "No telling what they might feel entitled to do now."

Gunnar nodded and Hakon left to gather the hirdmen. Only Aren remained, and his face burned red now. "Are you mad? Hrolf could hang Father if he wanted. Are you daring him?"

"I'm buying us time," Gunnar said, not looking at Aren but at his mother. Runa stood alone, arms wrapped around herself and head lowered. He wanted to comfort her, but understood she needed a moment alone.

"Time for what? Do you think Hrolf is going to change his mind? Or do you think we should fight him? What can be gained by insulting the new Count of Rouen?"

Hakon led a column of hirdmen along the trail, nodding to them as he passed. Gunnar returned it, then put his arm around Aren's shoulder. "Remember your plan, that I would organize a response if things went badly for Father? Well, that is what I am doing. I need time to send word to the other jarls and to await Einar's arrival. Once they learn of Father's fate, they will rise up in his defense and pressure Hrolf to reverse his judgment."

"Did you not hear that the bishop was a relative of his wife's?" Aren pulled out from beneath Gunnar's arm. "It's worse than pressure from the Church, but his own family relations are part of this problem. He can't excuse Father so readily."

Gunnar walked off, letting Aren trail him. His brother was correct, as he always was, and the sense of helplessness drowned him. Were they so readily defeated? Was everything he achieved in this life dependent upon the whim of one man? There had to be a way to fight back and not just meekly pack a cart and drift away.

"This is all that dog-shit Father Lambert's fault. He lied about his leg. I just know it." He stopped, and Aren, who followed behind, bumped into him. "He couldn't have been present for Father's hearing. Hrolf would have seen the priest had both legs and the Church's lies would've been revealed."

"Men in power make their own truths," Aren said. "It doesn't matter what facts are presented to them."

"It would have to Hrolf. He can't possibly have wanted Father's downfall. He would've taken any chance to forgive him this accident."

Aren tucked his head down as was his custom when considering new information. As his brother debated, Gunnar realized what he had to do.

"I'm going to find Father Lambert and bring him to Hrolf. That will prove he had been deceived."

"What?" Aren shook his head as if awakening. "There's no deceit in the bishop's corpse. Father killed him. No one can deny it."

"But the reason for the whole accident was based upon the lies Father Lambert told. Don't you see? It was a trap."

"I see the trap, but don't see how producing Father Lambert will change Hrolf's mind. If anything, it may anger him more."

Gunnar left Aren to his worries, knowing his solution was the right one. Once Hrolf saw how they had all been deceived, he would throw out his father's sentence. He only had to locate the priest before Hrolf's patience wore out.

He went to his mother, gently touching her arm so as not to shock her. She lifted glittering dark eyes to his. "You have that mischievous look. Please don't do anything to get your father killed."

"Nothing of the sort. I have the answer to our problems. Don't worry, Mother, I will have Father freed and our name restored."

Runa gave a feeble smile. For the first time in years he noticed how old his mother seemed. The lines between her brows were deep, and more gray than brown spiraled through the tight curls of her hair. "Don't risk too much. I am happy just to have my family back."

19

Aren was not used to having to take charge. Yet as he sat in the hall, a horn of mead clasped in both hands, Hakon and Finn both staring at him expectantly, he found himself with no other choice. His mother had gone to lie down, claiming the news had exhausted her. The hall was empty of even servants. No one was to know his father's fate, not yet, so words echoed like they were plotting in an underground cave. Only three conspirators gathered at the table, with Aren at the middle. Oil lamps lent an unearthly glow and fetid taint to the hall.

"So Gunnar doesn't even know where he's searching?" Hakon asked the same question for the third time. His brother, Hakon, was a brave but simple man, and Aren loved him for it. Yet now it grated on him.

"He couldn't be persuaded to change his mind," Aren said. "And Mother was too shocked to try. She's the only one he'll listen to."

"His wife, Morgan?" Finn asked.

"Of no account," Aren waved his had dismissively. "Gunnar has gone to do what he thinks is right. We have to work around that."

"That's always been his way," Hakon mumbled. "Gets a fire in his belly and flies off in whatever direction he's facing. Last time Father disappeared he was gone for five years."

Aren drank the mead to buy a pause in the discussion. He savored the sweet taste of it, but a hint of bitterness lay beneath. It was an apt comparison to their recent life. After the peace and the handing out of rewards all was sweet, but underneath that was the bitter taste of jealousy and betrayal. Why no one else recognized the hidden rancor was a mystery to Aren. He and Vilhjalmer seemed the only two people aware of the anger lurking in the hearts of men. Aren had seen men stare greedily at his father's success, and Vilhjalmer heard the grumblings of those who thought they deserved more. Yet neither of their fathers had deigned to hear of it. Perhaps as men aged they ignored troubles rather than face them. Yet now their self-inflicted blindness trapped them, and Aren had to seek a way out for his own father.

"What are we going to do?" Finn asked. He had been an innocent, freckle-faced boy when his father had met him, but Aren only knew him as a cunning woodsman and hunter. He respected Finn for his loyalty and even-handedness, both of which were needed now.

"I fear Gunnar may bring us more trouble. Kidnapping a priest can go wrong in so many ways." Aren sighed, dreading to state what everyone had understood. "And if anyone is hurt during it, Hrolf could take it as an excuse to execute Father."

Finn shook his head. "I just can't see Hrolf doing that to Ulfrik. He was in tears when they reunited. How could he want him dead now?"

"It's the Church," Hakon said. "And his wife. I guess the bishop was her cousin."

"The fact remains that Father is now a hostage and we are all outlaws." Aren set his drinking horn aside, the dregs flowing over the table. "We have to consider securing our wealth before Hrolf or the Church decides to claim it. We also must spread the word of Father's captivity. At the least it will prevent further aggression toward us. Right now the Church has a free hand to work in secrecy, but a spot of light upon them will bring modesty."

"So we hope," Finn said. "They seem to do as they please no matter who is watching."

"All men have limits, and we will find the Church's," Aren said. "Einar should arrive at any time, unless he has been intercepted. That is very likely given Magnus's arrival today."

"But his father's body is here?" Hakon said. Aren blinked at him until Hakon lowered his head in shame. "Of course, they won't care about that."

"Now we have to plan on Gunnar's actions to worsen matters."

"It's an ill thing to assume disaster," Hakon said. "But Gunnar has a history of rash action."

"So that means Father will be in greater peril," Aren said. Both Finn and Hakon were staring intently at him, and for the first time he felt truly like a leader. They expected a plan from him, one based on reason. "He must be safeguarded against whatever might come. Contacting the other jarls favorable to our side will help, but take too much time. We possess no way to help Father directly."

Both Finn and Hakon slumped in defeat and stared at the floor. He had not provided what they had hoped, yet his mind churned over the options. They sat in silence while he dredged his thoughts, and when the plan emerged from the muck of his confusion, he shot up straight on his seat.

"Of course! I'm such a fool," he said. Hakon and Finn looked up, smiling. "I will go to Vilhjalmer. He is not yet in his full power, but he has sway with men who expect him to succeed his father. He loves Father like an uncle, and thinks him a hero worthy of a saga. If anyone could appeal on his behalf, Vilhjalmer is that man."

Finn fell back laughing. "A brilliant idea!"

Hakon frowned and folded his hands on his lap. "How are you going to contact him? You're an outlaw, remember?"

"I'm also just one young man. Hrolf and his lackeys are watching for armies of men, not a lone traveler."

"You can't go alone," Hakon said flatly. "Even in times of peace that's dangerous, never mind after today."

"I will take a small escort. You pick the men. I know how to find

Vilhjalmer, trust me. We both had ways of escaping his mother and teachers when we wanted time for mischief."

"You and mischief?" Hakon raised an eyebrow. "Did it involve women? Do you even know what to do with one?"

"This is no time for jest," Aren said airily. "I'll enlist Vilhjalmer's aid. He might not even be aware of what is happening. Finn, you are a like a forest spirit when you set your mind to it. You should discover what happened to Einar, and give him our news. Make sure he can ride to our aid, and that he spreads the word. Ull the Strong is still his neighbor, and has ever been a supporter of our father. Those two alone can make trouble for Hrolf."

"And my role?" Hakon asked. "Shall I work the loom or spin wool like an old crone while you have your adventure?"

"News is going to reach our men sooner or later. You have their respect, so you will organize them. Start with the most loyal, so you have backup if others choose to revolt. You must be our jarl, Hakon. There can be no other."

"I'm delighted you elected me to the role," Hakon said, then stood. He reached across the table and mussed Aren's hair like he used to when they were children. "You are king-maker now, but I'll be rolled in horse dung if your plan doesn't work. Refill your horn and let's drink to its success."

Finn snatched the horn then refilled it. He thrust it into Aren's hands and slipped his arm about his neck. They all raised their drinks and Hakon made the toast.

"To the safe return of our father!"

When they had guzzled the mead and set their horns upon the board, they all laughed. Aren, though, could not stop thinking how much of their plan relied upon good luck. He prayed the gods they still had it left to them.

20

Gunnar arrived on the Seine with thirty of his own hirdmen, and stared across the cloudy water to the opposite shore. A ferry rowed toward them, halfway across the expanse. His own ship was moored to his father's dock where three other ships sat patiently waiting for their owners to take them to sea. Gunnar recalled a time when the open sea had been his only home. Seeing those masts all grouped together brought back memories of fleets taking to open water to find adventure and plunder.

"I've spoke with the guards," Bekan said, approaching from the docks. The high afternoon sun filled the sockets beneath his heavy brow with shadow. "Magnus's men passed both coming and going, but did not cause trouble. They left the ships alone."

"You might think they wanted us to do this," Gunnar said with a smile. "We can't land across the river where Hrolf's men could see us, but will have to sail upriver to cross."

Bekan scratched at the jagged white scar in his brow. "As long as we're still priest-hunting."

"That we are, old friend."

They sailed toward Paris. River traffic had increased now that Hrolf had pledged himself to Charles the Simple. A single longship was no longer a threat to anyone, and so they rowed against the current to a landing on the northern tip of Hrolf's lands. Beaching the ship, Gunnar left ten men to guard it and took the others inland. They followed the banks back west before cutting inland where sentries on the river might spot them.

"Do you know where this village is?" Bekan asked.

"I've an idea," Gunnar said. In truth he had a vague notion of its position. He had beaten one of the men who still lingered around Hrothgar's farm for the location of Father Lambert's church. At the time the directions seemed easy enough. Gunnar had been so filled with hate for this man, blaming him for all that had happened, that he split the man's head open with his ax. Now he wished he had taken him along as a guide.

They entered a light wood for cover against discovery by travelers or sentries. They stumbled through this wood and it grew thicker, not lighter as he had expected. The trail he had hoped to pick up had not revealed itself, and they had to double back to try once more. At last they did come to a path and followed it until a farmhouse appeared above a rise ahead. Gunnar smiled and pointed, as if to assure himself he had not gotten them lost.

"This must be the place," he said.

"Wasn't there supposed to be a giant elm by the farm?" Bekan asked.

"Maybe they cut it down," Gunnar said. His heart began pounding, realizing he might have followed the wrong path. The land was crisscrossed with them, worn into the dirt by villagers traveling to different towns. Nothing was laid out in any plan, and picking the wrong path was not uncommon.

"Let's send someone ahead to discover who's up there," Gunnar said. "If this is not the right village, we must learn where we are."

They retreated down the path until the farmhouse disappeared, then two men headed up the trail. No one spoke while the men were gone, as if speaking might cause them to become lost. Gunnar paced, holding his stump arm behind his back. While he paced, he noticed a shape atop the hill. He stared at it, not sure of what he was seeing.

Then the form burst into a run, and fled over the horizon.

"Shit! We've been seen." Gunnar pointed at the crest, as did another of his men.

"Should we run?" Bekan asked, and the men all turned to him.

His temple throbbed. If they had to retreat in failure, with Father Lambert just over that rise, he would never forgive himself. His father's freedom depended upon this decision. "Are we women to run from shadows? Do you think our swords and mail are not good enough to face a farmer's rake?"

The men laughed and shook their heads. Gunnar pulled the ax from his belt loop and pointed ahead, and with a roar led them up the track.

They piled over the ridge, where he stopped to examine the landscape. His eyes settled on a large elm tree and his body flooded with relief. His two men were chasing someone into a barn. He had no time to see who they pursued, but the door slammed on them and they began to kick. Gunnar called out for them to stop.

"It's the church we want to find," he said as he joined the rest of his men to the two he had sent ahead. "What did you learn?"

"Only that these are suspicious folk," said one of the men.

Gunnar scanned the rest of the farms, and saw people running out of the fields or fleeing the area. He had no way to contain all of them, but he did spot the stone building he had hoped to find.

The church was a small and simple structure, the only stone building in the entire village. The steeply pitched roof had been newly thatched, and Gunnar imagined it burning. Around the church were neatly trimmed shrubs and a small grove of trees behind it. People were fleeing to it now, as they always did when raiders came. He remembered his raids fondly as well.

"Let's go see if Father Lambert has both of his legs," he said.

They marched directly toward the church which seemed to huddle in fear in the open field. Gunnar sent his younger, faster men to sprint around the rear and cut off anyone trying to flee that way. The main force hit the front door, a heavy wooden affair with iron bindings. He tried it, and it was barred as expected.

"Looks like we're not welcome," Gunnar said, stepping back. "And I thought they wanted to make us Christians."

His men laughed and he gestured at Vigfus, one of his strongest men, to take his two-handed ax to the door. The wide-shouldered man hefted the ax overhead and slammed it into the door. Muted screams followed the thud of the ax head biting into the wood.

"We're getting inside no matter what you want," Gunnar called through the door while Vigfus pried out his ax. "So why anger me like this? Just open up. We only want to talk to your priest."

He shared a wry smile with Bekan, but when no one answered he had Vigfus continue to chop the door. By the time it splintered open, Vigfus was streaming with sweat. "Must be a pile of gold in there to have a door like this," Vigfus said as he used his ax to widen the hole he had broken.

"All churches are filled with spoils," Gunnar said. "After we take the priest, we'll help ourselves to some of his riches. I'm sure he won't miss it."

Having cleared a hole large enough to see through, Vigfus stuck a section of splintered door through the opening. It was an old trick used against desperate villagers. They might be hidden against the side of the door with a blade to stick into the first arm through the opening. Their fright normally caused them to strike at the first thing through the hole. When nothing struck Vigfus's decoy, he put his arm through and pulled up the bar. It clunked to the floor and more women screamed inside the church.

"I hate screaming women," Gunnar said. "Reminds me of my wife. Always screaming about something."

Bekan chuckled. "Morgan's a steady woman. I think it's you who does all the screaming."

"I've got two daughters. Between them and my wife there's enough screeching in my life."

The door burst open and the screams hit him with full force. Vigfus stepped aside to allow Gunnar the opportunity to enter first, which he did with his ax ready. He confronted a single man with a dull iron sword so tarnished he did not think the weapon had been used since Charlemagne ruled. Behind him were two other men with wooden rakes held like spears. Clustered against the altar were all women and children, their dirty faces white with fear. The tiny church might fit twenty people with comfort, but now it was crammed with bodies. The place smelled like sweat and manure with the rotten odor of tallow candles.

"Where's all the gold?" Bekan asked as he stood to Gunnar's left. "A Church without gold is like a woman without tits."

"Like a woman, they won't show it without no one," Vigfus said, standing to Gunnar's right.

"All right, boys," Gunnar said. "We'll get to the spoils in a moment."

Despite the banter, Gunnar's head throbbed. He did not see Father Lambert. He did not even see a priest. A throng of filthy, scared farmers was no help to him, and without Father Lambert for evidence, Ulfrik would be doomed. He leveled his ax at the man holding the sword.

"Stop waving that shit excuse for a weapon at me. Do you want to get hurt?" He spoke in Frankish, and the man stared back at him with wide eyes. Gunnar rolled his own and drew closer. The man still did not move. Gunnar's ax flashed as it struck out, hooking the blade and yanking it out of the farmer's hand. It clattered to the wood floor and bent. The women screamed again, but Gunnar laughed and kicked the ruined blade away.

"Did you steal that from a grave? Never mind. Where is Father Lambert?"

His men dragged the benches aside to allow more of Gunnar's crew to force into the church. The two men with the rakes stood protectively before the women and children while the disarmed man trembled, staring at Gunnar like he was a wolf.

"All right, do you have a priest here?" Gunnar asked. He used his ax head to hook the disarmed man's shirt and pulled him closer. "If you don't answer, you're no use to me. So speak or die."

"I am the priest you seek."

Gunnar tore his ax from the farmer's shirt and looked back

behind the altar where a middle-aged man in black robes stood with his arms folded. He was thin and wrinkled, but his hair and eyes were nearly as dark as Gunnar's. His left eye twitched rapidly, making it hard for Gunnar to focus on anything else. He wore no riches, only a simple wooden cross hung from his neck. Behind him, a larger wooden cross adorned the stone wall of this plain church.

"You're not Father Lambert. Where is he?"

The priest stood straighter. "I do not know of a Father Lambert. This has always been my church."

Gunnar sighed and slumped his shoulders. "This is the game we're going to play, then? You've been told to hide him from me, and you'll pretend not to know anything about him. I'll start killing these good people until you can't bear the guilt anymore, and then you'll finally tell me. So why not just tell me now?"

The women screamed and even the men flinched at Gunnar's threat. The priest's mouth dropped open and he slowly shook his head. "I really have never heard of Father Lambert."

"Let's just check your honesty."

Bekan and Vigfus each grabbed the armed men and Gunnar hooked the last one with his ax. He did not want to kill these innocents, so he raised a brow to the priest. "Last chance to save someone's husband?"

"Father Lambert has not returned." One of the women blurted. She was weed thin, twisted from labor and browned from the sun. Her blue eyes burned out from her muddy face. "He went to found a church but never came back."

Gunnar smiled. "Thank you. See how easy that was? Now we just have to talk to the priest for a few more details."

The priest wavered as if about to pass out. Bekan forced through the crowd and seized the priest by his throat, then dragged him to Gunnar.

"Since you're a liar, we're doing this the hard way."

"I didn't lie. I've always been a priest here."

Gunnar punched the priest in the stomach, doubling him over.

"Put his right arm over the altar," he said. "Hold back the others. Gut them if they resist."

The priest struggled as Bekan pulled his arm out and Vigfus pressed his face into the altar. Gunnar leaned beside him and showed him his stump.

"Some Frankish prick cut this off when I was just a boy. My sword hand. But see, it never stopped me from doing as I wished, and I've been killing Franks ever since. But since we're at peace, or so our leaders tell us, I'll give you one last chance. Tell me where I can find Father Lambert and you keep your right hand. Is that so hard?"

"I don't know where he is. He didn't tell me anything. Just left and never came back." The words rushed out in a bubbling torrent. Gunnar shook his head.

"Wrong answer." He raised his ax and slammed it down on the priest's forearm. It sunk deep into the bone but did not cut off the limb. The priest shrieked as did nearly everyone inside the church. Gunnar ducked his head at the screaming, grimacing as if he had been struck himself.

"You might be able to save that hand if you'd just be honest and give up Father Lambert. Where is he?"

The priest sobbed, echoed by the women and children watching in terror. Gunnar lifted the priest's face with the bloody ax head.

"They took him to Rouen. That's all I know."

"Did he have both legs?"

The priest continued to sob.

"Did he have both legs?" Gunnar put the ax blade into the cut on the priest's forearm and pressed. The priest thrashed and screamed, but Vigfus smashed him into stillness.

"His leg was hurt. I never saw him. You must believe me."

"I do believe you. One last question. Who took him?"

"Men from the archbishop." The priest's words were punctuated with sobs. "That's all I know. They gave me charge of this church and said he would not return and never to speak of him again."

Gunnar nodded and Bekan awaited a sign to release him. "You've told me what I must know."

Vigfus released the priest and he collapsed in tears. Gunnar nodded to his men to begin stripping any valuables, then he waited outside. Bekan joined him. Both stared at the closed door, listening to the shouting and smashing beyond.

"Father Lambert has slipped our grasp, and now we've sacked a church on Hrolf's land." Gunnar rubbed his face. "This is not good."

"What should we do?" Bekan asked.

"Burn the church and village. Then we track down anyone who might've fled and kill them. After that, we'll have to return home. To do more will only invite disaster."

Gunnar ran his hand through his hair and turned aside from the church. If anyone lived to identify him, he had just killed his father.

21

Mord approached Hrolf's great hall beneath a sky of patchwork clouds that threatened rain. In the distance, thunder rumbled and he took it for a good sign. The wind gusted, blowing his hair across his face and ruining the careful combing his wife, Fara, had done for him before answering Hrolf's summons. A new green cloak set with a gold pin fluttered from his shoulder as he greeted the guards at the doors. A cold drop of rain struck his cheek.

"You should be expecting me," Mord said. Chest puffed out, he presented his sword and daggers to the guards. "I was told to come in haste."

"Jarl Hrolf awaits you inside." The guards swung open the doors to the blackness beyond. For the first time in years he was entering not as a failure or disappointment, but as a man of regard. Fara had already learned he would be named to Ulfrik's lost property after concessions to the Church. She had worked her way into the good graces of Poppa, Hrolf's wife, and used her friendship for both gossip and influence. Now Mord stepped across the threshold, placing feet on the wooden floor of the front room, and he did so with confidence.

Passing through to the main hall where the floor became

pounded dirt covered in straw, he found it well lit with oil lamps and hearth fire. The heat threatened to overwhelm him in his new cloak, but he ignored it as he crossed the open hall to his jarl. His father already sat beneath the high seat, for now that Hrolf was a count none could sit equally with him as in the old days. Hrolf lounged in his giant wooden chair, and his confessor hung in the shadows behind him, ready to serve. The confessor smiled peacefully at Mord. They had an understanding bonded with gold and favors, and Mord was grateful to see him in a fine mood.

"Jarl Hrolf, how may I serve?" Mord said, as he knelt before him.

"Stand. I wish to make this as quick as possible."

Mord stood and found Hrolf frowning at him, which turned his hands to ice until he realized Hrolf was not mad at him. Ulfrik's rash behavior had fouled his temper and having to confront anything about it made him surly, or so Mord believed.

"You know Ulfrik Ormsson has been stripped of his lands and declared outlaw."

"So I have heard, Lord."

"Please, your nose is so deep in this shit it's a wonder you don't stink of it yourself."

Mord's stomach dropped and the icy feeling returned to his hands. He lowered his head to avoid the giant jarl's glare.

"But I've not seen your hand in any of this. Your hatred for Ulfrik is well known, to both him and me and anyone with eyes to see. So I'm certain you are delighted with his downfall. I will warn you to keep your celebrations to the privacy of your own hall. When word gets out, there will be unrest. I'm expecting you, as the son of the man who has mentored me my whole life, to do everything to bring peace. Do you understand?"

"Yes, Lord."

Hrolf's frown deepened and he stood. "Lands held by Ulfrik and Gunnar the Black will soon be vacated. I am awarding you both of these territories. You may collect taxes, raise warriors from the people, and rule in my name until such a time as I withdraw that right from you. The Church must be paid for their loss, and so it will come from the land in the form of churches to be constructed. Ulfrik will be made to pay for those costs before he is released, but you will be responsible to ensure those churches are built and that they prosper. Do you understand?"

Mord swooned with the success. He had just been awarded the best lands beyond Hrolf's own personal holdings. "It will be an honor, Lord."

"Good, your good relationship with the Church is why I am granting this to you. None of my other jarls have done as well embracing the change as you have. We need a strong relationship with them if we are to grow successful and bring the native Franks firmly under my rule. Churches are what the people want and my penance for all the churches I've burned in my day. So we build churches and cultivate good relations, then one day we are both looking at better lands farther east."

He gave Mord a small smile. Hrolf's ambitions were boundless. Already a year into the peace and he was considering his next moves into the Frankish nobility. "I will do all that I can to strengthen those ties."

Again Hrolf's confessor gave a small smile, but Mord averted his eyes. He had donated much gold for him to whisper good words on his behalf, and it had all been repaid today. Now the confessor would be expecting another reward for closing the bargain. Mord would be glad to pay it.

"Your former lands will be absorbed into my own for now. I need you focused on settling Ulfrik's people and not having to contend with your old holding."

Mord tried to hide the disappointment, and lowered his head with a nod of understanding.

"Good, then I am done here. You may visit with your father, if you wish. I have other matters needing my attention."

All stepped aside as Hrolf strode from his hall, the confessor scuttling behind him with a final wink at Mord before leaving. Now only his father remained behind. He rushed over to him, his heart beating with joy.

"We've done it," he whispered. "Can you believe it?"

His father's milky white eye fixed on him as he stood. Age and sickness had robbed him of strength and speed, so he struggled up with great effort. Once at his full height, he scowled and slapped Mord across the face.

Stomach tight with anger and his face stinging, Mord touched his cheek. "What was that for?"

"Ulfrik was banished and he'll be allowed to take whatever men will follow him. Do you know how many that will be?" Mord shook his head. "All of them except the ones not worth having. He's a warlord, a gold-giver, and a beast of the shield wall. Men follow glory even into exile. So what is there to celebrate?"

"But all these years, we've waited for him to make this mistake. He can't escape from this now. I've got everything you've wanted me to have."

Gunther violently shook his head and held up his gnarled hand. "You have the land. You are still not Hrolf's right hand. Did you not hear what he said? He barely trusts you. He would not even allow you to keep your old lands. That's an insult."

Mord knew it was true, but had not wanted to believe it. "But I've been awarded the best part of his territory."

"And Ulfrik will return for revenge. He will give you no rest, no enjoyment, no success while he lives."

"He brought this on himself. Why would he suspect me?"

"Oh, let my old, weak mind think of how that could be?" Gunther tapped his cheek with his finger in mockery of deep thought. "Think on this, you fool. Whose man shot his son in the face only a year ago, in what looked like an attempt on his life? He was just short of accusing you then, but thought better of it. Let's not stop there, though. Who has opposed him at every turn, and tried to make him appear foolish before others? Who is inheriting his wealth now that he is gone? Do you think he is stupid? Never underestimate that man. I did, and he came back from the dead. He will find out that you've been agitating for this. He will find out we sent Father Lambert to cause trouble with his son."

"But he made the decision to kill the bishop."

"Fine luck for us, but we put him in harm's way and we are doing everything we can to ensure he meets a bad end. If left alive he will hound you until one of you is dead. If the two of you ever cross swords, he will win."

"Father, he's getting old."

"He will win!" Gunther's shout echoed through the hall. "The gods favor him. Even now, I don't know why, they granted him a second chance. He killed a bishop, Hrolf's relation no less, and he's going to live. If it were you or I we'd have been dead a week ago."

Mord fell into a sulky silence, turning aside from his father's blind stare. How Ulfrik could ever connect him to his current misfortunes was a mystery to him. Yet he could not deny Ulfrik's luck. "What do you suggest I do?"

"What do you think?" Gunther hissed. "Remove him from the game board. Your work is hard enough without Ulfrik attacking from behind. He climbed too high for his station, overtook you and me, and now has finally earned his punishment. But it's not enough. You have to make sure he is dead."

"Once he is released from Hrolf's protection, he will be an outlaw," Mord said, staring up at Hrolf's banner of yellow lions on a red flag. It hung from the rafters and swayed lazily as air rose toward the smoke hole above. "I will have him ambushed and killed. But his sons remain a problem. Getting all of them will be difficult."

Gunther snorted. "The sons can be dealt with in time. Gunnar is too wild to be a serious threat, and he might scatter to where he has better luck. The middle child, Hakon, poses the bigger threat. He is steady and men like him, but he is not the force of battle that his father is. Kill him and you will remove the biggest threat to your peace. The youngest one was a strange child I never knew well. It is said he is weak, not of Ulfrik's blood. He is friends with Vilhjalmer, but I would not fear him. Kill the two oldest sons and you shall have peace when Ulfrik is dead."

Mord sat on a bench that had been cleared to the side of the hall. "Now I only have to find the men to do the job."

"Plenty of men have no love for Ulfrik. You don't rise so high without making enemies. For the right rewards they will do all you ask." Gunther now faced him; even though blind, he apparently could still see shadow. "You've made a good start, now finish it. Hrolf will need you to hold together, and in that you can be the hero you should have always been. Then with the land and Hrolf's favor, you will make our family a power to be remembered. You just need sons, and lots of them. That will be your greatest task after Ulfrik is gone."

"Do not worry for it, Father. Fara will give me sons or I will find another woman that can. For now, let me concentrate on removing Ulfrik from the board. I know who I can use for this purpose."

22

The trader's ship glided alongside the docks under the assured guidance of an old professional. Aren stood in the prow with his three guards, veterans of long service with gold armbands and faded scars as proof of their bravery. As the trader's crew moored the ship, Gunnar scanned the bustling dock for any familiar faces and saw none. Slaves and freemen alike labored with bales, crates, casks, and barrels. Being the first great city along the Seine, Rouen's docks were constantly filled with traders moving wares in and out of Frankia. A cluster of masts pointed at a gray sky and the thick scents of river mud and fish filled the air. Aren heard the gangplank drop to the dock, and so turned to his guards.

"You three must wait aboard the ship for me. I've paid the trader until tomorrow at noon, and I am certain he will linger no more than that." Aren searched their faces, and they all gave him a firm nod. "If I am not back before that time, you must leave without me. Return to Hakon and tell him I have been captured. Let no one come after me, for that will be expected. If I'm captured I will find my own way out."

The three guards exchanged glances. The leader, Gils, a brown-haired man with a shock of gray in his neatly trimmed beard, put a knobby hand on Aren's shoulder. "You are braver than men give you credit for. We will wait, and wish you luck on your task."

He entrusted his sword to Gils, for weapons were not allowed in the city except for Hrolf's men. Besides, he was no great fighter and he preferred to use his wits to win his battles. He mounted the gangplank, his guards slapping his back in encouragement, then left the docks toward the main city of Rouen.

If Paris was grander than this, he could not imagine what it would be like. Rouen always amazed Aren. The area surrounding the river docks was all ramshackle buildings with faded signs, broken barrels, and rusting debris. Racks of fish dried in the sun, adding to the aroma already filling the air. Laborers and fishermen in drab clothes traveled along rutted and meandering tracks, each lost in their own business. Yet beyond this drudgery was the excitement of the walled city of Rouen. He moved quickly among the low town people, squeezing past carts piled with goods and through crowds of merchants haggling over prices. He chased a goose that had wandered into his path, until he finally arrived at the gates.

Now he only had to find Vilhjalmer. Over the years they had developed means of contacting each other when Hrolf's only and most precious son wanted to be free of his minders. Aren gambled that Vilhjalmer had been excluded from anything related to his father. He was no longer a young boy, but a man of eighteen years, and if he chose to oppose his father's decisions, his words would carry much weight. If Vilhjalmer was in the dark, then their old ploys would succeed.

Paying his gate tax and providing an excuse for business beyond the walls, he entered into the shadow of the gate along with dozens of others traversing both directions. He kept his head down and found the palace where Vilhjalmer resided. He had used to stay in Churches, but now as the son of a count he had access to better living quarters. The stone building towered above him, not as grand as the cathedrals the Christians built but close to it in scale. The guards outside stood four at each entrance, but Aren ignored them and proceeded to the servant's entrance on the side where only two guards sat on stools in the shade. One was chatting with a bashful young servant girl while the other idly cleaned his fingernails with a dagger.

"Hail, Fulbert," Aren said to the guard cleaning his nails. The man did not stir, but only raised one eye to regard Aren. He went back to cleaning his nails when he saw Aren.

"Haven't seen your ugly face in a while," Fulbert said. The other guard and his girl glanced at him, but decided he was not worth their attention. Aren was glad for it.

"Always a pleasure to see you, too." Aren approached Fulbert, who seemed lost in ill-fitting mail that swallowed up his thin body. His helmet sat on the ground beside his spear. "I've a message."

Fulbert's eye raised again, but then flicked to his hand. Aren withdrew half a gold coin from his pouch and pressed it into his palm.

"Tell him that I've got a redhead from Ireland this time. Everything he's ever wanted and more. I'm at the usual place." Now Aren extended his hand to Fulbert, who snatched away the palmed gold coin before his companions noticed.

"Redhead from Ireland?" he asked as the half coin disappeared into his cloak. "Big tits?"

"Like melons." Aren winked and Fulbert smiled.

"Wish I was a rich prince to have someone find me a girl like that."

"Save your coins, Fulbert, and one day it may be so. Send him quickly. The girl can't wait long."

Fulbert laughed, which devolved into a choking cough. Aren left to find the tavern where they started their meetings. Again, no one had heard of his banishment yet so old acquaintances were glad to accept his gold and make the arrangements they had come to expect when he showed up. He expected at least two or three hours waiting, but was shocked when the doors opened to the large room where only one other man drank in sullen silence. Vilhjalmer and his personal escort entered.

He disguised himself in simple clothes, though his armored escort was a give-away to his importance. Vilhjalmer had his mother's eyes and his father's winning smile. Not as tall as his father, but every inch as royal and proud in his bearing, Vilhjalmer could never disguise his nobility even in drab clothes and a plain wool cloak. He strode across the dirt floor of the tavern, arms wide to greet Aren.

"A redhead from Ireland, with tits like melons? My dear friend, you know how to capture my attention."

They embraced and Vilhjalmer patted him on the back, then looked around for the girl.

"There is no girl this time. I have urgent news and we must speak in private."

Vilhjalmer's brilliant smile faded and he stepped back, his brow furrowed. "I dislike this serious tone. I've enough of that from the priests and nobles polluting this city." He studied Aren's face, then turned to his escort. "Clear this room and block the door. Wait for me outside."

The armored guard glared at the owner, who ducked away into a back room as he hustled a serving girl away with him. The other drunken patron protested when the guard lifted him by his shirt and dragged him to the door. He flew outside and the guard followed. The door slammed shut and Vilhjalmer gestured they should sit at one of the dozen tables in the room. Aren had already paid for a jar of ale and poured two mugs.

"What have you heard of my father?"

"Nothing recent. He is a popular man, but we find other people to talk about, believe it or not."

Aren fortified himself with a slug of the sour ale. Vilhjalmer did as well, and both grimaced as they set their mugs aside. "Pure goat piss," Vilhjalmer said. "But it's the taste of some great memories we've had here. You sure about that Irish girl?"

"This is no idle jest. My father killed a bishop, Burchard was his name. Your mother's cousin. Against my counsel my father went to your father to present his case, and now he has been declared outlaw and banished. As were all of his sons. So you are treating with a bandit now."

He laughed at referring to himself as a bandit, but Vilhjalmer sat back in shock, eyes wide and mouth agape. "My ears must be blocked. I don't believe I heard you correctly."

"You've heard it rightly, but let me tell you all of it." Aren leaned on his elbows on the table and proceed to reel out the story of the past week, leaving out no detail. By the end, Vilhjalmer had his head in his hands.

"Do you think Gunnar will find Father Lambert?" Vilhjalmer asked hopefully. "You might think it a stupid idea, but it has merit. If it can be shown the witnesses were false, my father could dismiss the crime."

"My eldest brother is ruled by his temper and his lusts. Whatever good he may do in finding Lambert he will ruin with some other rash action. That has always been his way. So I've come to you for help instead."

"You want me to help?" Vilhjalmer sat up, his head tilted to the side like a puppy trying to understand a new command. "How could I do that?"

"For starters, my father's situation is being kept secret until the sentence is carried out. So if others learn of what has happened, we might gain support for my father that could alter Hrolf's decision. Otherwise, you could use your influence with your father to get him to deal less harshly."

"You want me to go against the Church? Have you gone mad?" Vilhjalmer poured another mug of ale and guzzled it. Aren waited, hands folded neatly before him. Vilhjalmer, for all his swagger, feared his father, and Aren knew this request taxed his friend's courage.

"This is a favor that will place me and Ulfrik in your debt. Stop thinking about the wrath of your father or the anger of a few old priests. Both can be consoled with other concessions. But think of what you will gain? You know my father would do most anything you ask of him, but with a debt such as this he would do even more. Then my brothers and I will owe you as well. Such favors are always useful to own."

He saw the wheels turning behind Vilhjalmer's eyes, and he grew distant, touching the back of his fist to his mouth as he considered. "Actually, your father rescued me from the Franks. If anything, this would just balance the scales. Yet I understand what you are suggesting, but I won't do it for that reason."

"But you will do it?"

"I'll do it for friendship," he smiled at Aren. "And because we need men like you and your father to keep our new lands strong. Your father's a master of battle. Why let that go, or worse yet, become an enemy? You are the cleverest bastard I'm ever likely to meet, and I need you around when I succeed my father one day."

Aren sat back in relief, tension flushing from his body. He laughed, then raised his mug to toast Vilhjalmer. "I swear I will find you that red-haired Irish girl."

"Save her for yourself. I've no trouble finding a woman when I need one. But you, well, if you can catch one I suggest holding onto her."

They laughed and drank deep from their mugs, then fell into thoughtful silence. Vilhjalmer opened his mouth to speak but hesitated. Aren allowed him to struggle until he found his words.

"The Church is all-powerful. Like you, I believe they wanted to start a conflict so they could grab land Ulfrik and Gunnar were not willing to grant. But if they want your father to hang, then I lack power to oppose them. I think my father believes he has already done the best he can in this situation. Maybe he has. I will try to do more. But I cannot promise you I will change anything."

"I am only asking that you try. My father is being held hostage until his men are all cleared away. Hrolf has set no definite time for this, which to me means he's delaying until someone can rescue the situation. I believe you are that person. You are a man now, so use your say as a man to sway your father."

Vilhjalmer narrowed his eyes as if in challenge to some unseen threat. "I am tired of being a pawn. Everyone wants to control me because I'm the future of Normandy. Even men I thought were friends turned out to be no more than leeches. I'm done with that."

"A wise choice," Aren said. He had never heard Vilhjalmer openly voice such thoughts, but he guessed being Hrolf's only son would bring such pressures.

"Do you know Harald Finehair took over his father's kingdom at age ten, and he still rules today?" Vilhjalmer folded his arms across his chest. "I'm eight years older than that, and I've only been in a shield wall once. And only against a cowardly foe that ran away. It's time things change."

"Are you saying you will replace your father?"

"No! I just need to stop being manipulated by priests and shoved at ugly daughters of Frankish nobles. I need to be my own ruler, and I'll start today."Aren laughed. "Well, here you are holding a secret meeting with an outlaw in a cheap tavern, plotting to undermine your father's command."

"Ha! I hadn't thought of it that way." Vilhjalmer slapped the table with his open palm.

Then, as if listening at the door for a cue, a man burst into the room followed by three others. They were armored, wearing helmets and carrying sheathed swords. The first was a strong man with frizzy hair and beard spilling out beneath his dented helmet. His eyes skipped past Vilhjalmer and landed on Aren.

"Aren Ulfrikson, you are banished from Normandy. What are you doing here?"

Aren's heart flipped in his chest. His legs tensed to run, but he sat frozen in terror. The three other men fanned into the tavern, Vilhjalmer's guard protesting behind them.

Vilhjalmer's face blanched and he turned to Aren. "Oh, and my father's men have come to collect me home today. I had forgotten about that."

The four guards did not draw their weapons, but they spread in an arc around Aren's table. They widened their stances, ready to pounce.

"Take him alive," said the leader.

Aren blinked and saw all his hopes vanish as the men drew closer.

23

"Wait!" Vilhjalmer shouted.

The four guards halted and Aren jolted in shock. In the pause, he searched for an escape but found no other way out of the tavern besides the door. He assumed the back room would have another exit, but knew he'd never reach it before being caught. His mind ran over half a dozen ideas, none of them plausible and all requiring him to possess strength he lacked.

The guards did not relax their posture, but did not move closer. Vilhjalmer stood to his full, regal bearing and sneered down at Aren.

"I can't believe you thought to trap me with your lies. You were my friend, and I have been deceived. This is most awful. Possibly dreadful." He shook his head and slapped his hand to his cheek. "How can I face life knowing even you would betray me?"

Despite the terror of being seized by these brutish men, Aren had to stifle a smile at Vilhjalmer's overacting. Impressed with Vilhjalmer's quick wits, he played along, slumping in his chair.

"It is for my father that I do this. It is only through your vile luck that you have been saved."

The four guards straightened from their crouches, the frizzy-haired leader pushing up his helmet to scratch his head. He waved

Aren up from his chair. "Well, you're right about that. You're to come with us."

"Be careful with him," Vilhjalmer said, as if they were about to grab a venomous snake. "Remember his father. The whole clan are full of rotten tricks. I bet this one is planning to kick you right in the stones, then he'll gouge this one's eyes, and be out the door before you two can do anything about it. Are you certain you know what you're doing?"

The four guards looked at each other. "Um, well, I don't think that will happen, Lord," said the leader. He grabbed Aren by the arm and led him between another guard. "We can handle one unarmed man."

"Of course you can." Vilhjalmer clapped his hands together. "I'm just glad you got here in time. How lucky am I that you happened along to my secret meeting place where you knew my life would be in danger from this outlaw that you called by name the moment you entered. Fate really is something!"

Aren pressed his lips together to avoid laughing. The second guard grabbed Aren's other arm, and both held him in a grip a child could escape. All four guards were overwhelmed by Vilhjalmer's verbal barrage.

"Well, we heard that this one might have tried to contact you. So we thought you might be in danger."

"Of course I would be in danger. Ulfrik's entire family has gone mad with killing lust, stabbing people without cause. If I had only known, I'd have never come out here. Who should I thank for warning you about this threat? And I won't overlook the four of you when I speak to my father of this."

The leader tilted his head back and smiled. "Thank you, Lord. You owe your safety to Gunther One-Eye. He told us that one of Ulfrik's sons might try to use you as a hostage against Jarl Hrolf and that we should protect you."

"That's not a bad idea," Vilhjalmer said, surprising Aren by looking at him when he spoke. "Though I doubt it would have succeeded. How did you come here so quickly?"

"A man named Fulbert," added a second guard. He seemed eager to add himself to the glory he imagined forthcoming. "We can't draw our swords in the city, but I showed what I might do with a sheathed one. Told us right away where you'd be."

"Well, normally that would anger me," Vilhjalmer tucked in his chin in a mock frown. "But since it saved my life, I shall forgive him. Now let's get this tricky bastard out of this hole."

The guards tugged Aren, and he acquiesced to their direction. They led him through the door, then held him surrounded as Vilhjalmer strolled out last. As the leader began to tug him into the rutted dirt track that passed as a street, Aren scanned the area for the best escape route. He could outrun four men in armor, but once caught again he would not escape. He'd have to hide and hope to return to his own escorts without being caught. While he had taken them for safety on the overland journey, he had not expected to need them once in Rouen. He promised himself to never underestimate the potential for bad luck again. His best bets were to keep to alleyways and find a wagon or barrel to conceal himself until the threat passed.

"Before you take him away, let me give him a something to remember me by." Vilhjalmer stepped in front of Aren and drew his dagger, smiling. If Aren did not know better, Vilhjalmer seemed eager for blood. "One of you hold him still for me."

The frizzy-haired leader gathered both of Aren's arms behind his back. Vilhjalmer put the cold dagger blade to Aren's cheek and drew closer. "I'd say we both learned a few important things from this."

Vilhjalmer drew the knife back and gave Aren a solemn nod, then spoke louder. "I'm going to drive this right into your eye."

"Um, Lord, be careful not to kill him," said the guard holding Aren. For an instant, Aren felt bad for the man.

"I don't think I will," he said with a smile.

He thrust at Aren's head and he leaned away as if dodging the strike. In fact, Vilhjalmer's dagger went wide and plunged into the biceps of the frizzy-haired guard. The scream shattered Aren's ear and he was suddenly free. Vilhjalmer fell forward onto the guard, shouting panicked apologies. The other three stood staring in shock, while Vilhjalmer's own guard laughed.

Aren darted away. Vilhjalmer crowded them, shouting. "By the gods, I'm sorry! He just twisted away at the last moment."

He was laughing even as his heart pounded in terror. The alley he had spied earlier was dark and narrow, filled with trash that he leapt with ease. Behind he heard angry shouting, but as he emerged from the opposite end of the alley, their voices were already distant. This street was busier, filled with men streaming both ways from the docks. Horses plodded along with wagons filled with barrels. Porters carried sacks of goods, and knots of grungy fishermen clustered at the sides of the road. Aren's only distinction was his clean clothing. He threw away his cloak and slipped into the crowd.

Looking back, he saw no one in pursuit. His violent push drew more attention than he wanted, and one burly porter slammed him aside with his girth, cursing him for a fool. He slowed down, wiping the sweat from his brow and stepping into the shade of a building that stunk of urine and fish. The afternoon sun was sinking and the city gates would close. If he could get back to the docks, then he could get the ship launched before being found.

His pounding heart finally calmed as he swam against the flow of late afternoon workers and returned to the river dock. By now he was strolling as if in a fine mood. He had secured Vilhjalmer's help and confirmed what he had long suspected about Gunther One-Eye. Convincing his father to accept this betrayal might be the harder part of rooting out Gunther's evil. Ulfrik was notoriously loyal to his friends, as his naively presenting himself to Hrolf's judgment proved.

At the dock where he had left the ship, he found Gils and the other two guards standing idly with their packs at their feet. They stood on the dock itself which was now empty of the merchant ship. He noted how they strained too hard to appear as if not searching the crowd for him. Gils appeared more nervous than the others. Aren considered leaving and contacting them after dark, but he suspected they did not have that much time left. He wandered over to them, and when Gils noticed him he only inclined his head.

"You lost your cloak," he said.

"The least of my worries now." Aren stood beside them, scanning around for what had unsettled his guards. There were dock patrols, but these were common soldiers more interested in kickbacks and finding shade for relaxation. A different set of Norse warrior in chain shirts had spread out into the docks and appeared to be straining to watch laborers and crews at work. "Where's the ship?"

"After you left, men from Hrolf the Strider announced to the docks that sons of Ulfrik Ormsson were fugitives from Hrolf's justice and that they might be seeking passage to Rouen. Anyone aiding them would be judged guilty as well. So our weak-bellied merchant decided his business could not afford to be ruined, and ordered us off the ship and left."

"But I paid him good gold." Aren winced at how childish his words sounded. "That bastard's promise is worth nothing. If ever I find him on this river again, I'll take my gold back before I have his head mounted on a spear."

Gils nodded, still scanning the crowds. "Did you contact Vilhjalmer?"

Aren told him all that had happened. "So it's only a matter of time before they warn their friends waiting here. They are going to accuse me of attempting to take Vilhjalmer captive and could use that as an excuse to execute my father. We have to get back across the river."

Now all three guards shared fearful glances. "That might be impossible," Gils said. "The borders to our lands are being closed down, and any crossing we make from here will be right into Hrolf's guards. Something seems to have quickened Hrolf's pace."

As Aren listened, his fist balled up and heat came to his face. Gils noted his anger and picked Aren's sword from the deck. "You'll need this if you expect to fight out of here."

Taking it in hand, he realized just how little he had practiced with it. Ulfrik thought it shameful that he was not better with the weapons, but unlike his real father, he did not pressure Aren to be who he was not. Ulfrik had always told him his strength was in his mind and not his arms, and such men were both rare and valuable. Though he had warned him being handy with a sword would serve every man, and now he wished he had heeded that wise advice.

"There were four men sent to find me, and at least seven others we can see here." Aren slipped the baldric over his shoulder and adjusted the sword at his hip. "These are hirdmen come to escort Vilhjalmer home, and so there are at least two times as many more we don't yet see. There's no fighting out of here, and if you're right about crossings into my father's lands, then we are stranded."

"We can't stay here," Gils said, and the other two guards agreed with him.

"Not even a moment longer. There is but one road open to us, probably just as perilous as the others. We will travel to Eyrafell where Einar Snorrason will shelter us. He will help me return to my family once this is settled."

With the decision made, Aren went ahead of his guards so as not to attract attention. Hrolf's men never noticed them, and by sunset they were on the road heading east for Eyrafell. It was their only choice, but Aren wondered if he would ever see his family again.

24

Hakon sat at the high table of his father's hall, chin resting in his hand and heart thudding in his breast. His mother sat beside him, her face hard and inscrutable as if searching a distant horizon and hoping to find land. The morning light filtered through the open doors at the front of the hall, filling the entrance with an impenetrable yellow glare. But for slaves and servants the hall was empty, all the benches and tables cleared to the sides. The hearth was cold and filled with ash, and the black cooking pot hung empty on its trestle.

"You have done your best," his mother said. Her voice was weary but resolved. Hakon knew she had not slept well, but yet held herself with confidence.

"How do you stay so strong? Just the thought of facing these men turns my stomach to water."

Runa smiled, but continued to stare into the morning glare. "Fate dictates our lives. Who are we to worry for it? These men all have a fate that either follows ours or separates from us today. We sacrificed riches to the gods in the darkness before dawn. We begged them for success and luck. You have spoken to these men as a brother and a jarl, and given them the truth. We have done what we may. Now the

Three Norns weave what fates they will from the fabric we have given them. Do not fear to face these men, for each will do exactly as he must."

She at last turned and placed her thin, warm hand upon his. His mother was old now, nearly fifty, and Hakon did not know how much longer he could lean on her. Not many other women lived to this age, and yet still appeared as healthy and young as his mother. She had always been his strength, and though he fought like a wolf in battle, for all other matters he looked to her for guidance.

"You always have the words I must hear," he said. "Of course you are right, and whatever I must face outside of this hall is what Fate has decided. We did all we could do. I put a good amount of gold into that bag, and I only hope it has persuaded Odin's favor."

Having seen the One-Eyed All-Father in his youth, Hakon believed he had a special connection to him. He often found when he begged Odin for aid, he would receive it. Why the god listened to him was a question none could answer, but even his father had asked him more than once to implore Odin for luck in battle. Each time Odin favored them with victory.

Today had to be the same.

His mother retracted her hand and smiled at him. "You look just like your father did at this age. When I found him in the forest so long ago, I was nothing but a scared slave girl running from death. He was like a golden god, full of young strength and power. Go show that to these men, and they will follow you."

"I can never imagine you a slave," Hakon said, then stood. He checked his sword, straightened his clean blue cloak, then ran his fingers over his hair.

He paused at the doors, turned back to see his mother sitting at the high table in a frame of golden light. From this distance she lost all age and all weariness, and again became the shield maiden men had once celebrated.

"You must come with me, Mother. The men will take heart as I do to see your strength."

At first she did not stir, then she rose and joined him at the door.

She gave a gentle, small smile to him and gestured he should step outside.

The fresh morning air of summer smelled of wet grass and the cool air braced him. He turned from the eastern sun to the fields north of the hall. He averted his eyes until the last moment, not wanting to see only a handful of hirdmen and bondi left to his command. But as he lifted his eyes, he gasped with shock.

Rank upon rank of armored men stood silently awaiting him. His father had commanded two hundred hirdmen, the professional warriors at the core of his force, and could summon half as many bondi from the surrounding farms to fill his rank with spears and swords. As far as Hakon could count, not one was missing from the gathering. There were more men than ships to carry them into banishment. Hakon opened his mouth to speak but no words exited.

Runa appeared behind him, but said nothing. Instead she touched Hakon's shoulder and prompted him to stand before these warriors. At the front rank Ulfrik's standard of black elk antlers on a green flag waved in the breeze. Finn held the pole, his freckled face wide with a smile.

Hakon stood before the ranks, his mother next to him. With this many loyal men, he felt nothing could prevent them from rescuing his father. He shook his head in amazement. At last he spoke.

"I have no words. Your loyalty is as fierce as your strength. You are invincible. You are the sons of Odin."

"We honor our oaths," Finn shouted, and the men behind him joined, raising their rough voices to the sky. "We go with Jarl Ulfrik, for where he treads victory and glory follow!"

After the shouting subsided, Hakon looked to his mother who simply raised her brow. "You don't want to say anything to these men."

"They know me only as Ulfrik's wife. You are their jarl now, so command them."

Hakon licked his lips and met as many eyes as he could, and the grim faces of hardened warriors stared back. "We must expect victory but plan for the worst. Be prepared to leave on a moment's notice. Finn Langson returned last night and reported warriors massing at our borders. If we cannot persuade Hrolf to relax his sentence, then we will have no choice but to seek new land. Again, for those who wish to stay there will be no shame and Jarl Hrolf will take you. But for those who remain, I can only praise your honor and assure you the gods will see how you have chosen and judge you worthy of Valhalla."

The men shouted approval or stamped their feet. Hakon raised his hand for silence, then continued. "Go now and prepare yourselves. Prepare your families. There will be hardships to face, but none that men such as you cannot defeat. Be ready to answer the call to glory and know you have the admiration and gratitude of your jarl. Your loyalty will never be forgotten."

After more shouting and back-slapping, the assembly broke into smaller groups that lingered and eventually wandered off in all directions. Finn joined with Hakon and Runa, a wide grin on his freckled-face.

"That's a speech worthy of your father," he said. "I doubt any man would shame himself by running away now."

"No matter what they say today," Runa said, all reticence vanished, "many will shift loyalties if Hrolf continues to push us into homelessness."

"We don't have enough space on the ships to carry all of them anyway," Hakon said, his laugh dying under his mother's glare.

"Those men on the borders are keeping away any aid we might receive," Runa said, then folded her arms. "And they cut us off from Einar. Are you certain you had no sign of his approach? He was not rebuffed at the borders?"

Finn shook his head. "I found nothing of Einar nor the men originally sent to tell him of his father's death. I doubt he ever got the news, but just returned to Eyrafell. If he knew his father had died and was awaiting a proper burial, then nothing would have prevented him."

Runa nodded, then searched the horizon again like a sailor seeking land. Hakon hated the pensive expression, for he knew his mother feared more than she said. Neither Aren nor Gunnar had returned, and no word had come from Hrolf. The dearth of news worked on all of their nerves, but his mother's took the worst of it. No one hated inaction more than her, but in this situation nothing else could be done without risking Ulfrik's safety.

"Gunnar has returned," she said. Hakon roused from his gloomy thoughts to see a line of men approaching from the north. Groups from the assembly had stopped to talk with Gunnar's men, no doubt sharing news.

"If he is returning, then he must not have his priest," Hakon said. He shared a nervous glance with Finn. "Let him greet us in the hall. If his news is bad, I don't want others to read it from our reactions."

Runa nodded and all three returned to the hall to await Gunnar. Hakon seated himself at the high table with Runa, and Finn sat beneath them on a bench at the side. He seemed to meld into the shadows, only his white face showing. The wait dragged on in tense silence, and the servants sat uneasily with the somber mood, searching between Runa and Hakon for a command. At last the doors opened and Gunnar was framed in the morning light, a lone black shadow.

He strode inside, turning his head side to side as if expecting an audience. He walked with the arrogance of first-born royalty, something Hakon wished he could emulate. His mother had always been after him to sit up straighter and hold his head higher like his older brother. Even after losing his hand, he had not bowed his head nor let it keep him from the shield wall. He had to fight from the rear, for he could not lock a shield, but any man who challenged his ability learned how much he had practiced. For years it was all he did. Now even as he returned clearly in defeat, he stood beneath them with his chin back.

"If you think to sit up there and have me kneel to you, you'll have to break my legs to do it," Gunnar said to Hakon, his smile never wavering.

"No foolishness," Runa snapped. "You've returned alone. Tell us what you have done."

Gunnar's smile vanished. "Father Lambert has been hidden in

Rouen. We found another priest who knew nothing else of use. We could never get to Rouen and so we turned back. Hrolf's men are patrolling your borders, so I went to my own home first then came here. There are fewer patrols around my lands."

Hakon watched his brother deliver his news and he wished Aren were here. He would be able to determine if Gunnar was withholding something from them, and guess at what it would be. Hakon just harbored an uneasy feeling that the story was incomplete.

"So you just left the other priest with his villagers?" Runa asked, voicing Hakon's concerns. "You did not kill witnesses or take hostages, but simply turned back?"

"The important thing is the number of warriors on our borders," Gunnar said. "They don't all appear to be Hrolf's men, which means they may be either bandits come looking to pick at us as we leave or men wanting to stake a claim to the land. We have to be ready to leave now."

"But Aren has not returned," Hakon said. "And we've heard no news from Hrolf."

"News from Hrolf are the men at the border," Gunnar said. His face now darkened and he pointed at him. "If you're playing at jarl, then gather all the treasure and men you can and start moving toward the river for a quick escape. That is what must be done. I'm returning to my family to do the same."

He stalked from the hall, ignoring Runa who called after him. He left the doors standing open, as if the hall wore an expression of shock.

"Shall I go after him?" Hakon asked.

"No, he has done something wrong that he will not admit." Runa removed her head cover and ran her fingers through the tight curls of her hair. "We best do as he advises. Our situation will only worsen now."

25

Ulfrik lay sleepless on the bed, staring into the midnight darkness above him. He had counted more than a week's passage for his confinement to this one-room home, but now he struggled to remember which day was dawning. Was it day eight or nine? He should have marked the time on the wood frame of the bed, or on the simple table and bench he had been provided. He did not believe he would be held long. So much for trusting Hrolf to make the right choice.

Sighing, he flipped to his side on the goose-feather mattress. Hrolf had at least provided the most comfortable prison he had ever been confined to. He picked at goose feathers peaking through the cloth, teasing one out and letting it float to the dirt floor. Day or night, he had nothing to do but think. He had come to anticipate the arrival of meals, for the servants and guards would speak with him. Now they would say nothing, just as children stop petting a favorite pig before the slaughter.

More than shock, disappointment at both himself and Hrolf filled his thoughts. He stared at the dark of the wall next to him, the gray of a discarded cloak on a stool the only relief to the black. He struggled to understand what had happened to turn Hrolf. He had not seen his jarl in the year since the peace began, but in such a short time he seemed to have changed. He was now fearful, desperate to hold what he had grabbed. Yet why did he need fear anything? If King Charles broke his word, all would go back to war. Ulfrik would actually prefer it. Only a year ago, killing a bishop was cause for raucous laughter, congratulations, and a gold armband. Today, it cost him his name and honor.

A knock at the door interrupted his thoughts. Ulfrik shot upright, hand vainly searching for a sword that had been confiscated. He waited as still as a cat hunting a mouse, staring into the darkness where dull orange light flickered around the doorjamb. He crawled out of bed, and took up the cloak as a shield and the stool as a weapon. He crouched as the bars on the door lifted away.

If killers were come to finish him in the night, he would not go meekly.

The candle was as bright as a bonfire after hours of darkness and Ulfrik could not penetrate the glare. At least two men stood in the small door frame, but only the one holding the candle entered. In the globe of golden light, Ulfrik saw Vilhjalmer staring at him with his face caught between shock and laughter.

"I don't want to ask what you do in here alone in the dark, but this is a strange sight."

Ulfrik lowered the stool, but held the cloak in his fist. "I was just preparing a seat for your royal ass. Pardon my lack of hospitality, but my room is bare and I have nothing but water to offer."

"And a cloak," Vilhjalmer pointed at Ulfrik's hand then set his candle down on the small table.

"This is for catching any knife that might come at me in the night. You wouldn't have one of those?"

"Not for you, old friend."

The two embraced, each slapping the other on the back.

"You've grown up," Ulfrik said. "You look more like a king every time I see you. I guess it's in your blood."

Vilhjalmer sat at the table and Ulfrik followed. The fresh candle wavered between them, and Ulfrik folded his arms.

"It's bad news, isn't it?"

"Worse than you know," Vilhjalmer said. He turned aside, studying the crowded room and frowning. "Aren went to Rouen to find me, and told me about the bishop. I can't blame you for killing him, honestly. I think they are all conniving snakes who no more believe what they preach than I do."

"He was your mother's cousin."

"Would knowing that have stopped you from thrashing him?" Ulfrik shook his head, and Vilhjalmer laughed. "That's good. I am here in secret, as you probably guessed from the midnight visit. Aren gave me the news four days ago, but I have delayed contacting you until I finished my arrangements."

Ulfrik leaned back and narrowed his eyes. "What do you mean by that?"

"You're on the edge of a cliff and about to fall off, but you can't see it from inside this room. My father does not want to do what his new responsibilities require him to do, so he wavers and creates an opening for you."

"He's being a fool. Is that part of his of new responsibilities?"

"Those words don't suit you, Ulfrik. You know as well as I that my family is now Frankish nobility, at least in title. There's nothing foolish in defending that authority. But let's talk of important matters. When Aren visited, he wanted my aid in speaking for you. Yet within the hour of finding me, my father's hirdmen tried to capture him. They had been told one of your sons would attempt to take me hostage and barter me for your release."

"What? That would ruin the agreement for a safe passage. My sons would not be so foolish."

Vilhjalmer gave him a skeptical look. "You might recant that in a moment. But, yes, Aren is the smartest man I've ever known. He wanted me to persuade Father, and that makes a good deal more sense. He evaded his would-be captors, but he could not go directly home. I'm not sure where he went, but my guess is he traveled to Eyrafell. It only makes sense."

"What's happening?" Ulfrik let his arms fall to his sides. "Why has

Hrolf done nothing to me yet, but is sending men after my sons and preventing them from returning home?"

"You are being set up to fall, preferably on a sword. Killing the bishop was the lightning strike that set your forest aflame, but someone has been wanting you out of the way for a long time. Those men got their warning not from my father, but one very close to him. Gunther One-Eye."

Ulfrik stared at Vilhjalmer, his hands turning so cold he tucked them beneath his arms. "Gunther has ever been a friend to me. His son, Mord, that I could believe. But not Gunther."

Vilhjalmer shrugged. "I've no proof he has done more, but of his orders I am certain. You do not doubt you've had a hidden foe working against you? No man climbs as high as you without making enemies."

"I know my enemies. They're on the opposite side of the shield wall." Ulfrik now looked away, his heart in his throat.

"Not every enemy is so easy to see. You are successful, and Gunther and Mord both are ambitious and greedy men. You may love Gunther, but I never have. He has always wanted to own me, to force me to befriend his unlucky and unlikeable son so that when I am grown into my inheritance I will favor them." He paused and leaned forward. "Favor them as I would favor you. Do you see how they may resent you?"

"Did you come here in darkness to turn me against my oldest friend?"

Vilhjalmer rubbed his face and sighed. "Of course not. I came to save your life."

"I'm at risk of dying from boredom. So thank you for the conversation."

"Your son, Gunnar, has made a mistake so big that I scarcely believe he's the same man I thought I knew. It is why I have decided to help my father make the right decision, whether or not he agrees with me. You must leave tonight. Tomorrow your head will be taken, placed in a sack, and sent back to your family. It will be escorted by an invading army and all your family will be put to death once they are captured. My father will weep in the deep of his heart, but to do less would ruin his reputation."

Ulfrik's bloodless hands clenched and he blinked at Vilhjalmer. "What did he do?"

"He left witnesses alive to his crimes, that's the short of it. But in detail, he took his men to Byrgisvik. Do you know the place?" Ulfrik shook his head. "Well, it is a hamlet of four farms with a church holding it together. Franks mostly live there, though our people have joined them. The church serves all Christians for miles around, and do you know whose church it is? Father Lambert's."

"Gunnar went to find Father Lambert?"

"He did," Vilhjalmer lightly slapped the table as if drawing the conclusion had been a challenge. "But Father Lambert was not there. He's been taken to Rouen to recover from his wounds. So Gunnar burned down the church with everyone inside, then tracked down any who fled and killed them as well. I don't know where he went now, but personally I hope he sailed off the edge of the world."

"He left witnesses, who happen to know who he is?"

Vilhjalmer snorted a laugh. "He did. A young girl hid in the underbrush while her brother was run down. The dark-haired man with one hand who led the group told him how he hated Franks. Then he chopped off the brother's hand before cracking open his head. The girl says she fainted and when she awoke her brother was dead and Byrgisvik a smoking ruin."

Ulfrik put his cold hands to his hot face. "He broke the terms and forfeited my life."

"No doubt intending to prove Father Lambert had not lost his legs. Aren voiced that doubt to me, and while it is a good thought, it is misguided. The Church has decided upon your death, and facts will not interfere with it now. You killed a bishop, and that's the only fact. Now Hrolf must execute you or he will never be able to take a hostage again."

Biting his lip so hard he tasted the coppery blood, Ulfrik stared blankly ahead, imagining how he would beat Gunnar to death if he ever saw him again. "That boy, he never grew up after losing his hand.

He became someone else after that. His temper rules him, and it has killed me, his mother, and his brothers. I'll kill him myself."

"I don't disagree, but now is not the time. At dawn you will be dragged out for a beheading. I'm setting you free before that happens."

"Why? Even if I escape, I am now wanted by your father. He will bring his full weight to bear. I am a burden to anyone allied with me."

A small smile appeared on Vilhjalmer's face. "I have admired you since the day we met, and every year since I've found a new reason to believe you are my father's most important man. He is being forced to part with you, but I am unwilling to let you go."

He stood then rapped on the door. The man outside entered, a young and strong warrior with the still smooth skin of youth. He kept his head down, but in his arms he carried a bundle of mail and three swords. These he placed on the table, and Ulfrik recognized his long sword and sax atop his mail coat. The man dropped a pack from his back, along with a plain wooden shield and leaned these against the table before closing the door and leaning against it.

Vilhjalmer picked up his own sword and carefully drew the gleaming blade with a metallic whisper. He held it low, its point to Ulfrik's feet.

"I have prepared a disguised escort to take you home. You will gather your wealth, family, and what men will follow, then leave these lands. I will ensure you that my father does not pursue or interfere with your departure in anyway. But before any of this is done, you must swear loyalty to me. Put your hands upon my blade and pledge to serve me when I call, and to do no harm to my father, his people, or his reputation."

"I am an old man now and my fighting days are close to an end. What good will I do you in the future?"

"Let me worry for your usefulness. You can teach me your secrets, for one. For now, you must decide if you accept my offer."

Ulfrik stared at the blade then up into Vilhjalmer's smiling face. He took it lightly in his hands. "I swear loyalty to you, Vilhjalmer Hrolfson, never to be broken but in death."

Vilhjalmer sheathed his sword and raised Ulfrik to his feet. "In time, my father will understand why we did this tonight. For now, find your family and flee this land. Go south and trouble the Danes and petty jarls who are always bickering and fighting. One day I shall conquer that land, and it would be good for you to be already among them."

"Is that your first command to me, Lord?" Ulfrik could not help but twist the title in jest, and Vilhjalmer smiled at it.

"Just a suggestion. As for Aren, I doubt he will rejoin you in time to make your escape. I will find him and watch out for him. He is still an outlaw, but I will ensure he finds his way back to you when all is settled."

Ulfrik picked up the bag and the shield. "You've packed for me. What about my men? You'll have them released?"

"It's already done. I knew you would not leave without them. Good luck to you, Ulfrik. You once saved my life, and now I save yours. Our scales our balanced."

They clasped arms a final time before the door opened and Ulfrik stepped outside for the first time in weeks. The air was surprisingly fresh on his face, and in the darkness he saw the dull gleams of mail in the dim light of Vilhjalmer's candle. He was returning home a fugitive, but smiled nonetheless.

"You're certain you can prevent your father from attacking?"

"First there will be a crazed hunt to find where you escaped to, then I will tell my father in private what has happened. He will be madder at my going behind his back than your escape. Knowing you are sworn to me will ease his mind. Besides, I half suspect he knows what I am doing. Yet do not waste time. The Church has its own resources to find you."

Ulfrik nodded, then turned to join his escort and his freed men. Despite the promise of safety, he recalled Vilhjalmer's warning and his stomach ached at the thought. Violence might follow no matter what anyone wanted.

26

"I want you to kill the mighty Ulfrik Ormsson," Mord said, standing on the bank of the Seine. He searched the black line of trees on the opposite shore, thick pines like sharp teeth against the stale morning sky. "My spy is certain he has escaped, but is not sure how. He will gather his men and ships, then flee out of reach. You must get him before then."

The bandit leader standing beside him was called Knut the Hound, a thin, nondescript man with a bald head and a scar on his crown that formed a crater. Mord wondered if it collected water when it rained. His beard was dirty blond and wagged when he spoke.

"No easy thing. He will be on alert and surrounded by his men." Knut kicked a rock into the brown water. "I could never get close enough."

Mord sneered at him. "You are supposed to be a great killer, capable of deeds unreachable to normal men. You have worked for my wife's family, and they recommended you. Have I contacted the wrong man?"

"I'm your man," Knut said. He turned from Mord and began walking down the shore.

The insolence stoked a fire in Mord's belly, but he held his tongue. He was out of options now that Ulfrik had inexplicably been freed. The servant in Mord's pay reported that Hrolf was in an uproar at the news, but later he appeared calmer and had no immediate orders for pursuit. Ulfrik, that lucky bastard, had evaded sure death and someone had given Hrolf reason to pause.

"Then you will kill Ulfrik and his sons?" Mord asked, rushing to catch up. "He has been gone a day already, and must be at his hall by now. Maybe you can do a hall burning?"

Knut stopped and regarded him with hooded eyes. "If it's such a simple thing, why not do it yourself? Why pay my price?"

"Because I can't be shown to have a part of this. I will be ruler in those lands after Ulfrik is gone, and it would not do to be known as a murderer. Yet Ulfrik must die, or he will hover around me like a moth to a lamp. And it is no easy thing to kill him. So I need a man of reputation to make it happen."

"I have worked for the Franks many times, but not our own folk. It's not our way, really. You should challenge him to a duel and kill him there."

Mord blanched at the thought, remembering his father's warning as well as Ulfrik's uncanny swordsmanship. "This way is more practical."

They both stared at the river flowing past. A fat, high-sided trading ship, a knarr, rowed upriver with an escort of two sleeker fighting ships. When it had passed, Knut broke the silence.

"They will all be alert for trouble, but they will also be in haste to escape. That will work to my advantage. Ulfrik and his sons will be easy to spot, but I cannot possibly get all of them in the time that I have."

"You must kill the sons," Mord growled. "They will come back for revenge."

"I have a plan for the sons, but it relies more on luck than skill. I will need aid and some simple preparations to make it work. If you provide this I will have an assistant set the trap. Even still, it may not kill all his sons."

Mord laced his hands at the back of his head and sighed. "All right. You kill Ulfrik and his sons are targets of opportunity. I will pay you extra for every son killed. We don't have time to haggle, so let me hear your plan."

Knut gave a faint smile. With his plain looks and unimposing stature he appeared more like a wainwright than a skilled killer. The bald head made him seem older than he was. "There are two points where he will be vulnerable. Leaving his hall and boarding his ships. Before or after he will have too many men surrounding him. I just have to get close enough to him to cut him, and he will be dead before the sun sets."

"I'd prefer him to die straightaway," Mord said. "Why the delay?"

"Poisoned blade. But I will usually strike a fatal blow in the first attempt. The poison is just a precaution in case circumstances force me to flee."

"And how will you get so close to Ulfrik?"

Now a wolfish smile came to Knut's face and the killer inside of him shined through. "That secret is what makes me useful to the Frankish nobility, and why you are paying me so richly. I will get right beside him and he won't know the threat."

The sun peeked through the clouds and bounced off Knut's bald head. Mord stared at him through the glare. "I suppose that's all you'll tell me. Then here's the first half of your payment. The rest comes after confirmation of Ulfrik's death. Remember, get his sons as well."

"I will speak to your men about the sons. They must work fast if we expect to catch them." Knut then grabbed the pouch of gold Mord offered and weighed it in his palm. "But do not worry. I've not failed any job before, and I don't take work I think I cannot do."

"Good, then I look forward to hearing of Ulfrik's death tomorrow."

They parted, with Knut saying nothing more and ambling down the riverbank to his rowboat as if going fishing. Mord watched him go and heard the crunch of approaching footsteps. He did not bother to turn, but watched Knut launching his boat. The rocky voice of Magnus the Stone came over his shoulder.

"He says he can do it, then?"

"Only Ulfrik is guaranteed. I worry for leaving his sons alive."

Magnus gave a derisive snort. "The sons are all fools. Gunnar is like a wild boar that you can bait into any trap. The young one would probably piss himself if you came at him with a sword. Only the middle one has some potential, but he's not his father. As long as Ulfrik is dead, you will have no worries with the brothers. We'll handle them one at a time."

"My father thinks differently."

"I love your father dearly, but he is old. He worries like an old man. I don't think you need to even kill Ulfrik, but I can see why it makes sense."

Mord faced Magnus and narrowed his eyes at him. "If Ulfrik lives he will hound me incessantly. I cannot have him nipping at my heels forever. Besides, if he hasn't yet learned how I've maneuvered him into this disgrace, he will with enough time. Then it would be open war."

Magnus shrugged, then pointed with his chin toward Knut's boat. "Your wife says he murdered a count in his bedchamber. Do you believe it?"

"I don't know. He seems like nothing, but I sensed evil underneath his skin. I think he will be ruthless enough to do what we need, and by tomorrow morning I will be rid of Ulfrik's influence for good."

27

Ulfrik walked through his empty hall, his hands brushing tables stacked with used wood plates. His footsteps rustled over the rotted straw on the ground, echoing through the milky light of the hall. He had a mind to burn this hall to ash, but considered one day he might return to reclaim it. A slave grunted from the far end of the hall, the bald, old Frankish man struggling to drag the iron cooking pot to the front doors where hirdmen would retrieve it.

Despite the frenetic pace of his return and his rushed reunions with everyone, he now moved with slow deliberation. Was he really dragging everything including the cooking pot off to a new land? He could scarcely believe he had to flee, but now understood he had evaded a far worse fate. He had lost Hrolf's support but gained Vilhjalmer's, trading king for prince, or perhaps a better thought was trading the past for the future. Hrolf was old, and while he might rule many years, his son would doubtlessly inherit his power. He might even usurp it, and Ulfrik would return to the kingdom he helped forge.

The doors opened and the exhausted slave cowered from the light spilling inside. Rather than hirdmen, the curves of Runa's shadow appeared. He stepped up to the high table and extended his hand to her.

"Come join me here one last time before we leave."

She stared at the slave as she walked past, then turned her bright smile to Ulfrik. No matter how she had aged, she was a radiant beauty as perfect as the day they had met. She still moved with the grace of the young, lacking the bent and painful tilt of other women her age. "What are you doing in here? We don't want to load the ships at night. There won't be a moon tonight for all the clouds."

"There are not many memories in this hall," he said, looking up to the rafter where his banner had hung and now only cut rope dangled. "Still, it is hard to leave. I am being chased out like a rat."

Runa took his offered hand. Her skin was cool and rough from the work of spinning and weaving, and hard calluses formed where she had taken up her sword practice again. He guided her to his side and slipped an arm around her.

"This is a setback," she said, fitting into the hollow beneath his arm. "But we have loyal men, ships, and plenty of riches. You have the jewels?"

He slapped his waist. "I'll carry them myself for now. They're seeds for a new life. I suppose it is what Fate had always planned for us."

She nodded. "Aren will be all right?"

"He's with Einar," he said with confidence he did not possess. "Vilhjalmer will watch out for him, and will help him reunite once we send word of where we settle."

"I am not afraid," she said, her voice barely above a whisper. "As long as we are together, it is all that matters to me. Do you think there is still land enough in the Danelaw?"

"We will make room if we must, but there is still much of Northumbria yet to conquer." Ulfrik had set his sights on England as a temporary landing for his people. "It will be good to take up the sword again. I don't know if I could settle for another year of peace."

Runa smiled, then squeezed him. "Strange as it seems, I don't think I could either. War is all we've known, and having you lying around the hall with no great plans to occupy your thoughts made for a hard year." They both shared a laugh, and she slipped from under his arm. "Be quick here. I will be with our grandchildren. They are excited for this."

"They don't understand what's happening." Ulfrik kissed Runa's forehead and walked her to the front door. "Go keep them from getting underfoot."

"And Ulfrik," Runa said as she paused at the door. "We are all angered with Gunnar, but he was trying to do what he thought would help. Do not humiliate him. I'm certain he's already feeling foolish enough."

"You said he was thinking. I don't think he was." She lowered her head and glared at him. "But I've not said anything to him, have I? Relax, Wife, I will keep the peace. I've learned a few things in my old age."

She gave him a slow nod, then smiled before exiting.

Ulfrik turned back to the hall, noting that the cooking pot remained by the door yet the slave had vanished. He owned a dozen slaves, and while they had been treated well. he wondered if they planned to flee. He never beat them, and he fed them well. Their clothes were plain, clearly the garb of slaves, but cleaned and replaced whenever they became too old. Still, people loved their freedom and he supposed they might slip away during the confusion. He would not have time to chase them down.

Leaving the pot, he again crossed the main hall and entered his private rooms. Runa had already stripped them and packed their valuables before he had arrived. Despite sleeping here every night, he struggled to remember how the room had appeared. He stared at his bed frame against the wall, which was too big to take but for the bedding. Snorri had died here, and now would not receive a proper burial until Einar could arrange it with whoever the new jarl would be.

He heard a foot slide across the wooden floor behind him. From its light touch he guessed Runa had returned and so remained staring at the empty bed.

"We had a few good nights in this, didn't we?" he said playfully.

"Ulfrik! Behind you!"

The warning exploded away the silence, and Ulfrik instinctively stepped forward and whirled, his hand already reaching for the dagger at his hip. The room was too small for a sword.

The bald slave faced him now, a long, shimmering dagger in his hand. His face was slack with surprise, and though he was only an arm's length distant, he remained rooted to the spot. In an instant, Ulfrik's own dagger flashed. The would-be assassin leapt back, his reactions snake-swift, and he scowled as he ran for the door.

Runa blocked it. Rather than crumble like a frightened woman, she raised the iron tripod from the cooking pot overhead and tried to club the assassin. Again he dodged, the heavy iron bars barely clipping his shoulder.

His blade flashed and he slashed in a wide arc, slicing Runa's ribs beneath her right breast. She screamed and fell aside with her hand pressed to the wound.

The assassin shoved past her out of the room. Ulfrik ran to his wife's side, but she was already batting him away. "Catch him before he escapes!"

He crashed through the doors and the slave was already to the hearth. Ulfrik gave his loudest battle cry, a fierce bellow that boomed through the hall. Then he launched himself off the stage of the high table and sprinted after the man.

To his shock, the slave spun and hurled the knife at him. The metal spun through the white light of the hall, end over end, an expert throw that sped toward his neck. Heedless of the danger, Ulfrik dove for the assassin's legs.

The knife swished past his face and Ulfrik roared with success as he collided with the assassin's legs. They both crumpled into a ball, rolling into the benches at the side of the hall.

Another blade appeared in the assassin's hand. Ulfrik did not recognize all his slaves as some never came to his hall, but this man could not be anyone's slave. He was strong and prepared. He did not cry out or struggle uselessly. He knew how to fight on the ground and had the strength for it. Ulfrik read cold calculation in the face only inches from his own. He saw the white flesh around the mouth and chin where the man had shaved his beard to affect his disguise.

Ulfrik climbed up on the man, grabbing his knife hand before he could strike. He pulled his head back, expecting a head-butt, and instead he got a knee to his in his crotch.

The pain rolled through his stomach, but the assassin could not get enough force into the knee to cripple Ulfrik. He had lost his own dagger in the dive and scramble to catch the assassin. He now pinned the man with his weight, but the would-be slave was slippery. He already wormed his way free and now they both struggled for the dagger in hand.

The assassin punched with his left hand, but Ulfrik blocked it. He threw a head-butt, but only succeeded in striking the assassin's cheek. He shoved at the assassin, as if to try to pin him down again. Yet when he pushed back to resist, Ulfrik surprised him by yanking him forward. Now carried by his own momentum, he came up to Ulfrik's face.

Ulfrik rolled back with the man atop him, but then flipped him over. He pinned the dagger beneath both of them, so that the assassin's arm was set to break if he struggled.

"You're done for," Ulfrik growled. "Give up or I'll make it worse on you."

The hall doors burst open. Hakon and three other hirdmen paused at the scene.

"Help me," Ulfrik shouted. "This one's a slippery bastard."

Iron hissed as they drew swords, and at last Ulfrik felt the assassin beneath him slacken. Now four sword points touched the assassin's body, and Ulfrik released him. Hakon lent a hand to help hoist him to his feet.

"Hold him steady," Ulfrik said. "Your mother was hurt."

He turned to the back of the hall, but Runa had staggered out of the doors. Her hands were clasped to her wounds, and her face was smeared with blood. Her skin shined with sweat and dark circles had formed beneath her eyes. Still she smiled as she leaned against the wall. "It's not a deep cut. I'll be fine."

Then she collapsed to the floor

28

Ulfrik rushed to Runa, who had crumpled into a pile at the door to their private rooms. Hakon joined him while the other men held the assassin at sword point. Her gray dress hung open like a leering mouth and dark blood splotched beneath it. Ulfrik held her head, and she gave him a weak smile.

"I'm too old for this," she said. "It burns like fire."

She winced and sucked her breath as he tested the wound. "It's not a deep cut, but a slash. Nothing worse than a bad scar will come of it. Here, put pressure on it and Hakon will get you patched up until we can sew it closed."

"That's right," Hakon said as he knelt beside her. His face was creased with worry. "You'll be fine, Mother. What were you doing to get yourself cut like this?"

Runa's skin looked pale and sweaty as if resisting agony, but she smiled blithely at Hakon's question. "I did not recognize that slave. He seemed familiar, but I thought he might've tended sheep and so I did not know him well. Something just felt wrong about him. And why was he struggling with the cooking pot all alone? When I left, I asked the hirdman at the door why he wasn't helping, but he didn't understand. I knew something was wrong. Back inside I found that man sneaking toward our rooms, so I grabbed the heaviest thing I could find. If you let me carry a sword, I'd have probably killed him."

Ulfrik kissed the top of her head. "You saved my life."

"Will I get a gold armband for it?"

"As many as I can fit on your pretty arms." Ulfrik stood and smiled. "If you can joke like this, then I'm not worried. Now let me ask our friend a few questions."

Gunnar had entered the hall, bringing more men. Two hirdmen were conferring with him in whispers while the bald assassin sat on a table with three swords touching his neck. He stared ahead as if he were bored and waiting for the fun to begin. Ulfrik picked his dagger off the floor, weighing it in his hand as he approached the man. Gunnar broke away and joined him.

"A professional, yes?" The man stared through him. "Let me be clear, you're going to die. So here's my offer. Tell me who hired you and it will be quick. Resist and I'm going to pour forty years experience with giving pain all over your scrawny body. Do you really want to know what it's like to have your balls nailed to a table?"

"They're right about you," the man said, finally shifting his predatory gaze to Ulfrik. "You're a lucky bastard when it comes to slipping death."

"I've been standing in front of enemy spearmen most of my life and death hasn't found me yet. The gods aren't done with me, but they are with you. Who sent you?"

"You know I can't tell you."

Ulfrik smiled. "What I know is you think you're tough enough to outlast me. That I'll be too pressed for time and just carry you along to question later. Maybe you could escape during the chaos. How's that for a guess?" The man's expression blanked but Ulfrik noticed his brow twitch. He had guessed correctly.

"Gunnar, Hakon, let me show you boys the fastest way I've found to make a man speak. And here's a hint, it's not nailing his balls to a table. Pain alone is not enough. You have to mix in panic as well. Blinding a man does both."

The assassin looked up wide-eyed. Ulfrik brandished his dagger. "Hold this fucking bastard down, and keep his head still."

A struggle broke out, with his hirdmen forcing the assassin onto his back while he tried to break away. He cursed and bit, but he was overwhelmed and pinned. Ulfrik forced his way through and put the dagger to the man's face.

"All right, I'll tell you the truth. Please, just put down your blade. Please!"

"Too late. I have to be sure you're serious and you need to know I'm serious."

Ulfrik slid his dagger into the soft flesh beneath the assassin's left eyeball. The man's scream was horrifying, but Ulfrik worked as if cutting the eye from a goat's head. He sawed around the socket as the man writhed and screamed and blood bubbled out over his face. When the eyeball loosened, he pried it free with his blade, fluid and blood splattering with a gentle pop.

"You tried to kill me and mutilated my wife. You don't think I'd just allow that to go unavenged." Ulfrik dangled the eyeball by a sinew over the assassin's head. "Did the man who hired you also lack one of these?"

"Mord Guntherson," the man said through his sobbing. His face was now slick with blood and his eye socket was raw red.

"Mord!" Ulfrik shouted. "I should've guessed. But how did he know where I'd be? Tell me how he knew, or I'll cut the other eye."

"A spy in Hrolf's hall. A servant. Gods, just kill me."

Ulfrik stared up a Gunnar, who had a splash of gore on his cheek. "That did work as well as you claimed, Father."

"Someone slit this dog-fucker's throat." Ulfrik tossed his dagger aside and stepped away. He heard the assassin grunt as one of his men cut the life from Mord's hired killer.

"Why would Mord want to kill you?" Gunnar asked. "We're leaving and he can be free to make a fool of himself in front of Hrolf as often as he wishes."

"Because he knows I'll be back if I live. Vilhjalmer suspected Gunther One-Eye as being part of this, too. I didn't want to believe him, but Mord could not have done so much without his father knowing." Ulfrik joined Hakon, who now had two of Runa's women helping to wrap her in clean bandages. A bowl of water with a bloody rag floating in it sat next to them. "Gunther knows everything that goes on in and around Hrolf's court."

"But why Gunther?" Gunnar asked, crouching next to his mother and brushing her hair from her face. She smiled at him, her eyes half closed as if about to fall asleep.

"Only he can say, but it must be connected to my rise over his son's. Mord had plenty of hope as a young man, but somewhere along the way he began to make mistakes. A lucky man can survive one or two missteps, but Mord made big ones. I think Gunther resents both me and his son for being who we are. No matter now, we have to flee before Hrolf is forced to search for us. So let's get your mother on a wagon and go. I'll plan my revenge on both Mord and Gunther later."

Once the women finished wrapping Runa's injury, a girl fetched her a new dress. The men turned away to allow her to change, and when she was ready to leave she appeared normal again. When Runa announced she was ready, she stood supported between her women.

"You can walk without pain?" he asked.

"I didn't say that. I can make it to the cart without screaming, I think. This burns like fire, though cleaning it helped." She stared at the assassin's corpse leaking blood all over the table. The dagger that had cut his throat stuck out of his empty eye socket like a knife left in a pear. "We just leave him here?"

"A gift for the new jarl. Let him know how much death this accursed hall has witnessed. Even when I return, I will not live again in this unhappy place. Evil spirits haunt it."

Runa agreed, then gritted her teeth as her sons and women helped her from the hall.

29

The sun hung low in the western sky, fighting to shoot its final red rays over the tops of dark pines and oak trees lining the horizon. Birds of all kinds settled in the distant trees, singing their evening songs. Ulfrik leaned on the last cart and studied the land. No sign of any attackers from across the Seine, though at this distance he might not see them. In the cart, Finn grunted as he handed down the casks to the men lined up to receive them.

"Good thing we didn't miss this cart," he said. "An army runs on ale. Can you imagine if we overlooked this? Whoever found it would've been one happy bastard."

Ulfrik glanced down the rows of empty carts. He could not take them onto his ships, for they were already overcrowded. Crossing the channel to Northumbria was dangerous enough without an overloaded ship, but he had no choice. The majority of his hirdmen and bondi were accompanying him, though some had chosen to remain behind. Those were the men with deep roots in Frankia and he understood their choices. Some were cowards, but those were not worth taking.

He had seven ships, three fewer than a year ago when he sold them to expand his hall. Two of his sleek raiding ships had already launched into the Seine and were waiting for his high-sided, fat-bellied ships, the knarrs, to be stocked with ale. Ulfrik marveled at the precision of his men and the organizational powers of his sons in organizing this retreat. It was not panicked even after the attempt on his life, and everything of value was loaded on ships or traded off. He wished Aren could have left with him, but Ulfrik was confident they would find him again.

"Do your young eyes see anything worth worrying about?" Ulfrik asked. Finn handed off a cask then stood straight and scanned the horizon. "A single ship in the distance, not a war vessel. No glints of iron hiding in the trees. I think Vilhjalmer was true to his word and Hrolf will let us flee."

"Only if we make haste, or he'll be forced to confront us. The Church might be taking its own steps to catch us, too. Are we prepared to leave?"

"Here's the last cargo to load." Finn handed off the final cask, then stared at his hands. He rubbed them on his pants, checked again, and shrugged.

Ulfrik was about to ask him what was wrong, but then heard his name called from the lead ship. A man stood on the rails, oblivious to its rocking at dock, and cupped his hands to his mouth as he shouted Ulfrik's name.

"Go," Finn said. "I'll finish up here."

He dashed the short distance to the dock and clattered down the loose boards to where the man extended his arm to help him aboard. His bright blue eyes were wide with panic. "It's your wife," he said. "She's vomiting."

"What?" Ulfrik forced through the crowd of crewmen and their families to where Runa leaned over the rails at the prow. He touched her back with a questioning hand as she dry-heaved. "What's this about?"

She shook her head, spitting into the river beneath her. "I don't know. I feel like I'm pregnant again."

"Really?" Ulfrik's voice rose in excitement, but when she turned to face him, he knew she had only toyed with him. The dark circles under her eyes had worsened and her skin was sweaty and bluish. "Gods, woman, I only left you alone for an hour. Are you sick?"

"I must be. My bones ache with fever. I feel sleepy. Short of breath."

"Then rest," Ulfrik said, touching her face and feeling a mild heat. Nothing like a fever. He gave her a skeptical look, which she dismissed with a huff.

"Let's get the ships underway. We don't have time to lose." She wiped her mouth inelegantly with the back of her arm, but Ulfrik still kissed her. Her lips were dry.

"This is not right," he said.

He moved to touch her face again, but she gathered his hands in hers and kissed them. "All of these people, our sons and grandchildren, are dependent on us getting these ships launched. Let's go."

The words had drained her of breath, and she collapsed against the prow as her women tried to hold her up. Ulfrik wrapped her in his cloak and kissed her again, then he gave the orders to cast off once Finn had boarded.

"Is she sick?" Finn asked as Ulfrik took up the steering board.

"Maybe the cut was deeper than I guessed. She has trouble breathing. Maybe her lung was hurt?"

Finn shook his head. "It could be, but that's not like any lung wound I've seen. She should be gasping."

"True. Maybe you should steer while I go to my wife."

Relieving him of the tiller, Ulfrik walked down the rows of crew seated on their sea chests as they pulled the oars. He offered encouragement and strong words to each of them. He passed through the recessed hold at the center of his ship, piled high with crates, barrels, sacks, and the recent ale casks. Women and children gathered there, trying to remain out of the way. He also offered them brave words.

Ulfrik's ship, one of the knarrs, nosed out into the Seine and the line of other ships followed. Hakon steered one directly behind his, and Gunnar's ship would be at the end of the line. He set his fighting ships on either flank of his knarrs and the line made an impressive display as it pulled into the current. One ship held mostly flocks of sheep and a few ponies. All other livestock would have to be acquired in Northumbria, but these flocks were a precaution. He heard the sheep bleating in the distance, the water heightening every sound.

He knelt beside Runa, who had grown still and quiet. The oars splashed the waters and the deck creaked as the current shuttled them down to the ocean. More than anything he listened to his wife's labored breathing. She seemed to be shrinking inside his cloak, as if she were melting away.

Once they had been sailing for close to an hour and the sun had set, Ulfrik ordered torches lit. Normally they would not sail at night, but he knew the Seine as well as the roads of his childhood home. There were few dangers now that Hrolf controlled the waters, and they had only to push through the defenses around the mouth of the Seine. If Vilhjalmer had truly convinced Hrolf to allow them to pass, then no one would intercept them before taking to sea.

Runa continued to wheeze, a dry and rattling sound from deep in her ribs. They did not speak, for Ulfrik feared his wife's illness might worsen if he forced her to waste energy speaking. Unable to stand her suffering any more, one of Runa's women fetched an old woman to examine her. Ulfrik had not realized he had a healer aboard, though the old woman made no claim to it. He had known her husband and her son, both long fallen in battle, but she had stayed on with the help of her cousins. She shooed Ulfrik aside with a wordless swish of her arm. Runa's women held the old woman's arms as she crouched. She peeled away Ulfrik's cloak.

He hovered at her shoulders. Runa's dark eyes were unfocused and her breathing labored. The old woman felt Runa's sides, pressed around the rust-colored stains of the bandage, then felt her neck. Runa did not even wince, but let the old woman roam all over her body. She peeled back Runa's eyelids the pulled open her mouth. Nothing was left unchecked, and she folded the cloak back over his wife's frail body.

Her rheumy eyes met his and she shook her head. Her cracked, aged voice was clear. "She has been poisoned."

Ulfrik's hands went numb and his first impulse was to deny the old woman's assessment.

"By the gods, I should've guessed," he pushed aside the old woman and knelt beside Runa, who stared vacantly. "What can we do to help her?"

The old woman shook her head. "I need to know what the poison was. A lot of poisonings look the same." Her wrinkled old hand touched his shoulder. "Jarl Ulfrik, she is far gone now. Cleaning the cut helped slow the poison's spread, but it's been in her blood too long."

"No," Ulfrik said. His voice was hardly a whisper. "Not like this."

From the ships behind his own, Ulfrik heard shouting. He continued to hover over his wife, fearing to touch her might plunge her into death. It was not until the shouts repeated on his own ship that he roused.

"Fire arrows!"

Ulfrik shot to his feet, just in time to see the third ship in line billow up in a ball of fire.

30

The heat of the fire slapped Ulfrik as he stood staring dumbfounded at the ball of fire lighting the night sky. He had never witnessed such a thing, a roiling ball of orange flame climbing the mast then flaming out into the darkness. Burning debris showered down, burnt rigging disintegrated in the fire. People screamed as they windmilled around the deck, many throwing themselves overboard rather than burn to death. The scent of burnt wood and flesh now rolled over him as the wind blew downriver.

He heard a sharp plop, then realized flaming arrows were screaming out of the night at his ship. They had just turned a bend to discover the shore lined with yellow fires at regular intervals. Shadows moved around the fires, pulling up dots of flame on the tips of their arrows before sending these streaming toward his ships. The bright fire of the burning ship lit the night, but he still could not see what he faced on shore.

Finn held the tiller loose, staring at the burning ship. The explosion had shocked everyone. Even the enemy on the shore paused at the massive fire. The ship and all the people on it were lost. Yet worse still, the fire spread to Hakon's ship.

The volley of fire resumed, yellow streaks tearing through the darkness to thud into wood or hiss in the river. He could not understand what had caused the ship to explode. He had never seen anything like it, except for once as a young boy. Again, it had been at the trade center Kaupang where people came from every corner of the world. A man had set up a stack of barrels and with one shot from a flaming arrow he had caused the entire stack to billow up in fire. At the time it has been a beautiful display to warm the night and begin a celebration. Tonight it marked pure terror.

The casks. He thought of the casks and remembered Finn rubbing his hands on his pants.

"Your hands!" Ulfrik shouted at Finn, who remained fixated on the massive conflagration. The burning ship listed right, its mast like a burning finger accusing the enemy on the shore. Ulfrik jumped the hold where women cowered over their children, then wove through the rowers who had turned to face the fire. The first flaming arrow to reach his ship drove into the deck at Finn's feet.

Ulfrik spun Finn around, his face yellow in the burning light. Ulfrik yanked his hands out and rubbed the palms with his thumbs.

"Your hands are slick with oil," he said. Finn stared at his hands as if they belonged to another man. "Where did you get those casks of ale?"

"The cart was just sitting with the others waiting to be loaded," he said, still staring at his shiny palms. "I thought we had missed it when we loaded the other cart of ale. Someone told me it was more ale to load, then he left. I—I didn't recognize him."

"And you didn't smell anything?" Ulfrik said, dropping Finn's hands. "Those casks were filled with oil. It's part of this trap."

As if to confirm his discovery, another ship down the line burst into fire, a brilliant cloud rolling up from the center of her deck. More shrieks and sparks filled the night.

"Row, you bastards!" Ulfrik screamed at his crew, then turned to the women in the hold. "Throw the casks overboard. They're filled with oil."

No one seemed to understand his directions. Ulfrik grabbed

Finn's arm and shoved him at the hold. "Show them what to do. I'll take the tiller."

Finn jumped down into the hold, while Ulfrik stepped onto the rail. Even in his old age his voice was powerful and strong. If ever he needed to be heard, now was such a time. He cupped a hand to his mouth as he shouted at Hakon's ship. "The kegs are filled with oil. Throw them overboard."

Hakon appeared in the prow, then waved before disappearing again. Within a moment Ulfrik saw casks flying over the rails of Hakon's ship.

The hail of arrows had petered out, and Ulfrik wondered at it. He saw his ships of fighting men had swept ahead to the fires and had chased off the archers. The enemy were few for the amount of damage they had wrought. The burning ships and the wind were doing the rest of the enemy's work.

"Keep rowing," Ulfrik shouted. Finn and the people in the hold were throwing casks overboard. "Put space between the ships."

The night echoed with dying shrieks, frantic rowing, and the awful ripple of burning wood. His own ship had black scars of fire arrows that had not hit the casks. He noted how all the burnt shafts clustered around his hold and the mast. Some arrows would break the casks and others would set the oil aflame. The plan was simple genius, and had succeeded. Were it not his own ships and people being destroyed, he would have admired the ploy.

His ship lurched ahead while those strung out behind avoided the two burning ships. The fire on Hakon's ship appeared under control, though pockets of flame still flickered along its length. The first ship to have caught fire was already on its side, crew and cargo dumped into the cold, unforgiving waters and dragged down to the muck to die. If anyone knew how to swim, it would only be a handful of people. Ulfrik himself had never learned, nor had any of his family. To fall into the water was death.

"Jarl Ulfrik! Hurry!" The women at the prow waved both hands overhead, their bodies outlined in wavering orange light. Ulfrik's heart sank and he abandoned the tiller to dash the length of the ship.

The women cleared away. Runa had kicked free of the cloak Ulfrik had given her, and the bandages on her torso showed fresh red through the dried blood. She had both hands at her neck, more like claws than hands. Her skin had turned dark blue and her eyes were wide with fear. She twisted and gasped as if drowning.

"No! Someone help her." He dropped to his knees and scooped her into his arm. Her breath was short and desperate in his ear as he clutched her to himself. "Stop it!"

"I ... am ..." Runa's voice was weak, nearly lost for the terrified screams of the women surrounding her. "Dying."

He set her down gently, his body trembling and weak, and tried to offer her a smile. He collected her twisted hands from her throat and gathered them in his own. "Don't speak. Save your strength."

She closed her eyes, gasping like a dogfish. "You gave me ... a good life. I ..."

"Runa, no. Hold on. We will get ashore and I will find something to cure this poison."

"... love my sons. I ... love you. I wish ..." More gasping punctuated her words. "To stay longer, but ... it's my time."

Runa's breathing became shorter, and he realized she would not survive. "I wanted you to be proud of me, to be a jarl's wife covered in gold and jewels. Without you I have no purpose. What will I fight for? What will I live for?"

Her eyes snapped open and she gulped like a drowning woman unable to surface. She withdrew a hand and grabbed him by the shoulder, then squeezed out her answer.

"Vengeance."

Her hand dropped, eyes lingering on his. Her flesh was the color of a bruise with ugly veins standing out on her neck and face. Ulfrik watched the light flee from her eyes, and the final breath wheezed from lungs that had failed.

He sat back, his body numb. The women around him cried into their hands. Runa stared at nothing, and Ulfrik gently shut her eyes before drawing his cloak over her body.

Without a tear shed, he stood and turned to face his crew.

Everyone held still, white fear written in their expressions. Behind them his ships burned like wild asters of fire in the night. Both of his fists balled up and he roared with the thunderous might of Thor's hammer.

"Mord!"

31

Ulfrik did not remember anything after Runa's death. Dawn had broken and he now stood on the northern bank of the Seine with five ships hauled up on the narrow stretch of land. People had disembarked and they milled about the grass that gave way to a thin line of poplar trees masking the horizon. He heard weeping and moaning, varied with cries of pain. A cool wind blew over him and he made to pull his cloak tighter, but he was not wearing one.

He remembered covering Runa's body with it. That was his last memory until he woke from a walking nightmare on the shore of the Seine.

The sky above was still blanketed in clouds but no rain came. It was as if the sky held its tears just has Ulfrik did. What good were tears? They fill a man's eyes and make his vision blurry. He can neither talk nor think straight when in the grip of tears. So he frowned at the glowing spot where the morning sun wrestled with clouds, then spit.

"I've the count of the dead from last night," Finn said from behind. Ulfrik had not heard his approach and did not turn to meet him. Instead he watched the brown water flow past him.

Finn paused at his side, stared at the water with him, then at last decided to deliver his news. "One hundred thirty-seven dead, including all the people on the two ships we lost. The burning of the two ships did most of the killing. Others either fell overboard in the confusion or arrows took them. There are more wounded, but they will survive."

Ulfrik nodded. He heard the numbers, recognized that one third of his people had been killed, but he could not summon any emotion. He knew the toll should pain him. Mothers and their children were in that number. Yet it remained only a number. He had no tears for that news either.

"She was a beautiful woman. Unlike any other," Finn said. "I will miss her."

They were simple words, but they defined Ulfrik's feelings. He found his hand covering his mouth and his eyes growing hot. Finn patted him on the back and left him to his thoughts. He struggled against his tears, not allowing a single drop lest the dam break and he shame himself before his people. The horrible, blue-veined visage of his dying wife haunted his sight when he closed his eyes. Would he ever see anything else?

Angry shouting roused him from his gloomy mood. He saw a throng of people up the shore, and others rushed toward them.

"Your sons," Finn shouted from the edge of the crowd. "They're fighting."

He bolted up the slope, across the grass to the crowd. At the rear, children hopped trying to see over the shoulders of adults. Ulfrik tore them back, grabbed hold of a burly hirdman and yanked him aside as if he were a sack of feathers. He pressed into the gap and found both Hakon and Gunnar circling each other. Hakon's face glowed bright red and his lip was bloodied and fattened. Gunnar, who had only one hand to punch with, had his eye swollen shut and blood streamed from his nose. Both of them seemed as if they had been dragged through the river from the disheveled state of their clothing.

"You fucking fool!" Hakon shouted. "All of this is your fault! Mother would be alive if it weren't for you."

"Crying like a baby won't bring her back!" Gunnar struck with his left, and a mix of cheers and hisses came from the crowd. Gunnar had taught himself to fight with an ax and specially crafted shield, but he never adapted to brawling with one hand. This was painfully evident to Ulfrik when Gunnar's clumsy swing missed.

Hakon weaved aside and planted a blow into Gunnar's ribs. More shouts went up and Ulfrik suddenly realized people were favoring Hakon over Gunnar. That galvanized him into action.

Ulfrik leaped into the circle and plowed between the two of them. Hakon bounced back, but the arrival of his father was no deterrent. He charged forward again, fists poised for another blow.

Ulfrik's fist slammed into the side of Hakon's head, and dropped him like a stone. Sharp pain lanced through his knuckles, but he had instantly silenced the crowd. Only Gunnar laughed. Spinning with a snarl, he drove his fist into the same ribs Hakon had just pummeled. Gunnar's laughter turned to a grunt of pain and he staggered back. Ulfrik was tempted to follow up with another strike, but Gunnar sank to his knees in submission.

He stood between his sons, chest heaving and legs throbbing from the sprint up the slope, and refused to look at anyone. The entire crowd stood in silence as his two sons crawled to the edge of the circle.

"Is this what you two think we need? Fighting with each other?" He turned to Hakon, who sat on his knees with his head bowed. "Is this how you'd honor your mother? Or the mothers of children who died last night?"

Hakon wiped his bloodied lip with the back of his arm. "Of course not."

"Then stand up and act like a man, not a child." He whirled to face Gunnar. "And you. You've a wife and children. Where are they? Are they safe? Comforted? Too busy throwing punches at your little brother to know? Gods, do I have boys or men for sons?"

"Morgan and the children are fine," Gunnar said, his voice a whisper.

"They must be splendid after witnessing two ships full of people burning to death. I'm sure the cries of drowning friends was nothing at all to them. Do the children even know their grandmother has died?" Ulfrik shook his head and turned from him. "Go to your family."

He looked up at the gathered crowd; hirdmen and craftsmen, farmers and their wives, all stared blankly at him. He turned in a circle to face them, his lip trembling with raw emotion.

"Do you all want someone to blame? Don't look to my sons. They have made mistakes. All of us have. But they did not shower us with flaming arrows, nor fill our holds with oil and pitch. We owe that to Mord Guntherson and his black-hearted father, Gunther One-Eye. Oh yes, I see the shock in your faces. But I know the truth of it. Before we set out, I was attacked in my hall and I kept it secret from any who had not witnessed it. Before he died, the killer admitted Mord's plan to kill me. It's not enough we leave this land, he fears my return."

Ulfrik paused and surveyed the crowd again. Some faces were shocked, others frightened, and still others unmoved. He knew not all the men would follow him after he made his next declaration, yet he did not care.

"Well he should fear my return, for I swear before all of you, I will destroy Gunther One-Eye and Mord Guntherson. I will drink a toast to my wife from their hollowed skulls. Anyone standing with them shall die. If Hrolf the Strider keeps such snakes at his side, then he is my enemy as well. I will tear the gates from Rouen's walls and gut him before his bitch of a wife. There is no rest for me until the land has forgotten the names of Mord and Gunther."

No one cheered, nor stirred. The sheer enormity of his revenge appeared to have overwhelmed them. Ulfrik himself wondered at the scope of his quest, yet if Hrolf stood in his way, then he was an enemy. Oaths to Vilhjalmer be damned. He wanted to ask who was with him and to cheer them onto a frenzy of revenge. Yet too many had died and the rest had not yet slipped from Frankia. Mord might have another attack planned, or the ambushers from the prior night might strike again and crush him. No one would feel capable of taking on the Count of Normandy when fighting off skirmishers was a challenge.

"We will honor the fallen, tend the wounded, then get back upon our ships and reach the open sea by nightfall." He met as many eyes as were willing to meet his, then the circle parted and he exited.

The rest of the morning passed with him shoring up support of key men. He was already formulating new plans for revenge, and he would need his best hirdmen to stay true to him. Fortunately, he had not lost many of his hird, but mostly his bondi who were the young and able-bodied who filled out his ranks and were not part of his regular guard. He avoided both Hakon and Gunnar, preferring to work everything through Finn. His young friend had done all the hard work of preparing a funeral ship for Runa and a few others who had died of their wounds during the morning. It was Hakon's ship, which had been burned too badly to chance the open seas.

By afternoon, the ship was filled with dried wood covered with oil and pitch that had not been discarded. The vision of another burning ship was not the best image for his people's morale, but Ulfrik could not stand to bury his wife without honor. A sea burial, even though this was a river, seemed more appropriate. Such a burial was rare for a woman, but Runa had been a shield maiden and had once fought in battle against other men. She deserved the respect owed her.

Now they stood by the tired, brown waters of the Seine, Ulfrik with his sons and Gunnar's family beside him. Rows of others had formed up along the banks, and despite their losses they still numbered in the hundreds. Runa's body was wrapped entirely in Ulfrik's cloak and her own. He did not want to see the horrible, twisted visage of his wife's poisoned face, nor did he want his family to see it. He preferred to remember the radiance of her smile, the clearness of her soft skin, or her tightly curled, full hair. But more than anything else, he would forever remember her bold spirit, her stubbornness, and her courage.

Besides Runa, two other bodies were laid out, a man and a woman, both who had caught arrows that eventually killed them. Their families lingered beside Ulfrik's and he nodded to them. All the families carried their dead aboard the ship. Runa was light in Ulfrik's arms. A single tear streaked down his cheek as he laid her on the deck, and he lingered when everyone else cleared.

"As you asked, I will have revenge for you," he said to the wrapped body. He placed his hands over the lumps where Runa's were bound. "Now you make me wish I had been a farmer, so that I could have spent every day with you. But I don't think you would've settled for such a life." He smiled and patted her hand. "You loved glory as much as I did. We were well suited in that, I think. We were just two children once, who dreamed they were more important than they really were. Somehow, along the way, we made it come true. I promise I will not lose what you built. I understand who I am now. I am not a farmer, nor a jarl, but a conqueror. I was meant for war, and I will bring it to our enemies. When they are crushed, I will find others to fight and bring ever more glory and riches to our family. When I join you in death, you will see what I have done and know it was all in your name. It has always been in your name."

He sat back and reached into his pouch of gems, the same gems they had hid for so many years. At last he understood why the gods had given them to him. An emerald the size of his thumbnail fell glittering into his palm. He tucked it into the folds of her wrapping.

"You always liked this one best, so keep it. I will use the rest of them to buy ships and men. I will raise my own great army, one to rival anything seen in Frankia. I will return and burn this land flat."

He kissed her forehead, the soft wool fabric cold against his lips. "Farewell, Wife."

Men launched the ship into the water, and once it took to the current, Ulfrik and his family threw flaming torches onto the deck. The fire caught in a whoosh, startling many of the onlookers. In the overcast light, the ship burned bright as it wandered into the main current and the wind billowed the flaming sail. They watched until the ship began to list and sink.

Faster than Ulfrik expected, the flaming ship slipped beneath the surface with a gurgling hiss. Without looking at anyone, he turned from the river and walked away.

32

Aren and his three escorts arrived at the gates of Eyrafell on a gloomy morning that threatened rain. Sparrows circled the high stockade walls and the dark shapes of men stared down. None hailed them or offered a challenge. Aren considered they were an unimposing group, but still raised his hands to show he came in peace.

"Hail, men of Eyrafell. We wish to enter the walls." He hesitated in shouting his name. Gils, the leader of his escorts, had warned him to take a false name, even though while traversing the interior of Hrolf's land no one seemed aware of the bounty associated with his name.

"We don't get many visitors," called one of the guards. A few other interested faces appeared over the top of the stockade wall. "Who are you and what is your business here?"

Now Aren would discover Einar's loyalties, or at least those of his men. He glanced at Gils, who gave a barely perceptible shake of his head. Aren licked his lips. "I am Halfdan Halfdanarson and these are my guards. I come with a message from Ull the Strong for Jarl Einar Snorrason."

The guards disappeared from the wall and Aren waited, his pulse quickening.

"A wise choice," Gils whispered while they waited on the guards.

"It seemed best not to announce our presence, even among friends."

The gates swept open and four spearmen stood inside. They dressed in mail and wore shields on their backs. They used their spears more like walking staffs than weapons, and Aren felt the tension in his belly release. He had not thought to raise the hood of his cloak, and to do so now would invite suspicion. So he kept his head down and entered along with his escorts. Gils had prepared the silver bits for the gate tax they would be expected to pay. Einar likely never saw half the silver collected this way, but Aren guessed he did not care.

As they paused for the collection of the gate tax, the three other guards told them to leave their weapons at the gates. "We'll keep them dry for you. If you want, while you're visiting, we could have Hogni the blacksmith sharpen your blades."

"That would be fine," Gils said on Aren's behalf. They started forward but one of the guards barred Aren with his hand.

"I recognize you. You're—"

"Yes. We held a drinking contest during Sumarmál and you outdrank me three times over. Where do you put it all?" Aren gently lowered the bemused guard's arm as he continued to walk past him. He had visited Einar enough times that his face would be well known. He had been so focused on the journey that he had not planned for the arrival. Until he knew where Einar stood, he could not have his name circulated.

"No, that's not it," the guard began, but again Aren cut him short.

"I can't blame you for not remembering anything after that day. Well, we do have important news for Jarl Einar. I'm sure he would not be pleased to be kept waiting while we remember old times."

The guard stared at him, plainly unsure of what to do. His companions had already walked off with their collected weapons. Before he left he narrowed his eyes at Aren. "Whatever you say, friend. I'm sure you have your reasons for it. Since we are old drinking companions, let me escort you to Jarl Einar's hall."

Again Aren breathed a sigh of relief. As they waited for the escort to confer with his peers, Gils leaned in and whispered. "Luck is with you today. May that continue."

The guard returned with a bemused smile for Aren, then showed them through the narrow tracks of Eyrafell toward the hall set upon a small hill. The tracks were paved with planks, and chickens wandered over them and pecked at the gaps. A dog barked in the distance and the banging and clanking sounds of men at work surrounded him. He had always enjoyed his visits to Eyrafell. It was a living town, full of people all contributing to the greater need of the whole. The sounds and smells reminded him of his childhood home in Ravndal. It lived as nothing more than a faded memory to him, but so many of the homes and fences that defined this place seemed like something out of his youthful remembrances. Threading the winding tracks and hearing the voices in the buildings that flanked them gave Aren a feeling of wellness he had not experienced in the weeks since he left for Rouen. It was good to be among a peaceful, friendly people again.

The great hall of Eyrafell was nothing compared to Aren's father's, but among the halls of other jarls it was large. The building showed its age in the gray, rain-stained wood, but a roof of new thatch gleamed like gold in the pale light. White curls of smoke chugged out of the smoke hole and a savory smell reached them.

While Aren could not identify the scent, it summoned to mind an association with Snorri. He had not considered whether Einar had received the news of his father's death, and knowing he might have to deliver it filled him with dread. Einar was a good man, and his father had been legendary for his age and his wisdom. Aren had heard from his mother that Snorri did not like him in his youth, but as he aged they discovered they had a great affection for each other. The full weight of Snorri's passing had not even hit Aren yet. Now, with the possibility of having to stay with Einar for a while, the hurt of his loss would be all the more keen.

They were let into the hall, where their escort left them with the hall's door guards. He gave Aren a sly look, then said to his fellow guards, "Here's Halfdan Halfdanarson and his companions. They come with news from Ull the Strong. I'm sure whatever he has to tell Jarl Einar must be important."

Aren inclined his head at the escort, and then waited to be announced to Einar. After long moments where Aren felt every passerby recognized him, the doors reopened and the guard called them inside. The darkness of the hall blinded Aren while his vision adjusted. He picked his way carefully into the main hall, where servant women tended a large iron pot that was lost in smoke from the fire. The hall was milky white with the haze, but Aren still clearly saw the giant shape of Einar at the far end of the hall. He had two other men in conversation with him.

"Halfdan Halfdanarson from Ull the Strong," announced the guard. Heads all turned toward Aren and his three companions, and they all knelt out of respect. Aren made certain to give a blank expression to Einar, who now peered down at them.

A faint ripple of surprise came over Einar's round face, manifesting in a slightly raised brow. He sat back on his bench and waved his guard away. "Thank you. I have been expecting this news. All of you, leave us."

The men at Einar's side huffed at the disturbance, and both glared at Aren. They seemed familiar, but Aren could not place them. The other servants and hirdmen left, leaving only a slave to attend to Einar's needs. When the hall had cleared, Einar finally let his smile break.

"Halfdan Halfdanarson? Did you just make up that name on the spot?"

"It was all that came to mind."

Einar stepped from the high table to embrace Aren in welcome. The giant man had once been his father's standard bearer, and later became a mighty jarl in his own right. He was old now, in his forties, but time had barely frosted his beard with gray and only touched his hair at the temples. His strength was undiminished by age, and he crushed Aren between his strong arms.

They stepped apart, and Einar's smile vanished. "I was only just at your father's hall weeks ago, but now you arrive unannounced under a false name. Whatever your news, it must be grave."

Aren had rehearsed his delivery of the news dozens of times since he had fled Rouen. In each imagined scene he had been articulate and bold, not timid and voiceless which is how he felt under Einar's questioning gaze.

"Have you heard no news in Eyrafell?"

Einar motioned them all to sit at a nearby table. Mugs of half-finished ale sat where hirdmen had left them. Einar cleared them aside with one muscular arm, then shook his head. "If anything, it has been too quiet. Seeing we are at peace now, I thought it was a favorable sign."

"Anything but that," Aren said. He shared a glance with Gils, who for lack of anyone else had become Aren's support since their flight from Rouen. "There is no easy way to begin all the stories. I will start with what concerns you directly. Your father took ill shortly after you left him with us. At first it was nothing serious, but he worsened. We sent a messenger to call you back, but it seems you were never contacted. Your father died about two weeks ago. We were all at his side. He wanted you to know how proud he was of you."

Einar's expression remained blank, as if Aren spoke a foreign language and he awaited interpretation. For an instant Aren feared he had done something wrong and Einar would blame him, but the giant man only blinked.

"It is hard news to hear," Aren said. "My father was greatly saddened, and he had Snorri laid to rest in a temporary grave until you could be contacted."

"Of course," Einar said, his voice a whisper. "He was old, but strong. If I had known it was his time, I'd have not left him."

"No one knows the time of a man's passing," Aren said, sounding now more like the voice he had rehearsed. "There was nothing for you to do. You will see him again in the feasting hall of heroes. I don't mean to be disrespectful, for you know how I loved your father, but this is only the beginning of the bad news. Worse must still be told."

Einar's eyes widened and he swallowed. Aren took a breath and delivered all the news of Gunnar's priest problem, the murder of the bishop, and his father's banishment. He told him of the attempt to frame him for a plot against Vilhjalmer and his escape to his hall. When all had been told, Aren himself could scarcely believe the world had changed so much in so few days.

"I cannot get back home," Aren said. "Hrolf has placed guards at all the best crossing points. For a short time, at least, I ask for shelter with you."

"Of course," Einar said. He appeared dazed, absently touching his beard.

"Don't be so quick to agree. While I want your hospitality, you would be defying Hrolf if you shelter me."

"How would I know what Hrolf demands? He has kept all of this from me." Einar rubbed the back of his neck and grimaced. "I doubt he has told anyone for fear of the resistance. The Church wants to force his hand, and to have that witnessed by his jarls would be a shame. There are men who would say your father was not wrong in what he did. If I were threatened in my own hall, I might do the same. Banishment is a heavy price, maybe even worse than death."

"My family will likely leave before I can return to them. Vilhjalmer knows where I am and will send me information as he can. I think it is best for no one to know I am here, so that I can plan to reunite with my father."

Einar nodded. "You have given me much to think on. I will have a servant see to your needs, but I must ask for time alone. Your news was indeed grave."

Aren stood along with Gils and the others. "I thank you for this. I only hope it does not bring you more troubles."

Then Einar froze in place and shook his head as if disgusted. "Those men who I spoke with at the high table earlier, did they get a good look at you?"

"They glared at me as if I had pissed on their boots."

Einar laced his hands behind his head. "We already have worries. They are visitors from Mord's hall, and I wager they are leaving with news of your arrival even as we speak."

33

Ulfrik now faced the open sea, standing on the beaches of Neustria with his four ships hauled onto the strand. A line of people threaded from the ships toward the tree line, where a path led back to a seaside village. They were farmers and their families, carrying their belongings on their backs and herding the remains of their meager flocks.

"Is it wise to let them go?" Gunnar asked. His sons, Finn, and other hirdmen stood behind Ulfrik as he watched the waves crash onto the beach. He missed the open sea for its salty flavor and cold winds. It rolled away endlessly, forever uncaring of men and their troubles. On it a destiny could be found or lost, depending on the whims of Fate.

"I will not drag them along with me," Ulfrik said. "If they claim I am unlucky and that this journey is cursed, then how can I deny them? It has not been a promising start, has it?"

No one spoke, but Gunnar renewed his questioning. "What of their oaths? Men cannot walk away from their promises, or what would happen to the world?"

Ulfrik laughed, a dry and bitter sound. "Men have broken oaths and yet the world endures. I have broken many. I'm breaking one now by standing on this beach and planning my revenge."

"We will need men to carry out that revenge," Finn said. Ulfrik turned to his young friend, his freckled face uncommonly serious.

"We need men willing to fight for no better reason than a desire for gold and glory. Those people leaving would fight willingly for their homes, but not for my revenge. For that, their reluctance would be my undoing." He paused and looked his sons in their eyes.

"I must shed the mantle of a jarl and return to my roots. I came to this land as a raider, and so must I return to it. For that, I need a new kind of men. My hird is strong and loyal, but they are not enough. So while it seems I am losing what I most need, it is not so. I am as a snake, shedding its old skin for the new. Let these people go back to Hrolf. I gladly release them from their oaths, but they are also no longer under my protection. When I return, if Fate wills it, I will find these people again and they will regret their decisions."

Ulfrik turned again to the sea and let his words sit with his sons. It was high tide, and they would have to launch back to the sea before it ended. He had only burned his wife the night before, and now stood with a world of new choices to make. Sleep had eluded him and he felt weary beyond measure. His left leg throbbed from the moisture in the air, and a dozen other old wounds pained him. How much more could his body withstand? He was prepared to find out.

"That's the last of the oathbreakers," said one of the hirdmen. "We convinced the smith to remain with us."

A thin smile reached Ulfrik's lips. "I hope he was convinced without fear of injury. There are many other smiths in the world, and we cannot carry a forge on a ship."

"He has no family ties to this land," said the hirdman. "Someone has to maintain our war gear."

Ulfrik now faced the remainder of his men. "Whatever bondi have remained, I will make them part of my hird. Let there be no man who stood by me today feel as though his loyalty was not recognized."

Approving nods circulated among the men who remained. Both

Gunnar and Hakon stood apart, with arms folded and sour expressions. Gunnar's eye was still swollen and Hakon's lip scabby and fat. Ulfrik realized a rift had widened between the two. Something had always existed between them. Years ago when Ulfrik was presumed dead, Gunnar's quick departure had angered Hakon, at least that was the story Runa had told him. His sons never spoke of it in front of him. The two had found a tentative peace, but the death of their mother had shattered it. He could not have that divisiveness in his family.

"I have a new plan," Ulfrik said. "But it requires us to rebuild our strength and then surpass it. If there is any man who doubts I can do this, speak now. I will settle your fears."

No one stirred, though he noted a half dozen of his hirdmen sneak glances to their sides. Ulfrik folded his arms behind his back and began to pace.

"All of my hirdmen will be awarded a share of silver for your loyalty today. For tomorrow, I promise you we will carry away the hoarded wealth of Mord Guntherson and his father, Gunther One-Eye. We will do better than this. We will extract from Hrolf a ransom worthy of the Count of Rouen, and if he fails to pay it we will do to him all that he inflicted upon the Franks."

Even his sons frowned in confusion, and a murmur circulated among the rearmost of his hirdmen.

"You have seen what wealth I carried from hall. It sits upon my ship, and you guard it with your lives. It is ours, after all. But there is my own wealth that I have kept since many of you were yet to be born." He held up a pouch heavy with jewels. "Here is the wealth of a king's gift to another king. Long ago, the King of the Franks sent the King of Wessex a gift of gold and jewels. Both kings are long dead, but the treasure they would have shared has remained with me. These jewels will buy us ships and men in the numbers we need to do as I have promised."

Every eye went to the pouch that he held before them. Even his sons, who had only known about the jewels in recent years, looked greedily upon it. Ulfrik suspected more than one among his hird might be tempted to steal them, so rather than display the gems, he put the pouch back on his belt. "Such wealth is the seeds of the future, and so I keep it close."

A rumble of excitement came to the group as men discussed the potentials of so much wealth. Hakon remained frowning, and when Ulfrik raised a brow to him, he spoke over the voices of the men.

"Gems only have a use if converted to gold. Who would buy yours and how can you be guaranteed a fair price?"

Ulfrik smiled, and wondered if Hakon asked the question for himself or the benefit of the men. "A good question, and it leads to the next step in my plan. We must raise ships and men, and that requires gold beyond what is packed upon my ship. So these gems must be sold, and my time on a merchant ship was well spent in this regard. I know where to take these for a fair trade. The markets of Hedeby in Jutland have all that we require, both shipbuilders and merchants prepared to trade. Of course, with such wealth at stake, I will need my loyal hirdmen to guard it. For that service, I shall decide upon a share of the gems' value to be given to all, after the final trades are made."

Now the hum of excitement grew louder and Hakon nodded with approval. Gunnar smiled at the other end, but he seemed lost in his thoughts. Once the rush of buoyant talk dwindled, he raised his hand to speak.

"So Hedeby for gold and ships, but what of men? To ensure Mord and Gunther's destruction and to challenge Hrolf, we will need hundreds of men. Maybe even thousands."

"Hedeby is also a hub of news. Trust me when I promise you our arrival with so much wealth will attract attention. We need merely to announce we seek fighting men for adventure in Frankia, and we will draw hungry swords from every corner of the world."

His men cheered the statement, but Gunnar pursed his lips and shrugged. "That may be true, but do we have time enough to wait for men from every corner of the world to arrive? And if word travels so widely, surely Hrolf will learn our intent and prepare to meet us. Wouldn't a surprise attack be better?"

"Good points all." Ulfrik stopped pacing and stood before Gunnar.

"I will announce an intention to invade Ireland or some other country instead. We can reveal our true purpose to the men once we are underway. Now as for enough men, we are at the mercy of luck. We cannot attack without sufficient numbers."

"I have an idea," Gunnar said. His smile reminded Ulfrik so much of Runa that he had to turn aside. "During my time a-viking, I made a name for myself around the Northumbria and the surrounding countries. Men owe me favors and my name should still be known. I could recruit from these places, and spread the news of our plans to the right places. It is better to take your offer into the places where men are prepared to sell their swords than it is to wait for them to find you. I can do that."

Ulfrik considered Gunnar's plans, and agreed with his son's logic. He needed as many men in as short a time as possible. He had to remain close to the shipbuilders and ensure their progress did not stall. "And your family? They should remain with me. It will be safer for them in Hedeby."

"Yes, that would be better. Some of the places I intend to go are dangerous."

"Then it is settled." Ulfrik clapped Gunnar's shoulder, who flashed a wide grin. "I will provide you gold gifts for the new warriors you will bring me."

"I will fill my ships with fighting men. I swear it."

"Excellent. Hakon will accompany you as well."

"What?" Hakon asked, frowning. "You will need me at your side for all this business in Hedeby."

"Yes," Gunnar agreed. "He would be better off helping you with the shipbuilders."

"You two will do this task together," Ulfrik said, pointing at each of them. "And you will return together, or do not return at all."

34

Ulfrik saw the village rising out of the horizon and called a halt to the column of men. The sun was bright and the sky clear, but he did not see smoke, white or black, rising from the dark rectangles that outlined the houses. The men groaned as they lowered the ships they portaged onto the grass. He had taken his two longships, which were sleeker and lighter than the knarrs he had given to Gunnar and Hakon. They dropped their burdens into the knee-high grass as well, collapsing alongside their companions.

"Do you want me to scout ahead?" Finn asked. "Were you expecting to find this?"

"Were you?" he asked. "You were with me the one time I made this journey. Do you remember a village?"

Finn shrugged. "Doesn't take long to throw together a few houses. They could've settled this route after we were here. I'll go have a look."

He waved Finn forward, then lowered himself to the grass and turned his face into the breeze. He smelled the earth and the grassy scents, and he could not help but think of playing with Gunnar and Runa in the grass fields surrounding the hall of Nye Grenner. The memory made him feel tremendously old. For a fighting man he was aged, but he still acted on the impulses of his youth. He wondered if men would look upon him as a broken relic and scorn his call to battle. Why should they follow a leader who might die before he ever delivers on the promises of gold? He turned away from the cooling breeze and stared at the ground.

He heard the swishing grass as Finn returned to him. "It's a shell of a village. Burnt out and looted long ago."

"Well, it was a poor idea to build a steading so close to these paths. As many raiders as honest merchants must pass this way. They wanted to profit from that traffic, I bet."

Finn offered his hand to Ulfrik. Once he would have scorned the help, but now his old bones were too grateful for it. He dusted off his legs, and without a word from him the men returned to the ships. With more than twenty men on each side of the hulls, portage still was heavy work.

"I misjudged the speed of portaging these ships. We should rest in those ruins. We will make Hedeby by late tomorrow, if we are on the right path."

With a leg up from Finn, Ulfrik mounted into the prow, then grasped the beast head set there. He ordered them forward and the ships lifted off the grass, and the men trudged ahead. The long, graceful ships bobbed over the fields as if in full sail. Their shields were on the racks, like the colorful scales of a great sea snake. The same distance that Finn had run took the men three times as long to traverse. The ships were loaded with war gear, supplies, and treasure. Normally they sang their rowing songs to aid their strength, but now crossed to the village with only grunts and curses.

They set the ships down at the center of the village. Ulfrik noted that most of the walls that had faced them were all that remained of some of these buildings. At best, the five buildings were nothing more than burnt-out frames or a place to set a lean-to. Still enough rubble and debris clogged the buildings to warrant a deeper investigation.

"Check all the buildings and we will make a fire. Gunnar's wife will cook for us tonight." Men cheered at that announcement. Morgan appeared at the rail of the other ship and smiled. She was one of only a handful of women accompanying them, and while

Ulfrik loved her as the wife of his son, he hardly knew the woman. He expected she would do as he told her while Gunnar was away.

Ulfrik directed but otherwise stayed out of the way of his experienced men. They showed the younger men to their duties, while others investigated the houses. He went to Morgan and helped his grandchildren to the ground. The girls, Hilde and Thorgerd, squealed as he helped them jump to the soft grass. The youngest, Leif, cried out in joy as his mother handed him down to Ulfrik's arms.

"I'm tired of carrying you all day," he said. "One day I will need you to carry me." Leif laughed as Ulfrik set him down. "You girls help your mother prepare. I'll watch your brother."

Leif took his hand and they went to supervise the men setting up the cooking pot.

Then he heard a woman scream. It was not from his women, but from one of the ruined buildings. He heard men shout. Ulfrik released Leif's hand, and he pointed at Finn. "Watch the boy."

He dashed across the brief camp toward the sound. In the evening light, he saw a shape dart out and one of his men chasing. The fleeing figure wore a plain gray dress but otherwise the setting sun blinded him to the details. He heard her distant screams as he passed the house. One of his hirdmen was kneeling with his hands over his face, but otherwise Ulfrik saw no blood.

The fleeing girl tripped and her pursuer was right behind. Ulfrik caught up to find his hirdman, Hamar, wrestling with a young woman who kicked and screamed, uselessly pounding the man's body with small fists. He did not understand what language she spoke, but he recognized curses in any tongue. Hamar finally wrestled her to stillness.

"Looks like we've caught a runaway slave," Hamar said as he hauled her off the ground. The hirdman presented her like a fat bass fish to Ulfrik. "A feisty one, too."

The slave's clothes were plain and dirty, and torn at the left shoulder. Her hair was cropped closed to her head, making it seem larger than the rest of her thin frame. The rusty collar and red marks around her neck confirmed the image of a slave. However, that is where the resemblance to a slave ended. She stared defiantly at him, as if he dared to touch her she would strike him dead. Her eyes were as clear as blue ice, and though her cheek was bruised he saw uncommonly clear skin for a slave woman.

She looked nothing like Runa, but he could not help but see her in this woman. She was proud, probably arrogant, hid her fear well, and spirited. She tugged at Hamar's grip, not to flee but as if desiring to stand on her own.

Grass crunched as someone ran from behind and her eyes shifted from Ulfrik to the approaching hirdman. Fear flickered across her face and Ulfrik turned to see a fist punching toward her head.

Ulfrik deflected the blow, then interposed himself between the woman and the hirdman. "Lord? The bitch hit me in the face with a timber. I think she loosened a tooth."

"She improved your looks, Thorbert. Lower your fists." Ulfrik placed a hand on his shoulder to calm the man. "She was frightened for her life, that's all."

"She's a slave, Lord. Look at her."

Ulfrik gave Thorbert a warning glare and the warrior relaxed but frowned at the woman. Others had gathered around the commotion, but most of the men tended to setting up their camp before nightfall.

Turning to the woman, Ulfrik met her eyes. She held them for a moment, then appeared to think better of it and lowered her head. Ulfrik smiled. "So, slave, do you understand me, or do you only speak a foreign tongue?"

She nodded and Hamar shook her. "Then address him as a lord or I'll thrash you."

"Yes, Lord. I speak your language." Her voice was bright and youthful, but her Norse was thickly accented.

"You are not one of my people. Your speech gives that away." He paused and glanced around himself. "Are you alone?"

"Yes, Lord."

"No one else escaped with you?" The woman shook her head. "No one is pursuing you?" Ulfrik lowered his voice and gave her a serious look.

"No, Lord."

"These ruins are safe, then. No one hiding over the next rise?"

"They are safe, Lord. I've hid here for many days."

"And where were you going?"

Now her defiance slipped and Ulfrik saw her shoulders slump. "I don't know, Lord. I wanted to go to the coast, but then thought I would be captured and sold. Seems I will suffer that fate anyway."

The woman's eyes glittered in the evening light. He could hear her imploring him for mercy, though she would not say the words. Such bold pride made his own eyes feel hot, summoning a memory of Runa. "No, you won't. I knew a woman just like you once, and she did not deserve slavery. Your pride reminds of hers."

Her eyes went wide and she looked up at him. He did not know her spirit, and realized his mercy was brought on from the grief of his wife's passing. Yet he could no more see this woman remain a slave than he could his own granddaughters.

"I claim you as my own slave." He looked to Hamar and nodded at him. "Release her."

The woman did not run, but cowered as Ulfrik stepped closer. She closed her eyes as he reached out for her slave collar. He plucked at it, feeling the warm, scaly touch of the rusted iron. He had seen hundreds of slave women in his life. He still owned a half dozen slaves, and two were women. Yet touching the collar around this slave's neck was like reaching back across the years. He remembered how Runa had begged him to cut the slave collar from her neck, and he had delayed. He had feared she would run from him with her newfound freedom, and he had wanted to keep her close. He smiled at the memory.

"As your owner, it is my right to grant you freedom. Which I do as of this moment. You are a free woman. These men are witnesses to it."

The slave's eyes opened and tears spilled. She crashed to her knees and bowed at his feet. "Thank you, Lord."

His two hirdmen blinked at him, and he smiled. "Thorbert, I'll find some silver to ease the pain of your lost tooth." He looked to Hamar. "I will pay for the capture and sale of this slave to me. Now take her to the smith and have him cut this collar from her neck. I will have Morgan find her better clothing."

The slave rose, her tears leaving muddy tracks on high-boned cheeks. "I cannot thank you enough, Lord. I dare not ask more of you, but I still have nowhere to go. May I stay with you?"

"Of course," he said. "We are going to Hedeby. I assume you escaped from there." The woman's bloodless expression confirmed his guess. "Well, you will be under the protection of Ulfrik Ormsson, and no man will challenge me over you."

She again thanked him, and as he turned to leave she stopped him with a question. "Why have you treated me so kindly?"

"I told you. You remind me of someone I once knew."

That night, she visited his bed. He still did not know her name. She must have felt obligated to comfort him, but he did not want the body she offered. He merely held her through the night, and hot tears streaked his cheeks as he remembered another slave woman who had once slept in his arms.

35

Aren pulled the hood of his cloak lower and tucked his chin down. The sun was gliding to the horizon and shadows grew deep and long. Ruts in the well-trod path through the light woods filled with black. Aren's hamstrings ached from riding the horses they left behind with Einar's other men and he wondered at how quickly they had managed to travel.

"You don't have to do that," Einar said. He stood beside him, a giant with arms folded and his massive ax resting against his hip. "No one is looking for you out here."

He put his hands down, running his palm over the rough grip of his sword. His thumb searched for the loop that kept the blade in place, and for the tenth time since sitting in ambush he confirmed he could draw his blade without hindrance. Einar, five archers, and Aren remained hidden among the trees. They had galloped along another path, one Einar claimed would cut ahead of the two men Mord had sent to Einar's hall.

As they had expected, Mord's men made hasty excuses to end their visits early. Einar was certain to let everyone witness his sending them off. Within the hour of slapping their backs, Einar gathered ten men and horses and left by his eastern gate to pursue them. Aren had reluctantly been dragged along, but he had no choice. What could he tell Einar? <u>Sorry that I have burdened you with sheltering me, but I won't aid you in my own defense.</u> Worse still, could he admit he had never fought in open battle, and that the only man he had ever blooded was his father—and even then it was a stab in the back that only crippled him. So he followed Einar in his hasty plan. The only contribution Aren made was to leave Gils and his escorts at Eyrafell to make it seem as if he had not yet left.

His heart pounded in his ears and his palms sweated. With any luck the archers would kill Mord's spies outright, but Einar had mentioned questioning them first.

"Don't worry so much," Einar said, his voice deep and confident.

"Am I so obvious?"

"You twitch at every breaking twig and keep touching your sword as if you're afraid it has vanished. We're only facing two men, and we have another five with horses down the path to aid us if that has changed. You are in no danger."

"I've heard too many stories of plans going awry."

"Thinking is good," Einar said, then unfolded his arms to lay a giant paw on his shoulder. "But thinking too much before a battle is the best way to get killed. You cannot die before Fate has decided your time. If tonight is it, then even should you survive these enemies you will be thrown from your horse, or Thor will hit you with a thunderbolt. So don't worry."

"How comforting," Aren said. He stared down the ever-darkening path. "If they take much longer arriving we won't have shots at them."

"We don't need accuracy. Just fill the area with two or three arrows from each archer. Something will hit."

They waited longer, and Aren began to worry their plans had been revealed. Twilight fell and the last diffuse light of the day was scattered in the trees. Einar hefted his ax, crouched, and pointed with its haft toward the path. "They come. Be ready."

"You can see them?" Aren peered into the indigo gloom but saw nothing. Only after concentrating did two loping shapes resolve from the shadow.

The archers placed arrows to their strings, but pointed them at the ground. The two shadows drew closer. They moved at a fast walk, neither speaking but both with heads down intent upon the path before them. Aren snapped back to Einar, who only peered from the underbrush like a wolf studying a wounded deer. None of the other archers moved.

He wanted to tell them to strike now or risk discovery. Surely Mord's spies would spot them. They were not well disguised and Einar's blade or the arrowheads must be sending telltale glints. How was it the two had drawn so close yet not spotted them? Then he realized his sword was still safe in its sheath. What if they charged for him? He would never draw it in time and they would cut him down. Dying with a sheathed weapon during battle was the mark of a coward. He wasn't a coward, just not suited for fighting.

Einar raises his hand and the archers raised and released their arrows. The air around Aren's head hummed with the snapping bowstrings. The archers already grabbed another shaft from their quivers before they saw where the first ones had landed. Their bow staves bent gracefully as they pulled back and released another arrow. Again the loud thrum made him jump.

The two men screamed and both had crumpled into a dark pile in the center of the track. Einar raised his hand a second time and the archers lowered their bows. After waiting a dozen heartbeats, Einar nodded for them to exit their hiding places. Aren stepped onto the track as if emerging from a nightmare. The two men were filled with arrows, a spiny heap in the gloomy light. A black puddle flowed out from beneath them, and Einar stepped away as it expanded.

"Well, that was good shooting," Einar said, prodding the pile with his ax. "Too good. I hoped one would be alive yet."

Aren's heart still pounded despite the passing of the danger. "At least they did not make it back to Mord's hall."

"They nearly did," Einar said. "Mord's land is not far down this path, just a bit farther north. Now let's strip them of valuables to make it seem like a robbery."

The archers began hauling the bodies to the side of the path.

Aren watched them at the gruesome work. Blood flowed steadily from one of the corpses and filled the air with its coppery scent. He had never seen such blood.

Then he saw the dark figures down the path. He tapped Einar's shoulder, who was bent over one of the bodies. The giant jarl followed Aren's pointing figure and he stood up from his crouch. "Looks like they had friends coming."

"Friends?" Aren's question was answered by shouts from the distant group. Aren's first instinct was to dash into the underbrush and get away. Who knew the enemy's number? They were a black clump of waving swords and spears. What if they were just the start of a column of warriors? Yet escape was not Einar's consideration. He bellowed a war cry and charged along with his five archers, who had drawn their swords. None of them even had a shield.

"Wait! This could be a trap," he yelled, but he might as well have warned the moon. Einar's men became an equally dark shape hurtling at the others.

They clashed together with a clang of iron and shouts of anger and pain. Aren stood frozen to his spot. He had never fought a battle. His real father, Konal, had not taught him much, and his stepfather Ulfrik had not put any faith in his fighting. If neither man believed he could fight, then why should he?

Screams echoed in the growing darkness. He saw men stumble and fall, but he did not know who. Only Einar was distinguishable for his great size and the two-handed ax he wielded with practiced skill. He did not chop, but hooked and stabbed with the sharp horns of his ax head. He appeared to prevail, but at this distance Aren was not sure which side would win.

He wavered, realizing his sword was still safe in its sheath. He put his hand on it. This is a test, he thought. The gods will decide whether to aid me or not based on what I do now. Cower like a child and they will scorn me like one.

The blade hummed when he drew it, and the blade flashed with the final rosy light of the day. He raised it overhead and roared.

He charged in beside Einar. Up close that battle was pure confusion. He did not know who to attack, until a man solved his confusion. A fearsome man with a double-braided beard slashed at him. Aren slipped back, feebly clanking his sword on the attacker's blade in an attempt to parry. The enemy laughed and pushed forward, now breaking through the line Einar's men had formed across the path. Aren was the easy prey and this wolf had scented him.

The enemy had a shield, but did not seem to wear any other armor besides a leather cap. His sword licked at him again, and Aren tried to remember what he had been taught. He again skipped back, and as the attacker roared for another strike Aren backed up, anticipating the killing blow.

He slipped into the underbrush, and the enemy growled with frustration. "Coward! Raven-starver!" he shouted. "I'll gut you yet."

Aren's foot caught on a rock as he backed up. The man was lunging after him, shield forward. Aren reached down and grabbed the rock just in time for the man to reach him. He fell back again, leading his attacker farther from the road.

"Stop and fight me, you goat turd!"

The man raised his shield and marched forward. Aren felt the cold, gritty weight of the rock in his left hand. He hauled back and let it sail.

In the gloom, the enemy did not see the rock streaking for his head. Aren assumed it would miss and was already crouched and searching for another. Yet a heavy thud and grunt caused him to look up. The man staggered and fell.

Aren leapt like a cornered rabbit, but unlike a rabbit he did not bolt for a hole. He sprang at the fallen enemy. He was already crawling to his knees when Aren plunged his sword to its hilt into the soft flesh at the enemy's neck. He growled with agony, the whites of his eyes bright in the dark, and blood bubbled up black from his mouth. Aren felt the man's pulse vibrating up the sword, and released it to let his foe drop into the dirt.

"Aren?" he heard Einar calling. He answered with a shout, but stood transfixed over the fallen enemy. Einar and another of his men arrived at his side. They were both splattered with blood.

"I ran away," Aren said, his voice small and defeated.

Einar laughed and clapped him on his shoulder. "You killed a foeman. Your first, yes?"

Aren nodded and Einar grabbed him close. The stench of blood was overwhelming, but Aren did not complain. "Congratulations, you are a man today! Your father would be proud of you."

"I don't think so," Aren said, not certain why he did.

"It doesn't matter how you killed him, only that you did. You used your mind against his strength. Such deeds are what songs are made from."

Einar clapped him again and laughed. "Come now. Mord's men are all dead and some of mine are hurt. Let's finish our work and be away."

Aren continued to stare at the dead man. He had killed an enemy and now the gods would aid him. He had become a man worthy of their favor.

36

Ulfrik stood on the hill and watched the shipbuilders below scurrying over the frames of his ships. They looked like ants picking clean the bones of a beached fish, carrying wood and tools back and forth from the rows of hulls. Behind the builders the Schlei Inlet sparkled in contrast to the green cliffs of Jutland, and hundreds of ships crowded the piers and jetties of Hedeby. He wondered at how many of those ships were fighting men answering his call. He inhaled the sharp sea air and turned to join his own men.

Behind him Finn and ten of his best hirdmen waited. The former slave woman, Elke, also had refused to let him out of her sight. She smiled nervously at him, seeming to debate hiding behind Finn or standing still. Ulfrik smiled but passed her as he returned to the main town.

"Two more crews are prepared to join us," Finn said as Ulfrik passed him. His freckle-faced companion fell in beside him. "When do you think the ships will be ready to sail?"

"By the fall we should have all we need," Ulfrik said. He stared ahead to the crowded town of Hedeby. Despite its cramped, ramshackle appearance, the town was home to many wealthy merchants. The ease at which he had haggled a price for his gems was a testament to the wealth concentrated here. Dozens of hearths chugged smoke into the air above it, and people wove through its maze of streets intent on their own business. Even from this distance the hum of people engaged in trade was like a buzzing fly.

"What are we going to do with all these men now?" Finn asked. "They'll be bored, and you'll remember we were warned about causing trouble."

"They arrived on their own ships? Then they can sail off on other adventure while they wait. I'll not bear responsibility for their actions."

They had been in Hedeby for close to a month, and Ulfrik hated the crowded, arrogant city. This was a place where all was weighed in a merchant's scale, and everything from one's boots to one's honor could be converted to gold. He preferred to stay outside the earthen walls, where his own ships remained beached beside the Eider River. They had followed the portage routes to the Treene River which dumped them in the Eider, and in turn brought them to the estuary in Hedeby. The river water reminded him of Frankia, and he preferred its muddy scent to the hot and foul stench of a crowded merchant town.

As they left the hill for the main track into the town, Elke let out a short gasp from behind. Ulfrik turned, finding her already pale skin grown whiter. The hirdmen around her continued past, but stopped when Ulfrik put up his hand.

"What is wrong?" He followed her gaze down the slope to where a group of men were climbing the path toward them. A rotund man in fine clothing waddled ahead of six guardsmen all wearing white and red surcoats over their mail. The man pointed at him, scuttled four more steps, pointed again, then continued his struggle to mount the hill.

"You know this walrus?" Ulfrik said. "From before I freed you?"

"Yes," she said. Elke had spoken little about herself since Ulfrik had freed her, yet he asked little of her. She had become a companion, following him like a lost puppy and as eager to please as one. He had pushed her off on Morgan and the other women as often as he could, not wanting to worry for her when dozens of decisions required his attention. She had only been a comfort in his bed, and then only as someone soft and warm to fill the emptiness beside him.

"Jarl Ulfrik Ormsson?" the fat man hollered from a distance. He waved at him, walked seven or eight paces, stopped to wave again, then continued his arduous trek.

"I'll die of old age before he arrives," Ulfrik said. "Finn, come with me and the rest of you protect Elke."

They strolled down the track, and the fat man was so intent upon his footing he drew up short when Ulfrik set himself before him. His blubbery chin quivered as he staggered back. Faded blue eyes wide with surprise were hidden behind puffy creases of pink flesh. He wore a heavy mustache that buried his mouth, but otherwise kept his head shaved close to the scalp. A golden crucifix swung from a chain across his chest, and beneath it a silver amulet of Thor's hammer twirled from another chain.

"Who are you to call my name so brazenly?" Ulfrik folded his arms, not even glancing at the guards behind the man.

"I am Udolf," he said, straightening the hem of his red linen shirt. His Norse was lightly accented, not his first language, but any trader wanting the best goods learned it well. "I have been searching for you for days."

"You can't have her," he said. "I found her and I freed her."

Udolf's mouth hung open and his arms hung limp at his side. He gasped soundlessly, like a fish left to die on the shore. "She told you about me?"

"No, but she's frightened of you and that means you either owned her or represent the man who thought he did. I don't need to know more."

"Well, that's a problem. I did own her, and she fled. She was never properly sold to you, and so that makes her stolen property. The law is clearly on my side in this matter, and I will have her back."

"So you're a slave trader?" Ulfrik picked up the cross from Udolf's neck. His guards bristled, but a glance from Ulfrik stilled them. He twisted the gold cross in his fingers. "Doesn't the Christian god despise your kind?"

"Jesus asks only that a slave be treated well. And Elke was treated well, better than I imagine you treat her."

"Ah," Ulfrik let the cross drop back to Udolf's chest. "You seem to know much about me."

"How can I not? Your name is everywhere, with your vast treasure of jewels, building of ships, bringing warriors in search of glory and gold. You came from nowhere and yet you are as a king to your people. That's worthy of gossip, don't you think?"

"It's worthy of a song," Ulfrik said. "So, how much for Elke? I would not steal from you."

Udolf smiled. "I am afraid that's not possible. I had a buyer, and he is quite set on having her. He has come from far away, a rich prince of the south. His buyer is patient but stubborn."

"How valuable could she be to you? I've been here nearly a month and you only now bring this to me. Elke is no more a slave, and is under my protection. If your southern prince wishes to challenge me for her, then he may try his best. I have not lived to this age and grown to such wealth because I am timid and easy prey."

"You do not wish to take this stance. These men are dangerous and will not be denied. I tell you this for your own good."

"She has been gone from you for over a month, walking Hedeby's streets for almost that whole time. You and your buyer are too stupid to deserve her return. Now unless you have something besides threats, waddle back down this track to whatever box you call a home. We are finished."

"You will regret this choice," Udolf said, his eyes lost in midday shadows.

"I regret nothing." Ulfrik's voice was low and full of threat. "Challenge me again and you will find your head separated from this sack of fat you call a body."

Udolf did not back down, but instead puffed out his chest. "You are not the first raider to sail into town with a bag full of rocks and think himself king of the world. If you think your foot is on my neck, then you are mistaken. Reconsider your decision, Ulfrik Ormsson, or you will not see your fine ships completed."

"Threatening my life? Talk about a foolish decision. Lesser men have died for that, so be grateful I'm allowing you to walk away."

Udolf stepped back and bowed. "My gratitude is endless, as is your arrogance." He straightened the religious icons on his chest, then gave a wolfish smile. "You don't understand how this town works."

Udolf and his guards swept back down the track, leaving Ulfrik with Finn to watch him depart.

"He's a lot faster running away than he was climbing," Ulfrik said.

"Do you think he means to kill you?" Finn asked. "We've still got months ahead of us, and your sons haven't returned with their extra crews. I think this man is serious."

"Of course he's serious. So am I." He turned back to Elke, who hid among his hirdmen like a child afraid to be punished. He extended a hand to her. "Udolf is gone, and if he comes back I will make it the last thing he does. Though I think you should stay close to me for now. No more playing with my grandchildren unless I am there."

Elke nodded and accepted his hand as he guided her to his side. "I will never be able to repay you for this."

"If Fate wishes it, then a way will be found. But I am content to know you are free. When we sail, I will take you wherever you wish to go."

She smiled then studied her feet. Ulfrik had expected her to ask to remain at his side, but perhaps she had been too shy. He renewed his walk into town.

"We need to send a message to Aren," he said. "It has been too long and he must know my plans. I need you to organize at least five men for the task, men he would recognize and trust. Traders are leaving Hedeby every day. At least one must be going to Frankia. He and Einar will need to prepare for my return and settle a safe landing for our new fleet."

Finn nodded and they all walked in silence into the shadows of the town. Already the babble of hawkers and merchants as well as the scent of waste made his head hurt. He glanced at Elke, who walked with hands clasped at her lap and head down. Her golden hair was still short after the fashion of a slave, but she would be beautiful when it grew back.

He felt eyes searching him as he crossed the streets of Hedeby, pushing through the crowds of self-absorbed craftsmen and traders. It was as if he were entering a thicket surrounded by prowling wolves. He held his head up and continued down the road.

37

"Is there no end to the bickering of these people?" Mord asked. He sat on a chair that mimicked Hrolf's high seat, but was far less ornate and much smaller. Beneath him the priest and his flock of laymen huddled in a tight knot. They were all Franks, each with pleading, wide eyes and drawn faces. They glanced down when he looked at them, suitably respectful of his authority, unlike their leader who had a habit of taking what was offered and asking for more.

"Hrothgar's farm is the most suitable location for a church," the priest said. He was a thin man with a hard, crooked nose and handsome smile. He looked more like nobility than a leader to farmers, but perhaps this was the manner of task the Church gave fledgling leaders. His simple black robe offset the shinning silver cross hung over his neck. Mord imagined it had just been polished to its current brilliance. "Father Lambert nearly died to secure it, and yet Hrothgar refuses to recognize the primacy of the church. We will pay him a fair price."

Mord doubted the price would be anything close to fair, but it was better than his dark thoughts on the matter. Ulfrik's former hall was now his own. The blood stain where Bishop Burchard had died was ironically a brown shadow beneath the priest's feet. While it was a grand hall, it was built with no inspiration, as if Ulfrik knew he would abandon it. Had he planned to leave it? If so, why? Mord did not have an answer, and knowing that Ulfrik had slipped all attempts to kill him filled him with rage. His hands gripped the rests of his chair.

"Jarl Mord?" The priest interrupted his thinking, leaning in with a quizzically raised brow. "Have you been listening to me?"

"How could I not hear the wonderful word of God that ever spouts from your mouth. You can't get rid of Hrothgar. The bastard should've followed Ulfrik when he left, but he's a coward and no friend of mine or yours."

"Do you make light of God's word?"

"Father Brice," Mord said, relieved he remembered the priest's name at last. "I apologize if I have been distant and rude. Only last night I received disturbing news about the intentions of an old enemy. It has stolen my concentration."

Nodding as if in the know, Father Brice lowered his voice. "So it is true that Ulfrik Ormsson did not die on those burning ships? While I am not a man of violence, I am sorry he did not meet his end."

Mord narrowed his eyes at the priest. "How is it you are so knowledgeable?"

The priest shrugged. "The burning ships were witnessed by locals and so they passed on their news. It has taken time, but word has traveled to me. It is not much to know."

"Very well," Mord said, leaning back in his chair. He caught the eye of one of his hirdmen. "You, take twenty men. Burn Hrothgar's farm to ash and kill him and his family. Put their heads on a spear as warning to others."

The hirdman blinked, but without a word left the hall to carry out the order. Mord did not doubt it would be done. His hirdmen were not local and were known for ruthless efficiency. Father Brice blanched and his followers wrung their hands.

"We don't want to build a church over the bodies of the dead," he said.

"Why not? Wouldn't be the first time. If my methods bother you, don't come to me for aid. Hrothgar has been like a pimple on my ass, and it's time he be squeezed." His hirdmen chuckled at the coarse joke, but the priest wrinkled his nose. "Go hide somewhere while my men solve your dispute, and once the embers have cooled you can begin laying your foundations."

The priest blinked half a dozen times, then inclined his head and left with his laymen in tow. Mord watched the hall door flash with yellow light as it opened and then close the room back into gloom once more. Only hirdmen and slaves remained, and they kept a heavy silence. As he was about to leave the hall and seek his wife, Magnus the Stone stepped forward.

"Jarl Mord, may I have a moment with you?"

"I was just about to go seek Fara. Walk with me."

They exited the gloomy hall for the bright day. Since acquiring the hall and lands, Mord had not experienced the anticipated thrill. He had a wider swatch of property and more people to plague him with complaints. Even his wife had not seemed happier. They walked from the hall and the surrounding fields were wide and empty. Ulfrik's former people were as suspicious of him as he was of them, and they avoided him. A sunny afternoon should have brought people to the fields, but instead he saw them all in retreat.

"Your father's messenger arrived early this morning," Magnus said in his gruff, rocky voice. "I did not want to disturb you, so I heard his news."

"Where is he now?"

"In the stables tending his horse. His news was not urgent but important."

They stopped once Mord noted Fara returning with her women from the stream nearby. They had baskets of laundry on their hips, and Fara's golden hair blazed in the sun as she approached. She smiled at him, but he instead looked to Magnus. "So what news from my father? Does he have another list of demands that I accomplish on his behalf?"

Mord could not help the bitterness seeping into his words. He had done all his father had asked of him and yet the old man was not happy. He would never be happy until Mord became someone else.

"His spy in Einar's hall has confirmed Ulfrik's son, Aren, still hides with him."

The news turned Mord's hands to ice, and he studied Magnus's face. This was no jest. "He did not flee with his brothers?"

Magnus shook his head. "He did not return home after spotting him in Rouen, and must've sought shelter with Einar."

"So they must have killed my messengers, and not bandits." Mord began to pace, worried at this new wrinkle. Aren was Ulfrik's weakest son, sheltered and unwilling to fight. His only threat lay in an inexplicable friendship with Hrolf's son, Vilhjalmer. For that relationship alone, Aren had to be handled carefully.

"What is Aren doing exactly?"

"I asked the same. No one knows for certain, but he appears to be working in a great deal of secrecy. Your father believes whatever his plan, it will be disruptive to you. It is best to eliminate him while no one knows he is there."

"Is that your opinion or my father's?"

Magnus blinked in a rare moment of surprise. "Your father's, of course."

"Of course, I could kill him, or expose Einar for harboring Hrolf's enemy, but I think it is better to learn what he is planning. You know I've also heard Ulfrik is raising a great fleet in Hedeby. Have you heard the same?" Magnus shook his head. "Well, I wonder then if even my father knows. He must, for the traders who shared that news are sure to have visited Rouen. Ulfrik claims he wants to settle in the Danelaw, but does one need to raise such a large army for that purpose?"

"If he wants to ensure his place," Magnus offered. Mord scowled at him.

"He plans to return here, and his son lingers behind to make the way for him." Mord rubbed his face and sighed. "If I kill Aren, it will alert Ulfrik and cut off our spy from Einar's hall. I'd rather know

Ulfrik's next step and be prepared for it rather than gloat of the death of his weakest son."

Magnus shrugged, a careless motion that dismissed Mord's words. "Your father wants to kill him, or at the least expose him so Einar is caught in the trap as well."

"Are you sworn to me or my father?"

Magnus did not answer, but his flinty gaze did not falter. Mord continued to hold it until the old hirdman relented. "I am your man, Jarl Mord."

"Then we will wait to see what else Aren might reveal to us. If we cannot learn more then we shall have him killed. That will satisfy everyone, would it not?"

Magnus nodded. Mord waved him off, and he went to meet his wife, content that Ulfrik's whelp would unwittingly betray all his father's plans. The afternoon had ended much better than it had started.

38

"I can't believe you led us into a trap."

Hakon sat against the rough wood wall of the small hut where he and Gunnar had been placed. He felt the cool damp seeping through his shirt, and the small of his back hurt from sitting on the hard-packed dirt floor. He pushed his feet against the stone of the empty hearth. The small room was gloomy, lit only by the light filtering from the smoke hole above. Gunnar was still trying to peer through cracks in the door, and for the twentieth time he pushed on it. The door rattled against the outside bolt, and he let his one good hand slide down the door.

"So much for all the goodwill and friends you had waiting for us in England." Hakon had held his tongue for as long as he could, but now that he was no longer certain of the days he had been imprisoned, his willpower vanished. He was going to beat Gunnar senseless once he regained his strength. They had not been fed more than hard bread and mead.

Gunnar did not turn from the door, but kept his head lowered and listened.

"Do you really think they're going to open the door and free us?" Hakon snorted a laugh. "You fucked the jarl's wife how many times?

There's no misunderstanding that. Wouldn't that have been a good thing to tell all of us before we accepted an invitation to his hall?"

What little Hakon understood of the situation had all come from Jarl Aslak when his feigned politeness erupted into raging violence. He had accused Gunnar of too many horrible acts to comprehend, but it was clear Gunnar once had a tryst with his wife that ended in a child. Gunnar had a bastard son in Northumbria.

"She was not his wife at the time," Gunnar said to the door. "Nor was he a jarl. I should've known better the moment I saw his smug face instead of Jarl Hord's."

"Knowing better is the very story of your life, brother. You should've known better before you carved up a priest, or before you burned one alive with an entire village. And that's only your recent achievements. Since we have the time, I may as well count them out for you."

Gunnar leaned his head against the door, and Hakon was glad his verbal beating hurt, for he had to conserve strength for whatever ordeals Jarl Aslak had planned.

"You are right to blame me," Gunnar said, his voice quiet. "This is all my fault. Mother is dead and Father has lost everything, all for my foolishness. I have never done a right thing in my life."

"Are you joking with me?" Hakon straightened his back against the wall. "It's not funny, if you are."

"No," he said, finally turning from the door. His eyes were rimmed with dark circles and his face seemed to sag as if about to slip from his head. "It is all true. I am sorry for all that I've done. I fear I may have led you to death as well. This is bad."

Hakon leaned forward. "Hold on. Aslak sent to our ship for ransom. They've got the gold to pay for it, and it's not like they're a mercenary crew. They'll pay it. So why should we worry for death?"

"Aslak is a jealous whelp," Gunnar said, slumping down to the floor beside Hakon. His brother's shoulder touched his, but Gunnar stared at the opposite wall. "He hates me for my success, if you can believe that. He'll take the ransom, kill the crew, and burn us alive in this shack."

"I don't think so," Hakon said. "He'd have killed us already if he wanted that. Again, you think you're more important than you really are. He sees a chance at a profit, and we foolishly gave him the chance."

Hakon paused and listened to the muffled talk of men outside the walls, but nothing intelligible penetrated. "To be honest, this is as much my fault as yours. I should've insisted we take more than three men."

Rather than disagree, Gunnar remained silent. They sat quietly and Hakon studied the room. Too much time had passed since their capture. The ransom should have been settled and they should have been freed. Hakon wondered if Gunnar was right and he was being foolishly optimistic.

"You know, I blamed you for this," Gunnar said, holding up the stump of his right arm. The skin was burned over the wrist bone, appearing as if it had been roughly pulled taut over the stump then pinched shut. Hakon had seen it enough so that he no longer felt revulsion at the disfigurement. He had witnessed far worse in the aftermath of battle.

"Me? Clovis took your hand. What would it have to do with me?"

"Uncle Toki and and I were rescuing you when I was captured. Clovis may have taken my hand, but it would've never happened were you not his prisoner."

"Really? Well, it was Fate's plan to take your hand. Were it not Clovis then you'd have lost it in battle."

Gunnar nodded and raised his brows, but still stared listlessly ahead. "You're right, of course, yet that did not prevent me from blaming you. I think I still do, even now that I know better. Old habit, I guess."

Silence again took over and Hakon rubbed his own wrist, feeling the itch of an imaginary dismemberment. His voice was a whisper in the still room. "I'm sorry for it."

"Mother was as cold as an iceberg to me, even after I lost my hand. She blamed me too, said I had been irresponsible with you. I think she actually believed I deserved to be maimed. She was right, of course."

"I don't remember that," Hakon said. "I think you imagined it. All she ever did was worry for you and dote over your hand. This is going to sound foolish, but I was jealous of you."

"For losing my hand?"

"You had all of Mother's attention, and with Aren being such a strange child, it was as if I didn't exist."

Gunnar chuckled. "I had her attention because I was always bringing the family troubles. Remember, I had fallen for that girl who was Throst's spy? Even back then, I was the doorway through which all bad things entered our hall. Look at us now. It's no different. It would be better for all that I did not live."

Hakon leaned his head against the wall. "A moment ago, I wanted to beat your face bloody. Is this some trick of yours to get out of that?"

"No, I've earned it." Gunnar ran his one hand through his wavy, dark hair. Hakon saw the gray mixed in with it, and despite it Gunnar still seemed no more than a lost boy. "I hope father will see to Morgan. She's a good girl, you know, better than I deserve."

"Now that's the last desperate word I'll tolerate from you." Hakon struggled to his feet, then rubbed his thighs. "We can't sit around and wait to die. You're right about Aslak, I fear. Paying a ransom should not take so long when our ships are only just at the river. We have to escape."

"Leave me behind. Aslak will be satisfied and you can get away."

"Gods, man, you are either as mad as a rabid wolf or as limp as boiled dandelions. Nothing in between with you, is there? Would you stand up and help me think of how Father would break out of here. How many escape stories has he told us? Got to be something we can use from them."

"Do you think they were all true? I have my doubts for some."

"Truth doesn't matter, it's the idea in the stories we need." Hakon dismissed the obvious ploys of luring guards with a fake emergency, or a heroic breakout when the door opened. Both would end in ruin. Nothing else came to mind, and Gunnar remained despondent.

Hakon stared at the empty hearth. Not even ash remained, and whoever had lived in this hut had long ago abandoned it.

Then he looked up and laughed.

"I wonder who is more stupid, Aslak or us?" Hakon grabbed Gunnar's shoulder then pointed at the smoke hole. Blue light shined down between the rafters. "It seems one of us should fit through, or could widen it if we don't."

A smile formed on Gunnar's face. "If I did not feel stupid before, I do now. It's not so high that you can't reach it. If you stand on my back, you should be able to pull yourself up."

Strength returned to Hakon's limbs as he realized Gunnar was right. He would have to crawl through, since Gunnar had only one hand and could not pull himself up. He would drop down and unbar the door, then they would slip away. "All right, can you balance on the hearth while I get up there?"

Gunnar got onto hands and knees like a table, and Hakon carefully stepped on his back. It was like trying to balance on ice and he jumped down twice rather than fall. The third time he held himself steady, then jumped for the rafters that were just beyond his fingers. Grabbing the rough, smoke stained beam, he pulled up, kicking his legs up until they grabbed another beam. He did not know what to do next.

"Stop pretending to be a bat," Gunnar hissed from below. "Let go with your legs and just pull up onto the beam. It should hold you."

He followed Gunnar's instructions and hauled himself onto the beam. He now sat on it like a bird hiding in the bough of a tree. He had to stoop to keep his head from hitting the thatch. The smoke hole's edge brushed his outstretched hand, and he had to jump to it and hope he could catch the rim. The fall was not far, but he did not want his struggles to attract guards. "Pray the gods this works."

His hand caught the edge of smoke hole and his feet were still braced against the rafters. He swung one leg to another beam and braced himself against both as he worked his hands through the hole. He pulled up and his head was through to the outside. Faded yellow thatch blocked his view of the surrounding area, but his shoulders caught as he struggled to shimmy through the hole. He heard Gunnar below, but it was all muffled words. His shoulders burned as he hauled himself through the hole and then rolled onto the roof. The thatch was hard and scratchy against his skin, and he had scraped his arms but was otherwise free. The cool Northumbrian air washed over him and he laughed.

He sat up and saw a line of three men in padded leather hauberks and leather caps. A woman in a blue dress followed with a child she guided by her hand. Hakon felt his heart leap into his throat as they disappeared from view beneath the roof. Scrambling to the hole he stuck his head through and saw Gunnar staring up at him.

"Three men with a woman and child."

They both faced the sound of the bolt lifting from the door. Hakon knew his only weapon was surprise. When he heard muffled voices below, he scrambled to the edge of the roof and jumped down on the first man he spotted.

The collision crushed the man to the ground with a cry of shock and pain. Hakon hauled back on the prone man's neck, but it did not snap. Instead he sought a dagger or other weapon on the man's body.

Without an ax, Gunnar was not a good fighter. Hakon glanced up and saw he had a stone pried from the hearth, but the two men were not advancing on him. Hakon felt the man beneath claw his shirt and pull.

The woman held both hands to her face, eyes wide with shock. Then she started to shout. "Stop it! We're here to help you. You fools!"

"Olga?" Gunnar said. "What's happening?"

The man beneath Hakon growled. "Get off me, oaf, or I'll change my mind about saving you."

Hakon released the man's neck and stepped back. The man rolled aside and rubbed his neck, giving Hakon a murderous glare.

"What are you two doing?" Olga asked. Hakon had not seen her at the welcome feast, mostly because Aslak was screaming death threats in his face. She would have been pretty in her youth, and before her nose had been broken. Her hair was thin and hidden beneath a stained head cover, but locks like golden baby's hair hung from the sides. Her eyes were puffy and small, making her seem as if she had been crying. From the red beneath her nose, Hakon guessed she had.

"We're getting away before your mad husband decides to cook us alive," Gunnar said. "What are you doing? And who is the boy?"

The question hardly needed asking. The young boy had his mother's silky gold hair but Gunnar's curls. His bent smile was Runa's, and to see it nearly made Hakon cry. Olga pushed him forward.

"He is Brandr, your son. He will be ten at Yuletide, if you can believe so many years have passed."

Hakon sat with legs splayed out in the dirt, leaned back, and watched the play of shock, denial, then horror play out on his brother's face. He began waving his hands. "I have enough children."

"I'm certain you have more than you know," Olga said. She spun Brandr around and hugged him. Tears leaked from her eyes. "Go with your Da. He'll treat you better than Jarl Aslak."

"Will you come?" the boy asked.

"I can't. You will be a man soon. Be a good one." She stood and shoved him off toward Gunnar, holding out a sack. "My cousins will take you to your ships. This is silver for raising my boy. Be good to him."

Gunnar accepted the offered silver, his eyes still wide. "Why are you sending him with me? He needs a mother."

Olga shook her head. "He needs a father. Aslak hates him, beats him. He will never have any kind of life here."

"I'm an outlaw," Gunnar said, watching Brandr step to his side. The boy smiled up at him. "I'll offer him nothing better, and I'm not sure my wife will accept him. I might not accept him."

Leaning in to Gunnar, Olga planted a brief kiss on his cheek. "If you are who I remember, then you will care for him."

In the distance, the doors to Aslak's meager hall flew open and a bloodied man flew backwards into the dirt. The man that Hakon had tried to kill got to his feet and said, "That would be the end of the distraction we made for Aslak. We have to leave now or risk being caught."

Hakon stood and in a whirlwind of confusion they were all rushing for the borders of Aslak's lands. When they came to the path through the woods, the men stopped but bade them follow the path until they reached the river.

Olga gave a final hug to her son, then spun away in tears. Hakon smiled at Gunnar, who stared horrified at his newfound son.

"At least we recruited one person," he said. Gunnar did not laugh.

39

Ulfrik paced the deck and a black serpent of anger coiled about his heart. Across the inlet where his ship remained anchored, the black town of Hedeby chugged white smoke into the morning air. The inhabitants were like colorful flecks tumbling around the drab blocks of its buildings. Ships glided in and out of the docks.

"Nails!" he shouted at the town. "No more nails! Is this possible?"

His fist slammed the rail of his ship and he stared down at the green sea water slapping the hull. Someone behind cleared his throat. Finn's steady voice was at his left shoulder.

"More nails are on order with the blacksmiths, but all construction of our ships has stopped."

"And before that it was not enough lumber, and before that the ship master was ill." A cold breeze slapped his face, and it smelled of the sea and smoke. "Feel this wind? The summer is finished but our ships are not. We were to have been sailing up the Seine by now. The men I recruited are being paid to stay out of Hedeby, but they grow bored. And then you two."

Ulfrik faced his two sons, Gunnar and Hakon, who had returned with barely a dozen new men the prior night. They seemed to hide behind Finn, who stood with his freckled face turned bright red. The rest of the crew either found duties to occupy them on the opposite end of the ship or hung their heads in shame.

"At least Gunnar and I have settled our differences. That's what you really sent us away to do, right?" Hakon's smile seemed so genuine Ulfrik nearly laughed, but then he remembered how his wife's dying wish for revenge was disintegrating like old cloth in a fire.

"I sent you to fill your ships with fighting men!" His voice echoed around the inlet. "You barely found replacements for the warriors we lost."

"You also have a new grandson to meet." Gunnar spoke to the deck and his face was as red as Finn's. Only Hakon seemed pleased at the news.

"Morgan was not with child when you left. You mean to tell me you spent this time searching for your bastard children?"

"Oh no," Hakon said. "There's a good story behind this one."

Ulfrik silenced Hakon with a glare, and his voice was low with threat. "I should throw the both of you overboard."

"He's a good boy. Got Mother's smile," Hakon said.

"You're in a fine mood for someone reporting failure." Ulfrik stood nose to nose with Hakon. It was like looking into a pond and seeing a reflection of his younger self, only he had not been this irritatingly optimistic. "What has brought you such a lift to your step on this wretched morning?"

"He met the Frisian girl, Elke," Gunnar said, a wry smile twisting his mouth. "I think our unmarried man might have found his match. It was like a lightning strike when the two saw each other."

A hot rock fell into Ulfrik's stomach. Elke had stayed with Morgan and his grandchildren on Gunnar's ship last night. He had brushed aside her advances all summer, unable to reconcile being with another woman so soon after Runa's death. He still felt as if Runa were only waiting at home for him. Besides, Elke seemed to offer herself as the only way she knew to repay him. Yet when he stepped back he realized from his son's foolish grin that he was jealous of Hakon. The moment he realized it, he felt ashamed.

"She told you she's a Frisian? Took me half the summer to learn that about her. She is a good woman, and grows more beautiful as she loses the marks of slavery. But I need you to focus on our troubles today." Hakon's smile widened and Ulfrik had to turn aside from him.

"While you two are discovering new love and lost children and having grand adventures with my gold, I have not forgotten my promise to your mother. You did not have to see what Mord's poison did to her. How she drowned in the clear air. How she gasped out her wish for revenge. Nor did you witness how the poison robbed her of her beauty and turned her into a hag. I did, and I will never forget. Mord and his father, Gunther One-Eye, killed your mother, and are the reason why I sleep on the deck of a ship rather than beneath the roof of a hall. So put aside your joy and remember your anger. Your mother and our honor have yet to be avenged, and there can be no happiness until that day has come. Do you understand?"

Both of his sons bowed their heads and nodded, and Hakon's silly grin had bent into a frown. He circled them, a plan forming as his boots thumped the deck.

"A slave trader and merchant by the name of Udolf had owned Elke and when I defied him he threatened me. I expected attempts on my life, or violence. I have much to learn. He did none of that. Instead, he has used his influence in this town to drain my money and keep my ships from completion. He mocks me from the shadows and all my sword-strength is nothing. I can't get near him in order to —persuade him." Ulfrik stopped before his sons. "But he doesn't know you or your ships. You haven't even docked yet. So I will go with you upon your ship, and you will bring him back to me where I will be hidden. We will take him out to sea to show him what a good sailing ship is like, if you take my meaning."

Gunnar was already smiling, but Hakon frowned. "Why not let us handle him for you?"

"Because it's my problem, and I will fix it. Now let's get about this or his spies will see you here."

The plan came together simply. Gunnar pulled his ship alongside Ulfrik's, took on supplies to pose as trade goods, and Ulfrik dressed himself as a plain crewman without gold or fine clothes. While Gunnar's ship was a sleek longboat, it was not uncommon for raiders to offload at Hedeby. As a last minute inspiration, Ulfrik took the smallest of the new men and tied them loosely. "Here are captives you wish to sell as slaves," he said. "That seems to be Udolf's favored good."

The new crew were reluctant to surrender weapons and let themselves be tied, however loosely, yet Ulfrik insisted they were best suited for it. Their companions teased them as the rest of the crew rowed the ship to the docks. Once moored, fees paid, and a quick inspection performed, Gunnar and Hakon took seven crewmen and left in search of Udolf.

Ulfrik waited in silence, seated on a sea chest and arms slung over the rails. The gentle rocking of the ship and the bustle of dock workers made him drowsy. It took all his control not to jump up when he heard Gunnar speaking over-loud. Instead, he lazily turned and pulled his leather cap down over his eyes. He skimmed over the group of armed men that accompanied Udolf. Both Gunnar and Hakon stood close to him, and each spoke over the other. Ulfrik pulled back to prevent Udolf from noticing him, but he loosened his sword. Conversation floated up from the dock, with one voice drawing closer.

"The bog iron we can speak of later," Gunnar said as he bounded up the short gangplank. "The slaves are captured Saxons. A few died crossing the channel, but these are strong. Have a look."

The rest of the crew had all loosened their swords and shared wide-eyed glances with each other. Gunnar stepped onto the dock, looked at him as if he did not matter, then grabbed the first slave. "If I bring just one down, you won't have a good idea of the lot. I don't want to sell one. I want to sell all of them. My crew is hungry for gold, Master Udolf."

The reply was indistinct, but from Gunnar's frown, Ulfrik understood Udolf was too canny to board a slave trader's ship. As Gunnar yanked one of the so-called slaves forward, he slipped the man a dagger as he pretended to untie him. Again he glanced at Ulfrik, and gave a barely perceptible nod.

As they disappeared down the gangplank, Ulfrik drew his sax, a short sword for close fighting, and his crew followed.

"Now!"

He leapt the rails like a man half his age. While he was in the air his heart raced with the pent up frustration of a wasted summer. When he crashed onto the deck, he screamed with battle lust and shoved the first of Udolf's guards into the water. The other crewmen sprang over the side to land among Udolf's guards. With their heavy chain shirts and long swords and spears, they had no room to fight. Gunnar was already hauling Udolf up the gangplank while Hakon drew a guard's own dagger and plunged it into his neck.

The battle was quick and decisive. Ulfrik thrust his sax into the leg of the next man when at last Udolf's guards regained themselves. He dodged a spear thrust, caught the shaft with his left hand. When the enemy pulled back on it, Ulfrik shoved forward and sent the guard splashing into the water.

"Cast off!" Gunnar shouted. The former slaves were already cutting the ties and jumping back up onto the rails, aided by their friends. Uldolf's guards tried to follow but the weight of their chain shirts left them stranded.

A sword stabbed at Ulfrik's gut and opened his shirt, slicing the surface of his flesh. He growled, and instead of stabbing with his own sax, he pummeled the man on the head, staggering him. He was strong but shorter than Ulfrik, and when he fell Ulfrik caught him under arm. Putting the sax to the man's throat, he swiftly interposed him with the last of Udolf's guards. He backed up the gangplank with his hostage, and fell onto the deck with the man atop him.

Next he heard alarm horns sounding and dock guards stamping along the docks. Security in Hedeby was serious, considering the amount of wealth and raiders that congregated there. Gunnar laughed as he steered his ship, and every man that wasn't working the sail hauled on an oar. The sleek, light vessel flew over the water, even as another ship gave chase.

"You'll never make it away," Udolf shouted. "You'll be hunted until—"

Hakon kicked Udolf in the head while he searched for rope to bind him. Ulfrik shoved his captive to the deck while he searched him for other weapons. Once both captives were bound, Ulfrik leaned over the side to see two ships giving chase. They were not of Norse build, but fatter and with a deeper draft. Their sails filled and their crews shouted curses, but Gunnar's ship was an eagle to their sparrows. They glided out of the bay and into the Schlei inlet, where cliffs brooded down on their left and open water invited them to the right.

"There are plenty of places to hide along these shores," Gunnar said.

Udolf had grown still once he realized Ulfrik had captured him. Once they were out of sight of pursuers, Ulfrik dragged a sea chest up to where Udolf sat on the deck.

"See how easy that was," he said with a smile. "You imagined yourself out of my reach, that I would not chance violence against you. And it was true all summer, until you pushed me so far that I had nothing left to lose. You might be a great trader, Udolf, but you are a fool in war. Once you cornered me, you created a desperate foe capable of anything. Always leave a way out for your enemy."

"Thank you for the lessons in war," Udolf said. His fat jowls quivered and his small eyes narrowed. "But you will regret this."

Ulfrik stood and drew a knife, placing it against the soft, yielding skin of the merchant. "You will instruct the guard that I have captured to use your authority to ensure my ships are completed before the next full moon. He will reveal nothing about me, and claim we are only pirates seeking ransom. You will remain captive until my ships and their new crews are leaving Hedeby. If anything happens to me or my people, you will tied to the anchor stone and dropped into the sea. I've seen many drown, and it is a horrible way to die."

Udolf swallowed as Ulfrik withdrew his knife. Whatever bravado he possessed had fled, and a dark stain bloomed at the crotch of his blue pants.

"I'll take that as agreement," Ulfrik said, sheathing the knife. "Welcome to your new home for the next month."

40

The masts of Ulfrik's fourteen ships and a dozen or more other masts of raider crews clustered off the southwestern coast of Jutland. Ulfrik climbed onto the rails of his ship, one hand balancing against the neck of the prow and another holding the rigging. Finn held the tiller and his crew sat ready at the oars. Gulls screamed over head, begging for food from the fleet assembled in the bracing cool of the morning. Both Hakon's and Gunnar's ships rocked on the waves next to Ulfrik's, and both his sons looked to him.

The day seemed it would never come, but capturing Udolf had been the key to unlock the endless delays with the shipbuilders. They had set the trader free only this morning. Gunnar had suggested Udolf be sacrificed to the gods for good luck, but Ulfrik had no heart to kill the man. He had proved easy to keep captive, as if he had practice in it. He lost weight from not eating, but had otherwise not sought to escape nor deviate from the terms of his captivity. Once he had resigned to his fate, he treated it much like any business deal. Ulfrik did not like him, and would rather they never met again, but he did not hate him enough to kill. So Udolf walked off toward Hedeby without anything more than the clothes on his back, and if the gods saw fit to allow him a safe return, then Ulfrik would not interfere.

"We will sail day and night until we make landfall south of the Seine," Ulfrik shouted to his sons.

They had reviewed the plans a dozen times, but nerves forced him to repeat them. Both Hakon and Gunnar waved then returned to their crews. In Gunnar's ship, Morgan and his grandchildren waved at him with bright smiles. Even his newfound grandson, Brandr, offered a fearful wave. They boy was timid, probably because his father had beat any boldness out of him. Ulfrik did not care for him, but did not dislike him either. He simply had no time to know the boy.

He turned to the next ship, where Elke leaned against the rails with Hakon. Her small, hesitant hand waved to him and he raised his own in return. Her hair now flowed down to her shoulders and she had sloughed off the vestiges of slavery, holding herself with defiant pride. She looked good beside Hakon. As Hakon led her away, Ulfrik wondered if he and Runa had looked so poised when they were young.

Shaking his head, he stepped down from the rail and relieved Finn at the tiller. His crew watched him expectantly, and a wide smile broke across his face.

"Row, you dogs! Row us to gold and glory!" And revenge, he thought. Now let my fury be poured out on my enemies, and let a tide of blood wash them from the land.

The fleet of nearly thirty ships launched to sea, dark faces eager for blood and riches. They plied the coast and threaded the channel toward Frankia. They sang songs of great battles and bawdy exploits. Their spirits were high and full of strength. No enemy would prevail against them.

Then the gods looked down upon their ships crawling across the face of the water, and grew jealous.

They sent storms.

41

Ulfrik had spent years at sea and knew the signs of a storm: high clouds like blue-gray fish scales covering the sky, a rainbow at dawn, red light on the horizon, or a ring about the moon at night. This storm exploded from nowhere. A sheet of clouds like Thor's hand stretching out over the water blocked the sun. The winds whipped the sea into rough waves, and thunder rumbled overhead.

"Can we make landfall?" Finn asked, yelling over the roaring wind.

"Tie down whatever you can," Ulfrik said. "Unstep the mast, then lash yourself to a rail. I will tie myself here."

Finn's hair blew flat against his head as he stared into the oncoming storm. Thunder growled as if reinforcing Ulfrik's order. "We do not deserve this."

Ulfrik agreed, but the gods were fickle and their whims whisked away the lives of men. He took a length of sealskin rope and tethered his leg to the railing. An arm could be yanked out of its socket when tossed about by wave and wind, but a leg was sturdier. His right leg was better than his left, so he tied it at the ankle.

The wind was like the roar of a dragon and the ship now crested high waves that sent it plunging into the trough. Sea chests and crates yet unsecured dragged across the deck. Ulfrik searched the water, seeing his fleet spreading out against the storm. Both Hakon's and Gunnar's ships flanked either side of his, and he wished he could offer his grandchildren comfort. He knew the terror the gods prepared to unleash on them. He heard it in the wind, the pleasure moan of the goddess Ran, the whore who dragged sailors down to her bed at the bottom of the sea. He tasted it in the bitter spray of sea foam carried off the hull. He smelled it in the loamy scent of rain. But worse than all, he felt it in the pit of his gut when the planks of his deck shuddered with the crashing waves.

The sun failed and day turned to night. Thor hurled lightning bolts with the carelessness of a child. Rain began to slash the sea, driven by a wind that tore at Ulfrik's clothes.

His crew huddled against the gunwales. He and Finn pulled the steering board onto the deck. Both stared into each other's eyes.

"I'm scared," Finn said. "I've never been in a storm like this."

"I have, and I am scared as well."

A wave crashed over the deck and the full horror of the storm was underway. Cold, foamy water doused the crew, knocking Finn to the opposite gunwale. Ulfrik opened his mouth to order him to tie himself down, but the next wave flattened him to the deck. For an instant he heard nothing but gurgling, rushing water and lay flat against the planks as the water pummeled his back. His shirt was over his head when the water receded, and he fought it down in time to see Finn holding onto the rail.

Only he was hanging over the water.

Ulfrik leapt to his feet, ran halfway across the deck before his right leg yanked back and he slammed to the deck again. His vision flashed white, and his mouth filled with coppery blood and salty water. The rain pooled and sloshed around his face and he lay stunned. He struggled to hands and knees, but relaxed when he saw another man dragging Finn onto the deck.

Ulfrik smiled and called out his thanks. In the next instant, the ship plunged into the trough of a mighty wave and the man who had rescued Finn disappeared overboard. Both Ulfrik and Finn screamed. The crewman had left too much slack in his rope. Ulfrik did not need to see what Finn did when he clawed up to the rail. The man would remain tied but still submerged in the water. Finn hauled on it in frustration, but it was taut and bending the rail. His curse was barely audible above the howling wind and hissing rain.

The rest of the crew huddled beneath their cloaks like barnacles on a hull. Ulfrik heard the distant crack and snap of a ship breaking apart. Shrieks and curses were indistinct in the terrible wind, and doubtless Ulfrik's imagination filled in much of what he could not truly hear. He knew all too well the horrid notes of that song. Ran sang a bitter tune to the new lovers sinking to her bed.

The ship rocked and tilted in the storm. After each breaking wave threatened to swamp his ship, he blew the sea water out of his beard and pulled the hair from his eyes to count the men. He could never finish the count before another wave doused him. His clothes were stuck to his body and his leg tingled from the rope tightening with each time he tumbled away. Chests and boxes had broke from their hasty ties and slid across the deck.

"Throw those overboard," Ulfrik screamed. Loose debris could kill a man as surely as drowning. But his strongest bellow could not defeat the volume of the storm, and those who heard him only glanced up before lowering their heads again. His men would laugh at a thousand spears arrayed against them, but none were brave enough to face the fury of a storm.

Grabbing the rails, he hauled himself to his knees and inhaled to shout his order once again. Instead, it died in his throat when a wave like a foaming fist of a sea giant loomed over his ship.

It punched down on him, flattening him into the midnight world of cold, tearing water. He flipped onto his back and twisted in the water like a fish on a hook. His tie pulled at his leg with enough force that he felt as if his foot would be torn away. Worse still, as he twisted, his knee buckled and a lightning strike of agony shot through his entire right leg. He opened his mouth to scream but water poured into it.

The wave washed over the ship, and while it was low in the water it had not swamped. The hold was a pond filled with shattered wood and his men were still aboard, though it seemed to him some had vanished. He noted a rope tied to the railing that fluttered in the wind.

Finn huddled against the rail, flopping as the ship violently rocked and rain stung them like tiny arrows. He would have seemed dead but for his tight grip on the amulet of Thor's hammer he wore at his neck. Ulfrik had no care for his. Thor had already decided what he wanted to do to Ulfrik's ships, and no prayer would persuade him otherwise. He felt bad for you his young friend, who was nothing more than a pale face in a gray world of rain. He called out to him, and when Finn finally noticed Ulfrik attempted a smile.

"This storm must soon blow out," he shouted, not knowing if he spoke the truth. "Hold steady a while longer. We will live, I tell you."

Finn smiled and it warmed Ulfrik to see it. He was truly a good man, one of the best to have ever served him.

Ulfrik nodded and crawled back to his place against the gunwale. Another wave slammed the ship and sent him sprawling head first into the deck. He rose again, each time more slowly than the last. He turned again to see his crew, but a wave counter-punched from the opposite side.

A cask launched into the air.

Ulfrik saw it, a smeary shadow careening for him. He scrabbled to his feet, but not soon enough.

The cask smashed into the deck before him, did not break, then bounced into him. It caught him flush in the gut, and like a blow from a giant fist it sent him flying back to the rail.

The small of his back flexed against the wood rail. His arms wind-milled for something to grab.

Then he plunged backward over the side and his leg yanked tight with another excruciating bolt of pain. His head slammed against the strakes of the hull and water splashed into his face. He could not see anything, but hung inverted over the side of the ship, his head dragging in the water.

When the ship rocked, he was plunged beneath the waves. His screams were a gurgle and his eyes burned with salt. He came up just when he feared his breath was out. Again he saw nothing.

Unless the storm did blow out soon, he would die hanging from the side of his ship.

42

Birds. Blue sky. Gentle rocking. A creak of wood.

Ulfrik raised his head and cold water crawled down the back of his neck. His mouth burned with the taste of salt. He was on the deck of his ship. His vision was blurred and cloudy and it did not clear with blinking. It was as if peering through a gap in raw wool. He felt a cooling breeze on his legs and hips, and again raised his head to see his pants had been pulled down to his knees. He began to pull them up, working slowly as every joint in his body fired with pain. The sopping fabric dragged against his flesh, but he shimmied the pants up to his waist. The effort spent him, and he lay facing the sky.

The dots of gulls overhead circled and he heard their faint cries. Land had to be nearby, but he was not certain. Part of him fought to look up and survey the damage and the other part suffered too much pain to move.

"Finn?" His words were feeble and he did not expect an answer. Were he not so exhausted he would have jumped in shock when a hand brushed his shoulder.

Ulfrik flopped his head to the side, and saw Finn lying facedown on the deck. His hair was flattened against his head and watery blood dripped from his nostrils. He smiled at him as if just awakening from a pleasant dream. Ulfrik struggled to his elbows and saw the rope still tied to Finn's leg, only it had been cut.

He remembered being knocked overboard and dunked underwater, but nothing more. Realization flashed and he gave an astonished look to Finn.

"You pulled me back aboard. Alone?" Finn closed his eyes and shook his head. Ulfrik's vision cleared though his eyeballs throbbed with every beat of his heart. Two other men lay unconscious near Finn, both facedown with their clothing torn and plastered to their bodies. All around debris shifted with the rocking of the ship and men sat or lay flat on the deck. Some were awake, staring listlessly into nothing as water dripped from their faces.

"You saved my life," Ulfrik said. Again Finn did nothing but shrug and kept his eyes closed.

Pulling himself up to the rails, he stared out across the flat ocean to the horizon. Faint dots marked ships, though he could not know whether they were his. Broken planking, lost shields, empty barrels, and other debris collected around the hull of his ship. He turned behind and saw a shore of dark pine trees where two other ships were already beached. Staggering across the deck, his legs lighting up with pain, he leaned against the rail, straining to see who waited on shore. Younger eyes might have determined who stood on the beach, but to him they were dots of color moving slowly. Several dots appeared to be waving both hands overhead, and he returned the gesture.

Now he returned to checking on his crew. By count alone he guessed seven men had been lost, which was better than he had expected. The hold was still flooded, meaning all of their armor and weapons would be ruined. His remaining gold, if it had not been thrown overboard, would also be submerged. The ship's boat still remained tied to the rack at the center of the deck, and enough oars survived so the ship could be rowed. The mast and sail were also in good shape. The fat knarr sat lower in the water, but she had survived admirably. He did not want to imagine the fate of his warships, for those smaller, lighter vessels would have fared much worse.

His activity galvanized the surviving crew to begin recovery. Soon men were bailing out the hold while others raised the mast and started work on the rigging. Finn and Ulfrik wordlessly set the steering board back into the water and used a length of broken rail to replace the lost tiller. They pulled together the remnants of their ship, and as the sun climbed to the top of the sky, they began rowing for shore. Another ship had beached farther north, and Ulfrik saw the crew filing down the strand toward the main group.

After pulling their ship ashore, Ulfrik and Finn both joined Gunnar who had come to greet them. He was as bedraggled as every other survivor, and he held Morgan to his side as if a breeze might blow her away. He did not smile as Ulfrik approached.

"Are my grandchildren safe?" Ulfrik asked as he worked through the loose beach sand. Each step was like a knife stab to each of his thighs.

"They are gathering wood for a fire," Gunnar said. "Have you seen Hakon's ship?"

Ulfrik faced the water. The waves lapped daintily at the shore, nothing like their monstrous shapes during the storm. Scattered shadows on the horizon had to be the remnants of his fleet.

"If he's not on the ship that landed to the north, then he must be one of those scattered to the horizon."

Gunnar lowered his head and released Morgan. She wiped a strand of hair from her face and gave Ulfrik a weak smile before leaving. "I don't know where we have landed. I sent men ahead to scout while we waited."

Ulfrik grunted. Broken shields and busted wood rolling onto the shore caught his attention. "The storm and the signs of wreckage will bring plunderers. Any wrecks will be claimed by the local jarls, or if this is Frankia, Hrolf will claim us. How are your weapons? My mail is ruined without careful drying and scrubbing."

"Same for us," Gunnar said. He waved at the ships leaning on the beach. "We had our extra weapons wrapped in sealskin, and those survived with only a touch of water. The rust can be cleaned from those blades, but like you our mail will need care or rust to nothing."

Ulfrik left Gunnar and moved among his people, offering what comfort he could. Men stacked casks of mead on the beach, at least half of which were tainted with sea water. Supply was enough to camp for three or four days, but they would soon be forced to move from the beach. Other men tested the sea-worthiness of their vessels, reviewing the hulls and sails. Two more ships joined them on the shore, bringing the total to seven.

By the late afternoon, Gunnar's scouting party had returned with news they had landed in Contentin where the locals still fell under Frankish rule. They warned off would-be treasure hunters, but Ulfrik still had men alert for danger. The news buoyed his hopes, as the peninsula that formed the bulk of Contentin was not far from his intended landing south of Hrolf's borders. Yet as the day wore on and many of those dots he had hoped were his own ships disappeared over the horizon, his stomach flared with burning anger.

"Of all the ships I returned with, only seven have landed," he said as he stood just out of reach from the lapping waves. He inhaled the crisp sea air, still scenting the rain that had scoured his fleet from the earth. "All either destroyed or scattered by Fate's plans. All my gold, sent to the bottom of the sea."

Finn and Gunnar stood behind him. Hakon was still missing. Finn broke the silence first. "But we are still strong enough to challenge Mord. We must have close to two hundred men, most of them warriors."

"Challenge but not crush," Ulfrik said. He smiled bitterly. "Then there is the matter of getting at Gunther One-Eye. He's the real force behind all of this. Mord is just living his father's dreams. We'll never get to him as long has he hides in Rouen behind Hrolf's throne. And there's the key—Hrolf. He will have to stand beside Mord in any battle."

"But he does not have to fight us," Gunnar corrected. "Unless Mord calls for his aid."

Ulfrik snickered at the comment. "Of course he would call for aid. He has no shame. He hired a killer to stab me in the back. What kind of man does that but a weakling and coward?"

The rolling waves and sounds of the camp filled the silence. A ship was in the middle distance, rowing for the billowing columns of smoke Ulfrik had set to attract his lost ships. He ran his fingers through his tangled, stiff hair. "I have no more than what I left with, and my fortune is spent. Fate has dealt me a harsh blow."

"But your sword is still sharp," Gunnar said. He grabbed his shoulder and spun him around. His son's face was puffy from injuries sustained in the storm, but his dark eyes were alight with ferocity. "Sharp enough to cut a snake in two. So we are no longer the mighty army we had planned to be." Gunnar spit on the ground. "That's what I say to that challenge. We are better than Mord, and our vengeance is righteous. I have made too many mistakes in this life. I will not make the mistake of leaving this chance for revenge. We are where the gods have placed us. So let us use that as we may, and gut that traitorous bastard Mord and his blind father."

Ulfrik hung his head. "I am shamed. You are right. We carry on no matter what the challenge. This defeat has shaken me, but I will not let it rule me. We will camp on this beach until we are sure all our surviving ships find us. After that, we will travel inland and meet the so-called free jarls who challenge Hrolf's rule. If we can ally with them, then we will have the numbers again to challenge Hrolf and avenge ourselves on Mord."

The ship drew closer and Ulfrik turned hopefully to it, both Gunnar and Finn straining to see who commanded.

"It's not Hakon," Finn said, his eyes sharper than the rest.

"He will return," Ulfrik said. "He did not die in the storm."

No one challenged how he could make such an assertion. In truth, Ulfrik did not know, but the statement was the only prayer he knew to offer his son. Not all ships were scattered and seeking a path back to shore. Some had broken apart and sank. He closed his eyes and imagined Hakon and Elke together on their ship, sailing for the signal fires.

He had to believe Hakon was not dead.

43

Four days after landing on the Contentin beaches, Ulfrik had his ships back in the sea. He stood once more in the prow and watched his vastly reduced fleet slip by him as he sailed to the front of the formation. Gunnar and his family stood proudly at the rails of their dark ship, its red striped sail full of an eastward wind that would carry them to their destiny. Of the nearly thirty ships that sailed from Jutland, only ten remained. The others had wrecked or been lost, their crews blown off course or otherwise fleeing the bad luck that hung over their journey.

Hakon and Elke again waved from their ship. They had returned only the day before, and Ulfrik's eyes were wet when he embraced his son on the beach. Even Gunnar wiped the corner of his eye. "And here I thought you dead just when I was starting to like you better," he had told his brother. They had lost most of their crew as well as their mast, making for a long journey. Ulfrik force-fit the mast of another ship that was judged unfit for open sea, and now they were rejoined in their journey home.

"I hope Aren will find us before we attack," Ulfrik said as he took the tiller from Finn. The ship slotted into the front of the others and gulls screamed overhead, racing with the ship as if to see it off.

Finn shrugged. "He is a canny man. I'm sure he has planned something for your return."

He left out the assumption that Ulfrik's message had even been delivered. Aren never sent a return word, nor did the messengers return. Their travels would have been fraught with perils in the best of times, and far worse in today's world. Ulfrik scratched his head and grabbed the tiller.

"He's a smart boy. He'll be ready for us."

"What about your oath to Vilhjalmer?" Finn rotated his shoulders and winced. Everyone still carried their pain from battling the storm.

"What of it? If it is convenient for me to honor it, then I shall. I'm an outlaw already, or have you forgotten? What worse can be done to me?"

They spent a day sailing carefully along the coast. Debris in the water could have been the remains of his ships or of another unlucky vessel. The floating garbage plunked against the hull as Ulfrik sailed through it. Once they came to an estuary, they slipped deeper into the woodlands of the Frankish coastline. The Seine lay further north and here was land ruled by numerous jarls that loosely respected each other but bent a knee to no man. They lived their lives like men of old in a system Ulfrik's father would have recognized. He would never have bent a knee to either the Franks or Hrolf.

Ten ships of fighting men were difficult to hide, and after an afternoon of rowing upriver, the local jarl's men formed up on the riverbank. Only every fifth man wore chain, though all carried shields of various faded colors and patterns. Ulfrik's men outnumbered them, though not by much. He had cut a hazel branch before setting sail and now had a man waving it from the prow of the ship. A lone figure, probably the jarl, dressed in mail and helmet, raised his open palm in acknowledgment. He stood before his men ranked up on a grassy bank, and behind them a forest of mixed pines and deciduous trees formed a black stripe.

"I will take ten men in the ship's boat to speak with their leader," Ulfrik said to Finn. "You will remain aboard and if trouble starts I expect you know what to do."

"I'd like more of a plan than that," he said. Ulfrik supervised his men untying the ship's boat and preparing the short oars. They lowered it over the side and dropped a rope down to it.

"There will be no trouble," Ulfrik said as he climbed down the rope to his waiting men. Gunnar and Hakon had similarly lowered their boats and now rowed for shore. The larger knarrs carried small rowboats, unlike the smaller longships whose main function was to deliver men to the place of battle.

Once ashore, Ulfrik led his group of thirty men up the bank to the waiting jarl. He was a tall man, though still shorter than Ulfrik. His stomach bulged against his mail shirt, but his arms showed firm muscles entwined with gold armbands. A wavy lock of his graying brown hair hung over his left eye; his eyes were large and piercing. Ulfrik raised his hand in peace.

"Hail, I am Ulfrik Ormsson and these are my ships. We mean no threat, though we come dressed for war." Ulfrik smiled at the way the jarl's eyes widened and his men stirred at the mention of his name.

"I am Jarl Oskar Scar-Foot and these are my men." His strong arm swept over his lines of troops. "And we mean to protect our lands."

"As well as you should," Ulfrik said. "You have heard of my name and reputation?"

"You were Hrolf's do—um, second. Your reputation is well known." Oskar gave a weak smile to Ulfrik's raised brow. Calling him a dog would be fitting for how these men thought about serving a high king, but it would still be an insult. Ulfrik realized changing their minds would not be simple.

"So then you know of my banishment?" Oskar nodded and the men lined behind him murmured among themselves. "Well, I have returned with an army at my back and an oath of revenge upon my lips. I need a place to camp my men before we head north to bring war and death to lands that once knew my protection. I would ask such a favor of you."

Oskar's eyes brightened at the mention of war, but he instead stroked his beard as if in careful deliberation. "You bring many men. How can I be certain you won't cause trouble in my land?"

"You have my word upon it. If you wish to exchange hostages, then we should discuss it."

Waving as if he smelled something foul, Oskar said, "No, I have heard rumor that you would return, but never guessed you would come here. I am not prepared to receive so many men, but I will make you and your guests welcomed in my hall tonight. You may find a place to camp, so long as you do not take from any man's property nor harm his home in any way. I must have your word on your good conduct."

"Of course, I give it freely," Ulfrik said. "And I am grateful for your hospitality."

He and Oskar grasped arms and his men relaxed their stances. Smiles went around both groups, and at last Ulfrik was back in country and ready to begin his revenge. Yet he was still not at peace, for Aren should have done more to prepare for his arrival here. He had specifically asked him to travel south to negotiate with the jarls there.

"Tell me, Jarl Oskar, has no one come to you before my arrival today?"

Oskar's wide forehead wrinkled as he raised a brow. "Nothing. You were first spotted entering the river, and the alarm was raised. I mustered every man I could find and rushed here, guessing this would be your best landing."

"It is the best landing," Ulfrik said, sharing a knowing glance with his sons. "I had planned to come to this land long before I set sail. I had sent messengers to warn you. I'm sorry for surprising you as I did."

"The greater the distance the greater the chance a messenger won't arrive," Oskar said. "That's been my experience."

"Well, no matter. I am here now. And I do not wish to be a burden to you, but I have one more favor to ask."

Oskar paused and stared, his big eyes of faded green searching him. "You'll have to provision yourself, if that's your need. There's plenty of men that'll sell to you."

"That is good to know, but not my need. I have something more to ask, something that would be of great interest to you and your fellow jarls in these so-called free steadings."

"Ah, so you want to strengthen your shield wall with more warriors."

"I want revenge, Jarl Oskar. I'm not as driven by gold as I used to be. I have found it does not keep me warm at night. The men I will make war upon will have much gold, and I should be glad to share it if men would fight beside me. For my part, I want to kill the men who ruined my name and murdered my wife."

Oskar's smile widened. "Let's talk about it in the hall. You might have my interest."

"I will need more than your interest alone, as welcomed as it is. I will not just take war to my old lands, but to the walls of Rouen itself. I need all the jarls to bring their spears and shields to this battle. I plan to tear down what I helped build and drown the land in blood. That is what I intend, Jarl Oskar."

The smile fled Oskar and he nodded. Ulfrik's plans would frighten even the mightiest jarls, for even the king of Western Frankia had not dared fight Hrolf. But Ulfrik did not dream revenge in small denominations. If revenge had become his life, then it would be the grandest revenge he could imagine. He only needed the aid of glory-hungering men to make it reality. Oskar Scar-Foot and men like him were not much different from the Hedeby raiders he had lost to the storm.

"Then we will have to gather the jarls and see how you might persuade them to your cause." Oskar pointed to the ships still in the water.

They returned to their ships with the good news. When Finn asked about Aren, Ulfrik shook his head and said nothing. He feared his son was lost.

44

Oskar Scar-Foot's hall was a meager building full of darkness and stinking of stale beer, smoke, and sweat. Six jarls and their closest hirdmen packed the hall, turning a chilly evening into a swelter. The light from the hearth embers throbbed as if gasping for breath. Ulfrik certainly felt as if he was, sitting at Oskar's right hand at his head table. He had no stage to raise himself above his men. The hall was not large enough for it.

His wife served both of them as a sign of respect, and slaves tended the rest of the guests. Oskar's wife would have been a beautiful woman but for a wall-eye that made holding her gaze dizzying to Ulfrik. He simply held out his mug for a refill of the poor drink that accompanied the tasteless meal of venison and boiled onions. Down the table Ulfrik saw Finn chatting with Oskar's eldest daughter, who had neither her mother's bad eye nor her otherwise good looks. She was Oskar in the body of a young woman. Despite her unfortunate manliness, beside Finn she had two other men competing for her attentions. Finn was emphasizing the gold armband Ulfrik had taken from his own arm and awarded Finn for saving his life. He had done the same for the other two men who had helped him. His own arm was lighter for it, but such dedication was never to be ignored.

"That gold has my daughter's eye," Oskar said, his breath a reeking blast on the side of Ulfrik's face.

"It was well deserved," Ulfrik said. "I would give a dozen such rings for one more man like Finn."

Oskar stared at him, his large eyes now red with drink. "You have that much gold?"

Ulfrik laughed, but Oskar continued to stare at him, expecting an answer. "I have lost much of it to this disaster my enemies have visited upon me. But were it only a matter of gold to find good men, then I should do all I could to gather it. Gold buys a sword for a short time, but not a man willing to risk his own life for the gold-giver. Finn and two more of my men were so willing, and have followed me through every hardship and shame a man can endure. Gold is a poor payment for such loyalty, but it is all that I may give with my hands. The rest must be repaid with my heart."

The circle around him had stilled at his words, and Ulfrik woke to the other men staring at him with admiration. Oskar slapped his palm on the table. "Now those are the words of a noble man! I drink to that!"

Mugs were raised all around and they toasted Ulfrik. He suddenly wished his sons were at his side to witness the small moment of glory. However, the ships and their valuables required guards and both sons had women to entertain them. So he raised his mug and toasted all the good and loyal men in the world, which to his mind could be counted on his hands.

"The night grows ever shorter, and we grow ever drunker," Ulfrik said. "It is time we discuss what we have gathered to hear."

The men close by growled their approval, but outside the circle, hirdmen continued to drink, share news, and boast as men from different lands often did when brought together under a peaceful roof. It took Oskar's standing on the bench and shouting for silence from his fellow jarls. When the hall settled into a low murmur and all eyes turned toward him, he finally addressed his audience.

"You've had enough of my hospitality tonight. Time you pay for your meals with some attention." Light laughter rippled up and

Ulfrik smiled. In truth, Oskar was not a wealthy man and his insistence on holding the feast was likely beyond his means. Ulfrik regretted his disparaging thoughts of the meal Oskar had provided.

"We all know the reputation of Ulfrik Ormsson," Oskar said. "If you're like me, then you've cursed his name and called him Hrolf's dog." More laughter followed and Ulfrik smiled placidly, understanding too well how these men felt about him. "And if you're like me, you're glad he never turned his fangs on you. If anyone has delivered Hrolf his kingdom, then it is Ulfrik Ormsson."

The laughter grew louder, a note of tension in it. Ulfrik surveyed the faces of the audience. Most were grim and weathered by years under the sun and scarred with marks of battle. None of them were rich faces. Gold and jewels did not sparkle in the low light, as they would have in a gathering for Hrolf's men. These were hard-bitten fighters who scratched their lives out from the land one sword-stroke at a time and received little more than blood and dust for it.

Oskar continued his speech, wobbling on the bench as he gestured to his audience. "News of Ulfrik's fall was a shock, but also expected when an ungrateful and uncaring bastard like Hrolf the Strider sets himself above all others. No one is safe from a man like that, even his greatest warrior. Never shall I kneel to him, nor any man who calls himself his servant. Today Ulfrik has returned, not sworn to any man, and he has a request of us. For my part, I have heard what he asks and I like it. You will like it as well, my brothers."

Oskar unceremoniously stepped off the bench before he fell from it. Heads turned to Ulfrik and so he stepped on the bench and spent a full minute looking over the men. The silence made many shift or look away. Those were the men he had to convince. Others held his gaze and were ready to hear the call to blood.

"I have been betrayed. Mord Guntherson, who Oskar tells me is now sitting in my old hall, sent a man to kill me. A poisoned blade." The audience hissed at the shameful deed. "I killed the man, but not before his blade cut my wife. Even from a cur like Mord, I'd have not expected poison, and my wife died in my arms before I realized what had happened. But the treachery is not with Mord alone. Gunther One-Eye plotted to steal my land. Hrolf the Strider was cowed by Christian priests. All these men deserve my vengeance."

The audience shouted approval and banged the tables with their fists. Not every man was so enthusiastic, but as Ulfrik waited for them to subside he noted which men still appeared reluctant. "I will not tire you with my woes. I have returned to kill Mord and Gunther for their treachery, and to tear out a bloody hunk of flesh from Hrolf's side. They are all war-weary men sitting in halls built atop their piles of gold. Hrolf cowers behind the walls of Rouen, too afraid to offend his new masters with a misstep. Gunther is bitter and blind, counting his riches in darkness. Mord is a spoiled fool who cannot hold his lands without a strong hand to protect him. There is much to take from these men, and I know how. For years I was close to them. I know their weaknesses. Join me in battle and we will take all of it. With all of our gathered strength, we could burn a path to the walls of Rouen itself. Hrolf would pay anything to have us leave, rather than embarrass himself before his new king. Think of the riches awaiting you."

More shouting and stamping feet filled the pause. Ulfrik saw a pinch-faced man frown and around the cramped hall at least two other men did the same. When the crowd settled Ulfrik left a gap for these men to speak and was not disappointed when the pinch-faced man shouted over his peers.

"We've all heard this before. Doesn't anyone remember Thor Gundarason? Where's he now?"

"Thor was a braggart and barely a man," Oskar said. "And he didn't have the numbers he needed to succeed. The fool earned his death."

Ulfrik had never heard of Thor, but did know the southern jarls had just as often attacked other Norsemen as well as their usual Frankish enemies. Hrolf and his jarls had put down a number of these raiding parties over the years.

"Still, it is the same promise of gold and land," the pinch-faced man continued. "But the gods have settled Hrolf and his dogs into their holes and now with a castle to shield him he will never be expelled."

"We're not talking about expelling him, Alvis." Oskar now stood beside Ulfrik on the bench. "And we're not talking about Thor Gundarason. We have Hrolf's greatest warlord to show us how to win. Thor was a boy, but Ulfrik is a man the skalds sing of in their tales of bravery. None of us have done the deeds he has, and none of us know Hrolf and his dogs as Ulfrik does. This is our chance for glory."

"It's too late in the year to be raiding," said the pinch-faced man, Alvis. "We should be preparing them for winter. It's going to be a tough one. I just know it."

Oskar waved Alvis's fears away like a buzzing fly. "You find one excuse after the next. You've no heart for this, so do not poison the thoughts of others."

"Let all men air their doubts," Ulfrik said. Oskar turned with his mouth open, but Ulfrik raised his hand for peace. "While I am certain of victory, men will be maimed and men will die. Let no one join me who is not willing to face those risks."

"We are not cowards," Alvis shouted and the two other doubting men grumbled in support.

"I would not call you a coward. You are all jarls, and your decisions affect the lives of those sworn to you. I have nothing but respect for a man who so carefully considers his duty to his people."

Alvis and his fellow protesters appeared mollified, and Oskar's open mouth closed. Ulfrik saw Finn smiling at him with Oskar's daughter leaning on his shoulder. He had to look away lest he laugh during this grave moment. Finn's bright red face and drunken smile brought a lift to his spirits.

"Now let's speak of those who will dare to plunder Hrolf and his dogs. You will all take a jarl's share and portion this to your men as you see fit. For my part, I desire only blood. I take only what I owe my men, the same as yours, and leave my share to add to your own. I ask only that you leave Mord, Gunther, and Hrolf for me and my sons. Who then will dip his hand into the treasure piles of Normandy?"

The hall reverberated with excited shouts as the men stood in answer. Oskar beamed proudly and Ulfrik smiled. Only Alvis and one of the two protesters remained sullen and seated. Ulfrik had reformed his army, however loose it would prove to be. He spoke so softly that no one but himself could hear.

"Your last wish will soon come to pass, dear Runa. A storm of blood and death awaits our enemies."

45

An army of nearly six hundred warriors marched north with Ulfrik and his sons at the fore. The land hushed as they trampled the small tracks wending through forests or along streams. The sun hid itself behind clouds and the wind refused to blow. The gods themselves seemed to hold their breaths as Ulfrik led his marauders to his old lands.

He now stopped the march, his scouts gone with Finn to lead them in assaying the resistance Mord had prepared. When Ulfrik built this hall he had not prepared defenses against the Franks and had not looked south for danger. Oskar and all the other petty jarls never united for anything, and even now they bickered about the right approach. However, experience had taught him caution.

"What are we waiting for?" asked one of the jarls, named Thorstein. He was a burly man with cheeks so red he looked like he had been slapped. His complexion matched his temperament, though men called him Apple Cheeks behind his back. Ulfrik had become so accustomed to that name he had to bite it back when he answered.

"We must be certain of our attack," Ulfrik said. "We do not charge the hall only discover Mord is gone or has dug a ditch or worse. We scout first, then attack."

"There are five of us for every one of their warriors," Thorstein said. "If he dug a ditch, we'll walk over the backs of the fallen and get him. Let's move now."

"Don't be hasty, Ap—Jarl Thorstein. You have trusted me thus far. Trust me a while longer."

Apple Cheeks stared at him before stomping off, waving his hand over his head and protesting to the air. Gunnar and Hakon both laughed after he was gone.

"These men are all about running in and dying," Hakon said. "But he does have a point. We should outnumber Mord, even if he has raised more men since we left. He can't have summoned all his bondi, and the hirdmen will be at their barracks or elsewhere. This should be an easy victory."

"Has it been easy so far?" Gunnar asked, and Ulfrik slapped his son's shoulder in agreement.

"Exactly, this is too easy. We're a quick march from the old hall. We will have to cross the fields I cleared, but then we will be upon the hall and presenting Mord's head to his wife."

"What are we going to do to his wife?" Hakon asked. "Should we kill her too?"

"Why not? It would be fitting," Gunnar said. "We should take turns with her and have Mord watch."

"None of that," Ulfrik said. "We will ransom her back to her family. I know what Mord did to your mother, and she would be the first one to cut off Mord's balls and feed them to him. But she'd not forgive the rape and murder of his wife."

"That's not what I remember about Mother," Gunnar said, sniffing.

"Runa the Bloody, I know the name. And I know she regretted it in her later years. I will respect her memory."

The silence grew between them and Gunnar drifted to find his own crew. Each jarl had taken fifty men, leaving only a token force at home. That made the bulk of Ulfrik's troops independent of his command, though the jarls had thus far been compliant with his battle plans. Though the men were hardened and experienced, they were better suited to raiding than military action. Ulfrik winced at the noise they made, drinking and boasting to prepare themselves for battle when they should have been silently awaiting the scouts' reports. Ulfrik smelled the faint notes of sweet hearth smoke in the air. Revenge was but a short run's distance, but he had to be certain.

Finn returned, appearing out of the woods into the flat light of the clearing where Ulfrik and his army idled. Behind him other scouts returned and headed for their own leaders. Ulfrik waved Finn closer. His freckle-faced companion still had the hood of his green cloak pulled overhead.

"They are alert and prepared for us," Finn said before he had finished crossing to Ulfrik. "The surrounding farms are cleared and both hirdmen and his levies have formed up behind the hall. They know the direction of our approach, since they are screening themselves from our view."

"How did he know?" Hakon asked.

"I couldn't get close enough to the hall to ask him," Finn said, finally pulling back his hood. "But he's known long enough to summon his levies."

Ulfrik brooded, rubbing the back of his neck as he considered how to divide his forces for the attack. "We still have more men than he does, unless he has sent to Hrolf for aid. I could send a flanking force to meet with the main body when we attack. It was always my concern with fighting in that field. The northeastern woods were thick and I did not see the need to clear it, even though it gave good cover to an enemy. That should be our approach."

"Father," Hakon said, grabbing Ulfrik's shoulder. "You had better share your plans now."

Half of all the assembled troops were running through the trees and heading north for the hall. Ulfrik sprang to his feet and began shouting at them. "Apple Cheeks, you stupid whoreson! Get your men back into line."

Yet not only did Apple Cheeks ignore him, but scores of other men drowned him out as they began screaming their battle cries. Ulfrik stood dumbfounded, with only his own men and those of Jarl Oskar awaiting his orders.

"All right," he said, then turned to his warriors. "Mord is ready for us. These fools will charge him head-on, but we will swing around the northeast and hit them in the flank. We take no prisoners and have no mercy on these dogs. Now follow me!"

Hakon and Gunnar passed the command onto their men and Finn joined Ulfrik at his side, now carrying his standard of black elk antlers on a green field. "We have to act fast or our numbers advantage will mean nothing. Mord will take us apart one half at a time."

"I understand that," Ulfrik said. He began jogging toward the trees and his men followed. "I cannot get us as wide as I had planned. I wanted to coordinate the charges, but now we make do with this."

They crashed through the woods, no care to mask their approach. Birds rushed into the air as they passed, and branches snapped as they charged toward their positions. The scream and clash of battle already washed over the woods. Ulfrik doubled his pace until they exited on the eastern flank of the battle behind his own men.

He did not see any standard flying nor any sign of Mord's command. Only a long strip of warriors clashed in the field outside the hall, two lines of mostly unarmored men shoving at each other with shields and spears. A dozen problems revealed themselves to Ulfrik's expert eye. The worst issue being these lightly armored men were not the anvil to his hammer. They were not large enough nor strong enough for Ulfrik's heavy troops to drive the enemy against. They would simply break apart into an open melee, and that would be the end of the battle.

"We have to charge from here," Ulfrik said flatly. "I don't see Mord's standard anywhere. He's not even here."

"Or doesn't want you to find him in battle," Finn said.

Ulfrik grabbed his horn and sounded the charge. His men knew enough to form ranks behind him as Ulfrik charged toward the clashing warriors. As he pounded across the hard ground, grass whipping his feet, he scanned for signs of reinforcements. Nothing before them indicated Mord had prepared more than this token force. He did not expect great battle tactics from Mord, but this was a poor strategy even for him. Ulfrik's legs continued to pump as he crossed the cleared fields, each footfall sending shockwaves through his knees. His face grew hot and his shield arm tingled in anticipation of the clash.

Then the sound of thunder.

He looked over his right shoulder, across the front of his line, as from behind the woods warriors on horseback charged. Their mail and conical helmets gleamed in the flat light. They wore surcoats covered in squares of blue and white or yellow. Hungry spears lowered as the horses pounded out from hiding.

"Cavalry!" he shouted. Franks on horseback were a mighty force when used correctly. In Ulfrik's long experience, the Franks misused their mounted troops in most fights. But today their timing was perfect.

Heads whipped around toward the thundering beat of the horsemen. On foot, the distance would be great enough to allow Ulfrik time to face a new enemy, but charging horses were already halfway to his position before all his men understood the threat.

"Shield wall! Spears!" Ulfrik ran toward the charging cavalry. Finn planted his banner and touched his shield to Ulfrik's. Men lined up with them, huddling together like children in a storm. No matter how well trained the horse or how bloodthirsty his rider, no animal would crash itself into a shield wall.

The first riders broke around them like a wave over a boulder. The snorts of the beasts and beating of their hooves were louder than a clashing shield wall. He could smell their musky scent as the wide-eyed animals flowed around them. Typical of the Franks, they hesitated to throw their spears and so repeated mistakes Ulfrik had expected.

The riders circled them, scores of horses with their colorful riders wheeling around them as if playing a children's game. Their banners cracked with their whipping speed. They waited for Ulfrik's men to break formation and give in to the temptation of an easy target. Then the riders would push into the gap and crack their shell as easily as crushing a snail underfoot.

"Tighter! Close the gaps," Ulfrik shouted, and the men obeyed. He smelled sweat and urine as he backed into the shadows of his shield wall. He only needed one horse to fall. "Give me a spear."

The smooth weight of it in his hand was comforting. The hoofbeats were like thunder. The whirling blur of brown, blue, and yellow dizzied him. He waited then thrust the spear low into the gut of a passing horse. The beast screamed and it stumbled. The other riders had anticipated this and their circle disbanded as quickly as it had formed.

The cavalry was not as interested in attacking them as it was in herding them. In the instant the horsemen galloped away to prepare a second charge, Ulfrik saw Apple Cheeks leading the flight away from Mord's levies.

"Run for the trees!" Ulfrik screamed, and the men needed no encouragement. In three heartbeats, his hundreds of men were fleeing for the safety of the tree line.

Mord's archers flooded out of the hall; at least thirty men shot arrows into Apple Cheeks's men. An arrow landed at Ulfrik's feet as he ran. He was not sure where it had even originated.

The screams of routing men was a horrible note in the song of battle. Ulfrik saw the tidemark of bodies left beside the hall. He saw men stumble with shafts quivering in their backs. He heard the rolling thunder behind him, and as the trees drew closer, he heard his own men's dying curses as they were run down.

He crashed into the underbrush. A quick survey revealed Gunnar and Hakon had likewise gained the safety of the trees, and Finn was close at his side. His banner dragged behind Finn, and the sight of that disgrace filled him with rage. He snatched it from Finn, nearly knocking his friend to the ground.

"What kind of scouting did you do?"

Finn's face was white with shock, and he had no answer. Ulfrik pulled his banner from its pole and continued to flee with his men. The Franks and Mord's warriors pursued them, their whooping victory cries echoing through the trees. Ulfrik's forces scattered, and soon he was fleeing with only a handful of his own men. He had not only been defeated, he had been broken. Broken like a piece of kindling to be thrown on the hearth fire. His hopes for revenge burned up just as fast.

46

Ulfrik awoke on the deck of his ship, a dream of clashing swords and dying men skittering away into the blackness of memory. He sat up with a start, and his cloak fell from his chest. He grabbed the sheathed sword lying beside him. As the sleep drained from his head, he realized the heavy weight was his mail shirt. He had not bothered to remove it before he had collapsed in exhausted sleep.

Struggling to his feet, the remainder of his crew was sprawled out on the deck, either in their sleeping sacks or using cloaks for blankets. The size of the crew had diminished once again. He had not counted his losses from the rout of the prior day. The survivors were uninjured for the most part. Men had either escaped or fallen behind to be run down by the rapacious enemy. As he buckled his own sword to his side, he realized he had not struck a single blow with it yesterday.

The sweet chirping of birds greeted him and the morning breeze was chill. A faint orange glow announced a new day, and Ulfrik rubbed his face as he surveyed the rest of his ships. They lined up on the riverbank, ready to launch into the water should another ignominious retreat be required. The scent of a cooking fire wafted from

Oskar's hall. It was a placid scene of a quaint hall with white smoke curling overhead while chickens wandered about it, pecking at the dirt. A rooster crowed in the distance. If Ulfrik did not know that scores of demoralized men had flooded this hall the night before, he would have smiled at this vision of the good life.

But his fists balled and he struck the rail of his ship. Mord had discovered his plans and laid a trap. He had enlisted aid from the Franks, not Hrolf as Ulfrik had expected. That was the worst insult of the entire disaster: a former ally using Ulfrik's former enemies against him. He bit the back of his hand thinking of it. Worse still, he had lost the jarls as easily as he had gained them. They had scattered, and survivors would find their way home, but they would never stand with Ulfrik again. He hung his head in frustration and defeat. He had nothing left to challenge Mord, and he had a handful of gold left from the sale of his treasures. Dreams of revenge were finished.

"Jarl Ulfrik," said a voice from the shore. "Four men are here to see you."

Ulfrik squinted up the banks to where two of the guards on watch stood with four men. At the middle was a wide-faced man smiling to display a broken front tooth.

"Aren!" Ulfrik shouted as he leapt from the rails. He scrabbled artlessly up the banks, heedless of decorum. He had shamed himself so deeply by now that stumbling in the dirt was nothing. They joined together in a long hug, and Ulfrik clapped his son's back while feeling heat welling in his eyes. "I thought you dead, lad. I'm so happy to see you."

They pulled apart, and Aren matched his smile. "You can thank Einar and the good work of these three men. I would not have lived this long without their help."

Ulfrik recognized the three men with him, and he gave each a solemn nod. "You have my thanks and gratitude. I will reward your loyalty, though right now the camp is in a mess. Please forgive it."

The lead man, Gils, inclined his head as he spoke. "Aren is a fine warrior, and I have learned much from traveling with him. That is reward enough for me."

"So you were with Einar? What has happened? Where is he?"

Aren's smile fled and left no trace of happiness lingering. "It has been a long and treacherous summer, Father. I have been busy making plans, and from the disaster you experienced yesterday, I see not all of them succeeded. You had no warning of Mord's preparations?"

Ulfrik shook his head. "I believed we were surprising him. Did my messengers reach you?"

"They did, but they did not return to you with messages of my own. Wake my brothers and let us share news. I have much to tell."

By the time Oskar's women were serving a breakfast of boiled eggs and cheese in the hall, Ulfrik had assembled all his sons and hirdmen. Both Gunnar and Hakon delighted in Aren's return. The news of Runa's death had somehow reached Aren already, and so spared Ulfrik the pain of describing the details. Aren had only been gone eight months, but he appeared a different man. He stood straighter, spoke with more confidence, and even smiled more frequently. As they sat at the table with Jarl Oskar, Ulfrik marveled at Aren's stories of escape and survival. It was not the contents of the stories, but the manner of their delivery. Aren had dropped his youthful shyness and now wore the mantle of confidence owned by true rulers. His youngest son had grown up at last.

After Ulfrik had described all his trials since fleeing to Hedeby and returning to defeat at Mord's hands, he returned to Aren. "So now you must tell me all that happened in Einar's hall, and why he is not with you today?"

"For one, we are all still outlaws," Aren said, spreading his hands in a gesture that reminded Ulfrik of himself. "He cannot be seen to aid us or else force Hrolf to take action against him. But even so, Mord and Gunther One-Eye have been matching wits with me all year long. In the battle over Einar's help, they have gained an upper hand. They've managed to get him recalled to Rouen and then sent on a strange hunt for so-called raiders in the north. The order came to him not from Hrolf, but from Gunther One-Eye with Hrolf's authority. Hrolf seems to issue many orders through Gunther, which I suspect might not all be true. It makes the game more difficult to manage."

"You've twice called this a game," Gunnar said. "But it is a battle to the death. Those goat-fuckers will both die."

Aren nodded with a look of patience. Ulfrik covered his smile by drinking his ale, the flat bitter taste erasing it from him. Setting the mug down, he answered Gunnar. "Your brother is fighting the battle that I so carelessly lost. It is a game of power gained not through might of arms but strength of mind. That is where you and I both failed, but Aren is best among us for such a challenge."

Expecting Gunnar to bridle as if insulted, Ulfrik was again surprised that Gunnar instead gave a sheepish smile. "I've shown I'm only good at knocking all the game pieces from the board. Go on, Brother, and pardon my foolishness."

"After we killed the messengers and returned to Mord's hall, I discovered that one of Einar's hirdmen had been turned against him. He maintained his ruse well, since Einar claimed the man had served him for years. Yet I could read the falseness in his actions, and I spied upon him sending secret words to new men who came in darkness to hear them."

"Who was it?" Hakon asked. "I might have known him from when I lived in Eyrafell."

"Gyrn Hagenson," Aren answered, and Hakon sat back with a frown. "He was a sly man, and Einar wanted to kill him before he killed me. I gambled that the wisest move Mord could make would be to continue to spy. So we acted as we normally did when Gyrn was around, and even when he was not. Only in secret did Einar and I plan for the future. News of Mother's death reached me not long before your messengers did. It was a hard time, but I turned my mind to planning. Einar journeyed to Mord's hall to collect Snorri's body for a proper burial. He took time to investigate what changes he made and the will of the people there. Best of all, we decided that I should befriend Gyrn, and so during Einar's absence he was assigned to protect me. We made him swear loyalty to the secret, and convinced him that we took a great chance with his confidence."

Ulfrik laughed and clapped his hand. "And so you drew your enemy out of the darkness and into the light, right beside you. That was a brilliant plan."

Aren smiled placidly, then continued. "I was never in fear, for Gils and my bodyguards were always near. The one gap in my plan was that Gyrn's protection was not needed, but he did not seem to realize this. He was all too happy to become my confidant. I told him of all the horrible things you would do to Mord. I made him believe in my helplessness, my weakness. I confirmed whatever low opinion he had of me. I know I am regarded as a weakling, but I am one no longer. The death of my mother and the ruin of my family has beat that out of me."

Both Hakon and Gunnar slapped the table in encouragement, and Aren again paused to incline his head. He blushed slightly, but continued in the same confident tone. "Once Einar returned and your messengers received, we set about planning according to your instructions. We made certain Gyrn saw everything he expected, and even let him discover things on his own. We were careful not to make it easy for him to pass his news to Mord, lest he realize how we used him. I sent your two messengers back with one message for Gyrn to hear and one true message for you. Their failure to reach you led to the disaster yesterday. I gambled too much on one task, and the gods repaid my folly with your blood. I am sorry for it."

"You did the right thing, but Fate was not on our side," Ulfrik said, waving his hand to dismiss the blame. "What was the message, though by now I can guess it."

"That we were deceiving Mord and he would be prepared for your attack and the direction of it, and that we were finding other help for you. I expected you would figure out the rest of your part in that ruse, to make a halfhearted attack that did not betray your foreknowledge. A message traveling so far had to be kept simple."

"If I hadn't been stricken by a storm nor cursed with foolish allies, I would not have needed such aid. How did you know to prepare help?" Ulfrik saw Oskar wince at his comment, but he gave his host an apologetic smile.

"I did not know you would meet such disasters. But when Einar was in Mord's land collecting Snorri's corpse, he did his own spying. He learned Mord's wife was using her family's connections to secure Men-at-Arms to aid him against your expected attack. He no more believed you were raising an army to invade another country than he believes the sun will rise in the west. If you had brought such a large army, it would force Hrolf to take action, and by engaging Mord's Frankish allies you would have drawn in King Charles the Simple as well." Aren leaned across the table. "You would have a much larger battle to fight than you had planned. You would need more allies no matter what size army returned with you."

Ulfrik sat back on the bench, rubbing his chin. He had expected to provoke Hrolf just by announcing his return, but had not expected the Franks to involve themselves. From the expressions on both Gunnar's and Hakon's faces, he surmised they had also never considered it. A battle among their own people had never involved outsiders. "I guess now Hrolf and his jarls are part of Frankia. To strike at them is to strike at the kingdom. Yet, I would not expect Mord to have such strong ties. He had at least fifty horsemen at his command."

"I don't know how he arranged it, or what he traded for it. I would not expect Mord to retain their services after he had sprung his trap. Such a large number of horses and their riders would drain his supplies."

"But we are so weak now, he no longer needs aid," Ulfrik said. "If he strikes at us today, that battle will be a near thing, and I'm not sure who would prevail."

"You will," Aren said with a smile. "The aid I planned for you is in place and ready to strike."

"Are you going to keep it a mystery?" Hakon asked, grinning.

"Though Einar has been sent north on a fool's errand, he never intended to heed the command. He went to gather his son-in-law's men. I have been busy all summer securing old allies. You will recognize the names. Ull the Strong, Ragnar Hard-Striker, Hafgrim Herjolfsson, all men who have fought alongside you down through the years. Seeing what happened to you and hearing of Mord and Gunther's treacheries brought them to our side. They are not happy with how Hrolf has given power only to a few of his men. They see what happened to you to be their fates as well."

"Those are powerful names," Ulfrik said. "They have fought long and hard to earn their lands. They risk much joining in my vengeance."

"They know unless Mord and Gunther are stopped, then they too will become victims. Hrolf must also learn to govern his best men with greater wisdom. He may be tied to the Church and the Frankish king, but he must never betray the men who helped him to his throne."

"And what of Gyrn?" Ulfrik asked. "How have you kept this from him?"

"We met in secret the night before my plans launched," Aren said, his hand balling into a tight fist. "Told him he had fulfilled his purpose, then cut his throat ear to ear. Gils helped me dispose of the body and it will never be found."

Ulfrik realized his mouth had dropped open. "You are a changed man after all."

"We must act fast, for soon Gyrn will miss his next report and Mord and Gunther will realize what happened."

The hall grew silent and Ulfrik retreated into thought. His sons and hirdmen looked to him, but his mind was already turning over new plans. He now had a formidable army led by men he had already trusted with his life too many times to count. He could not ask these men to destroy their futures to aid his revenge, but he could not insult them by sending them away.

"What are the details of these men? How many and where are they now?"

Aren placed his mug at the center of the table, then he gathered other mugs and arranged them around it. "This is Mord's hall, and your old friends have camped in these three places, all to the northeast. They've left a corridor open here for the Franks to return home without running into them. Einar will gather his own men after collecting his son-in-law's, then they will move to the Seine and keep a path open for you to cross. Altogether, the jarls have three hundred men and Einar will add another two hundred. With what remains of your army, you will have seven to eight hundred warriors, enough to crush Mord and threaten Hrolf."

Ulfrik closed his eyes and imagined the forces at his disposal. He heard the men around him murmur with hopeful voices. Such numbers were a true army capable of handling Mord and forcing concessions from Hrolf. Yet they would all have to return home after the battles, and he would have no lasting surety of anything he extracted from Hrolf. Nor was the size of his army a true threat to Rouen. He had to take his revenge and then assure himself Hrolf would not move against him.

The plan emerged out of the darkness of his mind, and he knew it was his best choice. It had bounced around his thoughts throughout the summer, half-formed and vague, but now all the parts fit into place. He opened his eyes and slapped the table. "I know what to do!"

"Kill Mord and send his head to Hrolf?" Gunnar asked, drawing chuckles from the others.

"Mord will die, make no mistake, but Aren has given me enough leverage so that I can have more than revenge." He let the words quiet the hall, and he regarded them all with a sly smile. "It will take all of you, and others too. But when I am done, both Mord and Gunther will be dead and Hrolf will have nothing to say for it. He will be at my mercy."

Faces shifted from interested to astonished. Even Aren blinked at his father. "We have a strong core force, but not enough to topple Hrolf."

"We don't need to topple him." Ulfrik stood up and rearranged the mugs Aren had laid out. "Gunnar and Oskar, you join with Ull, Ragnar, and Hafgrim. They attack this way." Ulfrik shifted mugs to indicate the direction of attack. "You attack this way, and crush Mord between you. Make his death miserable, for I will not be there to do it myself. Hakon, you will take my men and meet Einar at the Seine crossing. Your task will be to draw Hrolf to battle. Demand Hrolf meet you and burn every farm and church you find until he answers. You will not fight him, nor will he fight you. I will tell you what to say during the parley before battle and it will stop the fight if Hrolf has any sense."

The men in the hall stared at him as if he had gone mad. Perhaps he had, but his heart felt light and beat with new purpose.

"Where will you be?" Gunnar asked.

"Finn and Aren, you will come with me. I will need help from Elke and Brandr, but that is all. We go to kill Gunther One-Eye and win peace between us and Hrolf."

No one spoke, until Finn cleared his throat and grabbed his mug back from the center of the table. "Well, let's drink to success."

Ulfrik roared laughter and the other followed, everyone grabbing a mug and raising it high.

No more setbacks, Ulfrik thought to himself. I either win all or I die.

47

Gunnar did not like Jarl Oskar. He decided this the moment his father left on his mysterious quest to avenge himself on Gunther One-Eye. Jarl Oskar sprung up like a weasel from its den, seeking easy prey. As they retraced the disastrous path of the prior attack, they found the detritus of battle: broken shields, abandoned weapons, snapped branches and rusty stains. Oskar marched his men right over these as if the warning contained within this wreckage had no bearing on him.

"Didn't he learn anything from the last attack?" Gunnar asked Bekan, his standard bearer and second in command. "Why do these southern jarls believe the approach to every battle is a charge?"

"They're simple-minded," Bekan said. "And they only raid Frankish farms or each other's flocks. Doesn't take much planning to do that."

"He won't listen to me. Look at him striding into the woods like there couldn't possibly be sentries watching for us."

Bekan shrugged and Gunnar grumbled. He had his men at his back, which were half the number of Oskar's. By numbers alone Oskar was the dominant force, and he was excited for Ulfrik's plans and the promise of help from legendary jarls like Ull the Strong and

Hafgrim Hard-Striker. They had relied on Aren's man, Gils, to send word ahead to these jarls, but they could not be certain of the timing. If they struck too early, they could be broken again.

The afternoon sun filtered between the trees, setting the forest alight in a patchwork of yellow and green. Birds rushed to higher branches or took to the sky, crying out as they flew. It would be a sign to both Mord and the other jarls of their approach, and was another reason for Oskar to slow down. Gunnar inhaled, smelling the earthy scent of rotting underbrush and pine, but he missed a key odor.

"No hearth smoke on the breeze," he said to Bekan, who also sniffed.

"The wind is not strong enough to blow it so far."

"No," Gunnar disagreed. "We are not far. Look around you, and see the signs of our flight and enemy pursuit strongest here." He picked up a broken limb with a patch of torn blue cloth hanging from it. "We had not scattered yet, and so we are close to the clearing. Oskar will reach it first. If there is no hearth smoke, they are waiting for us. They should be readying cooking fires for the evening meal."

Pulling up short, Gunnar decided Oskar should march wholeheartedly to his death. The big-eyed jarl cut an imposing figure, dressed in his mail coat and brandishing his flashing sword. His graying hair flowed out from beneath his helmet to lift in the breeze. He disappeared from view as he entered the clearing.

"It is shameful to cower in the rear while Oskar charges toward glory." Bekan's words were flat to Gunnar's ears. He studied the scene before him.

"There is a difference between fool-hardiness and glory, and our friend Oskar cannot find it." He tugged the strap tighter on his arm, drawing his custom shield firmly onto the stump of his right hand. He then pulled his ax from his belt and jumped the handle in his hand, warming his grip to it. Without his shield and ax, he was a handicapped man unable to defend himself, but with them he was a force of destruction. Unlike any other shield, his was rimmed with iron instead of leather. His ax was for hooking and holding his enemies, and he used his shield to bludgeon his foes to the ground where they readily died. It was heavier than any shield and in a long fight grew wearisome to bear, especially if it caught enemy arrows. But right now it was light on his arm.

The sounds of blaring horns echoed, and across the distance others matched. Gunnar's heart leapt at the far off note. "The others are here. Let's go!"

He jumped through the rough ground, avoiding the roots and rocks that had tripped him in retreat the last time he was at this battlefield. He emerged from the woods to find Mord's warriors lined up beside the hall in a long shieldwall. Oskar's men had not yet charged it, being outnumbered still.

At the center of the line, unlike last time, was a standard of a wolf's head with bloody fangs. Mord would fight beneath that standard, and Oskar was already blocking Gunnar's path to it.

"Charge!" Gunnar shouted to Oskar's men, yet they remained at a distance and taunted their enemy. Both sides had flung spears already evidenced by the crisscross of shafts in the space between them. Yet they did not budge.

"Mord's life belongs to me," Gunnar shouted. "Now let's get this fight started."

Nearly eighty warriors at Gunnar's back roared battle cries and charged. Again in the distance he heard horns blaring but did not see his allies emerging across the field. Mord's line stepped back as Gunnar charged, normally a weak action to take when faced with an onrushing army. Yet Gunnar was hitting Mord's line on the flank, since Oskar blocked the front.

The familiar thunder sounded again and Gunnar felt as if a hot rock dropped into his belly. Frankish cavalry in a thin column of two abreast burst from behind Mord's hall. They galloped between the gap in Oskar's and Mord's lines, their brilliant colors a smear atop their swift horses. Oskar's line flinched away but Gunnar had no more time to see if they broke.

"Hold fast and throw your spears," he shouted. Gunnar had no skill with a spear, so instead braced his shield for the oncoming rush. The horses screamed and their riders cursed, but their column broke apart as spears sailed overhead and sank into horseflesh.

A giant chestnut crashed to its front knees before Gunnar, flinging its rider flying to their line. Gunnar stepped out of line to strike the struggling rider on the back of his head, his helmet lost in the fall. He collapsed flat into the grass with a heavy crack and the killing fire ignited in Gunnar's heart. The horsemen plowed into their shield wall where men had fallen or faltered, and soon the animal stench of horses pressed Gunnar from all sides.

"Kill horses before riders," he shouted, then broke from his position beside Bekan to attack the first horse he found.

The horses were wild-eyed and frightened, but their riders handled them with skill. The beasts snapped at enemies and kicked out. From experience, Gunnar knew to attack them from the side, where the horses could not easily strike and the riders were the only defense. He swung for the horse's neck, but it lurched forward. Instead he chopped the thigh of the Frank and the ax sank to the bone. The rider did not even yell, but wheeled his horse to slash down with his own sword.

The shouts and screams were deafening, and the hideous squelch of hacking flesh surrounded him. Blood and musky horse spoor filled his nose. The rider's sword clanged on the boss of Gunnar's shield, sending a shiver to his shoulder. The Frank's horse nipped at Gunnar's face, barely missing him. He stepped back, expecting the horse to rear at him. His footing slipped on a dropped spear and in that instant he saw the Frank striking again.

He stumbled beneath his shield and the Frank drove him down with his horse, the great beast not rearing but slamming Gunnar. He landed on his back and panic seized him. A man laid out in battle counted his life in heartbeats. Feet danced above his head and the rider's horse now reared up, its hooves dropping clods of earth as it prepared to stomp him into the grass.

Rolling away, the horse came down hard. His shield had spun on his arm, but still held, and Gunnar now had his chance. The rider was already turning his mount, but Gunnar struck snake-swift. He hooked the rider's arm with the beard of his ax, then pulled down with all his strength. The rider tilted in his saddle but did not fall, so Gunnar pulled again as if hauling an anvil with one arm. The rider finally collapsed to the ground and his mount, now confused, kicked out at the closest person. The hapless victim was another dismounted Frank and the hooves struck him across the head and neck, crushing the enemy flat.

Gunnar slammed the iron rimmed shield on the head of his enemy. The Frank, whose leg had nearly been severed without a cry, now screamed as the blow did not kill. Releasing his ax, Gunnar chopped down a final time on the Frank's neck and a satisfying rush of blood sprayed across the grass.

The chaos of battle swirled, and Gunnar was ready to leap on his next enemy. They found him first, two Franks battering him back. Horses dashed about without riders, biting and kicking anyone they encountered. Gunnar stepped aside from the first sword, deflected the next one with his shield, then melted back to let his attackers pursue. The press behind him resisted him as good as any wall, and he found himself back to back with his men combating their own enemies. The Franks had compressed his force into a tight ball.

The two Franks lashed at him together, and one point crunched against his mail shirt. A link snapped with a metallic ping, and hot pain bloomed beneath it, yet Gunnar again hooked the attacker's arm and yanked him forward. The startled Frank flew past Gunnar, who used the man's momentum against him while catching the other attack on his shield. With only one man for the moment, Gunnar now stood a chance. He hooked his ax over the rim of the Frank's shield and pulled down. This revealed an angry, blond man with a stream of blood flowing from his scalp. Gunnar barely heard the foeman's curse before he slammed the iron rim of his shield into the exposed attacker's face. He collapsed and Gunnar pummeled him flat with his shield edge until he lay still. He whirled for the return attack, but none came. The Frank had either died or been consumed into another struggle.

Gunnar strained to see across the madness of the tiny world of his own combat. Spears, swords, and axes swam through a sea of helmets and horses and Gunnar saw nothing of Mord. His banner, however, rocked and shook as if in battle high above the fray. He screamed out, "He's mine! This is my revenge."

Trying to shove through the combat, he met thick resistance. Bodies littered the ground, friend and foe intertwined like firewood stacked for winter. Blood slicked the grass and he skidded as he sought the edge of battle. More horns blared, but their notes remained distant and Gunnar was no longer certain of their direction through all the grinding noise of battle. A man with his face cut open from chin to eye fell on him, screaming and spraying blood over his chest. Gunnar shoved him back into a press of enemy, then forced through the opening to the edge of the battle. Horses galloped around the field, some with spears hanging from their bloodied flanks. Fleeing men from both sides ran off into the surrounding woods. The other jarls had not arrived as Aren had promised.

He was trapped in a churning combat with Franks while Oskar and his men shoved against Mord's warriors. The back of Oskar's lines was breaking off and fleeing, like a honeycomb dissolving in a running stream. At first the edges broke, but soon all of it would wash away.

The grunt behind him warned Gunnar to jump forward, and he felt the wind of a sword strike that would have lopped off his head. He turned to face a lithe Frank, his beautiful surcoat of blue and white now torn and splattered with blood. He carried no shield and wielded his blade with both hands.

Gunnar dove into battle with him, realizing Aren's help was not coming and he would die unfulfilled on fields that had been stolen from his family. Fate had indeed planned a cruel end to his life.

48

"Who is it I am to see?" Finn asked Aren for the third time since leaving the jetty and joining the flow of traffic heading into Rouen.

"Fulbert is his name," Aren said. "I cannot guarantee his loyalty, but if you arrive with Elke and a bribe he should be wise enough to fetch Vilhjalmer."

Aren's chest beat so hard he felt unable to breathe. The Rouen docks were as alive with trade as ever. The formerly bare-backed dock laborers of summer now wore drab woolen shirts, but they hauled what seemed the same crates and barrels and shouted the same uninspired curses at those in their paths. Dockside hawkers laid out their catches of stinking fish and wilting vegetables, but women still picked these over with discerning eyes and frowning expressions. Guards slumped into their cloaks, half awake on duty in a city that had brooked no threat in the decades since Hrolf arrived in Frankia.

"Every city stinks like this," Ulfrik said, wrinkling his nose. Only his gray hair and the tip of his wagging beard hung out from the drawn hood of his green cloak. Aren thought his father had dressed plain enough to avoid notice, but he still stood with pride uncommon for the low-born he was mimicking, and his movements were too confident. His father could never truly bend his back in shame. Such towering pride was what had made him great, but now also made him difficult to hide.

"Father, you should stoop more and keep your head bowed. More like this." Aren demonstrated the look he wanted and received a thin smile from Elke and an outright laugh from Brandr. His face burned but he kept everyone moving through the crowds.

"I'm doing well enough," Ulfrik announced. "Elke and Finn have all the hard work to do. We just get to sit and drink until Vilhjalmer shows himself."

They filtered past the three guards who were clustered in conversation with a skinny woman. One saw Elke and immediately Aren saw the oncoming storm. The guard's face lit up and he was stumbling over himself to catch them.

"Trouble has found us," he whispered. "I told Elke to cover up."

The childish woman had insisted she had to be appealing to Vilhjalmer, and Aren had wondered if she was truly interested in helping them or more interested in impressing royalty. Now they were about to pay for her vanity.

"Hold on," called the guard. "Where are you going?" Aren could not determine who the guard addressed, for he was fixated on Elke's form-hugging dress.

"We are on business," Aren said, and held out a wood chip inscribed with Hrolf's mark. "And we've paid our dock fees. Here's our pass if you need to see it."

The guard glanced at it but smiled at Elke, who returned a dumb smile. "I wasn't asking for the pass. What's your business here, and who is this fine lass?"

"My wife," Ulfrik said, interposing himself between the guard and Elke. "So you'd do well to cease undressing her with your eyes."

Aren's knees weakened when the guard broke into a gap-filled, yellow-toothed smile. "Well, old man, I was just asking a question, and you're a bit defensive. Maybe I need to take a closer look at you."

Aren nearly fainted when Ulfrik pulled down his hood and got into the guard's face. "Is this close enough? Do you want to know who I really am?"

By all the gods, his father was going to announce himself. Aren's heart raced so hard he became faint. This was just the sort of madness that always filled his father's stories. He would probably grab the guard's sword and gut him with it. Aren searched for escape routes.

"In fact, I do. Who are you to stand in my face?"

"I am Jarl Ulfar the White, and I am here with a gift for Hrolf the Strider, one that you are despoiling in your thoughts."

"Never heard of you."

Now the two other guards joined their companion, forming a rough triangle around them. Ulfrik lifted his cloak to reveal his gold armbands. Aren's eyes felt ready to burst out of his skull.

"Know I've been awarded these by Hrolf himself. I stood with him beneath the walls of Paris back when you fools were sucking your mother's tits. I'm not surprised you've never heard of me, since Hrolf would only put his stupidest men to guarding the docks."

The guard bristled but seemed to hesitate. Aren saw how they began to doubt themselves, the way they touched their beards and noses, and pointed their bodies away from his father. "If you are so grand, then why only two guards and a child?"

"Use what brains of yours that aren't soaked with ale to think it through." Ulfrik grabbed the guard by his arm, and for a moment Aren believed they would all draw weapons. But Aren recognized how this gesture transferred control to his father. "Look at this beautiful woman. Hrolf is married to a Frank, is he not? Should this gift be given to him openly or more discreetly?"

The first guard shifted uneasily in his father's grip, but the second one had his own questions. "Why were we not warned of your coming? Anyone seeking an audience with Hrolf has to notify the guard."

Ulfrik shook his head. "Lad, you are only trying to do your duty. I understand that, but just think for a moment on all I just said. This beautiful woman is not my wife, but in fact destined to serve our jarl. First he would appreciate some time with her, but I'm certain his shrew of a wife will have much to say. So instead we must do this quietly and with care. Since you fools have now involved yourself in this, you may as well come with us to the palace."

Aren's pounding heart subsided as the guards stared at each other and slowly nodded. Only one chose to accompany them. His father gave Aren a wink and their new escort began clearing a way for all of them. Once they were halfway to the palace, Aren whispered to his father, "Are you going to change any more of our plans today?"

Ulfrik smiled and shook his head. "Only when the gods throw obstacles in our path."

Now Aren pulled his hood over his head as the guard took them to Fulbert, who sat at his traditional post at the servant's entrance. He stumbled over himself to appear more alert than he had been, but their dock guard took no notice. He explained their need and waited for Fulbert's answer.

Fulbert examined Elke like a hen for sale at market, then nodded. "I know what to do from here."

Finally rid of their dock guard escort, Aren breathed easier. He averted his face from Fulbert, who had once given him away to Gunther One-Eye's men. He had probably never realized what he had done, but Aren could not chance the guard's loyalty. His father spoke the words Aren had taught him. "A visitor for the young master. I've brought this one to his door. Saves him some time, eh? You'll be kind enough to tell him Ulfar the White sends his regards. Here's payment for your troubles."

Fulbert hissed at him. "Don't flash your gold, you oaf. Just set the pouch on my stool. I'll have to check her for hidden weapons."

Elke stepped back and put her delicate hand to her neck, but Fulbert just waved it down. "It's a precaution. Your man knows the right words, but I've not seen him before. Just roll up your sleeves and show me your boots."

Satisfied, he guided Elke toward the door. "All right, be gone with the rest of you."

Elke disappeared inside, and Aren thought she seemed too wide-eyed and excited. "You are certain she can be trusted to remember the message?" he asked as they walked out of Fulbert's hearing.

"She is just young and excited to be able to repay me for rescuing her. She will remember my message to Vilhjalmer. It is simple enough."

Aren shrugged. "Hakon seems quite taken with her. Do you think they will marry? He is long overdue to find a wife."

"As are you. Your mother would've liked more grandchildren."

His father's quip embarrassed him, and they walked in silence to the tavern where he and Vilhjalmer traditionally met. Inside they ordered ale and began their long wait. Ulfrik searched the dark room, nodding appreciatively. The sweet scent of burning wood mixed with the stale scents of spilled drink. "So this is where you two got up to mischief?"

"It was Vilhjalmer's idea, of course. I have no imagination for getting into trouble."

Ulfrik barked a laugh, then grew quiet and thoughtful. Finn sipped at his drink, swirling the liquid and humming a quiet tune. Brandr sat quietly staring at his hands. They had ordered a third ale by the time two guards entered the room, hands on sword hilts and their mail jingling. They stared at Ulfrik, and Aren's heart again leapt to his throat, but then they exited and Vilhjalmer swept inside. The tavern owner and the handful of other patrons fled the room like rats leaving a sinking ship.

Aren stood along with everyone else. Vilhjalmer's smile was wide and happy. He threw his arms wide and embraced Ulfrik first, patting him on the back. He then did the same for Finn and Aren. "Old friend, we've not seen each other since that misunderstanding with the guards. I see you've done well."

"I have survived, if that is what you call well."

Vilhjalmer laughed. "In these times, I certainly do call it so. Ah, but you selected a rare woman for me today. You always knew what I like best. This one I may keep close by."

"She's to be wed to my son, Hakon," Ulfrik said flatly. Aren detected the slight twitch in Vilhjalmer's otherwise unchanged demeanor.

"Ah, well, there are many beautiful women in the world, and I am sure to find another. But such a Frisian beauty! You mock me, then, with your choice of messenger. She will be well protected while we speak." Vilhjalmer now frowned and pointed at Brandr. "Who is this?"

"Gunnar's bastard son," Ulfrik said. "He's here to help me with what I've come to ask of you."

Now Vilhjalmer faced Ulfrik with narrowed eyes. "Coming here was bold, but I should have expected it. What would you ask of me that you risk so much? Have you remembered your oath to me?"

"I do not forget my oaths," Ulfrik said. "And I do not take risks lightly. You know what happened to my wife?"

Vilhjalmer's expression softened and he lowered his head. "She was a beautiful woman and a rare spirit. I was saddened to learn of her death."

"And you know how she died and who killed her?"

"I would make a poor count one day if I did not know all that happened in my lands. It was the plotting of Gunther One-Eye and Mord Guntherson that did this to you. Gunther has ever been jealous of your success and the lack of his son's. He thinks you've overstepped yourself."

"Maybe I have," Ulfrik said. "But that is not for Gunther to judge, but for the gods alone. My wife drowned in the open air, dead from a poisoned blade meant for my back. He maneuvered the Church into my path, and made certain I would lose everything. But it is not the first time he has tried this, is it? He was the silent hand that moved all the pieces against me, and sent me to meet death at the hands of Throst Shield-Biter."

"I was too young to remember," Vilhjalmer said, looking away. "But I have surmised as much."

"So I am here today to ask one thing of you, my oath-holder. Give me Gunther One-Eye."

Vilhjalmer raised his head and set his jaw. "That is too great a request. My father would never forgive me. He might even disown me or worse. Gunther is like a father to him."

Ulfrik smiled. "He's like a father to us all. Let me tell you how we will do this thing, and how you shall benefit. Sit and listen."

49

Gunnar stabbed the horn of his ax-head into the eye of the Frank, smashing his enemy's head into blood-slicked grass. He ground it in the socket, dragging on bone and delighting in the scream of pain. Metal clanged and wooden shields thudded; men screeched in pain and death. Gunnar choked on the stench of spilled guts and dead horses. He straddled his enemy, bashing his head for good measure with the gory edge of his shield. An iron strip had bent up, becoming a wicked spike that tore the Frank's skin. When Gunnar finally shoved off the corpse, the face was little more than red meat on bone.

Blood drizzled from his nose and flowed into his mouth, and he spit bloody phlegm onto the ground. His face throbbed and eyes watered. His nose had been broken despite the face guard of his helmet. He blinked through the swelling flesh cutting down his vision. Deciding his vision was too restricted, he tossed his helmet into the grass. The battle flowed against him, all his men brawling with Franks either mounted or otherwise, and Oskar's warriors flowing away toward the woods.

Mord's standard had lowered and now wavered as it bounced

through the press of men surrounding it. Mord, if he stood with his banner, was retreating.

Gunnar bellowed his fury, then ran toward the banner. Today was the day of his death, but he would not go until Mord Guntherson lay dead beside him as well. He swore it to himself. With every footfall he repeated his oath. "Mord dies today."

Oskar's men blocked the path to the front of the line where Mord's banner struggled to flee. Gunnar hooked men by their collars, his bloody ax dripping a gory warning for them to part. "Get out of my way! I've got to reach Mord!"

Pulling men out of line invited them to continue to fall back. Gunnar no longer cared what happened. Aren's promises of help had proved false. He had trusted his brother, seeing a different man from the hesitant boy that had left them only last summer. Yet in the end it had been misplaced. Whatever loyalty Aren thought to command from others had been a delusion. These men would not risk so much for so little in return. What good is gratitude when it has cost you all your wealth and fame?

He reached the front at last, but the space he found was vacated by a man collapsing with a sword stuck through his neck. Gunnar had no footing amid the sea of red-faced madmen attempting to break each other's resistance.

Gunnar did not function in a shield wall's front rank. His right-hand shield made him unable to fit with his sword brothers. So his presence disrupted the line and forced a wider gap than was needed. His very act of pushing into Mord's line weakened his own. He let his shield lead him, and used his ax like a hook to yank away striking weapons. He thought he saw Mord's treacherous face beneath his wolf head banner.

"Mord Guntherson, you gutless pig! Fight me! I am Gunnar the Black and I challenge you!"

A challenge had to be answered or else the man who cowered from it would forever live in shame. Mord apparently decided his life had been one long shame and to shirk the challenge offered no more shame than he already bore. His standard continued to float away like driftwood from the hand of a drowning man.

"Fight me, you whoreson! Raven-starver coward!"

Gunnar slammed his shield into the line and hacked like cutting through underbrush. Combatants from both sides flowed into the gap. Seven positions down the row Oskar called for his men to push harder. "They're nearly broken, boys! Crush them!"

The wedge Gunnar drove into the opposing shield wall penetrated the rear ranks and the resistance ebbed. A spear point sliced the outside of his left calf and drew a line of burning pain. Gunnar howled, hooked the spear, and tore it aside, then shoved deeper into the ranks until he broke through the rear. His companions cheered, but Gunnar was all grim determination. Mord's standard dropped lower and Gunnar lost sight of it.

Once in the clearing, he spotted Mord fleeing with a group of men. The line he had shoved through now broke into clusters of individual combats, and the rear ranks now followed their leader in retreat. Gunnar did not warn Mord, but charged him with shield forward and ax poised for a chop to the neck.

His vision blurred from both fury and sweat dripping into his eyes. His racing pulse and thundering footfalls sent quakes of pain through his broken nose. Mord continued to flee, unaware of approaching death.

Gunnar's ax blade flashed.

Mord's hirdman shouted a warning and he spun with his shield raised.

The ax crashed home into Mord's shoulder the same moment his shield collided with Gunnar's arm. Mord's mail shirt crunched and snapped and the ax bit deep. Gunnar felt it shudder as the blade dug into the bone. Gunnar's arm went numb as Mord's shield slammed into his elbow and the ax haft slipped through his hand. Mord fell back, screaming in agony and the ax lodged in his shoulder.

The hirdmen now crowded Gunnar. Shoving him back with his shield and prodding him with his sword. The others grabbed Mord and carried him with Gunnar's ax still buried in his left shoulder. While Gunnar blocked his attackers' weak blows, he roared in frustration. "You can't escape! I'll kill you, goat-fucker! You killed my mother!"

Tears threatened to blind him. Mord's men carried him away while Gunnar tried to skirt the man left to delay him. Why Mord would flee confused Gunnar until he realized the sounds of battle were even fiercer behind Mord's line. He blocked another strike, the shield catching the blade with a dull bump, then looked to the east. At the edge of the tree line, formerly out of sight, were dozens of banners flying over the heads of raving Northmen engaged against more Franks. Here were Aren's allies, fighting their own battle against reinforcements that had never deployed against them. Mord had prepared the same trap again, but this time had not expected he was at the center of one himself.

Gunnar laughed as he watched the Franks scatter and fall, a crowd of Norse helmets and colorful shields rolling over them like a locust swarm. In his moments of inattention, the enemy he fought melted away. Gunnar turned back for Mord, began running yet did not know where his enemy had gone. As the Norse reinforcements swarmed across the battlefield, they sowed confusion and death. Mord disappeared into this crowd. For Gunnar to find him again would be like wading across the Seine and just as impossible. Mord had escaped. Gunnar's only consolation was he might have yet delivered him a lingering, mortal wound.

With the breaking of the better-trained Franks, the battle ended in a rout. Gunnar found a quiet patch of grass to sit and watch men flee or die. Years ago he would have sought wounded enemies to finish, cutting off their sword hands first. Yet today he was soul weary and injured. His nose continued to drizzle thick blood, and every beat of his heart hurt like a backhand slap to the face.

The ground was littered with dead bodies from both sides, corpses that sprouted bent swords, broken spear shafts, or ax hafts. Shields were scattered over the grass like colorful autumn leaves. Groups of men chased down stragglers, while others stooped over corpses to begin looting. Gunnar loosened the strap of his shield and let it slide off his arm. At last Bekan found him and he had with him two men who Gunnar instantly recognized. The first was Ull the Strong, a tall man with a build to match his name. His hair and skin had been pale since Gunnar was a child, but age had whitened his beard and thinned his hair. He glittered with gore. Next to him stood Ragnar Hard-Striker. He too was a strong man who stood with pride. His hair had also turned gray, but his green eyes were alight with the killing lust, making him appear much younger. A red scar crossed his cheek, and according to his father's stories, Ragnar was also missing his left ear, though his helmet covered it now.

"You came at last," Gunnar said as he struggled to his feet.

The two jarls laughed and Ull folded his massive arms. "What are you doing sitting in the grass when there's a hall to be sacked?"

"The fields are full of plunder," Ragnar added. "The Franks bring us good weapons and strong mail, though they seem not to know how to use these best."

The jarls laughed again and Bekan now examined Gunnar's face, pulling it side to side, exposing his teeth and peering inside his mouth. "You'll live, and you might actually look better after your nose heals. Last time it broke it turned out crooked. Maybe this'll knock it back in place."

Gunnar smiled, unable to laugh with the others. "Mord escaped. He took my ax with him, buried in his shoulder. But it was not the revenge I wanted."

"Mord's destroyed," Ull the Strong said. "Hafgrim is leading his men in pursuit. He'll probably catch him and drag him back. Mord's men can't get too far if they're carrying him in a mail shirt and an ax stuck in him. Too heavy and they're too tired."

"Fear gives men strength to flee," Gunnar said.

Ragnar blew a sigh through his heavy beard. "We can only see what Fate has planned. For now, though, that hall is quiet. Mord defended it personally, which means something of worth must be inside."

"His wife? Gold?" Bekan asked. Gunnar shrugged then waited as the jarls rounded up men to clear the hall. Other parties were kicking in the door of other distant buildings, but Gunnar heard none of the expected screams. Bekan soon presented him with a scavenged ax, one with blood still on the blade, then refit his shield to his arm.

"I've always wanted to see this shield myself," Ull the Strong said. "I hoped to see you fight with your left hand. You should be proud that you learned to keep fighting. Losing a sword hand ends most men's fighting days."

Gunnar allowed Ull to examine the straps and the iron rim of his shield. They chatted about the details while thirty men surrounded the hall. Gunnar's parents had once lived there. Snorri died there. It seemed wrong to slam open the door and storm it with bloody weapons. "This was my father's home. Let me enter first."

The doors were not barred, and once inside Gunnar found a familiar scene. It was as if Mord had only lived in the hall on borrowed time, and now left everything as he had found it. Gunnar walked to the stain where the bishop had bled to death while other men checked out the rooms at the far end of the hall. Nothing was left behind, and anything of value cleared away.

"He didn't expect to win," Ragnar said. "He has probably fled to his wife's family."

Gunnar flipped over a table with a roar. No one approached him as his mind buzzed with a hundred murderous thoughts. How had Mord managed to escape? Not even a slave had been left behind. He kicked benches and flung wooden plates. Men abandoned him to his rage, but soon he heard Bekan calling his name. He whirled on his friend, but stopped when he saw Bekan's face. "They've found Mord?"

"No, but very close. His second was wounded in battle. I thought you might want to speak with him."

They rushed outside, and before the hall doors Mord's second, Magnus the Stone, hung between two men. His right leg had been hewed at the knee, turning it into a bloody mess bent at the wrong angle. He bowed his head and Gunnar suddenly felt much better. He smiled and stalked over to Magnus. The jarls and their hirdmen looked on impassively.

He lifted Magnus's head with the blade of his bloody ax. The old warrior stared through him. "So you're the one who shot my brother in the face trying to kill my father. You would do such a shameful, cowardly thing in service to a man who would abandon you to your enemies? Let me teach you to regret your choices."

Gunnar stamped on Magnus's wound, who fell from between the two men holding him up. He screamed as Gunnar ground his heel into the shattered knee.

"Where did Mord go?"

"I don't know."

"That's the wrong answer." Gunnar glanced at Bekan, who knew this drill well. He pinned Magnus down while Gunnar adjusted his grip on his ax handle. "Say farewell to your sword hand."

The blade slammed down, but it was dull and only stuck in Magnus's wrist bone. The old warrior howled in agony as Gunnar wrestled the blade free and chopped again. It took four gory strikes to break through the bone and remove the hand. By this time, Magnus was delirious with pain.

"Tell me where Mord and his wife went, or I'll use this dull ax to cut off your head. Cooperate and I'll have a fresh blade readied to make it easier." Gunnar retrieved the hand, its flesh now bloody gray. He slapped Magnus's face with it. "You deserve a lot more suffering for what you did to my family. But I am generous today, as well as tired. Speak."

"The lady Fara went back to her family. Mord may follow. I don't know. We weren't supposed to lose."

"Then why clear out the hall?"

"She didn't want to be close to the fighting. Took everything and left."

Gunnar knelt beside Magnus, who now lay facedown in the grass, and pulled up his head. "I will have a fresh blade prepared for your beheading, but before that you'll suffer well."

He stood, tossed the ax aside, and wiped the gore from his face. He looked to Bekan. "Find a tree and hang him. Make sure he takes a long time to choke to death. Then keep my word and find a good blade to sever his head. We'll set it on a spear along with the heads of every dead enemy we pick off this battlefield. I want this land to stink of death and be smothered in flies and crows. Let them know Gunnar the Black has come to avenge his family."

Bekan nodded as if the command were not unusual, though Ull, Ragnar, and Oskar regarded him with raised brows.

"They don't call me black just for the color of my hair, but for the flocks of crows that follow my path." Gunnar's quip drew an evil smile from Ull and Ragnar, and both nodded appreciatively. Oskar remained with his brow raised, and Gunnar pointed at him.

"Get me thirty good men. I know where they are taking Mord, and I mean to see him dead. We don't have far to go, but must hurry."

50

Ulfrik's hands trembled and were cold. He sat in the audience hall inside the palace that Hrolf called home when he stayed at Rouen rather than his traditional hall. The floors were covered in wood planks that servants had scrubbed smooth, and the exterior walls were of fitted stone and mortar that crumbled into piles at the corners. Rectangles set high on the walls provided light, and Ulfrik had noticed a sparrow's nest in one of them. The whole place smelled faintly of dust, and beyond the stone walls in the courtyard a dog barked. All the hallmarks of a lazy morning in a sleepy palace belied the upcoming tumult.

Three tables were arranged around each wall save the one where the double doors were set. Benches were placed between table and wall, so that no guest would have his back to another. Ulfrik liked that idea, and felt that men would enjoy their feasts more if all could see each other as well as their host. At the head table, he sat with Aren at his right and Finn on his left. Elke and Brandr cowered at the far end of the bench, and clung to each other as if weathering a storm.

So many for something I must do alone, he thought.

Aren sat quietly, eyes lowered to his hands folded on the table.

His careful planning had freed Ulfrik to focus on revenge. Despite having sat for at least an hour in the room, Finn still drank in his surroundings with wide eyes and looking very much the boy he was in his heart. Were it not for his mastery of concealment and skill as a scout, they could not have made it across the Seine to Rouen. Elke stroked Brandr's curly gold hair. She had blossomed to her full beauty now, and Ulfrik felt foolish both for having had her in his bed and not doing more than he had. She was charming in her simple way, and her smile had so won over Vilhjalmer that he was ready to do anything to please her. Without her charms, the doors to Rouen's palace might yet remained closed.

At last Ulfrik considered Brandr, the shy, broken child Gunnar had by another woman. With only Leif for a grandson and so young, Ulfrik was glad to find another of his blood in this world. He had studied the boy and wondered at the heart of this child. He had not wanted to leave his mother, but had been obedient to her wishes. Ulfrik now had to test that obedience to him.

He extended an arm to Brandr, "Come here, lad."

The boy reluctantly slid from Elke's arm and presented himself to Ulfrik. The boy faintly reminded Ulfrik of Gunnar, but he must look more like the mother than anyone else. That did not endear him to Ulfrik, though he was his blood. "Do you remember why I've taken you on this journey?"

"Yes, Lord." Brandr's voice was small and he lowered his eyes.

"You will be brave. I've no use for a frightened child, for they grow up to be frightened men. You are not frightened, are you?"

"No, Lord."

"That is good. There will be much to frighten you, but you must remember your blood. Who am I?"

"You are Ulfrik Ormsson, Lord."

"Is that all I am?"

"No, Lord, you are a vengeful jarl and a nightmare to your enemies."

Ulfrik laughed. "And your grandmother was named Runa the Bloody. She is why we are here today, and part of why you must do what I ask. Your father is Gunnar the Black, and not for his hair but for his vengeful heart. So with family names like that, you cannot just call yourself Brandr. What shall you call yourself?"

The boy's eyes widened and a smile grew. He looked off to the side as considered. "They will call me Brandr the Brave, Lord."

"A fine name, Brandr the Brave. Grow into that name and the skalds will add it to their songs of our family's deeds. Now sit with Elke, and be brave for what you are about to witness. It will be a terrible sight for even the strongest of hearts."

His grandson retreated to Elke, who smiled and mouthed a word of thanks to him. Both Aren and Finn regarded Ulfrik with cool smiles. All of them needed to hear those words and be reminded to remain brave as they sat in the hall of their enemy. If Vilhjalmer suddenly changed his mind, they were all as good as dead in a room with only one set of doors.

The silence dragged out until they heard voices at the door. Ulfrik's sword was already drawn and resting at his leg. He placed his shaking hand on the hilt and his breath grew ragged. The doors shook as someone stood before them and the voices grew louder. Both Aren and Finn picked up their weapons. The doors thumped opened. The darkness beyond yawned then Vilhjalmer entered, not even glancing at Ulfrik or the others lined against the far wall. He assisted a tall man inside, guiding him by the hand.

Gunther One-Eye had aged far worse than Ulfrik had expected. Though he still stood tall, he had shrunk to little more than bones. Ulfrik remembered a hulking giant with a wolf pelt tossed over broad shoulders. He remembered a man who had drank with him, encouraged him, fought beside him, and had been his friend. The hateful thing framed in the doorway was not that man. His skin sagged, blotted with brown patches and moles. His hair had thinned and left him bald on top. A single eye glowed with the strange bluish light of a thick cataract. Gunther swept the room with a frown Ulfrik recognized from their long association.

"What are we doing in this room?" Not even the voice remained the same. Gone was the sonorous, commanding voice of a warrior and jarl. In its place was the weary, suspicious voice of an old traitor. He sniffed the air. "Are we not alone?"

"Come in, Grandfather," Vilhjalmer said. He gently tugged Gunther's hand and he hobbled inside.

"I don't understand. I hear other people in the room." Gunther faced Vilhjalmer. If he were not blind, he would see Vilhjalmer's evil smile.

"You will understand in a moment," Vilhjalmer said, then lifted the bar into place across the doors.

Ulfrik stood, sword in a cold hand, and cleared his throat. "Hail, Gunther One-Eye. Welcome to our final meeting."

51

Gunnar drove his pack of thirty men as fast as they could march. The gentle slopes were as challenging as mountains to their battle-weary muscles. The bittersweet scent of burning farms and barns followed them as they cleared through the light woods and into the pastureland that had once been Gunnar's holdings. Rolling grasses now browning with the onset of winter spread before them, curled and dead leaves rolling like a tide. Throughout their chase they found signs of fleeing warriors everywhere. They glimpsed corpses in the underbrush, wounded men who had escaped but never found help. Even this far from the battle, a shield had been discarded. Its leather rim torn away and the wood splintered. Gunnar kicked it.

"Mord's men came this way," he said, then spit on the shield. "I'd bet my reputation on it."

"Then we should pause for a breath," Bekan said. He had insisted on accompanying Gunnar rather than remain behind butchering corpses, and Gunnar was grateful for a trusted face among strangers.

"We can breathe while we walk. There's every chance Mord got away, and we can't risk it." The men with him gave him weary glares but followed as he pressed into the fields. Atop a rolling hill he looked down on what he expected to find.

"Hrothgar's farm is no more, but a stone church is nearly finished." He pointed down the slope at the building of warm gray rock. It had no thatch yet, but it seemed the builders would have it completed before winter. Two wooden buildings with bright golden thatch roofs sat in easy reach of the church. There was no sign of life, no livestock or servant showed outside the buildings, nor did any birds sit on the roof.

"Blood in the grass," Bekan said, kneeling to touch the droplets with his fingers. "You were right."

"Of course I was right," he muttered. "Now that he's out of tricks, he'll be as predictable as the tides. Surround the buildings and if anyone comes out or struggles, kill them where they stand. I may have once ruled here, but there are no friends left in this land."

They rushed down the slope, Gunnar experiencing a renewed vigor having trapped Mord in the only refuge he could find. Thirty men did not feel enough to surround both buildings, but he doubted Mord had taken more than a dozen during his escape. Gunnar stood before the largest of the two buildings, shield strapped on his arm and ax in his cold hand. Despite the jingle of their mail shirts and the murmur of voices as they surrounded the buildings, no one emerged. All eyes waited on Gunnar's signal, and he gave it as a nod to Bekan at the door.

Bekan raised his foot and kicked on the door. It flung open and someone within screamed, man or woman Gunnar could not tell. He charged in with shield forward and ax raised. At the other building, men roared as they too burst through the doors.

Inside the choking, trash scent of burning tallow candles assailed him. His eyes wrestled with the darkness, but shapes flashed before him and the unmistakable glint of iron struck for his exposed side. He turned aside, bounced the strike off his mail shirt, and cut down with his ax. The attacker grunted as Gunnar felt his blade sink into soft flesh, then the shape thumped to the floor. Bekan roared for the enemy to surrender, and to Gunnar's surprise they did. As his vision adjusted to the light he saw two men set their weapons down and back away.

Now in the low candlelight of the windowless hall his sight came into focus. Two men already bandaged, one about his head and the other on his leg, stood back. Three other men lay side by side on the floor, their wounds more grievous. One had a stump of his left hand wrapped in bloody cloth. Gunnar grinned at that, but it fled him when he saw who stood at the rear with two women cowering with him.

"Father Lambert!" Gunnar shouted. He stalked toward the priest, and the surrendering men parted for him. Stepping over the injured men, he pointed his bloodied ax at the priest's chest.

"You snake! You returned after all to claim your prize." Father Lambert's pasty flesh turned whiter still as he stared down at the dripping ax poised over his heart. His mouth opened but he had no words. "Speechless, eh? Never expected to see me again, did you."

The priest still wore his hair short, but it had grown over the tops of his ears now. His melon-shaped head shook in answer to Gunnar's question.

"Where's Mord? Is he in the other building?" Gunnar swept his shield arm over the injured men, who Bekan and others were already guarding. "These are his warriors."

Father Lambert's eyes were fish-wide and a dark stain appeared at the front of his black robe. Gunnar gave a disgusted laugh. "You've pissed yourself! Oh, but you must know how I am going to hurt you, priest. We'll start with those two good legs of yours and work up to your lying tongue. Don't make me angrier than I need be or I'll get more creative. Where's Mord?"

"He's dead." The answer came not from Father Lambert, but from one of the prisoners. Gunnar faced the man. He was fat but strong, curly brown hair stained red with his blood. The bandage on his forehead hung over eyes like a bear's.

"Did you see him die?" Gunnar asked. "Be honest with me and you will live."

The man raised a paw-like hand. "I swear it to you, Jarl Gunnar.

He commanded us to take him here, but along the way he died. We could not carry him any longer. We were all hurt. We threw his body into a gully in the woods and covered him in branches. There is still much light left to this day. If you retrace our steps, you will find the body before the wolves get it tonight."

Gunnar's ax lowered, and his body drained of fight. "Thrown in a ditch for scavengers to devour. A fitting end to a traitor."

Bekan put his hand on Gunnar's shoulder, but he pulled away. He suddenly felt unable to stand and sat on a bench. "I killed him, I suppose. But there was no joy in it. He should've screamed more. Begged me to stop. Something."

"Your father bade you kill him, and you did. That was your ax in his shoulder."

"I will see his corpse myself. I will still have his head."

The captive spoke up. "I can take you to the body. I remember the way."

His companions hissed at him, the man with the wrap on his leg cursed him. "You traitor. You've no honor."

"He's dead!"

Gunnar silenced them by raising his ax. He now turned to Father Lambert. Tears streamed down the priest's eyes. Tormenting him felt meaningless now. He nodded to Bekan. "Let the priest witness the death of everyone you find here, destroy his church and burn his houses. Then cut off both his legs and hang him up to die. I will take five men and this prisoner to find Mord's corpse."

Father Lambert screamed along with the women at his side. The prisoner with the leg wound tried to grab a weapon and was as swiftly struck down. Now two bodies lay bleeding over the dirt floor. Gunnar took the prisoner and his five men, then exited into daylight. The air was cool and fresh on his face, but his heart was heavy and black. The prisoner went in front and began guiding them.

"If you are leading us into a trap, you will die before you can be saved," Gunnar warned.

But the prisoner had been sincere. After a long search and

doubling back, they came to a steep ledge where a stream flowed through below.

"We threw him down there and fled," said the prisoner. "There is his corpse."

Gunnar stared down from the ledge, which dropped twice his height. Mord lay on his back, foot in the stream, Gunnar's ax in his shoulder. His eyes were closed as if he were only sleeping beneath a blanket of pine branches covering up to his chest.

"We could gain the stream farther west, then follow it down to the body," said one of his men. Gunnar shook his head.

"The sun is already low in the sky and I have seen what I needed. That is Mord." He stared for a long time while his men waited. Mutilating the body was more effort than it was worth. Presenting the head to his father would have been a nice touch, but he did not know when they would next meet. Instead, rotting in mud while animals and worms gnawed Mord's corpse was just as fitting. So he pulled down his pants then urinated down onto the body. When finished, he turned to the prisoner.

"You've earned your freedom," Gunnar said. "If you are caught again, I will not be so generous."

"Thank you, Lord!" The man bowed and started to back away. The prisoner was already fleeing deeper into the woods when Gunnar recalled he meant to cut off the man's sword hand. He shook his head, then spit over the edge.

"So ends Mord Guntherson's worthless life," he said, then looked north and wished his father's revenge tasted better than this bitter draught.

52

Gunther stiffened at Ulfrik's voice and his confused expression grew resolute. Ulfrik stepped from behind the table, his white knuckle grip tight on his sword hilt. The scent of dust hanging in the air filled his nose as he inhaled deeply then sighed.

"You are surprised to find yourself in a room with me?" Ulfrik stopped in the center of the floor, the wood boards creaking beneath his weight. "Yet you had to know this day would come."

Gunther's frown faded to a smile, and for a moment Ulfrik glimpsed his old friend beneath the mask of this bitter old man. "I had often worried for it, imagining a dozen ways this might happen. You impress me still. I'd have not guessed you'd be so bold."

Ulfrik smiled. "Then you do not know me as well as you thought."

"May I sit?" Gunther asked. "My old legs pain me and I expect you have questions. I will think clearer if I am seated."

Already moving toward a bench, Ulfrik blocked Gunther. "You will stand."

Gunther smelled of age and his cloudy white eye searched Ulfrik's face. If he could see anything through it, Ulfrik believed it could only be shadows. Gunther nodded his bald head and turned back. "I see. So, Vilhjalmer, what is your part in this? I understand Ulfrik's reasons, but not yours. You led me to this trap, but why?"

"Grandfather," Vilhjalmer spit the word like a curse. "You are not nearly as wise as you claim to be. Do you think I have not felt your hand upon me long enough? I know how you connive with my mother to keep me under control. You and your son have had hooks into me long enough. To control me is to control the future of Normandy, is it not? No one has abused my father's trust as much as you, yet no one is more deceived by your lies than him. You are a blight to my father's rule and a blot on my future. You and your son are no better than scheming rats. No one controls me. Not my father, my mother, and certainly neither you nor your son. I am my own man, and I will rid myself of those that believe otherwise."

The echoes of Vilhjalmer's impassioned speech bounced around the room. Gunther bent his mouth appreciatively. "And here I thought as long as you were buried in women and drink you would have no eyes to see the greater world. Good job, boy."

"But let us not forget, this day is mine," Ulfrik said. He turned Gunther's face toward him with the flat of his sword. "And you have but one chance to earn yourself a swift death."

Gunther gently pushed Ulfrik's blade aside, his smile condescending. "Death is death. I am not afraid of what you will do to me."

"Then what about your son?" Ulfrik asked, and Gunther paused. "I turned him over to Gunnar, and he will make your boy suffer. He'll cut off his sword hand, at the very least. It's a problem he has had since losing his own. Seems to think no one else should have two hands."

"Empty threats," Gunther said. "I know who you've allied with, and know those southern jarls for the cowards they are. You have nothing to challenge us with."

"Ull the Strong, Ragnar Hard-Striker, Hafgrim Herjolfsson. Do these names sound familiar? They have journeyed south to fight Mord and his Frankish cavalry. Einar and all my men have struck for the Seine crossing at Rouen. Hrolf has already gone to meet them. Your son is finished. You are finished. So save me the bold act.

Answer my questions, and I will respect our old friendship. I'll make death quick. We were friends once, weren't we?"

Gunther nodded, his head lowered. "We were, until you placed yourself above everyone else. You climbed into Hrolf's bed, and tried to become his top man. You were nothing when I found you. You were a slave, then the jarl of a poor island lost in the sea at the top of the world. You were no better than a farmer, but I lifted you up. I put you before Hrolf. I fed you from my hand. And then you bit it."

"Whatever bite you imagined, was it worth all your honor to avenge it? Had it been a true offense, there would not be a man in the world to deny you revenge. You could have challenged me to a duel, to the death even. But your motivations were far more base." Ulfrik touched the edge of his sword to Gunther's neck to prevent him from turning aside. "You were jealous and you saw that your son climbed no higher in Hrolf's esteem. You moved in shadows, working on Konal's fears and his worries, twisting him until he bent to your traitorous plans to send me to Throst."

Gunther closed his eye and Ulfrik lowered his sword. He had held that suspicion in his heart for the entire summer. Aren had known much longer than he, and now he turned to his son who watched on with a drawn sword. His face was unreadable, but his cheeks had flushed red. He was as eager for revenge as anyone.

"Do you know how I suffered? Do you know the madness I endured for years after?" Ulfrik felt his anger rising, and he checked it. "But I came back, and even with me gone for so long you and your son still achieved nothing. Was I such a threat that even now you conspired to kill me? What would make this time any better than the last? Mord is a fool. The spark that lit your fires never ignited his. He is as colorless and cold as ash. You can give him my lands and put him in front of Hrolf, and all he will do is prove himself worthless."

"Your speech tires me," Gunther said. "If you mean to kill me, do it before you are discovered. When Hrolf learns of what you've done, he will avenge me."

"You dare smirk at me, you shameless bastard? You think I will allow Hrolf the chance to raise a hand to me? Hakon and Einar are right now ensuring he will not so much as spit at me when we next meet. I have it in mind to present your head to him."

"Then do it," Gunther said, his face warping into a mask of hate. "You overblown, pig-fucking farmer! You and your slave-bitch wife strutting around in your great mead halls, covered in gold and jewels. How much of that did you share with me? The very man who plucked you out of the slop! Where did all those riches come from? You would not have possessed them without me."

Despite his blindness his single eye bore into Ulfrik's and his age-blackened teeth were gritted in hate. Ulfrik dropped his voice to a low threat. "You got what you deserved of me. The rest of my wealth was my own business. So it was greed, after all?"

"Greed? You should be one to speak of greed. It rules your heart. You forget your friends and don't know your place. I regret the day I called you to Frankia. I should have left you and that whore to wallow on your rock in the sea."

Ulfrik narrowed his eyes. "She died from a poisoned blade meant for me. You are a shameless, gutless, old man, and it will be my pleasure to kill you."

Gunther spit in his face, the warm, thick spittle spraying his eyes. "You'll be hanged and I will laugh at you from Valhalla as you rot in the fog of Nifelheim."

"There's no place for you in Odin's hall." Ulfrik wiped the spit from his face. "Traitors are not heroes."

His sword plunged into Gunther's soft gut. He drove it to the hilt, snarling with the effort. Gunther's eye went wide and his mouth opened. He clawed Ulfrik's face with a weak, shaking hand, but it fell away as he sank to his knees.

Blood flowed onto the floorboards from Gunther's punctured stomach. Ulfrik followed him to the floor, then put his boot against Gunther's shoulder and pulled his blade free. A gout of blood sprang up from the wound. Ulfrik knelt beside him, setting aside his sword and drawing his dagger.

"Runa died choking on the air itself," he whispered into Gunther's ear. "I know of no way to make you suffer as she did. This is the best I can do."

He placed the dagger to the rough, loose flesh of Gunther's neck, holding his head back to expose it. Ulfrik began to saw, knowing it would hurt more than a clean cut. Gunther struggled and screamed, but Ulfrik worked with professional calm. Blood gurgled up in Gunther's mouth, turning his screams to gargling panic. Hot blood splashed onto Ulfrik's face and rolled over his hand. Tears stung his eyes. When Gunther's throat was laid open and filled with blood, Ulfrik stood again.

The old man clawed at the floor, twisting in agony that quickly subsided into twitching, and then stillness. He had no weapon at hand to grasp. The last of his blood bubbled in his throat, and he lay still in an ever-widening pool of dark blood.

"May worms eat your flesh until Ragnarok." Ulfrik dropped his knife and picked up his sword. Aren, Finn, and Vilhjalmer joined him over Gunther's corpse.

"Revenge is done," Aren said. "My only regret is he did not suffer longer."

"He suffered with his shame," Ulfrik said. "Longer than we know. Maybe I am wrong, but I don't believe he was always such a monster. Somewhere he lost sight of honor and gave in to his jealousy. The warrior that he had once been must still have lived in his heart and probably tormented him all these years. I do not excuse him, nor pity him. But he was once a friend and I owed him much. Today is a bitter day."

"Well, I feel better for it," Vilhjalmer said. "Are you really going to give his head to my father?"

Ulfrik looked up at Vilhjalmer, then touched his bloody sword point to the young man's throat. "I will give him something else instead."

53

"I never thought to see it from this side," Hakon said.

"Nor I," Einar agreed. "A terrible and mighty sight."

Both men stood at the front rank of their gathered hirdmen and faced north. They had secured high ground, knowing they would have to use every advantage they could muster. The hill swept down to a carpet of yellow grass that waved in the cool afternoon breeze. Clouds floated in clumps through a blue sky and cast spotty shadow over the land. Hrolf's massive army stood half inside shadow.

Line upon line of mail-clad hirdmen ranked up at the foot of the hill. There were easily two of them to every of Hakon and Einar's men, their weapons glinting in the sunlight. They stood in perfect squares and did not make any more noise than the clinking of their armor or knocking of shields. Hakon admired their discipline, which was reflected in his own men. After all, his father had instilled that thinking into both bodies of warriors and it gave them advantage in every battle they fought.

"I've been looking for a sign from the gods all morning," Einar said. "But I've seen no omens."

"No signs are better than bad omens," Hakon said. "I'm certain the gods will choose us over Hrolf. He has abandoned them for the Christians. How will they feel about that?"

Einar chuckled and they continued to wait for signals from Hrolf's lines of either an attack or parley. Hakon had wanted to force Hrolf to a meeting, which was customary before most battles of this sort. The Franks did not always parley, even when it would have been in their interest. So perhaps Hrolf was adopting more of Frankish customs than was good. Hakon certainly felt he was. His magnificent, new standard of red with two golden lions lifted in the wind, and even at this distance Hrolf stood out both in height and grandeur. His armor gleamed brighter than anyone around him.

"If we stand here all morning nothing will be accomplished," Hakon said. He glanced toward the horizon where treetops faded out to white, yet the highest towers of Rouen stood as a blue line in the distance. "I hope Father is all right."

He worried more for Elke than his father. He had not wanted her to take this risk, but with Gunnar sending his son, how could he protest? Besides, Elke wanted to go, and that worried him more than if she had begged to stay.

"Your father will handle himself," Einar said, breaking into his thoughts. "We have our duty today, and how we carry it out will either save us all, or get everyone killed. So forget him for now."

Hakon lowered his head, chastened. "Of course you are right. But Hrolf is too proud to come to us first; let us go down and parley with him. I cannot stand this wait any longer."

"Well, it was not my choice to wait," Einar said, a small smile lifting his lips. "You wanted to make the Count of Rouen come to you."

"Then let this not be our omen, for it has failed." Hakon turned to his men and gathered five from his front rank. Einar did the same, and his son-in-law picked guards from his own hirdmen. He was a short man, broad-shouldered with hair so pale as to be white. Men called him Hauk Pale-Hair, but Einar called him Hauk the White. He had mild success as a war leader, but his marriage to Einar's eldest daughter had raised his status. Hakon was surprised that he would risk it all to follow them in this gambit.

Once they had assembled, Hakon ordered his father's banner pulled up and carried with them to the parley. "Let Hrolf not forget who he is truly bargaining with when he speaks to me."

They stopped halfway to Hrolf's line. For a long while it did not stir, but then Hrolf broke off an honor guard of equal size. They strode across the grass to meet with Hakon, who waited with arms folded. His mouth had gone dry and his stomach burned. Hrolf was like a giant among dwarfs and the royal life had agreed with him. His gleaming mail was covered by a newly dyed red cloak, and his clothes were all brilliant blue. Gold and silver sparkled about his limbs and neck, and his heavy hands were crusted with jeweled rings. A frowning face sat beneath a helmet rimmed with a crown, and the deep lines of his cheeks collected shadow.

"Hail, Jarl Hrolf. I am Hakon Ulfrikson. You know my companions well, I think."

Hrolf looked up at the green standard showing black elk antlers, his frown deepening. He did not glance at Hakon, but instead stared at Einar and then Hauk. He shook his head. "You ally yourselves with outlaws and betray me? Then you insult me by sending the outlaw's whelp to me instead."

The fire in Hakon's stomach flared. He was no whelp and Hrolf knew it, but he reconsidered his outburst. Of course, it was a parley to Hrolf and insults were expected. Hakon had a different purpose for this meeting. "Jarl Hrolf, my father has left me all his men. You will treat with me as you would with him."

"Is that so?" Hrolf now finally looked at Hakon. His clear eyes were full of anger. "Being that he's an outlaw, I'd treat him no differently. You and all of the men on that hill will be dead before the sun reaches the crest of the sky. That is my promise to you, and of all people you should know I will make it so."

"Your skill at war is never questioned," Hakon said, warming to his role. Hrolf would bristle and bluster, but Hakon had to remain strong but respectful. "But it is my hope that no man on either side of this line need spill blood in battle today."

Hrolf barked a laugh. "You have strange hopes, boy. You have brought an army to fight, and corrupted two of my jarls. Blood must flow from that."

"They are here to seize your attention, Jarl Hrolf. Would you sit and listen to me any other way?" Hrolf snarled, but he did not answer. "I intend to negotiate a peace for all sides today. Many have died already, good men and women whose lives have been ruined for the Church's ambitions on my father's land. My mother was killed by an assassin's blade covered in poison."

"That was nothing of my doing," Hrolf said, and Hakon thought he heard a note of genuine sorrow beneath the bluster. Hrolf had always liked his mother, as far as Hakon knew. "I would never stoop to something so base."

"Of course you would not," Hakon said. "But Mord Guntherson would, and it is his plotting that has forced us to meet today as enemies rather than as the friends we have always been. He was not content to see us forced out, but wanted my father dead. I know you must deny your knowledge to the people, but among us we all know you are well aware of what happens in your land."

Hrolf's protests again stumbled and he did not shame himself with an answer. Hakon stifled a smile. "By now Mord Guntherson is dead. His lands are smashed, the Franks who aided him are destroyed. My brother, Gunnar the Black, even now is burning Mord's hall to ash and hoisting his corpse onto a tree so that ravens may pick his bones."

Hrolf glared at Hakon, then turned to Einar. "Were you part of that?"

"I only wish that I could have been, for Mord is a rat deserving of death. Others gave their aid, names you would recognize as long-serving jarls. There is greater discontent with some of your choices than you realize, Jarl Hrolf. Ulfrik is now returned and focusing that anger. You would be very wise to listen to all that Hakon will offer today. For while you may have the strength to fight us, you would falter in your duty to your new king. How can you protect his coast while you war with your own people?"

"My father and I have spread the call to battle far among the world," Hakon said. "We have drawn hungry men to Frankia, and many more are yet to arrive. You can either turn them back with the full support of your people, or you can beg King Charles for help in fighting one or both. Either way, you have lost face. Let me help you avoid that."

"Your charity is commendable," Hrolf said through a sneer. "But it is you and your father who will need help. I am sorry you returned, Hakon, for you were a fine warrior in your time. You as well, Einar. Both are a loss to me, but a loss I can replace. Make your threats, but I will not be swayed."

Hakon looked to Einar, and he gave a slow nod. Hakon let the silence speak for him and Hrolf's sneer began to melt.

"Do you not wonder where my father is? You believe he would set his family and most loyal friends in opposition to you with only what you see here? I would never have thought to call you a fool, Jarl Hrolf, but I can think of no other word to fit. Here is what has been done to you already and my offer of terms to you."

Hrolf's face grew red and Hakon realized he had pushed Hrolf far enough.

"Ulfrik is right now leaving Rouen with your son, Vilhjalmer, and your wife, Poppa. Gunther One-Eye's head has been placed on your throne, so that you might remember what happens to those who betray my father. Your family will be treated well, but if you fight me today, you will lose your wife and son."

Hrolf's face dropped and lost all color. "This is a lie."

"Go back to Rouen, Jarl Hrolf, see if we have lied or not. I swear to you on my honor that we will cease attacking your farms and people, and will pull back beyond the Seine. When you are ready to talk, Ulfrik will offer you a truce. Poppa will be returned to you, but Vilhjalmer will remain a hostage to peace for three years. Ulfrik has left you his oldest grandson in Rouen as a show of good faith. We have come to the edge of a terrible decision, Jarl Hrolf. You must either rescind your decrees, forced upon you by the Church, or stand with the priests and watch your kingdom splinter. Take the easy path. Speak to my father under a truce."

Hrolf's jaw ground and his face burned red. His nostrils flared as he leaned close to Hakon, his voice rough with threat. "When I see your father again, it will be to tear his head from his shoulders with my own two hands."

"That is an unfortunate choice," Hakon said. "I was fond of your son. But his death will not pain me as much as the death of my mother. We will drop the body on your land, so you may bury him with dignity."

"I will dine on your heart tonight, Hakon Ulfrikson. Your father has made an enemy this day that will fill his future with sorrow."

Hrolf spun away with his men, and Hakon felt himself sinking. Einar and Hauk both also slumped in defeat.

"Let us prepare for battle," Hakon said, then turned up the hill knowing he walked to his death.

54

Ulfrik sat with his sons at the high table for the last time. Gunnar sat at his right, a gloom hanging over him that no amount of good news could relieve. Hakon sat at his left. He smiled with the joy of a man who had escaped death. Despite his threats, Hrolf had withdrawn back to Rouen and Hakon had not lingered to see if he would return to make good on his threats. Aren stood behind him, pacing with worry for the final details of this plan. Reunited as one family, Ulfrik swelled with pride for what his sons had done together. They had brought the mightiest jarl ever known to heel. Hrolf's messengers had promised he would arrive with only an honor guard of one hundred men.

Mord had kept his hall in good condition, and it looked much like it had when he had abandoned it. Ulfrik had feared to return here, expecting to see ghosts of both Runa and Snorri hovering through the darkness. The first night sleeping alone in his former bedroom was too hard to bear, and Gunnar sent a woman to comfort him the next night. After business with Hrolf finished he would burn this hall and never think of it again.

The rest of the hall was a mixed mood of optimism and fear. Finn and Oskar remained close, Finn eager to impress the jarl in hopes of wedding his daughter. She had captured Finn's heart and Ulfrik was glad for them. Oskar smiled often, but when he believed no one looked his brow creased with worry. No doubt he wondered if he had joined the wrong side in this clash. Beyond them Einar and Hauk shared a drink of mead together, each man sitting silently with their thoughts. Einar had sacrificed more than anyone, and his loyalty and friendship had touched Ulfrik. Einar's family had even journeyed south to show support, and to be nearby if an unexpected retreat was needed. Finally, his three oldest companions in arms, the jarls Ull, Ragnar, and Hafgrim, laughed and boasted with their men as if enjoying a visit with an old friend. Ulfrik supposed it was nothing more for these men. Like him, they did not know what to do with peace, and the recent conflict had raised their spirits.

"If only Runa were here to see this," Ulfrik said, more to himself than anyone else. "She would be amazed at what we have done despite everything placed in our way."

"Well, it's not done yet," Aren said. "Hrolf could be preparing a trick of his own. He's had weeks to do so."

"No tricks," Ulfrik said. "We have his family, and if he has calmed himself by now he will realize this has all been done for his benefit more than mine."

"He'll thank you for kidnapping his family?" Gunnar asked.

"I don't expect that, but he has lost face with his jarls for bending to the Church." Ulfrik paused to drink the last of the mead plundered from Mord's holdings. "He can set things right with them and still make it seem as if he was coerced. His beloved Church will also have to understand. It's a perfect escape for him. He won't bungle it with a surprise attack. Who would trust him again?"

Doors to the hall hung open and beyond them the shadows grew long. Hrolf would arrive before twilight, and Ulfrik wanted to check Vilhjalmer and Poppa before he arrived. He stood and excused himself. Outside the scars of battle still remained etched into the ground. Horse tracks and a crisscross of ruts marred the earth. The ground had drank the blood and the bodies cleared, but still packs of crows pecked around the dirt discovering missing fingers or bits of hacked flesh. Splinters of broken shields or spear shafts littered the fields, mixing with the autumn leaves rolling over them.

Hundreds of tents housed the various jarls' warriors while they awaited Hrolf's decision. Ulfrik moved through the camp for a barracks that had survived Gunnar's destruction. It was surrounded by thirty guards on duty, and the camps around it were positioned to face the building. Ulfrik took no chances with his royal prisoners. At the doors, he nodded to the guards who lifted the bolt.

Inside, the long hall smelled like fresh lilac and the sweet scent of burning wood. The central hearth burned low, and beyond it a group of women surrounded Hrolf's wife, Poppa. With these women were both Elke and Morgan, and his granddaughters Hilde and Thorgerd. The conversation was low and amicable. They faced Ulfrik, all the women standing but for Poppa whose smile turned to a frown. Ulfrik nodded to them, but instead looked to Vilhjalmer who sat on a bed with his legs tucked up to his chest.

"Your father will be here soon," Ulfrik said to him. "Speak with me for a moment?"

He slipped off his bench without a word and they both went outside. The guards barred the doors behind them as they left. They walked into a field when Ulfrik stopped and faced Vilhjalmer. "I expect your father to agree to my terms. So you and I will be spending more time together than you expected."

"I've been thinking about that," Vilhjalmer said, his expression unreadable. "When you swore loyalty to me, and I helped you escape, did you know this would happen?"

"Never. Until Runa was murdered, I expected to resettle in England or elsewhere, then once your father cooled I would contact you again to see what we might do together. Now, I have given myself over to revenge and nothing more."

"I see." They continued to pace in silence, but Vilhjalmer seemed more set on leading this conversation. "So you have broken your oath to me?"

"I can't very well keep you hostage and be sworn to you at the same time."

"You can if I command you so." Vilhjalmer smiled. "I've spent weeks imagining how I was going to kill you when this was done. But now I realize this is what I actually wanted. As your oath-holder, I demand you and I turn our sights on new conquests. You could wrestle with my father for your old lands, but I think it's best if you plan to relocate. There is a group of foolish jarls who abandoned you, yes? I say it's high time one jarl set himself over all. Let that be you, and let me fight at your side."

"I agree," Ulfrik said. "But if you were to die in battle, then what? I cannot allow that risk."

"No man dies before his time," Vilhjalmer said. "If I am to die in these next three years, then it will happen no matter your worries. Better I fall in battle than fall off a horse."

They stared at each other in the late afternoon light. Vilhjalmer smiled like a child about to receive a long-awaited gift. "And of course, with me sworn to you, the lands we take will eventually become part of Normandy. That is how you bring me back into the fold."

"See? You can be smart and strong after all!" Vilhjalmer slapped his shoulder. "It's not only good for you, but good for the future of your sons and grandchildren. You don't want to be left in dishonor, not for all you've done. And I get out from beneath my parents and earn a name for myself, as well as join new lands to my father's. No one loses."

Ulfrik opened his mouth to agree, but blaring horns announced the arrival of Hrolf. Instead, the two shared a knowing smile, and Vilhjalmer clasped arms with Ulfrik. He said, "My father will curse your name forever, but I think even he would agree to this."

Hrolf was preceded by thirty men who prepared the way, inspected both Vilhjalmer's and Poppa's conditions, then returned to escort Hrolf. Ulfrik awaited him outside the hall, with his sons and allies flanking him. All the camp stood ready for this meeting, and when Hrolf the Strider finally entered with his one hundred men, he had Brandr following him in the care of a priest. That made Ulfrik's stomach turn, but he ignored the boy for now.

They met as equals and neither spoke, Hrolf glaring down at Ulfrik. He was dressed in mail, covered in jewels, and his helmet was rimmed with a crown. Ulfrik held his steely gaze but decided he had best give in first.

"Welcome, Jarl Hrolf, and my thanks for making this long journey."

"Fuck the pleasantries. Where is my family?"

Ulfrik's smile faltered, but he regained himself. "They will be returned to you once we have agreed to terms. Hakon has explained these to you."

"Three years of peace. Vilhjalmer remains with you. I keep your grandson. Then we return hostages and I proceed to tear your heart from your chest. Yes, he told me all about it."

"You've added some of your own imaginings, but yes, those are my terms. Also, I wish to remain on this land until I secure another home. There will be peace and I will not even look toward Normandy nor Frankia. There are other lands ripe for conquest."

He watched the familiar display of Hrolf calculating what this meant to him. His eyes fixed on a distant place and darted side to side. Hrolf might not know of his oath to Vilhjalmer, but the southern jarls would have to be dealt with soon, and with his reputation already strained, having Ulfrik do it for him would be ideal.

"We have a peace and I will agree to your terms. Any harm comes to my son, no matter what the cause, and your grandson dies, then I will destroy you."

"That is always the way of these agreements. I needn't remind you the same fate awaits your son should my grandson be hurt or killed."

"He'll be receiving a good Christian education. No worries for injury there." Hrolf smiled, and Ulfrik did not respond.

"Then we have agreement?"

"I swear to the terms as we have discussed," Hrolf said.

"As I do swear."

A cheer came up from both sides, surprising both Ulfrik and Hrolf. Poppa and Vilhjalmer were led out. Hrolf greeted his wife with respect, and gathered her back with her captured ladies as if recovering a bit of stolen jewelry. For Vilhjalmer, they stood aside and spoke privately.

Brandr wandered forward, not sure who he should see. Ulfrik pulled Gunnar's arm, and he went to his son. After they traded a few short words, Ulfrik knelt beside him. "You have been brave?"

"Yes, Lord."

"That is good. I want you to take something." Ulfrik lifted the silver amulet of Thor from his neck, made certain the priests were not looking, and pressed it into Brandr's hand. "Every time you pray to their god, you also pray to Thor. Do not let the priests find this, but keep it and remember your family. You will return to me a man, and I will reward you for good service. Do you promise to be good?"

"Yes, Lord." Brandr kept his head lowered, but Ulfrik raised it by the chin.

"Look at me. You carry my blood, the blood of jarls. You must look men in the eyes when you make promises. You fear no one, even me. Remember that."

"I will, Lord," he said, and looked Ulfrik in the eye.

With Poppa returned, Hrolf had no more cause to linger. He glanced between Vilhjalmer and Ulfrik and flashed a thin smile, then turned to the assembled jarls.

"Mord Guntherson was a vile schemer. I consider your actions here a service to me in ridding him from my land." He paused to let the murmuring crowd quiet. "But if any of you ever think to challenge me, I will tear you up like a wolf does a fawn."

The jarls lifted their heads, but none defied him. Hrolf now turned and pointed at Ulfrik.

"You and I are done. Your name will never be spoken again, and if I should hear it in song or conversation I will have the speaker's tongue cut out. It will be as if you had never lived, and I shall not remember you again when our dealings are finished."

Hrolf stalked into the setting sun with his hirdman and wife, leaving Vilhjalmer at Ulfrik's side. Ulfrik watched his former lord and friend vanish over a crest and knew he would never see him again.

55

For three years a tide of fury and blood rolled from the Seine west to the Contentin Peninsula. Ulfrik and Vilhjalmer rode that crest of violence, but beside them his sons and allies brought spear and shield in support. Einar Snorrason, Ull the Strong, Ragnar Hard-Striker, and more swelled his ranks with bloodthirsty men. The so-called free jarls who had once allied briefly with Ulfrik were swept aside by sword and fire.

Life without battle meant nothing to Ulfrik. Men called him Ulfrik the Old now, but his enemies called him War-Tooth for his insatiable hunger for battle. Vilhjalmer proved a worthy companion, leading men and fighting in the front ranks alongside Ulfrik. He earned the name Vilhjalmer Longsword, for his weapon was ever ready to carve a path through enemy ranks.

The Franks and Hrolf, more commonly called Count Rollo in these days, watched with guarded optimism. As long as Vilhjalmer associated with Ulfrik's victories they did not fear the conquering army rampaging at their borders. They welcomed the fear Ulfrik's armies struck into other Norsemen invaders, and a peace settled over the interior of Frankia.

He never intended to stop, but to fight every day until he died. He laughed at death, dared it to find him, but the more he dared, the less willing anyone was to battle him. With territory to rival Hrolf's, he considered whether to push on to Brittany. With such success he might gain the same recognition from the Frankish king and be named a count himself.

It all changed the final summer of Vilhjalmer's so-called captivity. The engagement was a small, cleanup action. No one expected serious resistance. Ulfrik led it personally, angered at the insolence of the young fool who had challenged him. That battle was sharp and short, and Ulfrik's men crushed their challengers. But Ulfrik was struck a blow that laid him low.

Age had slowed his reactions, and though his reputation frightened men enough that they faltered in combat with him, this young fool knew no fear. He struck beneath the shield, driving his blade deep into Ulfrik's left thigh. He cut the artery, and were it not for Finn's quick aid, Ulfrik would have bled out in three heartbeats. From that day, Ulfrik could not move with any speed. The leg had suffered a terrible break years ago, and now this wound nearly lamed it. He walked with aid from a staff, and though he bragged he would recover, all knew he would not.

The season of Ulfrik War-Tooth had ended.

His men settled their conquered lands, Brittany sent armies to their borders, and the Franks moved to contain him. No one would have guessed he could have forged a kingdom almost equal in size to Hrolf's in such a time. Though he would not be recognized by the Franks nor Hrolf, he did not need their accolades. He had secured himself a place in history even if no one would remember him.

Now the day to return Vilhjalmer to his parents had arrived, and the young man whom he had taken hostage now stood stronger and bolder than ever before. Hrolf had dispatched a guard of fifty men to escort him home and deliver Brandr.

Ulfrik stood with Vilhjalmer, and all his sons had come to send him off. They each embraced him, and when Aren came he had a tear in his eye. The two had grown to be like brothers. Vilhjalmer patted his back. "I will call for you one day. I will have need of your sharp mind when my father hands rule over to me. This is only goodbye for a short time."

Brandr was unrecognizable, taller and golden hair grown darker. Ulfrik saw that he wore a heavy silver cross over his new, white shirt. Brandr smiled as he returned to him, and without a word he lifted the cross from his neck and withdrew the amulet Ulfrik had given him years before. It was tarnished now, but he held it in his upraised palm. "You can have the cross for the silver, but I will keep this."

Ulfrik laughed and sent his grandson to see Gunnar, who waited behind them. At last he slipped his arm about Vilhjalmer's shoulders and walked him to the line of guards. He had to lean on his staff and he cursed the pain. The cold air bit his flesh as he walked.

"Three years were like no time at all," Ulfrik said.

"I will remember them with great fondness," Vilhjalmer said. His voice had grown deeper and more commanding. "You've taught me all your tricks, and showed me how to stop a sword with my thigh."

Ulfrik chuckled. "Don't try that until you're ready to see your whole life pass through your thoughts."

"We will continue to have peace," Vilhjalmer said. "Put down your sword and enjoy what you have wrought from this land. It's better than what any of us imagined."

"I am passing command to Hakon," Ulfrik said. "But I shall always be ready to aid him. It's time I let someone else enjoy the burdens of rule."

Vilhjalmer smiled. "Then we shall one day speak with Hakon and see if he can be enticed to join with me."

Again Ulfrik laughed. "Not while I live, dear friend. This is my kingdom and shall remain with my family."

They grew silent and Vilhjalmer suddenly embraced him. They had shared life and death struggles together for three long years. Parting hurt as much as losing a lover, for they were even closer when their lives depended upon each other's swords.

"Find a woman," Vilhjalmer said. "Have her warm your bed, cook your food, and massage your leg. You've earned this much for yourself. I've seen the light fade from your eyes now that the fighting is over. But life does not end here. You are a hero, and nothing will ever change that."

Ulfrik smiled, returned the embrace. "Go back home to Normandy. May your days forever be filled with glory. You will be a great leader one day."

They parted with a nod, and Ulfrik hobbled back to his hall alone, unwilling to watch a young man embarking on the adventure of his life when his own twilight had fallen.

56

Ulfrik closed his eyes and ran his hand along the cold stone, feeling the engraved lines of the runes. Birds chirped in the surrounding trees, singing their songs of springtime. From behind he heard his grandson, Leif, laughing as he teased his Uncle Aren. Both had insisted on accompanying him on this walk, but Ulfrik asked they give him this time alone.

"Five years," he said to the stone. "Has it been that long, dear wife?"

He opened his eyes and tears threatened to erupt. Instead he brushed them dry with the back of his hand, and leaned on his staff as he remembered Runa. The stone had already gathered green and white stains of lichen, though he had only raised it a year ago. He read the inscription, filled with red paint to make it bolder. <u>For Runa the Bloody, Wife and Shield Maiden</u>. He could have written much more, though he simply wanted a place to visit her memory. Ulfrik did not know whether from Freya's hall she could see this stone set for her. It only mattered that he and those who traveled through these lands did.

"Leif wants to go the creek and catch a frog," Aren said,

approaching from behind. "Will you be all right to find us there when you are done?"

Ulfrik nodded and Aren stood beside him in silence. "Your mother would have liked your wife," he said. "She is a smart woman, ambitious too, but not so much that it wears on you. Some grandchildren would be nice."

"We're working on that," Aren said, his face reddening. Ulfrik laughed.

"I don't remember the exact day, but I will never forget when your mother told me she was having you. I was worried about feeding three boys in winter back then, and wondered if we would even make a home in Frankia. Strange how Fate weaves our threads, is it not?"

"I miss Mother every day," Aren said. They stared longer at the rune stone until Leif ran up and joined them. "All right, we will see about capturing frogs. Come find us when you are finished. It's not far."

"I know where the creek is," Ulfrik said. "It's not far for your two good legs, but for me it's a walk back to Norway. Go on and find a big frog."

Leif hugged Ulfrik's leg and the two departed. Ulfrik rested his palm against Runa's stone and closed his eyes, remembering all her beauty and strength. Many women wanted to sit at his side, and he had allowed a few to share his company, but none would ever mean anything to him. Runa had only ever been the one woman who mattered. He bowed his head and remembered her and their life together until his arm tired.

He heard a swish of grass behind him, but he did not turn. "Decided against frog hunting?"

A sharp point dug into his back, and terror seized his stomach. He wore a dagger and a sax, but found a sword too unbalancing to carry. The point dug deeper when his hand fell toward the hilt of the sax. Raising his hand, he slowly turned, the point dragging across his clothes.

A spear tip now pressed against his stomach. He followed it up to the man gripping it.

He was gaunt, with milky eyes that sat deep in his head. His hair was greasy and graying, and flowed wildly from beneath a leather cap. His clothes were dirty and torn, a gray shirt and faded brown pants beneath a faded brown cloak. He stared at Ulfrik with yellow teeth bared. His face was familiar, like an old friend remembered in a dream. As it came home to Ulfrik, the man began to smile. The moment he spoke, Ulfrik knew who it was.

"Took a moment for those old eyes to recognize me, didn't it?"

"Mord. Gunnar killed you. Am I seeing ghosts?"

Mord's laughter turned to a cough. "I'm returned from the dead. You're not the only one who knows that trick."

The spear tip pushed deeper into Ulfrik's stomach, pinching the skin beneath his shirt.

Ulfrik raised his hands. "Gunnar saw you with an ax in your neck and lying dead in a creek. Was it not you?"

"It was," Mord said, then released one hand from his spear to pull aside his collar. He revealed a horrid, red lump of scarred flesh over his shoulder. Ulfrik noticed now how his body hunched around the old wound. He had been lamed but not killed by the strike.

Ulfrik thought to bat aside the spear while Mord had removed his hand, but he was not fast enough. Mord read his intent and set both hands back on the shaft.

"Gunnar did come to find me, and pissed all over me. That woke me up, but I knew enough to lie still. He had made another mistake too. He let one of my men go, who came back to find me. He also thought I was dead, and only wanted to rob me of my mail and weapons. But I grabbed him when he did. I thought he'd die right there from fright. He carried me to safety and so I lived."

"Have you really lived?" Ulfrik asked. "You seem a ruined and desperate man. What of your wife?" He did not care for the answer, but only delayed in hopes Aren would return to distract Mord. Right now, with a spear point at his gut, his best chances were to keep Mord talking.

"My wife! Ha! Her father got a priest to proclaim the marriage was not real. No children, after all, and I was a ruined man. I guess I got most of her father's men killed too. But that was your doing, wasn't it?"

"That was a long time ago," Ulfrik said. He studied Mord, watching for him to signal his intent. While Ulfrik might be slowed by old injuries, he was still sharp with battle-sense. Mord, however, seemed to have lost most of his skill. It made their match-up roughly equal to Ulfrik's mind. He only needed a moment's distraction to draw his weapon.

"I never wanted this," Mord said, his horribly aged face wrinkling in disgust. "My father pushed me to it. Said I deserved it and you did not. He made me hate you, made me want to kill you."

"Well, your father is long dead," Ulfrik said, slowly lowering his hands. "You are no longer beholden to him. Leave that all in the past, and put down your spear. There is always time to do the right thing."

"Is there? Not for me. I lost everything. I lost myself." Mord's eyes welled with tears and Ulfrik noticed that both of them were filmed with the beginnings of the cataracts his father had in his old age. Mord was going blind, and much earlier than his father had. "But look at you. You're a great jarl now. How is it you did not lose all as well?"

"That is Fate," Ulfrik said. His hands lowered toward his weapons. If Mord were going blind, he only needed to disarm him to strike him dead. If Aren returned in time, he would have no worries. "I have been reduced to nothing many times in my life. If I can tell you anything, it's that you can begin again. Put down the spear, Mord, and step into a new life. It's what you want."

"How would you know what I want?" Tears flowed freely now and it was as if their touch upon his cheeks woke him up. He blinked and straightened himself. "You're delaying me. You think help is coming."

"I will need no help if you would only accept your life can be different today."

Aren and Leif appeared as blurs in the distance. Ulfrik's own eyes were no longer sharp enough to tell. A wisp of a smile came to his lips, but then Mord roared.

"You killed my father, you whoreson! Die!"

The spear plunged into his guts. A hot pain rammed through his core and his vision hazed. He looked down and the head of the spear was gone. Dark blood bubbled up around the shaft protruding from his body and drizzled onto his feet.

His staff fell from his hand and he blinked. Mord stood with teeth clenched, staring in disbelief. His hands were white-knuckled on the spear.

Ulfrik marveled that he still lived. His heartbeat filled his ears and his face grew hot with rage. Power flowed into his old limbs and he grabbed the spear shaft with one hand and pulled himself closer to Mord.

With his right hand he drew his sax.

His teeth were clenched. Blood filled his mouth with the taste of copper. He spit the gore into Mord's stunned face.

"Vengeance at last, you coward!"

Ulfrik plunged the sax into Mord's heart. He felt it sawing on bone, plowing into his black heart and rupturing it. Brilliant red blood sprayed from his wound and he released the spear, both hands clawing at the sax. Mord's arterial spray dashed red onto Ulfrik's face as both staggered away from each other. The weight of the spear in Ulfrik's gut dragged him down, but he would not fall until he watched Mord die.

Mord collapsed, blood pumping furiously into the grass, his eyes wide. "You ... killed me. Father said ... you would."

Then his eyes rolled back and his head fell to the side.

Ulfrik thought to laugh but only spit blood from his mouth. Next he knew he was staring up as if looking through water. Two faces hovered over him and he felt a tugging at his stomach. The screaming was a faint echo and Ulfrik realized he was dying. Mord's blood was cooling on his face, and he grabbed the hilt of his dagger wishing he had a sword instead.

"My enemy's blood upon my face," Ulfrik whispered. Aren said something, but he did not understand it. "This is good."

Then Ulfrik knew no more.

57

Aren washed the blood from his hands and face, staring at the ribbons of red floating in the bowl. That was his father's blood, and he could not think of anything else. A servant snatched the red-stained rags beside him and set a fresh cloth for him. He let the water drip from his face into the bowl, watching the reflected candle light ripple on the surface. The hall was a tumult of activity, even hours after the attack it seemed as if he had just rushed inside with his father dying in his arms. Hirdmen and servants alike rushed about on tasks Aren did not understand. How could any of this be saving his father's life?

He wiped his face and sat on a bench out of the way of traffic. The hall was gloomy now that the sun had fallen below the horizon. Gunnar had just burst through the doors, which still hung open and unguarded. Such a grand hall, filled with captured standards and prizes of battle, had now become a gray smear to Aren. He had let his father be murdered, right before his own eyes. The vision of Mord running him through was as vivid as if he had just witnessed it. Mord had pushed through his father as if he were no more than a cloth sack. The bloody tip of the spear caught the sun as it popped out his father's back. He closed his eyes as if it would prevent him from witnessing the horror again, but it did not. In his mind's eye his father crumbled to the ground with a moan and he felt the hopelessness once again.

"You better come to his bed." Aren opened his eyes to find Hakon standing over him. His fine white shirt was speckled with blood and his face had red smears where he had touched his face with bloodied hands. "He was just holding on until Gunnar arrived."

Even with the magnificently sized room his father had built for himself, it was still filled with people. Gunnar knelt at the bedside like a Christian at prayer. Ulfrik's grandchildren huddled with their mothers, both Elke and Morgan holding them away from the bedside. Servants and healers moved among them, but now they carried baskets of gory bandages or basins full of blood-fouled water. Their lowered heads told Aren all he needed to know. The room stank of sweat and blood and oil lamps shed a flickering yellow light. Hakon put his cold hand on Aren's shoulder and guided him to the bedside. No one but the women wept, yet Aren felt like joining them.

His father glistened with sweat from the effort of staying alive. His shirt had been cut away to treat his wound, and the stump of the spear shaft still remained protruding from his body. They had been able to cut the spear down to relieve stress on the injury, but none dared pull it out. If anyone had, Ulfrik would die instantly. So now the shaft was packed with bloody bandages to slow the bleeding. It seemed to have stopped, but his father continued to weaken.

"Is he awake?" Aren asked. Gunnar kept his head bowed, but Hakon nodded in answer.

Ulfrik's right hand gripped a magnificent sword placed beside him in his bed. It was a long, thin blade of gleaming iron. The hilt was plain but a green gem winked from the pommel of the sword. Aren let his eyes skip over it, for it meant his father was prepared to leave this world for Odin's feasting hall.

"Why do I hear weeping?" Ulfrik's voice was weak and far older than only just this morning. It reminded him of his father's real age, which he had never shown until he had been injured in battle. No one knew his exact years, but he had to be more than sixty. Even at the edge of death, he seemed far stronger and younger than the few others who had lived so long.

No one answered Ulfrik, and his eyes fluttered open as he appeared to genuinely expect an answer. Gunnar sat up now, placing his hand over Ulfrik's. "Save your strength."

Ulfrik's chuckle was strained with a cough. "For what? Even weaklings spend no effort in dying. It's the easiest thing I'll ever do. But there is still weeping? I'll not hear it. No tears for me. I am happy today."

Aren swallowed hard and rubbed his face, then he approached his father's bedside. "Dying is hard for the rest of us. We are not ready to let you go."

"Why? I have lived my life. I have entertained the gods for the last time. Now they grant me a final boon, to die surrounded by my family." He broke into a fit of coughing and blood flecked his beard as he did. A servant leaned in and wiped it away, but Ulfrik turned his head.

"Father, don't force yourself," Hakon said, gently pulling the servant away.

Ulfrik raised his left hand and grabbed Hakon's shirt. "Listen to me. I have only so many breaths left and will not spend them to argue. Hakon is jarl, has been for a while. But with my death, let there be no confusion I expect him to rule. Gunnar, you have your lands and your ships. Aren, I will never see those grandchildren, but I'll not relieve you of the responsibility. Your children are coming too late in life, so be quick."

He flashed bloody smile, and Aren struggled to match it. "I will, Father."

"We'll lock him up with his woman until she gives him a son," Hakon said. Aren knew his smile was forced as well. The only one showing his true feeling was Gunnar, who now let his tears flow openly.

"You are a hero, Father," Gunnar said. "Your name and glory will live on forever."

"I do not think so, not if Hrolf has his way. That is my one regret."

Ulfrik's hand fell from Hakon's shirt. Aren held his breath, believing his father had died. Yet his chest still rose and fell. After a few moments, he spoke again.

"You three brothers must work together to keep what I have built. The world is cruel and many will try to steal what is yours. Be wary of those closest to you, and do not tolerate jealousy. Remain strong, my sons. I've shown you how to live life, and now I show you how to die. I go with sword in hand and my foeman's blood on my face."

Tears blurred Aren's vision and he wiped his cheeks with the back of his wrist. Both Gunnar and Hakon had bowed their heads. His father coughed, then lay still. His eyes searched a place no one could see. His hand tightened on the hilt of his sword.

He smiled.

"So many friends ... Runa ..."

And he fell still.

Ulfrik Ormsson had passed from the world.

58

The night was deep blue and scores of torches winked in the dark, sparkling off the flowing waters of the Seine River. The funeral ship sat high on a stand constructed for this occasion, a giant silhouette against the moonlit evening. The crowd murmured in a hush, quiet for its large size. Gunnar drew his brothers away from the crowds gathered to send his father to his final rest. He put an arm on each of them and met their eyes. They both looked like great lords, dressed in shining mail and glittering gold. Aren and Hakon stared expectantly at him.

"The night is finally at hand," he said. "Something has weighed upon me that I must confess to you both."

Hakon and Aren shared a glance, then Aren licked his lips. "As do I."

"Me as well," Hakon said.

"Well, a night for truth then. No better way to honor our father." Gunnar chewed his lip and considered his brothers. He had kept this inside long enough. "I wanted to tell you both that I take responsibility for Father's death. I was given the task of killing Mord and I failed. Why I did not behead him as I planned, I cannot say. Had I not been so lazy, Father would be alive. I accept your scorn and blame."

"No," Aren said. "I am at fault. I accompanied him the day he was killed. Had I not left his side, or reacted faster to what I saw, he would still live. It is me above all that deserves blame."

Hakon laughed. "Are we going to argue who is to blame? For I would confess the same sin. I had heard complaints of banditry that I did not pursue. A stolen hen. A prowler around barns. Of course it was Mord, and had I only investigated as I should have then he would've been caught. I carry the blame."

"So we are united in guilt," Gunnar said. "But I feel no better for sharing it with you."

They stood quietly, Gunnar unsure of what to say next. He felt his brothers deserved more from him as the oldest, yet he had no words and only rage. His father had been torn from the world by the man Gunnar was to have killed. He would never forgive himself. He rubbed the stump of his right arm as he lingered in shameful silence until the giant shadow of Einar approached them.

"Are you three ready? It is time to send your father on his final voyage." Einar's eyes shined with points of orange light reflected from the bobbing torches surrounding them. "What is this? You must not show such long faces to your men. Let your father's passing be one of dignity and honor."

"It is hard to hold up my head when I feel nothing but shame," Aren said, blushing.

Einar clipped Aren's shoulder with a gentle punch. "I loved your father as much as my own. He was a glorious leader and a legend in battle. He was still fighting when most men are bent over their drinking mugs and complaining of times long past. I will miss him as keenly as you do. But now is not the time for sad faces, and truth be said there will never be such a time. He goes to the feasting hall, Valhalla, and meets with all the fallen heroes this night. We are all good men, and shall join him there before long. So tend to your people, and show a proud face. There is much to be proud of. And there is much to be done now that he has died. You three must hold together what his sword and blood forged. If you must fret on something, then let it be that."

Gunnar felt the sting of Einar's words. He was first to raise his head. "Let us send off our father."

They went to the funeral ship. Gunnar nodded to Morgan and all his children, each holding a flaming brand. Elke stood nearby as well, her baby cradled in her arms. Beside her Finn held both sword and the battle standard of black elk antlers on a green flag. Stretched out along the shore were hundreds of hirdmen, farmers, and others who had come to honor Ulfrik's passage into the otherworld.

Stairs were set against the hull of the ship, and Gunnar took a torch from a hirdman and mounted to the deck. His father's corpse, blue in the moonlight, lay stretched out on a bed set where the mast would have stood. He wore new-made clothes and his hands were folded over the sword with the green gemstone in its pommel. Stacked all around him were treasures great and small, as well as kegs of ale, piles of horseflesh, wheels of cheese, and racks of salted fish. His mail coat and helmet were set beside him. He had all that a hero required to journey into the worlds of the dead.

"You will never be forgotten," Gunnar said. "Go now, and wait for me in the feasting hall."

He climbed down the stairs and let each of his brothers share a final word. At last Finn mounted the stairs, for he had considered Ulfrik as close as a father, and he set the standard over Ulfrik's body. Once he climbed down, Gunnar touched his torch to the oil-soaked wood. Fire rushed up and began to lick the hull of the ship. He stood back, feeling the heat on his face, and set his chin against the sorrow he felt. They all watched as fire climbed onto the ship, blazing bright in the night.

Once the heat became unbearable and the fire consumed everything, he threw his torch into the fire.

"Farewell, Ulfrik Ormsson," he shouted. "You shall live on in song and memory."

Hakon and Aren threw their torches into the blaze, and soon all others passed before the ship to toss their brands into the fire. It swallowed the torches, and the intense fire would burn both Ulfrik's body and the ship to nothing but ash come morning. They had decided to cremate him beside the Seine, which to Gunnar at least would always represent the road Ulfrik had followed to his destiny. It seemed fitting to send him off beside it.

He lingered while others filtered away into the dark of night. He stared at the fire and roiling smoke until it stung his eyes, only interrupted when Aren tugged at his sleeve.

Gunnar roused from his thoughts, and followed Aren's pointing finger across the Seine.

On the opposite shore were dozens of flaming torches, and in their light Gunnar saw a red and gold banner lifting in the gentle night breeze. A horn sounded, low and mournful, then all the glowing points of torchlight arced into the air and extinguished in the Seine.

The funeral ship groaned then crashed into the fire, sparks showering into the darkness.

Gunnar smiled and felt tears heavy in his eyes. His father had waited for one last friend to visit him, and now he was gone.

AUTHOR'S NOTE

In the spring of 911, Hrolf the Strider led his thousands-strong army in an attack on the area surrounding Chartres and later assaulted the city. What began as a hopeful bid to bring a major Frankish city under his domination devolved into a siege. By July the defenders had managed to hold Hrolf at bay long enough for the Franks to mobilize aid. King Charles III of the Western Franks, also known as Charles the Simple for his straightforward manner, sent an army to break the siege. Hrolf's warriors put up a vicious defense, but legend has it that when the Bishop of Chartres revealed the Virgin Mary's Veil, the garrison sallied forth to join the relieving army and drive off Hrolf's forces.

Hrolf organized a fighting retreat to a nearby hill and set up camp. However, the Count of Poitiers encircled Hrolf and threatened to annihilate his army. A conventional attack on the Franks would only result in the circle tightening around them, therefore Hrolf needed another plan. He sent picked men into the Frankish camp and had them blow on their horns to create the illusion of a surprise attack deep in their ranks. The Franks responded with shock and panic, thrown into chaos. During the confusion, Hrolf slipped his army off the hill and into the night.

By the next morning the Franks pursued Hrolf along the Eure River, but later ran into barricades constructed from trees, bushes, even dead animals. Anything that could slow the Franks was thrown against them. Hrolf had made good his escape, though he lost his bid to expand power to Chartres. On the opposite side, the Franks were thrilled with their victory. King Charles decided to put his victory to good use and negotiate a peace with Hrolf.

King Charles and Hrolf met in a small town known as Saint Clair sur Epte. The king offered Hrolf control of Rouen and the coast of Neustria, which the Franks had no reasonable chance to recover in any case. He additionally expanded Hrolf's territory to include Evrecin, which gave him new land south of the Seine, and Vexin which pushed Hrolf's border farther east. The only condition was that Hrolf swear loyalty to King Charles and convert to Christianity. This was King Charles's attempt to create a buffer state between the heart of Frankia and other Viking incursions.

Hrolf accepted the terms. To ratify the treaty, the Franks insisted that Hrolf kiss King Charles's foot. He refused to do it himself, but all agreed he could delegate a representative to perform the act of fealty in his place. This unnamed man lifted the king's foot as if to kiss it, but then instead threw King Charles backward into the grass. Hrolf and his warriors roared with laughter. Of the Franks' reaction there is no record, but one imagines their indignation would be inflamed by such an act. So the province of Normandy was born in July 911.

This initial grant of territory would not be the final shape of Normandy. By 923, Frankia erupted into civil war that gave Hrolf a chance to expand his lands by grabbing what is now lower Normandy. Hrolf eventually broke his treaty outright and attacked other provinces, and again ceded more lands. By 925, he had grown too old to rule and passed control to his only son, Vilhjalmer Longsword. Vilhjalmer continued the expansion of Normandy, bringing the Contentin Peninsula into the fold. Vilhjalmer's bastard son, Richard, would also continue the expansion until Normandy reached its final shape.

No one knows the exact date of Hrolf's death, but he was already frail by the time he passed Normandy into his son's care. Scholars agree that he had died by 933 at the latest. Prior to his death he was believed to have gone mad. Feeling guilty for having abandoned the old gods, he ordered the execution of one hundred Christian priests. It was his final act of violence before his passing. His son, Vilhjalmer, never produced a proper heir by his legally married wife, but had a bastard son, Richard the Fearless. Vilhjalmer himself was murdered in a ruse by the Count of Flanders. He was tricked into attending a peace meeting to settle disputed territories when the count's men attacked him. His sudden death left Richard in a precarious position, but he had the support of King Louis IV to help him maintain his grip on Normandy.

After Richard the Fearless, the people were no longer Vikings but fully assimilated Franks identifying themselves as Normans. Hrolf's great-great-great-grandson was the famous William the Conqueror. While the Norse identity had long since been shed, Hrolf's noble blood still lived on in history. In fact, Britain's current-day royal family can trace relations to Hrolf himself. The bold Viking jarl left an indelible mark on Europe.

I have taken the history of Normandy far past the life of Ulfrik and his sons. Ulfrik's life traversed a vibrant period of Viking history. Over the course of these seven volumes he has witnessed the birth of a united Norway (a union that did not survive Harald Finehair's death at age eighty), the settlement of the Faeroe Islands, the great Siege of Paris, the Viking annexation of the western Seine, Norse migration to Iceland, and finally the birth of Normandy. That is an admirable breadth of history for one man.

Ulfrik lived a long life for a man of his day. At last, he had to pass on to Odin's feasting hall, Valhalla. Of course his sons and grandchildren will live on into the interesting times I outlined previously. Perhaps one day we will see what names they have made for themselves and what their contributions to history were as men of their time. However, this was Ulfrik Ormsson's story, and we have followed his life of setbacks and triumphs to its conclusion.

The joy I have taken in relating Ulfrik's story to you cannot be understated. I have enjoyed following him into uncertain seas, shadowy mead halls, and chaotic shield walls. I hope you have as well. As the Norsemen would say, Far vel vinr! Farewell, friend!

∼

If you would like to know when my next book is released, please sign up for my new release newsletter. I will send you an email when it is out. You can unsubscribe at any time, and I promise not to fill your mailbox with junk or share your information.

To subscribe go to http://eepurl.com/ZDbpP and follow the instructions.

You can also visit me at my website for periodic updates at https://jerryautieri.wordpress.com

If you have enjoyed this book and would like to show your support for my writing, consider leaving a review where you purchased this book or on Goodreads, LibraryThing, and other reader sites. I need help from readers like you to get the word out about my books. If you have a moment, please share your thoughts with other readers. I appreciate it!

ALSO BY JERRY AUTIERI

Ulfrik Ormsson's Saga

Historical adventure set in 9th Century Europe and brimming with heroic combat. Witness the birth of a unified Norway, travel to the remote Faeroe Islands, then follow the Vikings on a siege of Paris and beyond. Walk in the footsteps of the Vikings and witness history through the eyes of Ulfrik Ormsson.

Fate's Needle

Islands in the Fog

Banners of the Northmen

Shield of Lies

The Storm God's Gift

Return of the Ravens

Sword Brothers

Descendants Saga

The grandchildren of Ulfrik Ormsson continue tales of Norse battle and glory. They may have come from greatness, but they must make their own way in the brutal world of the 10th Century.

Descendants of the Wolf

Odin's Ravens

Revenge of the Wolves

Blood Price

Grimwold and Lethos Trilogy

A sword and sorcery fantasy trilogy with a decidedly Norse flavor.

Deadman's Tide

Children of Urdis

Age of Blood

Copyright © 2015

by Jerry Autieri

All rights reserved.

No part of this book may be reproduced in any form or by any electronic or mechanical means, including information storage and retrieval systems, without written permission from the author, except for the use of brief quotations in a book review.

Printed in Great Britain
by Amazon